Praise for *Death's Way*

". . . Valen is a master of words, of plots and subplots, and subplots within subplots. In *Death's Way* Valen has once again crafted a spellbinding tale of mystery, murder, intrigue and the unexplained. His readers, both old and new, will not be disappointed."

—*Rebecca's Reads*

". . . This carefully plotted police procedural deals with the sex trade from Costa Rica, drug trafficking, a wrongly convicted murderer, and murderous drug cartels. There are numerous turns and twists in this carefully plotted police procedural. Secrets and the meaning of life and death drive this intriguing and fast paced mystery . . ."

—*Reader Views*

"Wow! Christopher Valen has done an extremely good job of making sure his latest offering, *Death's Way*, keeps you glued to the book till the end. The methodical way in which John Santana goes about piecing together the evidence in the case holds the reader's interest all the way. The author has researched his story well and ties up all the loose ends beautifully. Kudos to Christopher Valen for having come up with a character like John Santana . . ."

—*Reader's Favorite*

". . . The tightly wound story moves at a fast pace, with each chapter ending on a cliffhanger so that the audience will want to keep reading . . . this novel represents a gripping offering from an award-winning author."

—*Foreword Reviews*

Praise for *Bone Shadows*

Midwest Independent Publishers' Association 2012
Best Mystery of the Year

Named Best Mystery of 2012
by *Reader Views* & *Rebecca's Reads*

". . . *Bone Shadows* is guaranteed to hold readers' attention until the last page . . . Valen's highly moral Santana character is golden . . ."

—*Library Journal*

". . .With a compelling and believable hero and a colorful cast of supporting characters, this turned out to be another superbly written tale of convoluted motives and surprising twists and turns. I would highly recommend Christopher Valen's *Bone Shadows* to anybody who enjoys a well-written, contemporary story . . ."

—*Reader Views*

". . . *Bone Shadows* has a well thought out plot that is up to date with today's society and current social issues. Valen writes with an easy to follow style and he is adept at keeping his tale interesting, intriguing and exciting. I appreciated the many convoluted twists and turns of the story . . . I am also certain that this book will elicit at least one or two gasps of shock/ surprise . . . *Bone Shadows* was a great read . . ."

—*Rebecca's Reads*

Praise for *Bad Weeds Never Die*

Named Best Mystery of 2011
by *Reader Views* & *Rebecca's Reads*

". . . The latest John Santana police procedural is an excellent investigative thriller . . ."

—*Midwest Book Review*

"Christopher Valen's third novel, *Bad Weeds Never Die,* continues the story of John Santana, a homicide detective in St. Paul, Minn., who was introduced in *White Tombs,* and whose story was continued in *The Black Minute*. The three novels are all great police procedural stories . . . I have thoroughly enjoyed reading Valen's novels . . ."

—*Bismarck Tribune*

". . . *Bad Weeds Never Die* . . . delivered on all fronts. Once again I enjoyed Mr. Valen's well-plotted and intriguing mystery for all the obvious reasons: flowing and well-paced storyline, great dialogue, multi-layered and vivid characters, a great sense of place and time, relevant issues and believable events . . ."

—*Reader Views*

". . . This is the first of Valen's books that I have read in the John Santana series and surely will not be the last . . . Valen's novel is gripping, fast-paced and will have you guessing until the end. The characters are intriguing and there are many plot twists and turns. It is a true page turner in every sense of the word . . ."

—*Rebecca's Reads*

Praise for *The Black Minute*

Named Best Mystery of 2009 by Reader Views

Midwest Book Award Finalist

"Santana—an appealing series lead, strong and intelligent . . . Readers who enjoyed *White Tombs* will settle easily into this one; on the other hand, it works fine as a stand-alone, and fans of well-plotted mysteries with a regional flair . . . should be encouraged to give this one a look."

—*Booklist*

". . . as in *White Tombs,* Valen writes well about St. Paul and surrounding areas. He gives just enough sense of place to make you feel like you're there, but he never loses track of his story's fast pacing. And he does a super job of keeping the suspense going as the action reaches a crescendo . . ."

—*St. Paul Pioneer Press*

"The second John Santana St. Paul police procedural is a terrific thriller . . . Christopher Valen provides the audience with his second straight winning whodunit."

—*Midwest Book Review*

". . . *The Black Minute* grabbed me from the first page on, and pulled me into a complex world of evil, violence, deceit, bravery and a search for justice . . . While the plot is complex and anything but predictable, his storyline stays comprehensible and easy to follow. The characters are well developed, very believable and constantly evolving. The setting of the story is vivid, detailed and engaging . . ."

—*Reader Views*

". . . There is not one reason why this book isn't a winner! Everything about it screams success. The book is masterfully written with a tightly woven plot, visually detailed settings and well-developed characters . . ."

—*Rebecca's Reads*

". . . John Santana was introduced in Christopher Valen's first book, *White Tombs*. This second book is just as exciting as the first and one that keeps the reader guessing right up to the final page. Either book can be read as a stand-alone, but I hope Valen brings us more stories involving Detective Santana."

—*Buried Under Books*

Praise for *White Tombs*

Named Best Mystery of 2008 by Reader Views

". . . Valen's debut police procedural provides enough plot twists to keep readers engrossed and paints a clear picture of the Hispanic community in St. Paul."

—*Library Journal*

". . . *White Tombs* is a superb police procedural starring a fascinating lead detective. Santana is a wonderful new addition to the subgenre."

—*Midwest Book Review*

". . . Santana is an intriguing character. St. Paul readers will enjoy Valen's sense of place."

—*St. Paul Pioneer Press*

". . . *White Tombs* is a promising start to a detective series. I thoroughly enjoyed reading it and look forward to future novels with John Santana."

—*Bismarck Tribune*

". . . Christopher Valen addresses a very wide range of extremely relevant social issues in *White Tombs,* and this book goes well beyond being just a detective story. The characters are fantastically well developed . . . the writing is solid an elegant without unnecessary detours. Any lover of solid writing should enjoy it greatly. *White Tombs* also screams out for a sequel—or better yet, sequels."

—*Reader Views*

"John Santana of the St. Paul Police Department is a man you will not forget . . . The book is a great read, and Santana is destined to become one of my favorite detectives. Truly a five-star read from this author."

—*Armchair Interviews*

To Jim

THE DARKNESS HUNTER

Best Wishes!

A John Santana Novel

Christopher Valen

Christopher Valen

Conquill Press

 For information about special discounts for bulk purchases contact conquillpress@comcast.net

THE DARKNESS HUNTER

Cover Design: Rebecca Treadway

Library of Congress Control Number: 2015937330

Valen, Christopher

The Darkness Hunter: a novel / by Christopher Valen – 1st edition

ISBN: 978-0-9908461-2-3

Conquill Press/September 2015

Printed in the United States of America

10 9 8 7 6 5 4 3 2 1

To Jim Anker, Lee Mosher, Dave Florenzano,
and Tom Driscoll,

For All the Years of Friendship and Laughter

Also By Christopher Valen

White Tombs

The Black Minute

Bad Weeds Never Die

Bone Shadows

Death's Way

. . . I had a dream, which was not all a dream.

The bright sun was extinguished, and the stars

Did wander darkling in the eternal space,

Rayless, and pathless, and the icy earth

Swung blind and blackening in the moonless air . . .

The waves were dead; the tides were in their grave,

The moon, their mistress, had expired before;

The winds were withered in the stagnant air,

And the clouds perished; Darkness had no need

Of aid from them—She was the Universe.

"Darkness"
Lord Byron

THEN

Chapter 1

Hot white lights illuminated the shallow gravesite where the half-naked body of the teen had been dumped and partially covered with dead leaves and black dirt. Red and blue flashers slapped the night sky, and the voices of radio dispatchers disturbed the humid stillness.

St. Paul Homicide Detective John Santana sat on his haunches, forearms resting on his thighs. He noted the black electrician's tape that bound the teen's wrists behind her and the blue bandanna stuffed in her mouth. Her face had been painted red, and her bare legs were the color of bone. There was a small incision in her upper right abdomen where the ME had pushed a temperature probe into the tissue of the liver. According to an ID found inside her purse, the young woman was seventeen-year-old Danielle Lonetree.

"Lonetree," Wendell Hudson said, looking at Santana. "Sounds Native American."

Hudson squatted next to Santana. He had large eyes and a thick mouth. He wore a short-brimmed tan fedora with a dark brown band that matched the color of his skin. His detective shield hung from a lanyard around his neck. He smelled of talcum powder and antiperspirant.

Since Hudson was the senior detective in the department, this was his crime scene. He shifted his gaze to Reiko

Tanabe, the Ramsey County medical examiner. "What's your take, Reiko?"

Tanabe was kneeling on the opposite side of the shallow grave, staring at the body through her wire-rimmed glasses. Specks of living light flickered in the darkness as fireflies circled above her head.

"No sign of rigor or putrefaction. Given the ambient temperature, I'd say she's been here for twenty-four to thirty-six hours." Tanabe touched the young woman's head with a latex-gloved hand. "Someone cut a lock of her hair."

"Might be a trophy," Hudson said. "I hope to God we're not dealing with a serial killer."

Santana looked at Hudson. "Why the red paint?"

Hudson shrugged. "Something we need to find out."

Santana picked up a handful of cool, damp dirt and let it run through his fingers as the detectives stood.

At a lean six feet three inches, Hudson was slightly taller than Santana. Despite his age and height, he moved with the ease of a much smaller man.

Santana watched as Tony Novak, the SPPD's forensic specialist, snapped photos, and Hudson made a quick but amazingly accurate sketch of the crime scene, depicting the layout and relationship of evidentiary items to the surroundings. Santana drew a sketch in his notebook as well, giving him a perspective that wasn't easily shown in crime scene photos. But Hudson's artistic skills were truly superior. Santana thought his partner could make a good living as an artist.

"Any reason to think the young couple who found the DB were involved, John?"

Santana shook his head. "They were pretty shaken up. Given Tanabe's TOD estimate, it's unlikely they had anything to do with Lonetree's death. They just stumbled on the dead body while out for a walk."

Hudson nodded and loosened the knot on his striped tie. "Let's look at the truck."

They had found an abandoned red pickup parked in a lot near the Mississippi River in Hidden Falls Park, only fifty yards from the body. As they walked to it, Santana took another cursory look around. Yellow crime-scene tape, wrapped around a series of tree trunks, cordoned off a large area. He knew a flashlight search in the dark would be a waste of time. The ground would need to be extensively searched in the morning.

Two crime scene techs were photographing the pickup. A flatbed had arrived to tow the pickup to the impound lot, where it would be dusted for prints.

DMV records had confirmed that twenty-year-old Clay Buck owned the pickup. The driver's side door was open. An empty bottle of cheap wine lay on the floor mat.

Hudson put on a latex glove and turned the key in the ignition. The engine clicked. "Well, now we know why Buck abandoned his truck."

"But why leave his keys in the ignition, Wendell?"

"Maybe he was in a hurry. Maybe he was drunk. We haven't got probable cause to arrest Clay Buck—yet. We can enter a formal 'pick-up' into the SPPD's e-brief system later."

Santana nodded. Once a detective had entered a "pick-up," the Ramsey County Communications Center would enter the information into the ALERT system and send a BOLO to departments throughout the state.

A small group of reporters and their news vans had gathered behind the crime scene tape in the parking lot. They began shouting questions at the detectives.

Just as Hudson turned back to address them, Santana felt a low-frequency vibration pulsing the air. The vibration increased in intensity. Then it exploded in a cacophony of sound as a news channel helicopter cleared the treetops and hovered overhead. A cone of light lit the parking lot. The downwash from the blades drowned out the reporters' questions.

"Let's talk to the vic's family," Hudson said loudly. "Then we'll see if we can locate Clay Buck."

As he and Hudson headed for their Crown Vic, Santana was thinking that there could be a number of explanations for Clay Buck's vehicle to be at the crime scene. Danielle Lonetree could have stolen or borrowed the truck and then driven it to Hidden Falls Park. The killer or killers could have taken Buck hostage, or they could have killed him and hidden his body someplace else. Buck could have fled the scene in fear of his life and was now on the run. In any case, locating him as a person of interest was clearly a high priority.

But Santana was also remembering something another detective had once told him. *Avoid the targeting fallacy.* Don't decide that you have a suspect and then see all evidence through that prism alone.

* * *

The tops of buildings disappeared in the mist that fell from low-hanging clouds and the tar pavement glistened in the streetlights as Santana and Hudson drove to a house on the east side of St. Paul.

The woman who answered the doorbell had long dark hair parted in the middle that framed her smooth, light-brown face like black silk. Her faded yellow cotton dress clung like wet tissue to her shapely figure. With her full lips, small nose, and large onyx-colored eyes, she conveyed both the innocence of youth and the allure of a knowing woman. But there was something in those eyes that was much older than her years.

"Ms. Sherilyn Lonetree?"

She nodded.

When Santana told her who he and Hudson were, her eyes glazed.

"Ms. Lonetree?" Santana said again. "We need to speak to you about your daughter."

Gnats swam in the yellow glow of the porch light. A gentle breeze rang the wind chimes that hung from a porch post. Sherilyn Lonetree's eyes refocused. Her gaze tracked slowly across Santana's face, as though reading his secrets. Then she turned without a word and headed into the living room.

The room had natural oak floors and was brightly lit, but Santana knew he was there to bring darkness. He closed the door behind him and sat next to Hudson on a cushioned couch with a spindle frame. An electric box fan pushed hot air from one side of the room to the other.

She turned off a radio that was tuned to an oldies station and sat down in a chair opposite the couch. On the wall behind her was a painting of eight tepees on a desolate prairie under a purple sky at sunset, the horizon streaked with a ribbon of yellow and orange.

Santana and Hudson each took out a spiral notebook and pen. Hudson had removed his hat upon entering the house, and Santana could see his partner's white hair had receded sharply on each side, leaving a point at his forehead.

"Do you have any children in the house?" Hudson asked.

"No."

"I'm afraid we have some bad news, Ms. Lonetree."

She nodded again, as if expecting this.

"Your daughter's body was discovered early this evening in Hidden Falls Park. We're very sorry."

She stared into space, her face creased with pain. Tears streamed down her cheeks.

Hudson and Santana gave her a moment.

Though death notifications were a regular part of Santana's job, they never got easier. "Could I get you something,

Ms. Lonetree? Some water or coffee, or maybe something stronger?"

She shook her head. "Thank you for asking." She took a handkerchief from her pocket and dabbed her eyes. "Did someone kill her?"

"We believe so."

"Do you know what happened? Was she in much pain?"

Santana looked at Hudson, who said, "No, there wasn't any pain."

She put her hands to her face. Her shoulders hunched as she sobbed quietly.

Santana knew it was a lie, but, like Hudson, he saw no point in describing the senseless brutally of her daughter's death. He felt compassion for Sherilyn Lonetree, but at the same time, with her face covered, he couldn't watch for tells or false mannerisms.

As she wiped her nose, he asked, "When was the last time you saw your daughter?"

"Yesterday."

"Did you report her missing?"

She shook her head. "Danielle called and said she was staying with a friend."

"What's the friend's name?"

She hesitated. "I didn't ask."

Santana thought it unusual that a mother wouldn't know where her daughter was staying.

Sensing his skepticism, she added, "Danielle was mature for her age. She never gave me any reason to distrust her. She always kept in touch."

"What about her father?"

Lonetree flinched, as if she had been poked with a sharp object. She looked at Santana for a long moment before replying. "She never knew her father."

Santana sensed there was something more behind her answer. Something she wasn't telling him. He wondered if Hudson felt the same, but he knew it was best not to make assumptions or jump to conclusions this early in the investigation. Still, he made a note.

"Do you know of anyone who might want to harm your daughter?" Hudson asked, re-taking the lead.

She shook her head.

"Do you know a man named Clay Buck?"

"Yes, I know Clay."

Hudson glanced at Santana, then eyed Lonetree again. "What do you know about him?"

"He and my daughter were dating."

"Could your daughter have been staying with Clay Buck?"

Santana had been thinking the same thing. He wondered if it was the reason Lonetree hadn't asked her daughter where she was staying. Maybe she already knew and didn't approve.

"It's possible." She blinked and her eyes widened as she stared at Hudson. "Is Clay dead, too?"

"We don't know, Ms. Lonetree. We're looking for him."

As Hudson closed his notebook, Santana said, "You and your daughter are Native American, correct?"

"Yes," she said. "We're part of the Mdewakanton Band of Eastern Dakota or Minnesota Sioux."

"Is Clay Buck from the same band?"

She nodded and sat still for a time, her eyes on Santana's. "You think Clay Buck killed my daughter?"

"We don't know."

"But you're thinking it."

"We found his truck near where your daughter's body was found. But Buck is missing and could be dead."

"Clay loved my daughter. He wasn't a violent person."

Santana nodded but offered no response. He didn't know yet whether Buck or someone else had murdered Danielle Lonetree. But he suspected that the killer had been someone for whom cruelty and sexual pleasure were interchangeable. Someone, he suspected, who not only killed for enjoyment, but who experienced an unnatural feeling of power and control over another human being, as if he believed he was God.

Chapter 2

Clay Buck lived in a doublewide modular home in a trailer park off Rice Street, directly across the road from a small strip mall. There was a screen door in front of a closed front door. Santana could hear a laugh track from a TV inside the trailer and the hum of a window air conditioner. The rain had stopped, but a lingering mist hazed and softened the streetlights, giving the city a ghostly quality.

Santana knocked on the screen door. Ten seconds later he knocked again.

Ten more seconds went by before someone inside muted the volume on the TV and a voice came from the other side of the door. "Who's there?"

"Mr. Buck?" Santana said.

"No. The name is Youngblood."

"We're from the St. Paul Police Department. We're looking for Clay Buck's residence."

"What's this about?"

"Do you know Clay Buck?"

"He's my nephew."

"We need to talk with you, sir."

"Clay in trouble?"

"If we could talk to you."

There was no reply.

"Mr. Youngblood?"

Santana heard the sound of the lock turning. The door slowly opened and a tall, thin man who appeared to be in his sixties peered out at them. He had shoulder-length silver hair and a tanned, leathery face. He wore a pair of well-worn jeans and a beige T-shirt. Imprinted on the front of his shirt, surrounding the face of a Native American man with a feather in his hair, were the words:

MAN BELONGS TO THE EARTH,
EARTH DOES NOT BELONG TO MAN

Santana attempted to open the screen door, but it was locked.

"Open the door," Hudson said. "Mosquitoes are eating us alive out here."

Youngblood lowered his gaze as he thought about it. "You have ID?"

Santana opened his badge wallet and held it against the screen door.

Youngblood stared at the badge wallet while Santana swatted mosquitoes away from his face. Then the old man unlocked the screen door and slowly pushed it open. "Hurry. I don't want those blood suckers in here."

Santana followed Hudson inside. He could feel the sudden cool temperature drying the sweat on his skin. The room smelled strongly of cigarette smoke and cat urine.

Youngblood quickly closed both doors. "Sorry the place is a mess," he said, clearing some newspapers off the couch. He turned off the television, lowered himself into a well-used chair, and set the newspapers in a magazine rack.

"No problem," Santana said.

He took out his spiral notebook and sat down on a couch covered with a tattered slipcover and cat hair, Hudson beside him. But his eyes were focused on the two glass frames that were hanging on the wall behind Youngblood. Inside each frame were locks of hair. Santana recalled that a lock of hair had been cut from the left side of Danielle Lonetree's head. He nudged Hudson, who was also staring at the frames.

Hudson cleared his throat. "My name is Detective Hudson, and this is Detective Santana."

Youngblood nodded and reached for the burning cigarette resting on the edge of the glass ashtray on the coffee table.

"How long has it been since you've seen Clay?"

Youngblood squinted as if he were staring into a bright light. "Two days," he said. "What's this about?"

"Is Clay the only one living here besides you?"

"Yes."

"Is there a Mrs. Youngblood?"

"Never was. No children either."

"Where's Clay's mother?"

"She left a few years ago. I don't know where she is now."

"What do you do, Mr. Youngblood?"

"I'm retired."

"Were you concerned that you hadn't seen your nephew for two days?"

He shook his head. "He sometimes stays with friends on the weekends."

"What friends?"

Youngblood shrugged. "I don't know."

"Maybe Clay's father knows where he might be?"

"Clay never knew his father. I never did either."

"Do you know a young girl named Danielle Lonetree?"

"Clay's been dating her. Why?"

"Her body was discovered earlier this evening in Hidden Falls Park," Hudson said.

Youngblood paused between puffs of his cigarette. He stared at Hudson without speaking. Then his gaze slid to Santana's face.

Hudson said, "Do you know Sherilyn Lonetree, Danielle's mother?"

"Not really."

"What does that mean?"

"It means I've met her but don't know her well."

"Your nephew's red pickup was left in the park near the body."

"What happened to Clay?"

"We're attempting to find out."

"Has your nephew ever worked as an electrician?" Santana asked.

"He did an apprenticeship for a time."

"What does he do for a living now?"

"He's between jobs."

Hudson pointed to the glass frames on the wall behind Youngblood. "Tell us about the locks of hair."

"Why?"

Santana knew neither he nor Hudson would reveal that the perp had cut off a lock of Danielle Lonetree's hair.

"Kind of an unusual collection," Hudson said. "I'm curious."

Youngblood thought for a moment before speaking. "It's a Sioux custom to remove a lock of hair from the dead. We believe it's the ghost of the dead person. For a deceased woman, a lock of hair is cut from the left side of her head. For a warrior, a lock of hair is taken from the top or scalp lock. Traditionally, the hair was wrapped in pieces of calico and muslin and hung in the lodge of the deceased."

"But now you hang them in frames."

"I do," he said.

"And whose locks are these?"

"My grandparents, my parents, a brother and sister, and other relatives."

Santana figured that whoever had cut the lock of hair from Danielle Lonetree's head either practiced or was familiar with the Sioux custom, which meant that the perp was most likely from the Sioux nation.

"What about your nephew, Clay Buck?" he asked.

"What about him?"

"Was he familiar with the custom?"

"Clay never followed the old ways."

"Were the faces of the dead ever painted red?"

"In some cases."

"And what cases were those?"

"In cases of murder."

Santana looked at Hudson. It might be reasonable to dispense with a written affidavit for a search warrant. But he would have to convince an after-hours duty judge of that. Then he would have to prepare a duplicate warrant and recite it to the judge, who would then tape record Santana's oral testimony and have it transcribed on the appropriate warrant form duty judges kept at home. All of this would take time. There was a quicker way if Youngblood would agree to it.

"Would you mind if we looked around, Mr. Youngblood?" Santana asked.

"Don't you need a warrant?"

"Not if you give us permission."

"There might be something that can help us find your nephew," Hudson said.

"Maybe he doesn't want to be found."

"What if he's in danger?"

"Or worse," Santana said.

Youngblood thought about it. Then he made a hitchhiking motion with a thumb. "Clay's bedroom is down the hallway. First door on the right."

The small, disheveled bedroom had a single unmade bed and bare walls. Clothes were strewn on the bed and the floor of a small closet. Hooked on one corner of the headboard was a seven-inch round metal ring wrapped with leather. The webbing was made of sinew. White feathers hung from the two leather strips tied to the ring's bottom. Santana had seen photos of something like this before and knew it was a dream catcher.

Pinned into the wall above a four-drawer dresser was an unframed color photo of Clay Buck and Danielle Lonetree. Buck had an arm around her narrow waist as her head rested on his shoulder. They were smiling.

Santana gloved up and placed the photo in an evidence envelope. Then he looked through the closet, dresser, and under the bed and mattress. In the nightstand next to the bed he found what he considered to be a key piece of evidence. He placed it in a second evidence envelope and listed both items on an inventory sheet. Nothing he had seen gave him a clue as to Clay Buck's whereabouts.

Santana removed the dream catcher from the headboard and carried it into the living room along with the envelopes.

"What's that?" Hudson asked.

"It's a dream catcher," Youngblood said. "Clay made it when he was a child. I think it's the only thing he ever kept."

"What's it for?"

Youngblood hesitated and bit his bottom lip with his front teeth, as though he were embarrassed to speak. "We have superstitions."

"Every culture does," Santana said.

Youngblood nodded his head slowly. Then he seemed to come to a decision. "We believe the night air is filled with good and bad dreams." He took the dream catcher from Santana's hand. "Dreams have to pass through the dream catcher to get to the sleeper. Good dreams know how to pass through the center hole in the web. Bad dreams get tangled in the dream catcher's web and disappear in the sunlight. But I never worried about my dreams."

"Did your nephew have many bad dreams, Mr. Youngblood?" Santana asked.

"When he was younger. That's why he made the dream catcher."

"And why would a child have so many bad dreams?"

"Maybe because he didn't know his father," he said. "But I don't know for sure."

But Santana heard no conviction in Youngblood's voice. "You told us earlier that Clay never followed the old ways."

The old man shrugged. "I don't know that he really believes in the dream catcher."

A moment of silence followed before Santana said, "Here's a receipt for the property we're seizing." He added the two glass frames containing the locks of hair and handed Youngblood a copy of the inventory sheet.

"Why are you taking the frames?"

Santana didn't answer.

"Thanks for your time, Mr. Youngblood," Hudson said. He handed the old man a business card. "You can reach me at the number on the card if your nephew turns up."

"You'll let me know if you locate Clay?"

Hudson nodded and took the two frames off the wall.

As they walked out of the trailer toward their Crown Vic, Santana said, "You find anything in the rest of the trailer?"

"Nope." Hudson nodded at the envelopes. "What do you have?"

Santana showed him.

"Maybe Forensics can link one of the locks of hair in the frame with Lonetree. And that blue bandanna is similar to the one that was stuffed inside her mouth."

"Exactly," Santana said.

"Enter a 'pick-up' for Clay Buck. We need to find him and have a chat."

Chapter 3

Late that evening, Santana had a drink with Wendell Hudson at Alary's, a downtown sports bar not far from the Law Enforcement Center. Alary's was a popular hangout for off-duty police officers, firefighters, attorneys, and city and state workers. The bar featured flat-screen TVs; police, fire and sports memorabilia; and young, pretty waitresses in tight T-shirts and short skirts.

Since they would be working the Danielle Lonetree murder investigation together, and because Santana did not want to get off on the wrong foot with the most senior homicide detective on the force, he felt obligated to accept Hudson's invitation. They weren't serving Sam Adams, so Santana ordered a bottle of Budweiser, Hudson the same.

A young, busty waitress brought their beers and some popcorn. When she left, Hudson raised his bottle in a toast and said, "Maybe we can close this Lonetree case quickly."

Santana nodded, acknowledging the toast. He always hoped for a quick resolution, but questions about the young girl's death lingered.

Hudson watched him for a while. Then he said, "Something bothering you?"

"The pickup truck."

"What about it?"

"You commit a murder and then leave your truck at the scene to implicate yourself?"

"Clay Buck couldn't get it started."

"Forensics called. They found the command wire on the solenoid was loose."

"They should've called me. I'm lead detective."

"The point is, how does that wire come loose unless someone pulls it off?"

Hudson hiked his shoulders. "Buck was drinking. Maybe when he couldn't get the truck started, he fooled around with the wire and accidentally pulled it off."

"I doubt it."

"You think I'm jumping to conclusions about Buck?"

"I never said that."

"You didn't have to."

"Look, Wendell. I respect your experience. You're the lead on the case. Gamboni just asked me to help out."

Hudson looked at Santana with a half-smile. "You still seeing her?"

"We quit dating when Rita became homicide commander."

"That's what I heard."

"Then you heard correctly."

Hudson ate a handful of popcorn and drank some beer. "I'll tell you what else I heard."

"Go ahead."

He pushed up the brim of his fedora and leaned forward, studying Santana's face before he spoke. "Word around the department is you're a guy who acts like he's got nothing to lose. I don't like having a partner with a death wish."

"Don't worry."

"I always worry, son. Worrying keeps me alive."

"We're on the same page."

"We better be. But before we set some ground rules, have you ever heard of the asshole theory?"

"Don't believe I have."

"It starts with the belief that there are a few assholes out there, and you need to watch out for them. Soon, you begin to think everyone but cops are assholes. Then it's everyone except your shift. Then it's everyone but your partner, and sometimes you wonder about him."

"Your point being?"

"Some guys I've worked with thought that a good partnership was like a good marriage. You had to share everything. Well, if you share everything with your wife, you can kiss your marriage good-bye. I know what I'm talking about. But if you stay in Homicide, you'll need a partner who'll help you bury the bodies. Only way to build that kind of trust is by talking through things."

"You mean about cases."

"I mean about everything. I've pretty much seen it all, John. But what we saw today was a bad scene, a bad body. The face painted red. The lock of hair cut from her scalp. The bandanna stuffed in her mouth. You see enough of that shit, it can scramble your brains."

"Psychiatrists call it acute stress disorder or street fatigue."

Hudson cocked his head. "How'd you know that?"

"When you're involved in a shooting, you have to see a psychologist for counseling. You pick up some terminology."

"Oh, yeah. That's right. You've had counseling."

Santana clearly heard the derogatory tone in Hudson's voice. Counseling was for crybabies, even if it was mandatory. Hudson's attitude was no surprise to Santana. Many in the department expressed the same viewpoint. Showing weakness or emotion of any kind, except in the case of a dead colleague, especially one killed in the line of duty, was frowned upon. It grew out of street confidence, the belief that detectives could handle anything, that they had control of their crime scenes. That sense of invincibility was continually supported by a fraternal culture within the department, a culture designed to trivialize the dangerous nature of their job and to contain their own fears. But a bad body could lead to a sense of powerlessness, of loss of control, the sense that a detective no longer owned the crime scene; the scene owned him.

"You ever shoot anyone, Wendell?"

Hudson shook his head slowly.

"Then you don't really know what the hell you're talking about, do you?"

Hudson put up his hands in a mollifying gesture. "Take it easy, John. We're just talking."

"No one knows what he'll do in a life or death situation. Believe me."

"I get that," Hudson said.

"I hope so." Santana finished his beer and stood. "See you tomorrow, Wendell."

"One more thing."

Santana waited.

"You stay in this job long enough, you'll learn that nothing else matters after working homicides. I know what I'm talking about. Be careful."

Santana understood Hudson's warning. Staying alive was one thing. Maintaining relationships and a life outside of homicide was another.

* * *

Santana drove to his two-story brick home situated on a wooded, secluded bluff overlooking the St. Croix River. His golden retriever, Gitana, or gypsy in Spanish, was happy to see him as always, her tail thumping excitedly against the hardwood floor as she leaned her body against him, kissing his face while he knelt beside her and stroked her head, speaking to her as he would a child.

"How's my girl?"

It bothered him that he often had to leave her alone for hours, even though she could use the doggy door in the kitchen to take care of her business and get some exercise in the enclosed dog run he had built for her in the backyard. On most days, he would take her for a long run before he left for work or after he returned.

He had adopted her after her owner had been killed during one of his investigations. She had saved his life on more than one occasion and helped fill some of the empty spaces in it as well. He owed her more than she would ever owe him.

He grabbed a Sam Adams, two chicken breasts on a plate from the refrigerator, and chips from a cupboard and, with Gitana at his heels, went upstairs and out the sliding glass door to the deck overlooking the river. He fired up a small gas grill, then stood at the railing and looked at the black ribbon of water while he waited for the grill to heat. Clouds slid across the face of the full moon. There was no wind, and he could hear the hum of tires along the interstate to the north.

Santana was uncomfortable sharing his thoughts and feelings with anyone, let alone a partner he barely knew. He hadn't appreciated Hudson's attitude about counseling, but he had understood it. Still, counseling after an Officer Involved Shooting was mandatory. What could he have done about it? Not gone? Turned in his badge?

But it was Hudson's question about Santana's relationship with Homicide Commander Rita Gamboni that had really angered him. Hudson, like everyone in Homicide, knew he was no longer dating her. Santana was aware that certain detectives believed that Gamboni treated him differently because of their past relationship. But Santana still had feelings for her and she for him.

He drank some beer, put the chicken on the grill, and closed the lid. Gitana was sitting on the deck, her head slightly cocked, staring at him with her big brown eyes. He would often catch her looking at him in this way, as though she understood his loneliness.

After dinner, Santana listened to Armando Manzanero's *Grandes Duetos* CD while he read the latest e-mail from his sister, Natalia, who was a pediatric surgeon at the Vall d'Hebron University Hospital in Barcelona, Spain. Following their mother's murder in Colombia when he was sixteen and Natalia seven, the Filipense nuns had hidden her in a convent in Spain after Santana had killed the men responsible for his mother's death and fled to the States, where he had changed his name from Juan Carlos Gutiérrez Arángo to John Santana. Twenty-one years later he had finally discovered her whereabouts while in Colombia on a case. Natalia had also changed her surname, but to Valencia.

To protect her from the Cali cartel and the assassins still hunting him, he and Natalia had established a private e-mail account. Only they, and an uncle in Bogotá, Colombia, knew the password to the account. Santana could not risk sending a direct e-mail to Natalia given that it might be intercepted, thus revealing her whereabouts to the cartel. They had worked out a system in which they would write each other e-mails but never send them. As long as each of them had the password to open the account, they could read the e-mails.

His sister wrote that she was dating a doctor from Barcelona who worked at the hospital. Natalia was young, smart, and beautiful. Many men would want to date her. Still, Santana was surprised by the unease he felt. He realized this feeling was common for a Latino brother. Most were very protective of their sisters. He hoped that she was involved with a good man, someone who would treat her with the love and respect she deserved.

He was also worried about his sister's safety. Would this man be able to protect her? No, he decided. He alone could protect Natalia. He alone would give up his life for hers. But upon further reflection, Santana realized that another feeling tarnished the concerns he felt for Natalia.

It was envy.

Chapter 4

The following morning Santana was up early, too revved up by what he had seen and learned to get much sleep, something that often happened whenever he began a new investigation. After a shower, shave, and breakfast, he drove to a tan brick building next to Regions Hospital. The one-story building had a front door for the living and a back door loading dock for the dead.

The dead were wheeled on gurneys from the loading dock through metal doors to an intake room with tile walls. Each body was then placed on a shiny silver metal cart and rolled into an autopsy suite. The suite was bright and clinical. Beside the autopsy table was a tray of razor sharp knives and scissors. A scale hung from the ceiling.

Rather than view the autopsy, some detectives preferred to hang out in the break room or nap in a sleeping room equipped with a twin-sized bed, a set of weights, and an inflatable balance ball.

Santana felt that it was important to remain with the victims. What he hadn't yet learned about them in life, he would learn about them in death. He would speak for them. It was his mission.

The bandanna found inside Danielle Lonetree's mouth could have accidentally worked its way backward, completely obstructing the airway. Most choking deaths were accidental in manner. In adults, choking almost always involved a piece of food wedged in the larynx. Such deaths had acquired the name of "café coronary." But it was far more likely that Danielle Lonetree had been bound and gagged to keep her quiet.

From experience, Santana knew that his role was more than that of an observer. He was an active participant, there to aid Reiko Tanabe in establishing the time, manner, cause, and mechanism of death so the case wouldn't get labeled as "Undetermined." After the autopsy was complete, he would write up an investigative report on the ME's findings.

Tanabe had checked the clothing for any fibers, droplets of blood, or residue, and the skin for bruises, wounds, or marks. She had photographed the body clothed and naked and had taken a blood sample and fingerprints.

She turned away from the autopsy table and looked at Santana through her plastic spatter shield. "The congested face, petechiae, and scleral hemorrhage indicate she was strangled, John."

"What about ligature marks?"

"There's a very faint mark on her neck. The perp probably used something soft like a towel and removed it immediately after death. There are no other abrasions or contusions of the skin of the neck. Typically in these cases, there's no fracture of the hyoid bone and thyroid cartilage. I found no hair in her hands. I'll take some fingernail cuttings, but we're unlikely to find any foreign tissue."

Most victims struggling to release a ligature ripped out strands of their own hair and often scratched the perp's face. But since Danielle Lonetree's wrists had been bound behind her, she was unable to use her hands. Santana hoped Tanabe could get some DNA off the bandanna.

"And the TOD, Reiko?"

While she thought about her response, one of the body snatchers assigned to pick up corpses pushed an empty gurney into the suite and then went out the double swinging doors again.

"You know the problem I always have with TOD, John. I don't know the temperature of the body at the actual time of death or the rate of cooling."

"Okay. Your best estimate, Reiko."

"Well, using the temperature I took at the scene, I'd say she'd been dead closer to twenty-four hours. That would put TOD at around eight p.m. the previous evening."

Tanabe's estimate fit the scene markers, Santana thought. Danielle's mother had talked with her daughter the day before.

Tanabe swabbed and then examined the genital area using a specialized colposcope equipped with a camera. She spoke into an overhead microphone as she noted tears and swelling, suggestive of insertion or attempts at insertion by a penis or foreign object into the vagina.

"So Danielle Lonetree was sexually assaulted," Santana said.

"That would be my conclusion."

Later, Santana forced himself to focus on the evidence rather than on his feelings of sadness and anger as he watched Tanabe remove the organs from Danielle Lonetree's body, weighing and bagging each organ that had once given life to the young Native American girl.

* * *

That afternoon, as rain beat on the Crown Vic's roof and lightning gashed the dark sky, Santana and Hudson drove south from St. Paul to Red Wing, Minnesota. It was a fifty-minute drive through flat farmland, where lighted windows were like distant stars in a dark, unending universe.

Santana gripped the Crown Vic's steering wheel. His eyes strained to see the center line. If the clock hadn't read 1:30 p.m., he would have sworn it was closer to midnight.

"We could pull over till the rain lets up some," Hudson said.

"If it gets much worse, I will."

Hudson unwrapped a stick of gum and put it in his mouth. "Juicy Fruit?" he asked.

"No, thanks."

Hudson wadded the wrapper, dropped it in a pocket of his sport coat, and chewed for a while before speaking again. "You think the dream catcher you found in Clay Buck's bedroom has any significance besides what his uncle told us?"

"I don't know."

Hudson chuckled. "Funny the superstitions people believe in. I had a Creole grandmother who always put a small bag of coins—or black-eyed-peas, as she called them—above the front door. She thought the coins would bring good fortune. Put them up in every house she ever lived in. Day she died, she didn't have a pot to piss in."

Santana's mother had done the same. He had grown up in a Colombian culture defined by superstition and the magical realism of writers like Gabriel García Márquez. From Ofir, the maid who had worked many years for his parents, he had learned the value of dream interpretation and intuition, skills that had helped him solve cases. But he saw no point in sharing these thoughts or his experiences with Hudson, a detective who was near retirement, a detective Santana would likely be working with for one case.

"Anything I need to know about the phone call from the Red Wing PD, Wendell, before we get there?"

A half-mile passed before Hudson replied. "Clay Buck refused to answer any questions during the field interview. He was told two SPPD detectives were picking him up."

"So the sheriff's department never Mirandized him."

"No. But as long as we were coming down, one of our detectives in CAP asked us to pick up a woman named April

Ford. She's wanted on identity theft and felony assault charges. Saves them a trip."

Santana knew Hudson was referring to the SPPD's Crimes Against Property division. "Anything on Danielle Lonetree's phone records?"

"She called her mother and Clay Buck the afternoon before her death. Nothing afterward. What about the ME?"

"Danielle Lonetree was strangled to death."

Hudson pushed back the brim of his fedora, peered out the rain-streaked passenger window, and blew out a breath. "Too bad Minnesota doesn't have the death penalty. Clay Buck should fry for his crime."

"We don't know that he killed Danielle Lonetree."

As Hudson shifted his gaze to Santana, approaching headlights created shadows like rivulets of rain on his face. He grinned at the corner of his mouth. "Sure we do."

Santana glanced at the darkness outside the driver's side window. He had fought the battle between the light and the darkness ever since he was sixteen and growing up in Colombia—ever since the demon of revenge had driven him to kill the two men who had murdered his mother. He knew the line between the two wasn't always fixed, that anyone could cross it, given the right circumstances and motivation. But he believed now that to be a good homicide detective, he had to become one with the darkness, without becoming the darkness itself. The best way to do that, he thought, was to understand that his job was as much about truth versus lies as good versus evil.

The rain slackened as they neared the town of Red Wing. Santana loosened his grip on the steering wheel and switched the windshield wipers to the intermittent setting.

Hudson chewed his gum and gazed out the passenger window again. "Think you'll ever get used to it?"

"You mean the bodies?"

"I mean death."

Santana sensed the intensity of his partner's gaze. "Death's no stranger."

"That right?"

"Fact is, death's the only certainty in life."

"Sure, when you're an old man or woman. Not when you're a seventeen-year-old child like Danielle Lonetree. Makes me question God's plan sometimes. But my faith keeps me strong. It gives me direction and purpose in life."

"Faith isn't what gives me direction."

"Then what?"

"Justice," Santana said.

Chapter 5

The Law Enforcement Center in Red Wing was the headquarters for both the Goodhue County Sheriff's Office and the Red Wing Police Department. The LEC was located next to the Justice Center, a few blocks from the center of town.

Santana had notified them that he and Hudson were coming. After parking in the sally port in the lower level of the building, they placed their weapons in small lock boxes embedded in the cement wall. A deputy in the master control room on the main floor monitored the cameras located throughout the building and access in and out of all doors. Once the door leading out of the sally port was opened, the detectives proceeded down a narrow cement-walled corridor to the elevator, where they waited again.

When the elevator door slid open, a deputy and two inmates exited and headed for the tunnel leading to the Justice Center. One inmate was clothed in a dark blue jumpsuit, the other in orange. Santana knew that orange jumpsuits were for inmates with discipline issues. He figured a judge would know that as well.

Santana and Hudson took the elevator up one floor to the intake center. Deputies had made sure that both Clay Buck and April Ford were waiting in individual holding cells near the desk. Santana filled out the release forms, acknowledging that Buck and Ford had been received into his custody.

Santana escorted Clay Buck to the Crown Vic in the sally port and placed him inside a dual-seated cage in the back of the sedan. The cage had a full roll bar, two doors, seatbelts, and a sturdy plastic divider. Buck wore blue jeans over a pair of Nike running shoes, a white T-shirt under a brown leather vest, and a blue bandanna tied around his neck. He had high cheekbones common to many Native Americans. His heavy-lidded, almond-shaped eyes were dark and intense. He wore his long black hair in a ponytail. His hands were cuffed behind him.

Santana watched as Hudson placed twenty-four-year-old April Ford in the cage on the other side of the divider. Her long black hair was streaked with bright red. She was dressed in a sleeveless cotton pullover and tight-fitting jeans that were tucked into high black boots. Dark roses were tattooed on her thick upper arms, and a barbell bead pierced her tongue. Her hands were also cuffed behind her.

By the time they were back on the road again, it was nearing 3:00 p.m. Dark clouds still clustered along the edge of the horizon. A V-shaped flock of geese soared across the purple sky like the black tip of an arrow.

"What's this all about?" Buck said.

Hudson half-turned his body toward the back seat and peered at Buck through a thick wire-mesh screen.

"The murder of a young girl in Hidden Falls Park."

"I didn't kill anyone."

Santana could see both sides of the cage in the rearview mirror. Buck was gazing at the back of Santana's head. But April Ford was staring at Buck. Then she looked at Hudson. "Did he kill someone?" Her blue eyes were dancing with excitement.

"Ask Buck," Hudson said.

She did.

Buck shook his head without looking at her.

"Where's your truck?" Hudson said.

"Parked near the river where I left it two days ago."

"Why park it there?"

"I went fishing. When I came back, it wouldn't start."

"And where specifically did you park it?"

"In a lot in Hidden Falls Park."

"Were you alone?"

Buck hesitated. "Yeah."

"So what did you do then?"

"I walked to a friend's house."

"And then what?"

"He drove me to another friend's house in Red Wing."

"You didn't call a service station about your truck?"

"I didn't have money to tow or fix it. I thought I'd borrow some from a friend in Red Wing."

"Did you?"

"We were on our way to the bank this morning when the cops picked me up. And here I am."

"Well, someone killed the girl," Hudson said. "You were drinking. Maybe it was an accident? Maybe you panicked?"

"And maybe whoever took her killed her."

Santana glanced at Hudson, who nodded his head in understanding.

"Who said anything about kidnapping a girl?" Hudson said.

Buck offered no reply.

"You have any more of those blue bandannas you're wearing, Mr. Buck?" Hudson asked.

"No," he said.

"A blue bandanna was found at the crime scene."

"Then whoever took her left it to set me up."

"Uh-huh," Hudson said. "Then how come Detective Santana found another blue bandanna in a dresser drawer in your bedroom?"

"Maybe I had another one."

"You catch anything the day you went fishing?"

"No."

"What did you do with your fishing gear?"

"I think I left my pole in the woods."

"Maybe if we drove by the park, it would jog your memory."

"I don't remember."

"You don't remember if you left your fishing pole in the woods, or you don't remember killing the girl?"

Buck offered no response.

"Think about your options, Buck," Hudson said. "You don't have many."

"He said he didn't kill anyone," April Ford said to Hudson. "Leave him alone."

"You should learn to keep your mouth shut, young lady."

"I will if you will," she said.

Hudson laughed and shifted in his seat and faced the windshield again. "You go down for murder one, Buck, you'll go away for life. You help us out, maybe there's a plea bargain in the offing."

Santana touched Hudson on the knee and shook his head in a silent warning. He knew that unless Buck had counsel present or was advised of his Fifth Amendment rights and voluntarily waived them, any confession they heard now would be tainted.

"Don't worry," Hudson said. "I know what I'm doing."

Santana wasn't sure, but he kept his thoughts to himself.

They were halfway home when Santana saw a white van ahead moving well below the speed limit in the right hand lane of the two-lane highway, water blowing in a vortex behind it. He let up on the gas pedal as he approached, flicked on his left turn signal light, and checked his side mirror. A dark blue Cadillac with tinted windows was sitting in his blind spot, as if it was about to pass. In his rearview mirror, he saw the headlights of a black pickup truck fast approaching in the lane behind him.

The hairs on the back of Santana's neck stood up. "We've got trouble."

Hudson turned in his seat and looked out the rear window, then at the Cadillac to his left.

It had pulled even with them now, but Santana couldn't see anything through the tinted glass. The pickup behind them was riding the Crown Vic's bumper. As the van in front of them slowed, Santana had to do the same.

They were boxed in and would soon be forced to stop.

Santana swung the Crown Vic's steering wheel to the right and pressed the gas pedal to the floor. The big sedan lurched off the road and bounced onto a dirt and gravel farm road.

"What's going on?" April Ford said in a voice filled with alarm.

The Crown Vic's rear window exploded and a bullet slammed into the dashboard.

April Ford screamed.

"Jesus!" Hudson yelled.

In his rearview Santana saw the three vehicles speed onto the farm road, led by the black pickup.

Hudson tried his cell to request backup. "No service," he said. "We must be in a dead zone."

"Not yet," Santana said, giving Hudson a little smile. He nodded at the radio.

Hudson shook his head. "The bullet. The radio is toast."

Santana glanced in his rearview again. The three vehicles were still a quarter mile back. Keeping ahead of them, he figured, would be no problem for the Crown Vic. But he had seen the yellow "Road Ends" sign a half-mile back and knew their pursuers had probably seen it too. If the road ended at a farmhouse, they would be endangering innocent lives.

He slowed and turned to the right, across a field, ripping through corn stalks and soft dirt. Gunning the engine, he held the wheel tightly, trying to keep the big car from sliding sideways. Fifty yards from the road the wheels sank into the soft earth. The Crown Vic would go no farther.

Santana killed the engine, shoved the driver's side door open, and then unlocked the rear driver's side door and the cage and pulled Buck out by the crook of his arm.

Hudson went out the passenger side and freed April Ford from the cage. Then he opened the trunk and grabbed a 12-gauge pump and two bulletproof vests before crouching behind the car beside Santana.

As they put on their vests, Hudson said, "I wish we had an AR-15."

"We don't have one?"

"You have to qualify to carry one."

"You never took the training course?"

"I don't have much time left, John."

Santana knew Hudson was referring to retirement, but the double meaning was not lost on him.

The three vehicles came to a stop along the road, and four people got out. Two had handguns, one carried a shotgun, the fourth an assault rifle with a scope. They all wore black ski masks.

Hudson chambered a round into the shotgun. "Maybe we can hold them off."

"Not with the ammunition we have," Santana said.

The one on the road with the shotgun went off to the left, and the one with the assault rifle went to the right. The two with the handguns started toward the Crown Vic. One of them was smaller than the other and had the figure of a woman.

"They're trying to flank us," Santana said. "Get us in a crossfire."

Hudson glared at Clay Buck and then April Ford. "Either of you know who these assholes are?"

Buck was stoic and silent. April Ford shook her head.

Santana had wondered at first if the four were assassins from the Cali cartel, but a lone assassin was their typical M.O.

Drizzle fell in the cornfield. It was, Santana calculated, maybe one hundred yards on a side. Just beyond the cornfield behind him to the south was a thick stand of evergreens, birch, and maple trees. To the east near the trees sat a small, dilapidated barn with peeling red paint.

"The cornstalks are over five feet tall," he said. "If we stay in the corn and keep the Crown Vic between us, we might be able to make it to the tree line." He gestured toward the trees with his Glock. "We've got a better chance of holding our ground there."

"Sounds like a plan," Hudson said. He looked at Clay Buck. "You copy that?"

Buck nodded.

"You'd better. Because if you run, I'll put you down."

Buck nodded again, but Santana saw no fear in the young man's eyes.

"Do you have any more of those vests?" April Ford asked.

"Sorry," Santana said.

"Then uncuff me," she said. "Give me a chance."

Santana unlocked her handcuffs. "Stay close."

She licked her lips and nodded.

"How 'bout uncuffing me?" Buck said.

Hudson looked at him as if he were crazy. "Not a chance."

"I can't run with my hands cuffed behind me."

Hudson swore under his breath and unlocked Buck's cuffs. "Let me see your hands."

"Why?"

"Don't argue."

Buck held his hands out in front of him.

Hudson cuffed Buck's wrists again.

"Let's go," Santana said.

They moved deeper into the cornfield, Santana in the lead, followed by April Ford, Clay Buck, and Hudson. Santana used his free hand to protect his face from the stalks of corn as he veered between them. It was raining harder now. Rain soaked his clothes and formed small puddles in the soft earth. The thick, humid air smelled strongly of sweet corn and damp soil.

Five minutes later, they came to the edge of the cornfield, where they stopped and sat on their haunches, fifteen yards from the tree line.

"We've got to run for it," Hudson said. "But not in a straight line." He was panting hard and sounded nearly out of breath. A faint sheen of perspiration had formed on his forehead.

"I'll go first," Santana said.

A second later he sprinted for the trees, zigzagging, intent on getting across the open field, where he would be most vulnerable, as quickly as possible. Even in the dim light and behind curtains of rain, he could see brown cones hanging from the evergreens as they loomed closer.

He was within five yards of the trees when the first shot sent a spray of mud and dirt into the air inches from his feet. A second shot struck the branch of a maple tree just above his head. Then Santana was among the trees, where he stopped and squatted down, catching his breath, laying cover fire for Ford, Buck, and Hudson till they reached the trees.

"Now what?" April Ford said. She was beside Santana, ten feet to Hudson's right. Buck was between Hudson and the girl.

"We wait."

"For what?"

"We've got the advantage of good cover. If they try and cross the open field, we'll see them."

"Except one of them has an assault rifle with a scope," Hudson said. "Probably the one that nearly took your head off seconds ago."

"Maybe the four of them will leave," Buck said, kneeling on the damp ground.

"Depends on how badly they want one of you."

"Why would they want me?" April Ford asked.

"If we capture one, we'll ask," Santana said.

"They want me," Buck said.

Hudson jerked his head in Buck's direction. "Why?"

"Because I saw them burying the body."

"Saw who?"

"I don't know who they were. But there were three men. They were the ones who killed Danielle. And I can identify them."

"Then you were with her," Hudson said.

"We drove to Hidden Falls. I was drinking some. Danielle didn't like it. We argued. I left her in the truck and went for a walk. When I returned, she was gone. That's when I saw them covering her body."

"They saw you?" Santana asked

"They chased me."

"Don't give me that," Hudson said. "You know damn well you killed her. Why else would you run?"

"I was running for my life." Buck clenched his fists, gritted his teeth, and started to rise.

Hudson grabbed Buck by the belt and pulled him down. "What'd you think you're doing?"

"I'm going to make them pay for what they did."

"Don't be stupid. You're handcuffed and you have no weapon. You'll be dead as soon as you step into the open."

Santana looked at Hudson. "They think we're heading for the barn."

"How do you know that?"

"It's the only place that has cover on all sides. The guy with the rifle will clear the barn first before he comes this way."

"What're you getting at?"

"I'll work my way east and see if I can neutralize him, get the rifle. That might even the odds."

"You get yourself killed, that leaves me here alone with these two."

"I'll try not to let that happen."

Hudson thought about it. "Remember what I said about a death wish?"

Santana nodded. "Remember, I told you not to worry?"

"Yeah."

Santana nodded once more and headed east, a shadow among the trees.

Chapter 6

Santana worked his way ten yards deeper into the trees and then stopped behind a birch to listen. He could hear drops pelting leaves, but nothing else. His skin felt warm in the high humidity and temperature. He was already soaking wet, and the rain showed no sign of easing up soon.

If killing Buck was the objective, were he and Hudson simply considered collateral damage? But killing two SPPD detectives made little sense. The heat generated by the murder of two police officers would be intense. Maybe the shooter with the scope on his assault rifle had deliberately shot low and then high. Maybe, like a pack of wolves, they were trying to separate their prey from the herd. If that were the case, then Santana had already made a mistake by leaving Hudson alone with Buck and the girl.

The dilapidated barn lay in a clearing thirty yards to the east. The red siding had faded over time to a washed-out brown color, like the rusted hull of an old ship. High grass grew around it. Just beyond and in front of the barn was a concrete foundation that Santana figured had once supported a farmhouse. Whoever owned the property now had built a larger barn and farmhouse seventy-five yards to the east.

He imagined the entrance to the old barn would be on the north side of the building below the gable. If he wanted the advantage of the high ground, Santana knew he would have to make it to the barn before the shooter. If he was late —well, he didn't want to consider that possibility.

He moved cautiously out from behind the birch tree, his Glock in his right hand, and quickly covered the distance to the barn. The main sliding door was slightly off its hinges and had no lock. Santana stopped and listened again. Raindrops rattled off the wooden structure and pinged off a leaky metal trough to his left.

He squeezed through the opening in the door and stepped inside the barn.

Immediately he dropped to a knee and scanned the area with his gun barrel. Empty cattle pens ran parallel along the walls to his left and right. Gray light filtered through small holes in the ceiling. A thick layer of dust streaked the windowpanes. The barn smelled of manure and old, damp hay that littered the floorboards.

A hayloft above him jutted out from the near corner to his left and extended halfway along the left side of the barn. Thick beams supported it. Santana saw no access ladder, but a long rope tied to a ceiling beam hung through a cutout in the loft's floor.

Kids, he thought.

He went to the rope and yanked on it. Satisfied that it would hold him, he holstered his Glock and climbed up, hand over hand, letting the rope fall across the top of one foot while he stepped on the rope with the other, locking the rope in place between his shoes and taking some of the strain off his arms.

From his perch in the left corner of the loft, Santana could see out a wide ten-foot door, where hay had once been loaded from wagons, and into the tree line that extended all the way to the farmhouse in the distance.

He waited three minutes before he saw a man dressed in camo raingear carrying an assault rifle. A hood protected his head; a black ski mask covered his face. Twenty yards from the barn and the end of the tree line, the man hunkered down beside a maple tree and scoped the area.

Santana ducked away from the open doorway and pressed his back against the wall. At this angle, he could still watch the man as he moved forward in a crouched position, taking cover behind individual trees. Five yards from the end of the tree line, he knelt and scoped the building one more time. Cautious. Professional. Seemingly satisfied, he ran toward the front of the barn.

He entered directly below the loft where Santana stood. One nerve-shattering moment later, Santana saw what the man below him must have seen.

The rope was swinging slightly, as if blown by a soft wind.

But Santana knew there was no wind inside the barn—and so did the man below him.

He leapt out the hayloft door a split second before the air exploded with a deafening roar as bullets split the wood floor. Bending his knees before impact, Santana landed on the balls of his feet in the soft ground, curled his body, and tucked one shoulder in as he rolled to cushion the fall. Then he was on his feet again, running for the northwest corner of the building.

Seconds later, bullets raining through the walls kicked up clouds of dirt and wood shards as they slammed into trees and blew out a large hole in the barn door, allowing the shooter to step through.

"Lose the rifle," Santana said from his kneeling position at the corner of the barn.

The man hesitated.

"I'll drop you where you stand."

The man squatted and set the assault rifle gently on the ground.

"Stand up."

He did.

Santana moved forward quickly and pressed the barrel of the Glock against the back of the man's head. Then Santana grabbed him by the collar and pulled him backwards.

The man did not resist.

Five yards from the barn door, Santana said, "Get on your knees, pull back your hood, and clasp your hands behind your head."

He calmly followed the instructions.

Santana removed a thirty-round magazine from the man's coat pocket. Then he searched the other pockets for an ID. Finding nothing, he moved in front of him and yanked off the ski mask.

The shooter appeared to be in his mid-to-late twenties. His dark hair was close shaven, and his body was stocky and powerfully built like a weightlifter's. Raindrops dampened his hard, pockmarked face.

"What's your name?" Santana said.

The man remained silent. His dark eyes were as dead as a charred match. They were focused not on Santana, but on some distant point.

Santana suspected he was ex-military and had been trained to resist questioning. Still, he tried one more time.

No response.

Then, from a distance, Santana heard the sound of gunfire, followed seconds later by two loud booms. *A shotgun.*

Santana cuffed the man to a leg of the heavy metal trough near the barn door. Then he picked up the AR-15, exchanged magazines, and ran toward the shots.

He was halfway back to the spot where he had left Hudson, Buck, and April Ford when he heard limbs snapping. He huddled behind a thick maple and peered through the rifle scope. It took a few moments to locate the figure heading toward him, but only a second to recognize Hudson. He was half-stumbling, half-running through the woods, his eyes focused on the ground in front of him, his fedora missing from his head, his left hand pressed against the bloody wound in his shoulder.

Santana bolted from his position and ran toward him. "Wendell! Over here!"

Hudson stopped and looked up. Then he spun around and went down as a shot echoed through the woods.

Santana felt a spike of adrenaline. He charged ahead and opened fire with the assault rifle, spraying the area behind Hudson with a long burst of bullets that ripped through branches and tore leaves off the trees.

Soon he was kneeling at Hudson's side, his breath coming fast and his heart beating hard. He scoped the woods before turning his attention again to Hudson, who lay on his back, squinting in pain.

"Wendell!"

He gazed at Santana with unfocused eyes. "I don't want to die."

Santana pulled back Hudson's sport coat. He could see an entrance wound in Hudson's right shoulder. Hudson groaned as Santana rolled him on his side. "The bullet is still in your shoulder, Wendell. The vest stopped the one in your back."

Hudson managed a weak smile. "Can't feel much." His lips and nail beds were turning blue, the first signs of shock.

"You're losing blood. You need a hospital."

"The guys behind me might have something to say about that."

"Not so much now that I have the AR-15. What about Buck and the girl?"

"They took off when I first got hit."

"Can you stand?"

"I think so."

Hudson let out a cry of pain as Santana helped him to his feet, his left arm draped over Santana's shoulders. "Where's your Glock?"

"I dropped it. Buck picked it up when he and the girl took off."

"Let's move."

"Where we going?"

"To the farmhouse."

"What about the residents?"

"We don't have much choice now. Even if we could get back to the car, it's stuck in the mud. Besides, we've got the firepower. And whoever is after Clay Buck is probably chasing him, not us."

"You better be right," Hudson said.

Chapter 7

In an interview room at the LEC in St. Paul, Santana looked across the table at the SPPD detective from Internal Affairs. The detective had jet-black hair, skin the color of saddle leather, and a nose like an eagle's beak. Rumors were that he was a descendant of Sitting Bull.

The detective flicked on the small tape recorder in the center of the table and said, "My name is Glen Tschida. I'm assigned to the Internal Affairs unit of the St. Paul Police Department." He gave the date and the current time. "The following is an interview with Homicide Detective John Santana. No other persons are present during this interview." His dark eyes peered at Santana. "For the record, will you please state your name, rank, and current assignment with the St. Paul Police Department?"

"Sergeant John Santana, assigned to Homicide."

"Detective Santana, do you understand that this interview is being recorded?"

"Yes."

"Would please raise your right hand?"

Santana did.

"Do you swear that the information you provide will be true and correct to the best of your knowledge?"

"Yes, I do."

"Okay. Prior to this interview, were you given the opportunity to read all relevant documents and reports?"

"Yes."

"Were you given an opportunity to consult with a representative prior to this interview?"

"I was."

Santana recalled the briefing with his union rep. The Officer Involved Shooting team had handled the initial investigation. Internal Affairs had been called in because there had been an allegation of misconduct.

Since Internal Affairs had never interviewed him before, it had been helpful to learn about the expectations and the dos and don'ts in answering questions. Santana had been counseled to think of the interview as giving testimony in court or providing a deposition in a lawsuit, something he was familiar with. The union rep had cautioned him to let the IA investigator complete the question and to think carefully before responding clearly and concisely. If he didn't understand the question, he could ask the investigator to repeat or rephrase it. If asked a multiple part question that could be answered in multiple ways, Santana had been advised to have the investigator break it down into single questions.

The key point was to answer only the question asked. If a question could be completely answered by yes or no, this was recommended. If he truly didn't remember or didn't know the answer, then he had been instructed to say so. He had been warned never to speculate. If he felt he had sufficiently provided an answer, there was no need to expound or elaborate. The goal was to provide a complete, clear, and concise short answer. It was the investigator's job to ask the proper question.

Santana was certainly familiar with posing questions to subjects and witnesses. However, turning the tables and becoming the subject or witness on the receiving end of those questions was not in his comfort zone.

"Let me advise you, Detective Santana, that this is an administrative investigation and is not criminal. You are further advised that truthful statements during this interview cannot be used against you in any subsequent criminal proceeding, except in the case of perjury. You are, therefore, required to answer all questions truthfully regarding this investigation. Any refusal to do so may result in disciplinary action. Do you understand?"

"I do."

"Do you waive your right to counsel during this interview?"

"Yes."

"All right," Tschida said. "Let's proceed. I'm going to summarize the incident and ask you some questions regarding the shooting and the allegations. These allegations are not about you, but about Detective Wendell Hudson. Do you understand?"

"Yes."

"Okay. Let's get started. On August twenty-fourth, a 'pick-up' was issued for Clay Buck, a suspect in the murder of Danielle Lonetree."

"That's correct."

"On the afternoon of August twenty-fifth, you and Detective Wendell Hudson drove to Red Wing, Minnesota, to get Clay Buck, who had been detained by the Red Wing Police Department."

"Yes."

"At the time, you also were requested to retrieve a woman named April Ford."

"Yes."

"According to the summary reports filed by you and Detective Hudson, on the return trip, the Crown Vic you were driving was forced off the road by three vehicles."

"Yes, it was."

"And why were you forced off the road?"

"I didn't know at first. Later, Clay Buck said the perps in the vehicles were after him because they had killed Danielle Lonetree and Buck could identify them." And if that were true, Santana thought, then Buck hadn't killed Danielle Lonetree. Maybe he had been framed to take the fall for her death. But Santana knew that was supposition.

Tschida took some time to review the report on the table in front of him and the questions he had written on a yellow legal pad.

Santana drank some water from a plastic bottle the investigator had provided.

"You stated in your report, Detective Santana, that there were four armed perpetrators in three vehicles and that you believed that one of those perpetrators was a woman."

"Yes."

"Once you'd reached the woods beyond the cornfield, the four of you decided to separate."

Santana thought about his answer before replying. "The four of us didn't decide to separate. I left the group to track the shooter with the assault rifle."

"And this was your idea?"

"The four perps had separated. They were attempting to set up crossfire. I figured the only chance we had was to neutralize the one with the assault rifle."

"So you left Detective Hudson alone with Clay Buck and April Ford."

"Yes."

"Was Buck handcuffed?"

"He was."

"April Ford, too?"

"No. I took off her handcuffs when we exited the Crown Vic."

"Did Buck ever request that his handcuffs be removed?"

"He did."

"But the request was denied."

"Yes."

"By you?"

"No, by Detective Hudson. But Hudson did cuff Buck's hands in front of him instead of behind."

"What weapons did you and Detective Hudson have?"

"We both had our Glocks. Detective Hudson also had a department-issued 12-gauge shotgun with pump action."

"You mentioned that one of the perpetrators pursuing you had an assault rifle."

"Yes."

"What about the other three?"

"From what I observed, two were armed with handguns. A third carried a shotgun."

Tschida looked at his copy of the summary report again and then at the legal pad before his eyes locked on Santana's once more. "I'm going to skip ahead to when you first heard what you reported were shots. This was after you'd disarmed the man with the assault rifle. How many shots did you hear?"

"As I noted in my report, I wasn't sure."

"But you did write that two rounds were fired from a shotgun."

"Yes."

"And you didn't know at the time if Detective Hudson had fired his shotgun."

"No. As I previously said, one of the perps pursuing us also had one."

"When you reconnected with Detective Hudson, was he armed?"

"No."

"Did he tell you what had happened to his weapons?"

"He told me he dropped his Glock and Buck picked it up."

"What about his shotgun?"

Having read the summary report, Santana knew that the shotgun had been found in the woods, but he didn't know that at the time. "I didn't ask."

"Did you ask Detective Hudson where Clay Buck and April Ford were?"

"I did."

"And what did he reply?"

"He said they ran off after he was wounded."

"Hudson said nothing else?"

"He said that he didn't want to die."

Tschida stared at Santana for a long moment before he spoke again. "After you arrived at the farmhouse, you were able to call 911 using a landline."

"Yes."

"When did you first learn that Clay Buck had been shot?"

"After the emergency personnel had taken away Detective Hudson, I spoke with Detective Flint from the Goodhue County Sheriff's Department."

"What did Detective Flint tell you?"

"That Clay Buck had been found dead."

"He'd been shot."

"Yes."

"In the back."

"Yes."

"And the bullet that killed him came from Detective Hudson's Glock."

"I didn't know that at the time."

"And the young girl, April Ford, was missing."

"That's what Detective Flint said."

Tschida nodded. "Let's talk for a moment about the man with the assault rifle."

Santana's hands were sweating. He drank some water.

"You wrote in your report that you'd cuffed him to a water trough."

"Yes."

"But when you eventually returned to the trough, he was gone."

"Yes."

"If, as you reported, the trough was very heavy, how was it possible for him to have escaped?"

Santana recalled that the man had been powerfully built and probably had lifted weights. He could have raised the trough high enough to slide the cuff off the leg it was attached to or picked the lock. But it was pure speculation.

"I don't know," he said.

"Was anyone with you when you returned to the trough?"

"No."

"And this man was never found."

"No."

"In fact, none of the four perpetrators or their vehicles has been found."

"No."

"You never got one license plate number?"

"They were smeared with dirt." Santana figured it had been done deliberately, but he didn't say it.

Tschida sat forward in his chair and rested his thick elbows on the tabletop. "Is there anything you want to add to your statements?"

Santana didn't feel there were any discrepancies or inaccuracies presented during the interview. He shook his head.

Tschida pointed to the recorder. "Please reply verbally, Detective Santana."

"No. There's nothing I want to add."

"I'll write a summary, have the recording transcribed, and forward all materials to your commander for review," Tschida said.

"Okay."

Tschida turned off the recorder.

Santana got up and left the interview room without thanking Tschida.

Chapter 8

Santana was sitting at a round table on the patio in the backyard of Wendell Hudson's house off Hazelwood Avenue in Mounds Park, a small neighborhood of houses built in the '40s and '50s. The houses sat on the Mississippi River bluff overlooking the city of St. Paul near Interstate 94 and six Native American burial mounds archeologists believed had been constructed over fifteen hundred years ago. He was drinking Sam Adams and listening to the hum of tires on the freeway and the sizzle of hamburgers on the grill. Hudson was drinking a margarita over ice and flipping burgers with a spatula.

Darkness was settling over the landscape. Despite the cool fall air, Hudson was sweating. Santana wondered if it was from the heat off the grill or from the wrongful death lawsuit Clay Buck's uncle, Chaska Youngblood, had brought against the department.

"You've made a good recovery, Wendell."

He offered a satisfied smile. "You saved my life."

"You would've done the same."

He nodded as if it were a given. "My shoulder is still sore, and I have a hell of a painful bruise on my back, but it could've been much worse."

"What are your plans after the trial, Wendell?"

"Depends on the verdict." He paused, frowning with concentration. "You know I didn't shoot Clay Buck in the back."

Rather than answer, Santana posed a question. "What happened after I left you in the woods? We've never talked about it."

Hudson closed the grill lid. Smoke leaked out from under the cover and rode on the wind. "Two guys coming in from the north started firing into the woods at us from the edge of the cornfield. I returned fire."

"What were Buck and the girl doing?"

"Taking cover in the trees."

"So you stayed where I left you."

Hudson nodded.

"I heard two rounds from a shotgun."

"The first shot came from the north, John. I fired back with my shotgun, but the shooter was too far away. I was wounded in the shoulder a few seconds later. I drew my Glock but dropped it. Buck picked it up and took off. The girl followed."

"Which direction?"

"West. Toward the highway."

"Why do you think they ran in that direction?"

"They knew you and the shooter with the assault rifle were in the opposite direction. Maybe Buck figured if he got to the highway, he could flag down a car—or stop one with my gun."

"He was still handcuffed?"

Hudson nodded.

"The prosecution is going to say you shot Buck when he tried to escape."

"Why would I shoot him? I was more concerned about my life at the time, not his."

"Buck's body was found in the woods where we sought cover, Wendell. How could that be?"

"I don't know. Maybe the perp who shot him brought him there."

"What do you think April Ford will say?"

"I'll tell you what she shouldn't say."

Santana waited.

"She shouldn't say I shot Clay Buck in the back because I didn't."

"What if she testifies that you did?"

"Then she'll be lying."

"Why would she lie?"

"Maybe a better question to ask, John, is why didn't I kill April Ford, too, especially if she saw me kill Buck?"

"I've asked myself that question, Wendell."

Hudson stared at the grill for a time and then at Santana again. "You don't believe me, do you?"

"I never said that."

"You don't have to. I can see it in your eyes."

Santana had some doubts that Hudson was telling the truth, but he had no solid evidence that Hudson had, in fact, shot Clay Buck. "I'm on your side, Wendell. Believe me."

Hudson nodded, but he didn't look convinced.

"Two things still trouble me about Buck being the prime suspect in Danielle Lonetree's murder," Santana said.

"What things?"

"The forensic report noted that a plug wire on Buck's pickup was slightly off. That's why the truck wouldn't start. Why would a plug wire be off unless someone pulled it off? Why would Buck disable his own truck?"

"We've been through this before, John. Who the hell knows? Buck had obviously been drinking."

"Think about it, Wendell. What if the perps who ran us off the road intended to frame Buck for her murder?"

"How did they know Buck and Lonetree were in Hidden Falls Park in the first place?"

"If they intended to frame him, they would be following him, looking for the best opportunity. After Buck went to the river, they took the girl and disabled his truck. When he came back and tried to start it, he saw them burying the body. He fled when they spotted him. They painted Danielle Lonetree's face red, cut off a lock of her hair, stuffed the blue bandanna in her mouth, and left the electrician's tape in the truck bed."

"Buck would say anything to save his neck. Besides, he knew Sioux customs, and he worked as an apprentice electrician."

"Leaving his truck and all those clues was like leaving a sign saying he did it."

"So maybe he's not the brightest bulb in the package."

"Then why would someone run us off the road after we picked up Buck in Red Wing? Why would someone attempt to kill Buck unless they wanted to silence him?"

Hudson shook his head slowly, as if he wasn't sure.

"I'll tell you why, Wendell. Because Buck might not have known who they were, but he saw their faces. He could identify them."

"Look, John, we're getting off track here. I'm facing a civil trial in six months, not a criminal one. The bar is pretty low. All the prosecution has to show is a preponderance of the evidence, not guilt beyond a reasonable doubt. The jury only has to believe that it's more likely to be true that I shot Buck than not true. You have to testify that I didn't shoot Buck."

"How can I do that? I wasn't there when it happened."

Hudson sipped his drink and thought about it. "Maybe you heard a final shot in the cornfield when you were helping me to the farmhouse."

"But I didn't."

"Are you sure?"

Santana nodded.

"But I did."

Santana knew it was a lie. "Is that what you told the OIS team and IA?"

"I did. What did you tell them?"

"Tschida never asked if I'd heard or seen the shot."

Hudson smiled. "There you go. He left you an out. All you have to say on the witness stand is that you heard one shot when you were helping me to the farmhouse. That might be enough to convince a jury that I'm innocent, which I am. And it'll save the city a lot of money. What do you say, John? You going to help me out?"

Santana drank some beer and looked at the horizon to the west as the last glimmer of twilight faded into darkness.

Chapter 9

Santana looked around the mahogany-paneled courtroom with the low ceilings and saw that it was half-full. Reporters, whom he recognized, occupied the seats along the back row.

The courtrooms in the Ramsey County Courthouse were modeled after the British system of justice. Attorneys from each side, along with the plaintiff and defendant, all sat at one long, rectangular table. But since the table was long and the courtroom relatively small, it had to be angled, meaning that one of the attorneys, and his or her client, had to sit with their backs to the jury. Experienced attorneys arrived early to secure the most favorable positions, where they could view the jury box.

Barry Kirchner, sitting beside Wendell Hudson, had secured the optimum position. At 5' 6" he appeared less than intimidating. Yet he had a reputation as a smart, tough defense attorney who wouldn't back down. Busts and paintings of Napoleon decorated his office. He shunned the title of litigator—someone he considered a backroom dealmaker—and insisted instead that he was first and foremost a trial lawyer. That was all he did. People either loved him or hated him. But in either case, there was no ignoring him. Santana hoped that Kirchner's confrontational style wouldn't hurt Hudson's chances.

Chaska Youngblood, seated beside his Native American attorney, Diane Wade, was a picture of stillness. In the seats behind Youngblood was a contingent of Native Americans. One of them was Carrie Buck, Clay Buck's sister. Santana recognized her from an interview on a local television station in which she had proclaimed her brother's innocence and blamed the department for his death.

The seats directly behind Wendell Hudson were empty.

Santana felt an adrenaline rush as Judge Robinson entered the courtroom. At 6' 4" he was a bear of a man. He had been a civil rights attorney before his appointment to the bench and, as a young African American man, had marched in the South with Martin Luther King, Jr. He was known as a tough but fair judge. Still, Santana thought Robinson, given his civil rights background, might rule procedurally in favor of Diane Wade and her client, Chaska Youngblood, whenever the opportunity presented itself.

Santana had followed the civil trial in the newspaper and had been surprised that Diane Wade had rested her case without calling him as a witness.

"If Wade were to call you to the stand, John, she would have to ask the questions first," Kirchner had explained. "That would give me more time to plot strategy and to discredit her case. By not calling you, she's reversed the situation. My choice now is to not call you and probably lose the case, or call you and give her the best shot at you. It's a smart move."

A law clerk gaveled the court to order, and everyone fell silent.

"You may call your first witness of the day, Mr. Kirchner," Judge Robinson said.

Santana heard his name read by the law clerk. He glanced at the jury of five women and seven men as he made his way to the witness stand. Three of the jurors were black and three were Asian. One was Latino and five were Caucasian.

Most civil trials in Minnesota were presented to a judge. Anyone requesting a jury trial had to pay a fee of $102 to the court in advance of the trial, except in trials involving the recovery of money or personal property, where defendants had a right to a jury trial unless waived. But Diane Wade had believed that her client, Chaska Youngblood, stood a better chance with a jury. Santana figured her assumption was probably correct.

Robinson administered the oath to Santana himself, rather than the clerk. It was something he preferred to do.

Kirchner stood and looked at Santana with his intelligent brown eyes. The courtroom's small size limited movement. No lawyer could approach the witness stand or jury box, so the lawyers remained at the table as they asked their questions.

"I would ask the Court's permission to let Detective Santana check his notes if need be."

Judge Robinson said, "Ms. Wade?"

"I have no problem with the detective checking his notes as long as I have copies of those notes. I assume I do."

"Very well," the judge said. "But before we proceed any further, will you inquire of the witness whether he has anything in his possession that has not been given to the plaintiff in discovery in this case?"

"Thank you," Wade said.

Kirchner turned to Santana. "Everything you've given to the county, you have given to the plaintiff, have you not?"

"Yes."

"If you will then, Detective Santana, please state your full name and your occupation."

"Detective John Santana, St. Paul Police Department, currently assigned to the Homicide and Robbery unit."

"Tell us a little about your background, Detective."

"I've been a police officer for sixteen years."

"How long before you became a detective?'

"Seven years."

"And how long have you worked Homicide?"

"Seven years. Prior to my current assignment, I spent two years in Narcotics."

"So Detective Hudson was not your first partner in Homicide."

"No."

"Had you known him before?"

"I knew who he was. But I wouldn't say that I knew him well."

"How long did you work directly with him?"

"Just a few days."

"Would you say you know him better now?"

"Yes."

"Would you consider Detective Hudson a good police officer?"

"Objection, Your Honor," Diane Wade said. "That calls for an opinion."

Kirchner faced the judge. "Your Honor, Detective Santana is an experienced police officer. Having worked with many other officers and detectives, he should be able to make a reasonable judgment."

"I'll allow it," Judge Robinson said.

"Thank you, Your Honor." Kirchner turned to Santana again and repeated the question.

"I would consider Detective Hudson a good officer, yes."

"Detective Santana, were you involved in the investigation into the death of Danielle Lonetree?"

"Yes."

"And when and where did you first become involved?"

Santana gave the date and time when he and Hudson had been called to the crime scene in Hidden Falls Park seven months ago.

"Would you briefly describe the crime scene?"

Santana did without describing it in graphic detail.

"You mentioned that you found a blue bandanna in the victim's mouth."

"Yes."

"Your Honor," Kirchner said, holding up a clear evidence bag containing a blue bandanna. "I would offer this into evidence, county exhibit number ten."

The judge said, "Any objection?"

"No objection," Diane Wade said.

"Exhibit number ten is received in evidence."

"Thank you, Your Honor. Now, Detective Santana, did the forensic technicians process a red pickup found in the parking lot near the crime scene?"

"Yes, they did."

"Whom did the truck belong to?"

"It was registered to Clay Buck."

"What did you find in the bed of the truck?"

"A roll of electrical tape."

"And was this tape later identified as being of the same type that bound Danielle Lonetree's wrists?"

"Yes, it was."

Kirchner entered the roll of tape into evidence.

"Tell us what happened after you left the crime scene, Detective Santana."

"Detective Hudson and I went to see Sherilyn Lonetree."

"The victim's mother."

"Yes. We informed her of her daughter's death."

"And did you learn anything about Clay Buck?"

"We learned that he and Danielle Lonetree and her mother were all part of the Mdewakanton Band of the Minnesota Sioux tribe. And that Clay Buck was dating Danielle Lonetree."

"Where did you go from there?"

"After leaving the Lonetree residence, Detective Hudson and I went to Mr. Buck's residence to question him."

"Was Mr. Buck home?"

"No, he was not."

"Was Mr. Buck living alone?"

"No. He was living with his uncle, Chaska Youngblood."

"And did you serve a search warrant on Mr. Youngblood?"

"No. We asked if we could search the premises. He gave his consent."

"What did you find when you searched the residence?"

"I found a blue bandanna similar to the one found in the mouth of the victim."

"Where did you find this bandanna?"

"In Clay Buck's bedroom."

"And what did you do with this item?"

"I placed it in an evidence envelope. I then wrote my initials, badge number, the date and the time on the envelope indicating that I had secured it, and I turned it over to Forensics."

Kirchner handed a clear envelope to Santana for his examination. "Is this the item you put in the evidence envelope?"

"Yes."

Kirchner placed the bandanna into evidence.

Wade raised no objection.

"Did you take anything else into evidence, Detective Santana?" Kirchner asked.

"We took two glass frames containing locks of human hair."

"What was the significance of the locks of hair?"

"Forensics noted that a lock of hair had been cut from Danielle Lonetree's head."

"Did you question Mr. Youngblood about the locks of hair?"

"We did."

"And what did Mr. Youngblood tell you?"

"He told us it was a Sioux custom to remove a lock of hair from the dead. The Sioux believe it's the ghost of the dead person. For a deceased woman, a lock of hair is cut from the left side of her head."

"Was the lock of hair removed from Danielle Lonetree taken from the left side of her head?"

"Yes, it was."

"So that suggests that whoever killed her was aware of the custom and belonged to the Sioux tribe."

"Objection, Your Honor," Diane Wade said. "Speculation."

"Sustained," the judge said.

"What did you do after leaving Mr. Youngblood's residence?"

"I issued a 'pick-up' on Clay Buck."

"Could you explain what a 'pick-up' is for the jury?"

"When an officer has probable cause to make a felony arrest, the officer is authorized to broadcast a 'pick-up' for the person's arrest. Then a BOLO is sent to counties across the state."

"And what's a BOLO?"

"It's an acronym for Be On the Lookout. Departments were authorized to detain Clay Buck based on the description we provided."

Kirchner glanced at his notes before asking Santana the next question. "When did you come into contact with Clay Buck, Detective Santana?"

"The following day. We were told that authorities in Red Wing were holding Mr. Buck. Detective Hudson and I drove down to pick him up."

"Was Mr. Buck the only person you picked up in Red Wing?"

"No. We also picked up a woman named April Ford."

"And why were you bringing her back to St. Paul?"

"Objection," Diane Wade said, standing. "Already asked and answered."

Santana knew that Kirchner wanted to remind the jury about Ford's record of assault and identity theft—a fact he had already elicited when Diane Wade put Ford on the witness stand—thereby undermining her credibility as a defense witness.

"You opened the door, Ms. Wade," the judge said. "Overruled."

"Thank you, Your Honor," Kirchner said. He looked at Santana again. "Why were you bringing April Ford back to St. Paul?"

"A detective in the Crimes Against Property Division asked us to bring her back. She was wanted on identity theft and felony assault charges."

"What happened on the return trip?"

Santana went through the incident in detail for the jury, including how he had found an unarmed Wendell Hudson wounded and stumbling through the woods.

When he had finished, Kirchner said, "I have no more questions, Your Honor." Santana understood that Kirchner's strategy had been to avoid any reference to the shot that had killed Clay Buck, leaving that up to Diane Wade during cross-examination.

She stood and glanced at a yellow legal pad on the table in front of her.

Santana had no personal experience with Wade and knew little about her skills as a lawyer. But the word in the department was that she knew her way around a courtroom and was meticulously well prepared. Kirchner had warned Santana that Wade's soft-spoken manner belied a killer instinct. Once she zeroed in on the jugular of her opponent's case, she wouldn't let go.

"Good morning, Detective Santana."

"Morning," he said.

Her short dark hair was brushed back from her pleasant face. She wore no makeup. Her nails gleamed with clear polish. A pair of half glasses hung from a chain around her neck. Her figure was hidden in the stiff lines of her gray suit.

"During the return trip from Red Wing to St. Paul, did you or Detective Hudson engage Mr. Buck in conversation?"

"Yes," Santana said. "Detective Hudson spoke with Mr. Buck."

Santana understood what Diane Wade wanted. April Ford had clashed with Wendell Hudson. Ford had testified of Hudson's efforts to extract a confession and admission of guilt from Clay Buck. In her opening statements and in April Ford's testimony, Diane Wade had used a broad brush to paint an unflattering portrait of Hudson. Now, Wade needed Santana to support that portrait.

"According to your affidavit, Detective Santana, Detective Hudson told Mr. Buck that the two of you were investigating the death of Danielle Lonetree."

"No. Detective Hudson told Mr. Buck that we were investigating the death of a young girl."

Diane Wade's cheeks momentarily colored, but she quickly regained her composure and moved on to her next question. "What rights specifically did you or Detective Hudson advise Mr. Buck of at the time he was told the two of you were investigating the death of a young girl?"

Santana glanced at Wendell Hudson. Hudson's eyes were steady on Santana's face.

"Please answer the question, Detective Santana," Diane Wade said.

"Mr. Buck was not Mirandized."

"Could you tell the jury what the Miranda warning consists of?"

Santana looked at the jury. "I'm a law enforcement officer. I caution you that you have the absolute right to remain silent. Anything you say can and will be used against you in a court of law. You have the right to the advice of a lawyer before and the presence of a lawyer during questioning. If you cannot afford a lawyer, one will be furnished to you free before any questioning, if you desire."

"So Mr. Buck was never read his rights, yet Detective Hudson still questioned him. Is that correct, Detective Santana?"

Santana shifted his gaze toward Wade. "Yes."

"Did you, at any time, question Mr. Buck?"

"No, I did not."

"And why didn't you, Detective Santana?"

"I was driving."

"So you would have questioned Mr. Buck had you not been driving."

"Objection," Kirchner said. "Speculation."

Judge Robinson thought about it. "I'm going to allow it, Mr. Kirchner. Answer the question, Detective."

Santana knew he had no room to maneuver. "No."

"No, what, Detective?" Wade said.

"No, I would not have questioned Mr. Buck had I not been driving."

"And why is that?"

"Because he hadn't been given his rights."

Wade nodded for the jury's benefit. "Did Detective Hudson say at any time that Mr. Buck had killed the young girl?"

Santana let out a slow breath. "Yes, he did."

"And what was Mr. Buck's response?"

"He said he hadn't killed anyone. Later, he said he didn't remember."

Diane Wade seemed surprised by Santana's second response. He guessed April Ford had told Wade only that Buck had denied killing Danielle Lonetree and not that he couldn't remember what had happened. Santana figured Buck had been referring to the whereabouts of his fishing pole, but the young man had never clarified his response when Hudson had asked him about it. Santana was happy he had made the point for the jury and, at least momentarily, thrown Wade off stride.

But Wade quickly recovered. "At any time did Mr. Buck say that he had murdered the young girl?"

"No."

"Did Detective Hudson extend to Mr. Buck any promises of any sort that if he were to speak at that time or at any later time, it would be to his advantage?"

"No. Detective Hudson made no promises."

Diane Wade collected her thoughts for a moment before rephrasing the question. "Did Detective Hudson say that if Mr. Buck cooperated, there might be a plea bargain in the offing?"

"Yes."

Wade flipped a page on her yellow legal pad and looked at Santana again. "When you, Detective Hudson, Clay Buck, and April Ford were fleeing your pursuers, did Mr. Buck attempt, at any time, to escape?"

"No."

"Was Mr. Buck handcuffed?"

"Yes."

"Was Ms. Ford handcuffed?"

"When we first picked her up from Red Wing. But I uncuffed her in the cornfield after we exited the Crown Vic."

"Did Detective Hudson at any time threaten to shoot Mr. Buck?"

Santana drank some water from a cup the clerk had left for him on the stand. He glanced at the jury and saw that all their attention was focused on the witness stand. "Yes," he said, "but only if he ran."

"So Detective Hudson told Mr. Buck that he would shoot him if he ran."

"Objection," Kirchner said. "Already asked and answered."

"Sustained," the judge said. "Proceed, Ms. Wade."

"When you were helping Detective Hudson to the farmhouse, after he'd been wounded, do you recall hearing any shots?"

Santana knew the question was coming, knew he could say he had heard a shot and no one would be the wiser. Glen Tschida had either purposely not asked him about the shot during the IA interview or had overlooked it. Santana would not be contradicting his past statements—but he would be contradicting what he knew to be the truth. He had not heard a shot.

He didn't look at Hudson when he said, "No. I did not hear a shot."

Wade paused and looked at the jury, giving them plenty of time to comprehend the significance of what had just been said before she turned to Santana again.

"Were Clay Buck, April Ford, and Detective Hudson in the cornfield when you left them?"

"No. They were in a thick stand of trees south of the cornfield."

"Where was Mr. Buck's body found?"

"In the woods."

"You mean in the thick stand of trees where all of you had taken cover."

"Yes."

"And not in the cornfield."

"Objection, Your Honor," Kirchner said. "Detective Santana has already answered the question."

"Sustained."

"Detective Santana, are you familiar with the term reasonable force?"

"Yes."

"When used as an adjective, the dictionary defines the word 'reasonable' as 'being in accordance with reason and not extreme or excessive.' Would you say that this definition fits with your understanding of the word 'reasonable'?"

Santana knew where this line of questioning was headed, and it angered him that he could do nothing about it. "Yes."

"The word 'reasonable' is also used in the Minnesota statute describing authorized use of force, Detective Santana."

"Is that a question?" Santana said.

"Your Honor," Wade said, blowing out a frustrated breath.

"Let's be respectful, Detective," the judge said.

"Sorry."

"Please restate your question, Ms. Wade," the judge said, peering at her over his half lenses.

Wade made a show of flipping through the pages of her notes. Santana knew it was a show because she had already made her point. Even if Clay Buck had fled, she had planted the seed in the jury's mind that shooting him in the back was excessive, not reasonable, force. Kirchner hadn't raised the issue of reasonable force since Hudson had testified that he hadn't shot Buck.

"Let's move on," Wade said. "According to the evidence inventory, you and Detective Hudson took two glass frames from Chaska Youngblood's residence."

"Yes."

"And there were locks of human hair in those frames."

"That's correct."

"Did the forensic lab compare the locks of hair in the frames to the lock of hair taken from Danielle Lonetree's head?"

"Yes."

"And did any of the hair in the frames match the hair taken from Danielle Lonetree's head?"

"They did not."

"No further questions, Your Honor," Diane Wade said.

Kirchner stood for re-direct, hoping to salvage something from Santana's damaging testimony. "Detective Santana, did you or Detective Hudson display a weapon or threaten Mr. Buck in any way that he would feel compelled to speak to you or Detective Hudson?"

"No."

"Did Mr. Buck understand that he was a suspect in the murder of a young girl and was being brought back to St. Paul for that reason?"

"Yes."

"So he voluntarily answered Detective Hudson's questions."

"Yes."

"Did Detective Hudson ask Mr. Buck where his truck was?"

"Yes."

"And what was Mr. Buck's response?"

"He told us that he'd parked it in a lot in Hidden Falls Park while he went fishing in the river. Detective Hudson asked him if he caught anything. He said no. Then Detective Hudson asked him what he'd done with his fishing gear. Mr. Buck said that he'd been drinking and thought he'd left his fishing pole in the woods."

"Was a fishing pole ever found in the woods near the crime scene?"

Santana peered at his notes a moment. Then he looked up and said, "No."

"When you and Detective Hudson picked up Mr. Buck at the jail in Red Wing, was he wearing a blue bandanna around his neck?"

"Objection, Your Honor. Mr. Buck is not on trial here. I fail to see how this line of questioning has anything to do with the case against Detective Hudson."

"Overruled. A blue bandanna has already been introduced as evidence."

"Thank you, Your Honor," Kirchner said.

The judge looked at Santana. "You may answer the question, Detective."

"Mr. Buck was wearing a blue bandanna."

"Did Detective Hudson ask Mr. Buck if he had more blue bandannas?"

"Yes, he did."

"And what was Mr. Buck's response?"

"His initial response was no. He said he didn't have any more blue bandannas."

"Then what happened?"

"Detective Hudson asked him to explain how I'd found another blue bandanna in his bedroom dresser drawer. That's when he said he may have had another one."

"All right. Was there any other conversation immediately after about this item?"

"Yes. Detective Hudson told Mr. Buck that a blue bandanna was found at the crime scene."

"And what did Mr. Buck say?"

"He said that whoever took the girl placed the bandanna at the crime scene to set him up."

"The word or the phrase 'whoever took the girl' was Mr. Buck's?"

"Yes. I wrote it in my notes."

"Had you, Detective Hudson, or any other officer to your knowledge, at that point in the investigation, ever told

Mr. Buck that Danielle Lonetree had been abducted, kidnapped, taken, or whatever the phrase might be?"

"No. We had not. Detective Hudson told him only that we were investigating the death of a young girl."

"His response was that the girl had been taken?"

"Yes."

"All right, Detective Santana. When you were helping Detective Hudson to the farmhouse, did you ask him what had happened to his Glock?"

"Yes."

"And what did he say?"

"Detective Hudson said that after he was wounded, Clay Buck had taken it."

"And how many wounds had Detective Hudson sustained?"

"Two."

"Did you ask Detective Hudson what had happened to Mr. Buck and Ms. Ford?"

"Yes. He said they had run off."

"Both of them?"

"Yes."

"And when did he say they had run off?"

"After he was shot."

"Thank you," Kirchner said. "I have no further questions at this time."

Santana wondered if Wade would ask the judge for permission to re-cross since his testimony might leave doubt in the jurors' minds. But past experience reminded him that he could not predict what was in the minds of jurors. Some of them might have had negative experiences with law enforcement. Some might have issues with the use of deadly force.

"Detective Santana," the judge said, "you may be recalled as a witness in this case. As a result, do not discuss your testimony or anything else about the case with anyone except for these attorneys. You may step down."

Santana had no problem with the judge's order. He never wanted to discuss this case again.

NOW

Three Months Later

Chapter 10

Jane Linden's U-shaped cubicle workspace in the Homicide and Robbery Unit at SPPD headquarters was decorated with photos of her and her husband and child, and her horse, Ravel, along with pictures of the victims whose cold case deaths she had investigated. Rows of thick blue binders lined the shelves above her station. The murder books were filled with notes, photos, diagrams, and transcripts of unsolved cases. Inside each binder cover a progress report gave a detailed account of everything that had been discovered about the case to date.

"I get a letter or a call every week from somebody looking for closure," she said, peering at Santana as she held up a letter. "The vic's friends and family have a difficult time moving on without it." Noticing that he was looking at the victims' photos, she said, "Getting a sense of a vic's life is my way of keeping them alive."

"You personalize them because they should be something more than a number or a file."

She nodded. "It's a connection, a way of showing respect." Her face became thoughtful, her hazel eyes looking off into space as she reflected. "Just because these cases haven't been solved doesn't mean the victims have no value and their families don't suffer."

Tall and attractive, with short hair the color of straw, Linden favored black T-shirts, matching jeans, and roper-style western boots with a shorter boot shaft. Her department ID hung from a crime-scene-tape lanyard, and her Glock was nestled in a close-fitting leather shoulder holster.

"That's why shutting down the cold case unit makes me sick to my stomach." She tossed the letter on her desk as though it suddenly had no value.

"I didn't know it was shutting down."

"The final decision hasn't officially been made. But there are budget cuts in all city departments. Plus, the mayor wants more officers on the streets."

"Shutting down the unit doesn't make sense."

She sat back in her chair and locked her fingers across her belt buckle. "The department got less than a quarter million to fund the unit. I reapplied for another federal cold case grant, but the available money was cut in half. We weren't funded a second time. Besides, in the only case we brought to trial in three years, the perp walked."

The not guilty verdict had surprised everyone, including the judge. Linden had collected solid physical evidence, fingerprints, and DNA. Santana had always wondered if someone had threatened a jury member.

"There's no money left to pay one detective to dig through the old files searching for new evidence," she said.

Santana knew the brass preferred not to discuss cost/reward ratio, particularly when it involved homicide cases. Still, he felt obligated to point out the obvious. "You can't put a price on justice."

"Tell that to Romano and the AC," Linden said, referring to Homicide Commander Pete Romano and to Tim Branigan, the assistant chief of the Major Crimes and Investigation Division. "If they won't dedicate resources to follow up on cold case leads, then justice won't be served."

"Closing the cold case unit isn't Romano's idea, Jane, even if it involves only one officer."

She shrugged. "Yeah. So Romano got creative." She gestured toward the newer of the two white boards hanging on the wall of the squad room.

Five Open-Unsolved cases were listed on the board. Santana saw that he and his partner, Kacie Hawkins, were the only two of the seven detectives assigned to Homicide whose names were written on the OU board.

Besides murders, robberies, and cold cases, the Homicide and Robbery Unit investigated suicides, unattended deaths, assaults on departmental personnel, kidnappings, terroristic threats, obstructions of the legal process, as well as impersonating a police officer, bigamy, drive-by shootings, officer-involved critical incidents, unlawful possession of tear gas and/or electronic control devices and bulletproof vests, certain types of harassment, and stalking. The unit averaged 2,300 to 3,300 cases a year.

The second white board listed the current homicide cases detectives were working. Santana could see five were in various stages of investigation. Romano had recently moved the boards out of his office and into the squad room where they would have more visibility.

"You come up with the list of OU cases or did Romano?" Santana asked.

"Not that it makes any difference, John, but Romano asked me to give him a list, as long as it included Sam Noor."

Santana looked down at the blue binder in his lap. "Why the special treatment for Noor?"

"Because his wife is pressuring the department to get it solved."

"How's she doing that?"

"She's rich and a big contributor to the police foundation. And her father was a former chief."

Santana could hear the bitterness in her voice. Because of his frequent contact with the victims' families, he was aware that keeping cold cases on the back burner sent survivors the message that the victims—many of whom were killed while engaged in prostitution and other crimes—were not important, which only compounded the pain.

"Have you spoken with Noor's wife?" he asked.

She shook her head.

When Santana had first joined the Homicide and Robbery Unit, administrative approval was required to show the victim's family the cold case file. Most senior detectives believed they needed to protect the family of the victim from all the sordid details of the still-open investigation. When a suspect went on trial, it was often the first time family members had heard the whole story.

That had all changed when Rita Gamboni became commander of the Homicide and Robbery Unit. She believed in keeping families informed. She also had applied for a federal grant that encouraged police departments to use advances in DNA testing to re-examine cold cases. Gamboni had recruited Linden, who in turn had recruited a few retired detectives to examine some of the unsolved cases. But the grant money had dried up, and Gamboni had accepted a position as departmental liaison to the FBI's Safe Streets Initiative. It pleased Santana that Pete Romano wanted to continue Gamboni's more open communication efforts with the victims' family members. Of course, the wheels of justice were often greased when the victim's wife was the daughter of a former chief—and she was rich.

"According to the case file," Linden said, inclining her head toward the blue binder in Santana's lap, "Sam Noor was hired by an environmental group opposed to silica mining in Red Wing."

"Any solid leads?"

She shook her head.

"Why me?"

She hiked her shoulders. "I don't know. But Romano specifically told me to give you Noor's murder book."

After talking with Linden, Santana believed he knew why the case had suddenly become a priority.

Linden leaned forward in her chair. "You could turn this all around, John."

"How do you mean?"

"If you solve this high-profile case, Romano might think twice about closing the cold case unit."

"You'll still have a job no matter what the outcome, Jane."

"That's not the point."

"So what is?"

"This job is one of the most important in the department. We need to keep the unit open. Not just for me, but for the victims and their families."

"I'll do the best I can."

"I know you will."

"But it won't be my fault if the unit closes. Don't lay the responsibility on me."

She nodded as her hazel eyes slid off his face.

"Something else you wanted to say, Jane?"

Her eyes held his again. Then she exhaled, as if she had been holding her breath. "The investigating officer on the Sam Noor case."

"What about it?"

"I thought you should know," she said. "Wendell Hudson was the IO."

Chapter 11

Santana took the murder book back to his desk in the Homicide and Robbery Unit, a large, brightly lit room filled with cubicles and workstations. Someone much higher in rank—or with more influence than Pete Romano—must have assigned him the Sam Noor case. And he figured he knew who that someone was.

Santana didn't like the idea of looking into an unsolved file and possibly proving a colleague was wrong or incompetent, especially if the colleague was Wendell Hudson. Despite his denial of guilt, Hudson had carried the baggage of Clay Buck's murder with him into retirement. Any contact Santana had with Hudson now would open up the festering wound that was Buck's death. Hudson also felt Santana had betrayed him at the civil trial. Santana had no desire to revisit the issue. But he had no choice in the matter. He would have to talk with Hudson. He had to trust that his former partner had done his job well and conducted a thorough investigation into Sam Noor's death.

The reports were filed chronologically in the blue three-ring binder. The narrative on the preliminary reports indicated that Sam Noor's body had been discovered in Hidden Falls Park. Santana found it curious that Danielle Lonetree's body had also been found in the same park a month before Noor's death, and that Wendell Hudson had worked both cases. But any connection between the two murders was pure conjecture at this point. Still, Santana filed it in his memory bank.

Sam Noor had been found in a shallow grave near the Mississippi River. The body had been discovered at 6:25 a.m. by a jogger. The reporting officer had quickly identified the vic because Noor's wallet and driver's license were found on him. The RO had interviewed the female jogger, as had Hudson, who concluded that she was not a suspect.

There were no witness statements since no one, apparently, had witnessed the crime.

Next in the binder was a group of summary reports on interviews conducted during the investigation with known associates. Most of the KAs were people with incidental knowledge of the victim and the crime along with friends and acquaintances. Hudson had interviewed the victim's wife, Kelly Noor, and the victim's son, Adam. Santana read the two reports carefully. Both wife and son claimed they were home alone on the night of the murder. Neither had witnesses to support their alibi.

Hudson had also interviewed Virginia Garrison, who headed an environmental group in Red Wing, Minnesota, that opposed silica mining, but that had led nowhere.

Forensics had pulled plants from the ground around the body. The plants were placed between sheets of paper and flattened in a book prior to submission to a forensic botanist at the University of Minnesota. On the submission form under TYPE OF ANALYSIS REQUESTED, Hudson had typed: *Check each to determine if any trace evidence can be found that could link any plant to the victim or suspects.*

Santana read the forensic summary report on the plants, but no trace evidence had been found.

No credit cards or cash was found in the wallet or in the victim's pockets. Noor's gold watch and wedding ring were also missing, which suggested robbery as a possible motive.

An eight-by-ten envelope contained the crime scene and autopsy photos. Santana studied each of the photos and then moved on to the evidence inventory list, which was stapled to a second envelope.

EVIDENCE RECOVERED
1 short-sleeved shirt, white—blood stained
1 pair of pants, khaki—blood stained
1 pair of underwear, white
1 leather belt with silver buckle, brown
1 pair of leather loafers, brown
1 pair of brown socks
1 leather wallet, brown

It was clear by the clothing and shoes that Noor was not jogging in the park when he was murdered. After removing the brown paper bags used to preserve any trace evidence on Noor's hands, the ME had examined and collected evidence from Noor's hands and clothing and placed it in manila envelopes, which were then sealed and labeled. Then the clothing items had been individually removed and re-examined.

Santana thought it odd that Sam Noor's cell phone hadn't been recovered, but if robbery was the motive, the perp might have taken the phone. He made a note to ask Wendell Hudson about it.

Hudson had obtained the call history logs from Noor's cell phone provider. Santana crosschecked the call logs with the phone numbers of KAs and family members he had written in his notebook. He assumed that he was covering the same ground Hudson had covered when he was the investigating officer. But Santana wasn't comfortable with assumptions, particularly when they involved someone other than himself.

Noor's last phone call on the day he was killed was to his wife. The call was made at 3:56 p.m. Credit card records revealed that Noor had purchased gas at a Mobile station in Mills Creek at 6:36 that evening.

Santana then reviewed the chronological case log at the back of the murder book. It was an investigative record listing the date, time, and result of each action taken. Santana often used the log to summarize investigative reports and analyze evidence, and as a reference in testimony. In reading through the log Hudson had created, nothing he saw struck him as more important than when it had originally been entered.

Next, he retrieved the evidence box from the property room. Each of the listed items had been placed in labeled paper bags inside the box. Removing Noor's shirt from a bag, he could see that it had been torn, possibly indicating that Noor had struggled with the perp. Santana wished more significant evidence had been recovered, but he moved on to the external and internal sections of the summary report of the autopsy.

The ME had submitted nail scrapings taken from Noor's hands and hairs found on his body to the BCA lab in St. Paul. But analysis by the state crime lab had determined that the hairs did not possess a sufficient number of unique individual characteristics to be positively identified as having originated from a particular person to the exclusion of all others. The nail scrapings had led to another dead end.

All latent prints belonged to the victim. The laboratory data and drug and bacterial screen results were negative. Blood samples had been placed on labeled Protein Saver filter cards. Each card was then sealed in a labeled manila envelope and given to Hudson, who had attended the autopsy. Separate cards were held frozen as per routine blood card storage.

There were multiple stab wounds, but no weapon was found. Prior to the autopsy report, Hudson's initial assumption based on the appearance of the body was that Sam Noor was the victim of a random robbery that had turned violent. But the autopsy report had changed his mind. Sam Noor had not died from the wounds. Santana thought the stab wounds also indicated something else.

He wanted to talk to the ME.

* * *

Reiko Tanabe's office reminded Santana of a relaxing study. Light gray carpet and whitewashed furniture brightened the interior of her windowless office. Dark green walls matched the lampshades over the brass lamps on the two end tables. A wicker basket in one corner held a tall silk plant. A glass framed anatomy chart and medical degrees covered one wall, a tall bookshelf filled with medical texts another. Because she often met with the victim's family to discuss autopsy results, Santana knew Tanabe had made a conscious effort to create a warm and comforting atmosphere.

"You wanted to discuss Sam Noor's autopsy report," she said, her brown eyes steady and unblinking behind the lenses of her wire-rimmed glasses. She wore no makeup and no jewelry, save for a thin gold wedding band. Just below the open collar of her white shirt, Santana could see the *café au lait* mark on her neck, the only blemish on her smooth, youthful skin that belied her forty-some years.

Santana nodded and opened the murder book in his lap. "You estimated that Sam Noor was killed around eight-thirty p.m."

Tanabe tapped the keyboard of her computer and peered at the large screen on the corner of her desk. "Yes. His body was in complete rigor mortis when discovered in Hidden Falls Park. He'd phoned his wife around four that afternoon and purchased gas at six thirty-six that evening. Figuring that rigor begins two to four hours after death and is complete in eight to twelve hours, that's a reasonable estimation. Plus, lividity was fixed, which usually occurs eight to ten hours after death."

Santana wondered what Sam Noor was doing in Hidden Falls Park that night.

"Noor was stabbed twice on the right side of his back," Tanabe continued. "The first wound penetrated the skin and the subcutaneous tissue before striking the seventh rib in a right-to-left and back-to-front direction. A second wound on the right flank also punctured the skin and subcutaneous tissue, but it didn't penetrate the chest wall or the abdominal wall. Neither had a third transversely oriented stab wound on the left side of the back. All three wounds measured three to three and one-half inches in depth."

"But you ruled all three wounds were superficial and non-fatal, Reiko."

She nodded. "Sand obstructed the trachea and lobar bronchi of both lungs. The victim's efforts to breathe against the obstructed airways caused congestion, cyanosis, and multiple facial and conjunctival petechial hemorrhages. There was evidence of brain edema as well. All other internal organs were unremarkable."

"So he suffocated."

"Yes." Tanabe swiveled her chair away from the computer screen and faced him. "Death usually occurs in three to five minutes after complete withdrawal of air from the lungs, John. The extent of the penetration of sand in Noor's lungs and nostrils, as well as the congestion and edema in the air passages, is consistent with his head being held down in sand to suffocate him. The stab wounds were post-mortem. The cause of death was due to asphyxiation by bronchial aspiration of sand."

The fact that the stab wounds had occurred after death raised another possibility in Santana's mind. Someone who attempted to disguise his or her involvement and motivation in the randomness of a robbery had murdered Sam Noor. Santana could think of only one reason for the misdirection.

The killer knew the victim.

Chapter 12

Later that morning, Santana met Wendell Hudson for breakfast at the Coffee Cup in St. Paul's North End, a working class neighborhood built along the Rice Street corridor. The restaurant had been around for over sixty years and had the feel of a small-town diner with a reputation for good, inexpensive food and fast service.

The front room where Santana entered had booths and two countertop dining benches that seated six on each side. The dining room around a corner had several wooden tables and led back into an atrium, where Hudson was seated at a table, drinking a cup of black coffee. He was wearing his familiar short-brimmed tan fedora, a bright orange polo shirt, tan slacks, and brushed-suede Hush Puppies. His face was gaunt, his body very thin.

"Place is always busy," he said, looking around. "We're lucky this morning. Usually have to wait for an open table or booth."

A waitress appeared soon after Santana sat down and took their orders. When she left the table, he said, "I'm working the Sam Noor cold case."

"And you want my help."

Santana nodded.

"Ironic, isn't it?"

"What is?"

"You wanting my help."

"Because you feel I didn't help you in the Clay Buck civil trial."

"Bingo," he said.

"I told the truth on the witness stand that day, Wendell."

"Maybe as you saw it."

"What I didn't see was the fatal shot that killed Clay Buck. I didn't hear it, either."

Hudson smiled with no hint of humor and shook his head, as if he had just heard something unbelievable. "Doesn't mean there wasn't one."

"No, it doesn't."

"City paid out a lot of money to settle that case. But you've done pretty well for yourself, John. Buck's case never hurt your reputation. Hell, it never cost you a thing."

Santana ignored the provocation. "There's always a price to pay."

"Clay Buck murdered that Lonetree girl. He got what he deserved." Hudson used an index finger for emphasis.

"We don't know that."

"Maybe *you* don't know that. Everybody else does. Whatever you think doesn't mean squat now." He drank some coffee and set the cup on the table again.

"You ever wonder why someone wanted Buck dead, Wendell?"

"Sure. Revenge."

"For Danielle Lonetree's murder?"

"You got it."

"And who might want revenge?"

"Someone from the tribe."

"Doesn't it ever bother you that we never found any of the perps who ran us off the road?"

"As long as Buck got what was coming to him, no. But, hey, John," Hudson said, raising his cup of coffee in a salute, "I say let bygones be bygones."

Santana knew Hudson was lying. He would never forget what he perceived as an unforgiveable breach of trust when they were partners. But Santana wanted to press on.

"You caught the Sam Noor case a month after the Lonetree murder."

"Yeah," Hudson said. "I'd pretty much recovered from the bullet wound. I hated to walk away from it when I retired. But after months of dead ends and the verdict in the civil trial, I figured it was time to pull the plug."

"Tell me what you know about Noor's murder."

"It's all in my summary reports."

"I read them. You never located Noor's cell phone?"

Hudson shook his head. "The perp probably took it."

"You looked at the data Forensics downloaded from Noor's computer."

"Of course. There was only his home computer. But there wasn't anything worth pursuing."

"According to a credit card receipt, Noor was in Mills Creek at 6:36 p.m. the night he was murdered."

"So what? If the ME's TOD estimate is correct, Noor was killed two hours later, plenty of time for him to drive back to St. Paul."

"Noor was an environmental engineer. A woman named Virginia Garrison hired him."

"She runs an environmental group down in Red Wing."

"You remember why she hired Noor? I couldn't find anything in your reports."

"I don't recall. But what difference does it make? She didn't kill Sam Noor. His kid did. I just couldn't prove it."

"What made him a suspect?"

"Some perp looking for a vic to rob in Hidden Falls Park would use a gun, not a knife. There was a struggle. The perp pushed Noor's head face first into the sand. Suffocated him."

"You ever consider any other scenario?"

Hudson drank another swallow of coffee and wiped his mouth with a napkin. "I wondered if it might be a hate crime, being Noor was originally from Iran. But when I interviewed the wife, I found out neither one is a Muslim."

"Maybe the perp didn't know that."

Hudson blew out a breath. "You read the reports. Do you make this a hate crime?"

"No."

"At least we agree on something."

"The stabs wounds were post-mortem, Wendell."

Hudson nodded. "I figured someone tried to make it look like a robbery, a classic misdirection if the perp knew Sam Noor. Tell me you haven't come to the same conclusion."

"I have. So you looked at Adam Noor."

"Sure. The kid's a schizoid."

"He's mentally ill."

"A basket case."

"You ever search his loft?"

"Never had probable cause."

"What about a motive?"

"Money. Sam Noor made his fortune the old fashioned way. He inherited it."

"Why didn't the kid kill his mother, too?"

"He nearly did."

"With a knife?"

"With his fists. That's how the mother got a court order to have him committed to a treatment facility."

Santana knew Minnesota law required that a mentally ill person had to cause or attempt to cause serious physical harm to another, or that there had to be a substantial likelihood of physical harm to another, before the courts would take action.

"Did the assault occur before or after the father was killed?" he asked.

"Shortly after."

"How come you left this information out of your reports?"

"You know that Kelly Noor's father is Ray Carver."

"I do."

Hudson chuckled. "Well, you don't accuse the former chief of police's grandson of murder unless you have solid proof. At least I don't."

The waitress arrived with their meals, Santana's juice, and a pot of fresh coffee. She refilled Hudson's cup and asked if they would like anything else.

"We're good," Hudson said with a smile.

She returned the smile and left.

"Why would Adam Noor take his father's cell phone?"

"You're assuming Sam Noor had it with him."

"Who doesn't carry one?"

Hudson shrugged. "Maybe there was something incriminating on it?"

He removed a small plastic vial from a pants pocket, opened the tamper-proof cover, and shook a pill into his hand. As he tried to recap the vial, he lost his grip, and the vial rolled across the table, scattering small round blue pills in its wake.

Santana grabbed the vial before it fell to the floor. "Oxycodone," he said, reading the label.

Hudson quickly gathered up the pills and gestured at Santana, his long fingers curling back toward his palm. "Give it to me."

Santana handed him the vial.

Hudson swallowed a pill with a drink of coffee, returned the rest to the vial, and recapped it.

"Pretty strong medication."

"I've had some back pain." Hudson had been looking at Santana straight in the eye, but now his gaze broke.

Hudson's waxy skin and thinning body reminded Santana of a burning candle slowly melting down. "When did you find out, Wendell?"

"Find out what?"

"That you had cancer."

Hudson started to protest and then stopped. "It's none of your business, Santana." His voice had an edge as sharp as a knife's.

"No, it isn't."

Hudson's sandy eyes remained locked on Santana's till the wave of anger that had washed over him receded. He shrugged his shoulders, let out a breath, and said, "Just after I retired. Liver cancer. Perfect timing, huh?"

Santana considered asking what the prognosis was, but he figured he already knew. "You have any family?"

"None who give a damn. But I'm at peace. I'm going to a better place—where they don't need homicide detectives."

Santana heard no anger in Hudson's voice, only resignation. "You know if Adam Noor is still in treatment?"

Hudson shook his head. "Don't know and don't care. My advice to you, John, is to stay clear of the kid. You go poking around at sleeping dogs, you're likely to get bit. But then, you've never been someone who listened to good advice."

"I'll let you know what I find out, Wendell."

"Better hurry," Hudson said.

Chapter 13

That afternoon, Santana drove to Kelly Noor's four-story Victorian on historic Summit Avenue in St. Paul. Cameras mounted on the ten-foot-high sandstone wall surrounding the mansion safeguarded her. Santana called the house and waited till the electronic security gate swung open.

A Latina housekeeper led him through a large foyer with dark woodwork and a winding staircase and into a living room with a high ceiling. The room had antique furnishings and rose-colored rugs over oak floors. Santana felt as if he had stepped back in time.

He sat on a couch beside a red brick fireplace. On the mantel was a series of framed photos of a woman dressed in period costumes. The woman pictured in the photos was a younger version of the same woman in a larger framed photograph on an end table taken with her husband, Sam Noor.

On the wall above the fireplace was a large black-and-white painting of a long-haired woman in a flowing white gown, backlit by gray thunderclouds. She was sitting on a flowered swing a few feet above a set of dark gravestones and white skulls that were nestled among gnarled branches and weeds. In her left hand she held a white lace umbrella. Her body was slightly turned to her right as though she were riding sidesaddle. But her beautiful, pale face was looking to her left, toward the dark leaves that framed the painting.

Santana had read that a previous owner, who had hung herself from a beam on the first floor landing, supposedly haunted the mansion.

The thought reminded him of his mother's murder in Colombia. He reached for his notebook in the inner pocket of his sport coat and refocused his thoughts on the current case instead of on painful memories from his past.

He waited five minutes before a tall, slender, and handsome woman with thick dark hair entered the room, followed by the maid and a slightly shorter blonde who had the streamlined shape of an athlete.

He stood.

"Detective Santana," the dark-haired woman said, offering a hand. "I'm Kelly Noor." She had long-lidded brown eyes and a soft grip.

She gestured toward the blond woman beside her. "This is my good friend, Susannah Barnes."

"Pleasure to meet you," Barnes said with a Southern accent.

Santana shook her hand. It felt cool and strong.

"Please, sit down," Kelly Noor said to Santana. "Can I have Maria bring you something?"

"I'm fine. Thanks."

"I'll have some tea," she said to the maid, who nodded and slipped quietly out of the room.

"I'll leave now, Kelly," Susannah Barnes said. "Call me later."

"I will."

"Good day, Detective," Barnes said, giving a little smile and wave as she headed for the door.

Kelly Noor sat on a love seat opposite Santana and watched him expectantly. Copies of *Vogue* and *Better Homes and Gardens* were neatly arranged on the coffee table beside a large decorative hourglass.

"You have a lovely home, Ms. Noor," he said, opening up the conversation.

She smiled weakly and looked at the hourglass, as if it were something she had suddenly discovered. "Yes, it is. But every house has its secrets, Detective."

Santana wondered if she was referring to the previous owner's suicide—or to something else.

"I noticed the photos on the fireplace mantel. Are you an actress?"

She smiled shyly. "Oh, my. Sometimes I forget those photos are still on display. I haven't acted since my early twenties. I really should take them down."

"Was an acting career your dream?"

She hesitated, her eyes looking at some distant point. "Not really."

But Santana caught the wistful tone of her voice.

"When you called," she said, turning her eyes on him again, "I was pleased to hear your department had decided to reopen the investigation into my husband's murder."

Given her father's former position in the SPPD, Santana suspected Kelly Noor knew perfectly well why the investigation had been reopened. He gave her a nod and flipped open his notebook. "You've probably answered most of the questions I'm about to ask, Ms. Noor, but I'd like to go through them again."

"Why you and not Detective Hudson?"

"He retired."

"So he's no longer involved in the case?"

"I plan to consult with him."

"Don't waste your time. Detective Hudson believed my son, Adam, murdered his father."

"Why would he believe that?"

"You'd have to ask him. But just because my son has some mental health issues doesn't make him a murderer. If your colleague had focused his energies on finding the real killer, we wouldn't be sitting here today."

The maid appeared with a silver serving tray holding a china cup, a saucer, and a pot of tea. She set it down on the coffee table and turned over the hourglass.

When she had left the room, Santana said, "You mentioned your son has some mental health issues."

Kelly Noor poured a cup of tea and nodded. "He suffers from depression and schizophrenia."

"I understand he spent some time in a treatment facility."

"And how would you know that?"

"Detective Hudson told me."

"Of course. Yes, Adam was in a treatment facility for a short time. But he's much better now."

"I'm afraid I don't know much about schizophrenia, Ms. Noor."

"You and most of the population." She set down the teapot and drank from her cup of tea before continuing. "Adam was nineteen years old when the first symptoms began."

"And what symptoms were those?"

"He was doing well in college and studying business. But then he became increasingly depressed and paranoid and started acting out in bizarre ways."

"Such as?"

She thought for a moment before responding. "First, he became convinced that his professors were out to get him. Then he thought other students were in on the conspiracy. Soon after, he dropped out of school. He stopped bathing, shaving, and washing his clothes. He started hearing voices. Imagine how you'd feel, Detective, if your brain began playing tricks on you, if unseen voices shouted at you, if you lost the capacity to feel emotions and the ability to reason logically."

"I can't imagine how difficult that would be."

"More than difficult," she said.

"I've heard schizophrenia runs in families."

"It can," she said without elaborating.

Santana moved on. "Did your son think you or your husband was trying to harm him?"

She took a deep breath and let it out. "I know where you're going with this line of questioning, Detective. Your colleague wanted to go in the same direction. Trust me. You can look all you want, but there's nothing to see. You'll merely be wasting your time like Detective Hudson wasted his."

"Trust is a two-way street, Ms. Noor. I'm making no judgment about your son. I'm trying to understand."

She stared silently at him. Then she set down her teacup and sat back. "Things came to a head when Adam acted on the voices."

Santana noted that some of the edge had gone out of her voice. "How did he act?"

Her eyes focused inward for a time before they settled on Santana again. "He smashed the TV in his room and screamed that he wasn't going to put up with the illegal spying anymore. I tried to calm him down, but . . ."

"Were you hurt?"

She shook her head. "I called the police and convinced a judge that Adam should be hospitalized. The doctors tried different drugs. Eventually, he was prescribed clozapine. But because of the possible side effect of loss of white blood cells that fight infection, Adam had to have a blood test every one or two weeks. Maintenance on clozapine is extremely difficult. His doctor finally settled on Risperdal. Adam started on one dose a day and then took two. It made him a little drowsy at first, and he gained some weight, but I think it has helped."

"You think?"

"After his discharge from the treatment center, he lived here for a while before moving into his own place. I don't see him often. I think he's dating some girl."

"What's her name?"

"I don't remember. But she's Mexican."

Santana could hear the disgust in her voice. He tried to keep his expression neutral, but she must have read something in his face.

"Oh, I'm sorry, Detective Santana. I meant nothing against Mexicans. Maria, my maid, is Mexican. I love her."

Santana wasn't certain that Kelly Noor was being honest about her feelings, despite having a Latina maid. "Actually, I'm Colombian, Ms. Noor."

Her smile looked forced. "I have nothing against Colombians either. I'm just upset that Adam is living with a girlfriend. It's so important that his meds are monitored."

"Is your son working?"

"No. He's been studying photography at the art institute in Minneapolis. It's such a waste." She shook her head in disbelief. "Adam is an extremely bright individual. He could do so much with his life."

Santana wondered what Kelly Noor would have thought had her son become a cop. Perhaps that profession would have been more acceptable, since her father had been the chief of police.

He peered at the next question he had written in his notebook. In most murder investigations, he'd had little time to write out questions in advance. He'd had to rely more on his experience and judgment. But a cold case gave him time to think, time to plot strategy. Now he wanted to make sure that he asked all the questions he had written down. He sensed that Kelly Noor would not agree to another lengthy interview.

"Your husband was an environmental engineer."

"Yes."

"And he was originally from Iran."

She nodded. "His family fled to the US during the Islamic Revolution. Sam was ten at the time. We met in college."

"What did your husband's parents do?"

"Sam's father was a Harvard-educated economist and later an investment banker."

Santana figured that's where Kelly Noor's wealth had come from.

"Sam's mother was a Middle East scholar and history professor at the University of Minnesota."

"You said 'was.' Are both of your husband's parents deceased?"

"Yes. Sadly, they were killed in a car accident when Sam was in college, just before we met."

"Your husband was the only child?"

She nodded.

"Were you aware that he'd been hired by an environmental group in Red Wing?"

"I was not," she said, "till Detective Hudson told me. Sam once worked for the state, but in recent years he'd formed his own consulting business."

"Did your husband talk much about his work?"

"No. I have no idea what he was working on when he was murdered." Tears welled up in her eyes. She picked up a napkin from the serving tray and dabbed her eyes. "I'm sorry. I still get emotional whenever I talk about it."

Santana watched the grains of sand in the hourglass on the table trickle through the narrow center before asking his next question. "Do you have any idea why your husband was in Hidden Falls Park the night he was killed?"

"He liked to walk. He liked the river. We'd often go there for picnics in the summer. That's the only reason I can think of for him being in the park."

"You spoke to your husband on the afternoon he was murdered. Do you recall the conversation?"

"Sam said he was finishing up some business and would be home later that evening."

"Did he say where he was going?"

"No."

"Did he say he was with anyone?"

She shook her head.

"How did your son react when his father was murdered?"

"Adam didn't react."

"Not at all?"

"Emotions tend to flatline, Detective, when you're taking heavy medication."

"Where does your son live?"

She hesitated before giving Santana the address. Then she said, "Just remember, Detective, my son is dealing with a mental illness. What you'll see is a different person than Adam once was."

Chapter 14

Adam Noor lived in an artist's loft on the third floor of the former Schmidt Brewery. The building was noted for its crenellated towers and Gothic details but had sat idle for years before a developer decided to renovate it for community use. It was located in a diverse neighborhood along West 7th street. Formerly known as Old Fort Road, 7th Street had once been a historic Native American and fur trader path along the Mississippi River from downtown St. Paul to Fort Snelling.

The loft had large windows, high ceilings, and polished concrete floors. There was a wall made of brick, stainless steel appliances, and quartz countertops. An alto sax sat in a stand near the brick wall. Santana stood near a built-in bookshelf. Among the books on the shelves were *The World as Will and Representation,* by Arthur Schopenhauer; Friedrich Nietzsche's *Thus Spoke Zarathustra*; and, to his surprise, the English translation of *Labyrinths,* by Argentinian writer Jorge Luis Borges, one of his favorite writers.

But what also caught Santana's attention were the framed photos hung on the inner walls of pretty, young women in chic floor-length gowns, posed in rooms filled with African sculptures, taxidermy animals, gilded furniture and chandeliers, and marble floors. The scenes of unabashed decadence were so over the top that it reminded Santana of something out of F. Scott Fitzgerald's *The Great Gatsby.*

Santana sat on a hardback chair across a glass-topped coffee table from Adam Noor, who was slouched on a dark brown leather couch. He looked a little ragged along the edges. Scraggly dark hair framed his puffy and unshaven face. He wore faded jeans with holes and a white T-shirt that looked a size too small. His feet were bare. Smoke from a burning cigarette in an ashtray in his lap snaked its way toward the high ceiling. Santana wondered if the heavy-lidded, glazed eyes that stared at him were the result of medication for the young man's schizophrenia.

"I'd like to ask you some questions about your father's death," Santana said.

Adam Noor's steady gaze became an oddly troubled squint. "Why keep harassing me?"

"This is the first time I've talked with you."

"When I said 'you,' I meant the police. You're the police."

"I wouldn't consider a conversation harassment."

"Maybe I would."

"You could've refused to see me."

"Yeah. Then you'd call my grandfather, the former chief of police."

"I doubt it."

"Sure." Noor took a deep drag on his cigarette and blew smoke through his nostrils.

"Your grandfather has influence over you?"

"Only because he and my mother could have me committed again."

"So your grandfather was involved in having you committed."

"I'm sure he was."

"You know that for a fact?"

"Look, Detective . . ."

"Santana."

"Yeah. Detective Santana. The police have already questioned me about my father's death. Don't you have reports you could read? Some kind of case file you could review instead of bothering me?"

"It's not the same as an interview."

"So this is an interview and not an interrogation?"

"That's right."

"I don't have to talk to you?"

"No, you don't. You don't have to help me solve your father's murder, either."

"Like you're going to solve it when no one else could."

"There's never a guarantee. Sometimes we believe we know who committed a crime and can't prove it. But what do you have to lose by helping me?"

"Okay," he said with a deep sigh. "What is it you want to know?"

"Did you get along with your father?"

He shrugged. "Most of the time."

"How did he feel about your illness and you dropping out of school?"

"He understood."

"What about your mother?"

Adam Noor rolled his eyes and offered a joyless laugh. "You talk to her?"

Santana nodded.

"Then you know how she feels." He gestured to the framed photos on the wall. "She doesn't much like my career choice either."

"These are your photos on the wall?"

He nodded. "I call them children of the rich and famous."

"Are they models?"

"No. They're real people. My father had lots of connections."

"Through his business?"

"Through his parents. They were wealthy. That got me a free pass to the private lives of my millionaire subjects and their extravagant homes." He glanced at one of the framed photos. "My images are really a study of consumption and greed."

"You play the saxophone?"

He nodded. "But I can't make a living at it."

"Are your paternal grandparents still alive?"

"No. You must know my maternal grandfather, Ray Carver."

"He was police chief before my time."

Adam Noor stared at Santana as though he didn't believe him.

"Your mother said you were dating someone."

Noor shook his head. "That didn't last. Most of my relationships don't. Women have trouble dealing with a schizoid. And I don't get invited to parties. We're not the best conversationalists."

"Is there any history of schizophrenia in your family?"

"My mother didn't tell you?"

"Tell me what?"

"My maternal grandmother had schizophrenia."

"Ray Carver's wife?"

Adam Noor nodded. "The illness occurs in one percent of the general population, but in ten percent of people who have a first-degree relative with the disorder. Guess I just got lucky." He laughed, but there was no humor in it. "Bet my mother didn't tell you my grandmother committed suicide either."

"No, she didn't."

"Her car was traveling one hundred miles an hour in broad daylight when it hit a bridge abutment. The roads and weather were good."

"So you don't think it was an accident."

"My grandfather had just become chief at the time. He made sure the cause of death wasn't listed as suicide."

Santana made a note before asking the next question. "You doing better now?"

"Yeah. I rarely have the feeling that people are out to get me anymore, or that people are watching me. Except for the police." A ghost of a smile appeared.

"You think we've been watching you?"

"Maybe that idea isn't so paranoid, huh, Detective?"

"We haven't been."

"Yet here you are." His eye contact suddenly appeared hypnotic. "I didn't kill my father."

"I'm not suggesting you did. But maybe his death contributed to your illness?"

"It wasn't like that. I was depressed long before my father's death and before the onset of schizophrenia. When my father died, I felt grief. Depression is a totally different sensation. Depression is like being trapped in bed for twenty hours a day with no mental energy to get out."

"So depression leads to schizophrenia?"

He shook his head. "Not for everyone. Still," he said with a shrug, "I'm surprised more people aren't depressed."

"Why's that?"

"Think about it, Detective. Psychiatry works on the assumption that depression and schizophrenia are abnormal. But what if normal means something completely different, something horrible?"

"Such as?"

"We're in an unwinnable situation in this world."

"And what situation is that?"

"No other creature even knows what it is to exist—or that someday it'll die. But some of us understand that consciousness is an evolutionary mistake, that we have to lie to ourselves and pretend we're not what we think we are."

"And what are we?"

"We're doomed creatures living on a lonely planet in a cold, dark universe."

"We all have to die."

"For most people, Detective, just living with that thought is a fate worse than death itself. So we've figured out ways to ignore it. But when alcohol, drugs, and one's own personal relationship with Jesus no longer disguise the painful truth that one will die someday, one tends to grasp desperately at the consolation prize, the truly big lie, that there's life after death. People like me threaten that house of cards. We're labeled depressed because we understand it's all a con game. You may convince yourself that your life has meaning. But if you're like me and you don't feel that meaning, then life itself becomes meaningless, and you're nobody. Emotions offer us the illusion of being a somebody among somebodies, Detective Santana. Depression and schizophrenia erased those emotions and allowed me to see that what psychiatry calls mental illness is simply a logical consequence of human reality and not a pathological state."

He fell silent for a moment, his eyes filled with remoteness as he smoked his cigarette. Then he came out of it, as if his mind had captured an elusive thought. "But no one wants to hear about the anxieties we keep locked up inside ourselves, Detective. They don't want to hear that the network of emotions designed to make us think we mean something is as fragile as overhead wires in an ice storm. Those of us who challenge the house rules are warned not to tell others of our living nightmare. If threats don't keep us quiet, we're given drugs designed to suppress our heretical thoughts and told to get on with things or the world will get on without us."

"What do you think would happen if everyone thought like you, Mr. Noor?"

He shrugged. "Who knows? Maybe we'd all decide that the real horror is human consciousness. Maybe we'd decide to do ourselves a favor and end the human race."

"Maybe whoever killed your father felt the same way you do."

"I don't mean we'd start killing each other. We'd just quit procreating. Leave this world to the animals that know how to care for it. But it's a moot point now anyway. The corporate fascists controlling the world economy are determined to destroy the whole planet regardless, and kill everyone in the process."

"You have any idea who might have killed your father?"

He gave a humorless snort. "You want a suspect, look no further than my mother."

Santana was surprised. "You think your mother murdered your father?"

"I think she had someone do it for her."

"Why?"

"My father was planning on divorcing her. You see the house she lives in? The money she'd lose? There's your motive, Detective Santana. All you have to do is prove it."

Chapter 15

The next morning Santana looked at the notes Wendell Hudson had compiled in the chronological case log and found the phone number for Virginia Garrison, the woman who had hired Sam Noor a few weeks before his death.

"You're re-opening the investigation into Sam's death?" she said after Santana identified himself.

"It was never closed."

"Well, I'm pleased to hear it. But I can't speak to you right now, Detective Santana. I'm leaving for a special council meeting at the city hall in Red Wing."

"Just one question. Why did you hire Sam Noor?"

"Come to the city council meeting and find out," she said.

The afternoon sun was like a flaming match set to paper, its intense rays burning away much of the morning's overcast.

Santana drove into Red Wing with the driver's side window open, his left forearm propped on the window frame, his mind reflecting on the past and the drive that he and Wendell Hudson had once taken with Clay Buck and April Ford.

But his thoughts kept returning to his conversation with Adam Noor and the young man's accusation that his mother had had something to do with his father's death. Maybe the kid had killed his father and wanted Santana looking in another direction. Maybe Kelly Noor had had something to do with her husband's death. Regardless, Santana knew that for his own peace of mind, he needed to look at her more carefully.

Santana parked near the Red Wing City Hall, a two-story Renaissance Revival building constructed at the turn of the 20th century. The building occupied half a city block and was set off by a large green lawn.

The meeting was in progress when Santana entered the crowded council chambers and stood against the back wall. On one side of the room, people held signs that read: STOP THE MINING, BAN FRACK SAND MINES, and NO FRACKIN' WAY. The folding chairs on the opposite side of the room were filled with people wearing green T-shirts with the slogan SAND = JOBS stenciled in black letters across the chest and back.

Near the front, eight city council members, including the mayor, sat at a long table facing the audience, their names and titles engraved on the nameplates in front of them.

An auburn-haired woman with a slender frame and high cheekbones stood beside a folding chair in the front row, addressing the council. "Residents have filed numerous noise complaints," she said, holding up a fistful of papers as evidence.

Shouts of agreement from supporters erupted in the audience.

"Please," the mayor said, pounding a gavel on the table as though he were a judge. "Let's keep the discussion civil."

A man seated in a chair on the opposite side of the aisle from the woman stood up. He was a tall man with a youthful face and a black mustache flecked with gray. His thick gray hair was longish and razor cut, and his pinstriped suit had not come off a rack.

"My name is Grayson Cole," he said, to a smattering of boos. "Select Sands has addressed those concerns, Ms. Garrison, as you well know. Since erecting a sound wall, they've received no further complaints." He gave her a placating smile and sat down.

"Well, Mr. Cole, what about the truck traffic that has tripled in the neighborhoods and the complaints of too much dust?" Garrison's hands were fisted on her hips, and her voice was louder now.

The man she had addressed as "Mr. Cole" rose to his feet once more. However, instead of responding directly to Virginia Garrison, he turned and spoke to the audience. "The trucks were rerouted away from the neighborhoods nearest the mine as soon as Select Sands received complaints. As for the neighboring streets, they are swept daily at the company's expense. The mining entrance has been paved as well to minimize dust."

The mayor said, "What exactly is it that you want this council to do, Ms. Garrison?"

"We'd like the council to issue a moratorium on sand mining permits until these and other issues can be studied further."

"We'll take your recommendation under consideration," he said, though his dismissive tone indicated to Santana that the council had already made up its mind.

"The dust blowing off the piles of fracking sand at the mine have such high levels of silica that respirators worn by the workers don't offer enough protection," she said. She turned and faced the crowd. "Nearly eighty percent of the collected samples exceeded the recommended exposure limit set by Select Sands. They're not following even their own minimal safety standards."

"Mr. Mayor," Cole said, "it's abundantly clear that Ms. Garrison and her supporters in this room want to undermine the work of the council by rewriting the county's nonmetallic mining ordinance. If that happens, it will be impossible for Select Sands to conduct business."

"You mean pollute the environment and injure workers," Garrison said, her supporters calling out in agreement.

The double doors to Santana's left opened. A big man in jeans and a T-shirt stood beside a large cage filled with a brood of clucking hens. When he opened the cage door, the hens scattered among the crowd. The big man followed the brood into the council chambers, carrying a sign that read: FARMERS AGAINST SAND MINING.

"What about our water and food supply?" he yelled, heading toward the council members.

Pandemonium broke out in the chambers as the hens scattered among the crowd. People stood and began shouting at one another. The mayor gaveled the table and declared the meeting adjourned. Then he and the council members rushed for the exits.

Santana kept his eyes on Virginia Garrison and waited till the room had been cleared of chickens before he approached her and introduced himself.

"Quite a spectacle," she said with slight smile and shake of her head.

"You know the farmer?"

"His name's George Nelson. He owns a farm outside of town. Select Sands wants to purchase his property."

"I'd be happy to buy you a cup of coffee if you have time to talk."

She glanced at her watch. "I need to get home." She rummaged in her purse and came out with a business card with her address and phone number. "Call me in an hour or so. We'll talk then." She turned and hurried out the door.

Santana wanted to speak to Grayson Cole, but he was nowhere to be found. With time to kill, he drove past Victorian houses, many with lawn signs that read SUPPORT SAND and LET'S MINE, NOT WHINE, and into downtown located below the sandstone bluffs along the Mississippi River.

Among the historic buildings, brick storefronts, and flowering planters hanging from lampposts, he found the Veranda patio restaurant at the St. James Hotel, near Levee Park and the Amtrak train depot. Sitting at a black wrought iron table under an umbrella, Santana could see the fountain across the street at the corporate offices of Red Wing Shoes, which had been manufacturing work boots for over one hundred years.

While waiting for his buffalo-elk burger, fries, and Coke, he took out his cell phone and located the Select Sands website. Their mission statement said that the company was dedicated to maintaining and sustaining the environment. Underneath their mission statement was a quote from a local farmer:

"Excavating the sand deposits on my farm has allowed me to keep my land and home. When you choose to support the local sand industry, you are supporting the economic future of our state."

Santana then found the number for Grayson Cole's real estate office and called. The woman who answered said that Mr. Cole was out at the moment, but she expected him back later that afternoon. Santana told her who he was and asked for Cole's cell number. The woman gave it to him without protest.

When Grayson Cole answered his cell phone, Santana introduced himself.

"What's this about, Detective?"

"I saw you at the city council meeting in Red Wing and wonder if I might talk with you about Select Sands."

"Is there a reason why you're interested in the company?"

"Curiosity," Santana said.

"And why would a homicide detective be curious about this particular company?"

"I'm investigating the murder of Sam Noor."

There was a short pause. "Who's Sam Noor?"

"He was an environmental engineer hired by Virginia Garrison."

"Oh," Cole said. "Her."

"Your secretary said you'd be back in the office later today."

"Actually, I may not. But what does Select Sands have to do with this man's murder?"

"Maybe nothing," Santana said.

"You have that correct, Detective." Cole paused again before he said, "Are you still in Red Wing?"

"Yes."

"Well, I'm at the mine site now and will be for a few hours. Why don't you drive out here? I can dispel any thoughts you may have regarding the company's involvement in Mr. Noor's death."

"If you'll give me the directions, I'll be there soon, Mr. Cole."

* * *

The mine was located three miles south of town near a small housing development and up the hill from a stream. Dump trucks rumbled past Santana as he drove along a winding county road toward bluffs that rose gently up from the rolling hills and farmlands. At the intersection of two county roads, the landscape abruptly changed. Bluffs had been turned into giant piles of sand. The landscape looked like the Arabian Desert—sand everywhere and piled up high.

Santana parked in front of a metal office trailer to the right of the entrance, went up a set of three aluminum steps, and opened the door. Inside to his left was a wide built-in desktop for blueprints, a two-drawer filing cabinet, and an overhead wire bookshelf containing manuals and three-ring binders.

Santana recognized Grayson Cole. He was standing in front of a metal desk. Up close, Santana noted the small acne scars on Cole's cheeks.

"Ah, Detective. Good of you to come." His handshake was firm and genuine and his eyes dark and unblinking. Cole gestured to the man seated behind the desk. "This is Ken Webb."

Webb stood and offered a hand. "CEO of Select Sands," he said in a heavy Southern accent. He was dressed casually in tan khakis and deck shoes. Santana guessed that Webb was barely 5' 7" in height. His white button-down shirt was open at the collar but stiff with starch. His blue blazer fitted across his small shoulders without a wrinkle.

"Please sit down, Detective."

Santana sat next to Grayson Cole in one of the two swivel chairs in front of the desk.

"What can we do for you?" Webb said, taking charge of the conversation as he sat down again.

"I'm investigating the death of an environmental engineer named Sam Noor."

"And when did this death occur?"

"Nine months ago."

Webb had his hands tented in front of him. He tapped his fingertips together while he looked at Santana. His black hair was cut short. His teeth were very white and even. "Is this what the police call a cold case?"

"It is."

Webb took out a thin cigar and used a double guillotine-style cutter to snip off the cap. Then he rotated the cigar as he held it into the flame of his butane lighter. He got it drawing and inhaled and exhaled and gazed for a moment at the glowing, cherry-red tip before looking at Santana again.

"Frankly, Detective, I know nothing about Mr. Noor's death."

"Did either of you meet him?"

Webb inhaled more smoke and let it out in a narrow stream. "I did. Mr. Noor took some ground and water samples around the mine. I had no objection since we operate an environmentally safe operation."

"Do you recall when that was?"

"I'm afraid I don't."

"Maybe Sam Noor called to schedule a time? Maybe you recorded the date somewhere?"

"I can check, Detective. But I doubt I'll find anything."

Santana doubted it, too, given Webb's casual attitude.

Webb blew out more cigar smoke. The room was beginning to fill with it. "Have you spoken with Virginia Garrison?"

"I have," Santana said.

"Has she made accusations against Select Sands?"

"Not that I'm aware of."

"Then I don't understand what your interest is in our company, Detective."

"Where are you from, Mr. Webb?" Santana asked, ignoring Webb's last statement.

"Midland, Texas. That's where our corporate headquarters is located."

"Been here long?"

"Ever since the mine opened." He shuffled some papers on the desktop. "Do you have any further questions for me, Detective?"

"Not at this time. But I wonder if Mr. Cole could show me around?"

Grayson looked at Santana and then at Webb, as if waiting for permission.

"All right," Webb said. He stood up and shook Santana's hand again. "I'll look for that date when I spoke to Mr. Noor. See if I wrote it down."

"I'd appreciate it."

"Make sure you wear a hard hat, Detective. It's a busy place. I wouldn't want you getting hurt," Webb said with a half smile.

Santana fell in step beside Grayson Cole as they exited the trailer.

"Select Sands bought one hundred fifty acres of woods, cornfields and bluffs," Cole said as he led Santana across a flat, sandy expanse of land that was rutted with heavy equipment tracks. "The company also bought land for a transportation facility on the Mississippi further downstream. But environmentalists, led primarily by Virginia Garrison, have been hauling us to court. They don't seem to realize that sixty percent of all the energy in the country comes from oil or coal. We need a cheaper and more sustainable source of energy now and into the future. Natural gas is the answer to our energy independence. I'll bet you use it to heat your home, Detective."

"I do."

"Then you can thank sand mining for helping to reduce the cost of supplies—and for the oil and gas boom in America."

Cole gestured toward the surrounding bluffs. "The gold in these green hills is sand. It gives the hard-working people in many of these small towns a chance to share in the wealth generated by the domestic production of energy. It's a perfect example of the capitalist model working as it should."

"Why the need for sand?"

"Not just sand, Detective. Silica sand. In the fracking process, its shape ensures that when the sand is injected into cracks in dense rock, the individual grains hold those spaces open, which allows the oil and gas to flow from deep inside the Earth. Hell, silica sand has been used for decades in glass making, toothpaste, and even Asian noodles."

Santana wondered if he had to rethink his opinion of Asian noodles.

They walked to the edge of a huge open pit mine. Santana could hear the rumble of truck engines and the sound of a large excavator as it scooped up sand and dropped a load into a waiting dump truck. Plumes of dust rose up from sand-handling machines.

"Open pit mining isn't unique to Minnesota," Cole said.

"But this type of mining is."

"Yes. Silica sand needs to be close to the land surface, roughly within fifty feet, to be viable to mine. There are hundreds of thousands of acres of silica sand layers at or near the land surface in Minnesota and Wisconsin, more than anywhere else in the United States. This particular facility has in excess of forty million tons of high quality Northern white silica sand and has the capacity to produce approximately five hundred thousand tons annually." Cole was speaking loudly now over the noise.

Santana could understand why neighbors might complain.

"Our white sand deposits are located near rail transportation so that we can ship it to the oil and gas fields in North Dakota, where it's used to blast oil from shale. We also have barge access along the Mississippi River, which means we can provide service to Southern Mississippi and into Ohio and Pennsylvania. You notice the sand isn't blowing around?"

"Not much wind today," Santana said.

Cole shook his head. "The piled sand doesn't blow around because workers saturate it with water, and they recycle the water used in the process." Cole pointed to a group of workers who were all wearing masks. "That's the area where we separate the different grains of sand. Occasionally, we have some blowing dust, despite our best efforts. But one hundred to two hundred trucks roll out of here each day with loads of sand. All of them are covered with tarps to keep sand from blowing around. The sand goes straight to a rail yard. And I haven't even mentioned the jobs that Select Sands has brought to this town."

Cole let out a breath and looked around at the landscape. "There's just no reason why anyone involved with the company would want to harm Mr. Noor."

"There's always a reason," Santana said.

Chapter 16

After leaving the Select Sands mine, Santana phoned Virginia Garrison and got directions to her home.

The two of them were seated at a table in an enclosed porch next to a window that faced the backyard. Sunlight beaming through the glass highlighted the red in Virginia Garrison's auburn hair and the sand-colored freckles sprinkled across her nose and cheeks. She drank from her cup of coffee with cream and sugar, Santana from a bottle of water.

"You're not a coffee drinker?"

"Never acquired a taste for it," he said.

She placed an index finger over the dimple in her chin and peered at him for a long moment, her soft, smoky eyes busy with thoughts. "You have a slight accent, but I can't place it."

"I was born in Colombia and came here when I was sixteen. And, yes, most Colombians drink coffee."

She shrugged and smiled. "It's good to be different."

Santana had a feeling that Virginia Garrison was speaking more about herself than him.

"Do you understand why we're trying to stop the silica sand mining and the fracking industry, Detective?"

"That's not what I'm focused on, Ms. Garrison."

"But you should understand."

"And why is that?"

"Because it might help you solve Sam Noor's death."

Santana drank some water and looked toward the wooden handicap ramp leading from the porch doorway into the backyard. Beyond the ramp, he could see a man sitting in a wheelchair in the shade of a large oak tree. The man's back was to the house. A woman Santana thought he recognized but couldn't place was standing in front of the wheelchair, talking to the man.

"My boyfriend, Sean Latham," Virginia Garrison said, tracking Santana's gaze. "He suffers from silicosis."

Santana looked at Virginia Garrison again. "From working in a silica mine?"

She shook her head. "Sean worked as a sandblaster after he got out of the military. The silica dust he inhaled caused swelling in his lungs and chest lymph nodes. He suffers from shortness of breath and fatigue."

"Can the disease be treated?"

"Yes," she said, "but not cured."

"And the woman?"

"That's Carrie Buck."

Santana felt like his heart skipped a beat. He remembered Carrie Buck's face now from Wendell Hudson's civil trial. She was Clay Buck's younger sister and Chaska Youngblood's niece.

Virginia Garrison stood up. "I'd like you to meet them."

Santana followed her out the porch door, down the handicap ramp, and into the yard. Sean Latham turned his wheelchair toward the door when he heard it slam. He was a solidly built, handsome man, wide in the shoulders and neck, with a heavy-jawed, dark-bearded face. Thick, wavy hair hung over his ears and touched his shoulders. He wore a white linen guayabera shirt, faded jeans, and leather sandals. Inside a cup holder attached to the right armrest was an open can of Budweiser.

"Sean," Virginia Garrison said, "this is Detective Santana. He's investigating the death of Sam Noor."

Latham held out a large, thick-fingered hand. "Pleased to meet you."

Santana noticed the dark, shallow rifts in Latham's nails as he shook the man's hand. He wondered if they would eventually crack—and if it was a symptom of silicosis.

Latham's brown eyes narrowed a little as he rested both hands on the armrests and gazed at Santana. "You any better than the last detective?"

"I'll give it my best."

Latham smiled. "Diplomatically spoken, Detective."

"And this is Carrie Buck," Virginia Garrison said, gesturing toward the statuesque young woman with long black hair so thick and lustrous that Santana wanted to touch it. The tails of Carrie Buck's white cotton shirt were knotted across her stomach, exposing the deep brown color of her skin.

She looked at Santana as if he were toxic. "I know you," she said.

Staring into her eyes, Santana thought, was like staring into the barrel of a shotgun.

"You were with the detective who killed my brother."

"What?" Virginia Garrison said.

Carrie Buck's dark eyes shifted to Virginia Garrison. "He was one of the detectives who picked up Clay in Red Wing when he was falsely accused of murdering Danielle Lonetree. His partner killed Clay."

Santana slapped a mosquito on his wrist and looked at the smear of blood on his hand. He wasn't about to get into a heated debate regarding Wendell Hudson's or Clay Buck's guilt or innocence.

"I'm working another case now," he said. "The death of Sam Noor."

A sudden breeze rustled the leaves on the oak tree rising above them. Latham began coughing hard, covering his mouth with his right fist as he fought to control it.

"Can I get you anything?" Virginia Garrison said, patting him gently on the back as she would a baby.

Latham shook his head. "I'm fine, Ginny." He was panting hard when he finally regained control. He reached for the beer in the cup holder and swallowed a gulp. Then he wiped his mouth with a forearm. "Disease is a bitch, Detective. You better make up your mind whose side you're on."

"I'll work this case whether I have an opinion on silica mining or not, Mr. Latham."

Garrison nodded her head as if she understood Santana's position.

But Carrie Buck said, "What's your opinion on your partner's guilt or innocence?"

"Hudson retired. He's not my partner now."

"So he's never going to pay for what he did."

"The city paid out a lot of money after the civil trial."

"That's not the kind of payment I meant."

"Carrie," Virginia Garrison said, "Detective Santana wasn't accused of killing your brother, was he?"

Buck shook her head. "But he knows his partner killed Clay."

"I don't know that, Ms. Buck," Santana said. "I'm sorry your brother's dead. But you heard all the trial testimony. An armed group of four ran us off the road. One of them could've easily killed your brother."

"It's not that your brother's death isn't important, Carrie," Sean Latham said, looking at her. "But it's a new day now. Detective Santana needs to know what we're fighting for."

"He's not even from here," she said.

"So what? If Select Sands is blowing dust in his eyes, he'll never see how to solve Sam Noor's death."

Santana shifted his gaze to Virginia Garrison. "Why exactly did you hire Sam Noor?"

"We needed research data that supported our position from an independent source."

"Your position being that you're against sand mining."

"We make no secret of our opposition."

"You said 'we.' "

"Sean and I and Carrie and her uncle Chaska Youngblood represent a group of concerned citizens. Many in town oppose sand mining."

"Appears from the signs around town and the people at the city council meeting that some are for it."

"It's the jobs," Latham said. "Select Sands hired a lot of the unemployed and are paying them good wages."

"But the industry is new and mostly unregulated," Virginia Garrison said. "There's little oversight. Select Sands isn't concerned about the environmental costs. They're in it for the short term and for the money. Once they've depleted the silica sand from the bluffs along the river, they'll pack up and let the town clean up their mess and the open-pit mine."

She pointed in the direction of the bluffs. "There's a sand-processing facility just across the river in Wisconsin. It can suck up over a million gallons of water a day out of a local aquifer to clean silica sand before it's loaded onto waiting trains. We've got sixteen thousand residents in Red Wing that use that much water in a single day. High water demand could dry up Mills Creek and ruin one of the best wild trout fisheries near the Twin Cities. And runoff from the bluffs could pollute the stream with chemicals or sediments."

"From what I heard at the meeting," Santana said, "it seems like Select Sands has made attempts to address your concerns."

Virginia Garrison laughed. "Attempt is a good word." She gestured toward Latham. "Silica sand dust is highly carcinogenic, Detective, and very dangerous. We want a statewide moratorium that blocks new mines from operating until communities have the facts regarding its impact on environment and health."

"So Sam Noor's data proved what you already knew to be the case."

"I only saw the data about the high levels of silica blowing off the sand piles. He was murdered before he finished his report."

Santana looked at Carrie Buck. "What's your interest in all of this?"

"In case you never noticed, Detective, Native Americans have an interest in making sure our lakes and rivers are not polluted and our wildlife and lands destroyed."

Santana turned his attention to Virginia Garrison again. "You're suggesting something Sam Noor found might've contributed to his death?"

She nodded. "I told that to the last investigator, but he never pursued it."

Wendell Hudson's case notes had confirmed that he had spoken to Virginia Garrison, but Santana recalled reading nothing that suggested Hudson believed Sam Noor's murder was connected to his environmental research.

"Wait a minute," Virginia Garrison said. "Wasn't the last investigator's name Hudson?"

Carrie Buck fisted her hands on her hips and glared at Santana.

"Noor's body was found in Hidden Falls Park in St. Paul, Ms. Garrison," Santana said. "That's a long way from Red Wing."

"Better for Select Sands if the body was found there rather than around here," Latham said.

"Why do you think Noor's murder is connected to sand mining, Ms. Garrison?" Santana asked.

"Companies like Select Sands stand to make tons of money. If Sam Noor found something we could use to stop the mining, the company could lose millions."

"But you have no proof."

"Maybe you can find some, Detective Santana."

Chapter 17

Though a little thick around the middle, Captain Doug Flint of the Goodhue County Sheriff's Department looked like he could do some damage. The burly man had a bristly porcupine of a mustache that offset his thinning dark hair, and his jaw was permanently set, as if he were trying to crack a walnut between his molars.

Out of courtesy, Santana had called ahead and set up a meeting with Flint. Poking around in another jurisdiction without notifying the local police department often caused problems, something Santana wanted to avoid. Besides, he felt Flint, who worked homicides, might know something that could help him with the Sam Noor investigation.

They were standing beside Santana's Crown Vic. The sedan was parked in a dirt lot outside Chaska Youngblood's trailer, one very similar to the trailer in St. Paul that Youngblood had lived in with his nephew, Clay Buck. The sky was the color of pewter. The breeze blowing out of the west smelled of fish and mud from the Mississippi backwater.

"We met before," Flint said, his gaze as straight as the creases in his trousers. "After Clay Buck was killed."

"I remember."

Santana's eyes followed Flint's as they swept the trailer park. Youngblood's trailer was one of a half-dozen older trailers with mobile home skirts set in the clearing of a wooded ravine, a mile from the Treasure Island Casino and the Prairie Island Mdewakanton Sioux Community, one of the smallest of Minnesota's eleven Indian bands. The community was located on an island in the Mississippi River fourteen miles north of Red Wing and thirty miles southeast of St. Paul, near the Xcel nuclear power plant, and only a fifteen-minute drive from Virginia Garrison's house.

Santana saw little evidence of casino gambling money, only grounds that were spiked with weeds and a tangle of debris and rusted vehicles, like the Ford pickup with one partially deflated tire parked in front of Chaska Youngblood's trailer.

Flint's attention returned to Santana. "Things are strained in the city right now. Residents are taking sides for and against silica sand mining."

"I got that impression talking with Virginia Garrison and Grayson Cole. You familiar with them?"

Flint nodded. "They've been battling for months at the city council meetings. Our former mayor was lobbying for the Minnesota Industrial Sand Council on behalf of the industry. Once the media got ahold of that story, he had to resign. It's gotten ugly."

"I'm not interested in debating the silica sand issue or who might be right or wrong. I want to know who killed Sam Noor."

"Probably your best course of action," Flint said. "You know much about Youngblood?"

Santana shook his head.

"He was one of the protestors at Wounded Knee, South Dakota, on the Pine River Indian Reservation back in 1973."

"You remember anything about it?"

"Appears there was an effort to impeach the tribal president, who was accused of corruption. Protestors also wanted to reopen treaty negotiations with the US government. They controlled the town for seventy-one days while federal marshals and the National Guard cordoned off the area."

"Why Wounded Knee?"

"It was the site of the 1890 Wounded Knee Massacre. Held a lot of symbolic meaning."

"How come you know so much about this?"

Flint tightened the corners of his mouth, relaxed them, and said, "I grew up in South Dakota, not far from the reservation. There's some Sioux blood on my mother's side of the family. My parents took a great deal of interest in the situation. It didn't end well."

"What happened?"

"Both sides were armed, and there was shooting. A US Marshal and two Native Americans were killed. A civil rights activist disappeared during the occupation. Rumor had it he was murdered, though his body was never found."

"So what about Chaska Youngblood?"

"After the protest ended, he enrolled at the University of Minnesota and got a PhD in Native American and Ethnic Studies. Taught there for a number of years before leaving. Don't know much about his later years."

"You ever have problems with him?"

Flint shook his head.

"How about Clay Buck?"

"The department has a good relationship with the Prairie Island tribal council, which isn't always the case on reservations. Only about two hundred fifty to three hundred of the tribe live on the reservation. There's a police force of nine officers. But we often handle crimes on the reservation. I checked Buck's record. Had one drunk and disorderly charge. Outside of that, we had no problems."

"Was he violent?"

"Quite the opposite."

"What about Chaska Youngblood?"

"He keeps pretty much to himself. You ever speak to him?"

"My partner and I interviewed him when Buck was suspected of killing Danielle Lonetree."

Flint nodded. "Want me to stick around while you interview Youngblood?"

"I'd rather talk to him alone, if you don't mind."

"No problem. You need anything else, let me know."

"There's a farmer from around here named George Nelson. Know where he lives?"

Santana wrote the directions in his notebook, thanked Flint, and waited till he drove away. Then he knocked on the trailer door.

When Youngblood opened it, Santana showed him his badge and said, "Remember me, Mr. Youngblood?"

The old man nodded. "What is it you want, Detective?"

"I need your help."

"I needed yours once."

"I wasn't responsible for your nephew's death."

"Perhaps not directly," he said with a shrug.

Trying to read the thoughts behind Youngblood's eyes was like trying to see through black quartz. Santana wondered if Youngblood would shut the door in his face. But then he stepped back and gestured for Santana to enter.

Two glass frames containing locks of hair hung on the living room walls, as they had on the walls of the trailer Santana and Wendell Hudson had once visited.

Hanging on a second wall was a brightly colored Native American blanket. The red and black vertical pairs of triangles joined at the apex reminded Santana of hourglasses. They formed a large image in the center of the blanket that he recognized as the Thunderbird.

Santana sat in a well-worn leather recliner and took out his notebook and pen. Youngblood lowered himself into a rocking chair across from him. He wore a blue denim shirt rolled up to the elbows, a sterling silver and leather bolo tie, jeans, and western-style boots. His long silver hair was tied in a ponytail. His leathery face looked no different than it had the last time Santana had spoken with him, as though the deep lines and wrinkles embedded there had been sculpted in granite. The room held the heavy scent of cigarette smoke.

"Why do you want my help, Detective?"

"I'm investigating the murder of Sam Noor. He was working for an environmental group that's trying to shut down the silica mine near town. Your niece, Carrie Buck, is involved with the group. I understand you are as well."

"My interests go well beyond the mine, Detective Santana."

Santana wasn't sure what the old man meant, but he intended to find out. "Why did you move here, near the reservation?"

Youngblood gestured toward some distant point outside of the house. "The city of Red Wing was named after one of the Mdewakanton Dakota chiefs. His Sioux name was Hupahuduta, or Wing of the Wild Swan Dyed Red. Later, he took the name Shakea, or The Man Who Paints Himself Red."

Santana remembered that Danielle Lonetree's face had been painted red either before or after she was killed, a tribal custom indicating that she had been murdered. He wondered if there was a connection.

"When I grew up on the reservation," Youngblood continued, "we had no electrical lights. Now the younger generation embraces the casino wealth. Many of the elders predicted things would change on the reservation. I'm worried that the band is losing its identity. The tribal council should invest more of our money in education and economic development."

"Why not live on the reservation?"

"Not everyone appreciates my opinions."

Santana glanced at his notes. "What did you mean when you said your interests go well beyond the silica mine, Mr. Youngblood?"

"You recall the Fukushima Daiichi nuclear disaster in Japan?"

Santana nodded.

"We live in the shadow of the nuclear plant. Nuclear waste is stored in large steel casks on Prairie Island in an area that is a floodplain of the Mississippi."

"I wasn't aware of that."

"You should be, Detective. It's thirty-nine miles from the power plant to the center of Minneapolis and thirty-two miles to the center of St. Paul. If there was ever a radiation leak, it could affect hundreds of thousands of people. Even without a leak, the plant has affected life on the reservation. Nobody swims in the river anymore. Medicinal herbs that were collected for generations no longer grow." Youngblood pointed towards the sky. "An electrical field from the power lines that stretch across the reservation causes hair to stand up and gives shocks to children on the playground. You can hear the hum of the wires."

"Is there any proof that the nuclear plant is to blame for any of this?"

"There's no proof that it isn't."

"Yet you're determined to stay."

"The Dakota have lived on these bluffs for centuries, Detective, since BC."

"Before Christ?"

It was the first time Santana had seen the old man smile. "Before casinos," he said. "But we have lived on Prairie Island for countless generations. Mdewakanton means 'those who were born of the waters.' Our burial mounds overlooking the Mississippi were dug about the time of the birth of Christ. My great-grandfather was among those imprisoned at Fort Snelling after we went to war with the whites over treaty violations in 1862. A bounty was placed on Dakota scalps. Thirty-eight warriors were hanged in Mankato. The largest mass execution in US history. Many believe it led to the state's eventual ban on capital punishment. Through it all, my tribe remained on Prairie Island. I'm one of the few fluent speakers of Dakota. Whether there's danger or not, this is my home. Many of the tribe feel the same, though less than half the band currently live on the reservation. My niece believes casino profits are the salvation and future of the tribe."

"I understand you were involved in the protests at Wounded Knee, South Dakota."

The pupils in Youngblood's dark eyes widened a moment. "That was a long time ago."

"And now you are involved in environmental concerns."

"There were similar concerns on the Pine Ridge reservation."

"With silica sand mining?"

"With the strip mining of the land, Detective. The chemicals used by the mining operations were poisoning the land and the water. People were getting sick. Children were being born with birth defects. The tribal government and its supporters encouraged the strip mining and the sale of the Black Hills to the federal government. They were nothing more than puppets of the BIA."

"The Bureau of Indian Affairs?"

"Correct. The sacred Black Hills became a wedge that tore apart the Lakota Nation."

Santana wrote a note and looked at the old man once more. "Perhaps I should call you Dr. Youngblood?"

"You have done your homework, Detective."

"You always struck me as an educated man."

A slight smile appeared again on Youngblood's face. "I am not the stereotypical wise old chief spouting clichés."

"No," Santana said. "You're not." His eyes drifted to the image of the Thunderbird. Something about it fascinated him.

"*Wakinyan Tanka*, the Great Thunderbird, is a powerful sky spirit of Sioux mythology," Youngblood said, following Santana's gaze. "*Wakį̌yą*, from the Lakota word *wakhą*, means sacred, and *kįyą* means winged. It was said that the beating of the bird's large wings caused thunder and stirred the wind. Lightning shoots from his eyes whenever he blinks. Legend had it that he once lived in his *tipi* on top of a high mountain in the sacred *Paha Sapa*, the Black Hills. But with the coming of the *wasichu*, the whites, the thunder beings moved to the farthest end of the earth, where the sun sets."

"There are similar legends and myths in South America," Santana said.

"You were born there?"

"In Colombia. The Ashluslay Indians in Paraguay believe in a similar bird."

Youngblood nodded and considered this. "Sioux people believed that in old times a dangerous serpent, a nameless, shapeless shadow, emerged from the cold waters of the far Northeast. In time the creature came to the *Paha Sapa* seeking a new home in the mountains. It caused great chaos and fear and was an enemy of the Thunderbird. Many warriors from the Lakota tribe challenged the dark monster we called *Unktehi*. Perhaps *Unktehi* has returned."

"I deal in facts, Mr. Youngblood. Not myths and legends. And I think you know more than you're telling me."

"Regarding what?"

"Did you ever meet Sam Noor?"

The old man nodded.

"Were you aware of what he was doing?"

"Testing soil and water samples, I believe."

"And you have no idea why someone might want to murder him?"

Youngblood sat still for a time. Then he rose to his feet and went out of the room. When he returned, he was carrying a small vial in his hand. He gave it to Santana and sat down once again.

Santana peered at the vial that was filled with a clear substance that appeared to be water. Then he shifted his gaze to Chaska Youngblood. "What is it?"

"I don't know. But Sam Noor gave it to me a week before he was murdered."

"Does anyone else know about this?"

"I don't think so."

"Why didn't you turn it over to the police after Noor was murdered?"

"How can I know it had anything to do with his murder?"

"Why didn't you have it analyzed?"

"You can trust only so many people, Detective Santana."

"And you trust me?"

"I believe I can."

"Why?"

"I remember your testimony at my nephew's civil trial. I believe you told the truth then, even if it did not help your partner. Plus, you are not white."

"You don't trust whites?"

Youngblood's eyes locked on Santana's. "I don't trust some of them."

Santana held up the vial. "You didn't tell Virginia Garrison and Sean Latham, or your niece, Carrie, about this?"

He shook his head.

"You don't trust them?"

"The *Unktehi* has killed once. He will kill again."

"You're afraid?"

Youngblood shrugged. "For others. I'm an old man." His gaze lingered on Santana.

"Is there something else?"

"Most things in nature move in a certain way, Detective. Whites call it clockwise. But thunder beings move in a contrary manner—counter-clockwise. That is their way. They do everything differently. They stand for rain and fire and the truth. They like to help the people. That's why, if you dream of the *Wakinyan*, you become a *heyoka*, an upside-down, hot-cold, forward-backward man. I think you are becoming a thunder being now, Detective."

"You still believe in legends, Dr. Youngblood, despite your education?"

"As do many. Becoming a thunder being gives you great power, Detective, but it is also very dangerous."

"And why is that?"

"When you seek the darkness, the darkness seeks you."

Chapter 18

George Nelson's farm was located six miles south of the Red Wing city limits near the small township of Mills Creek. Santana drove along a dirt and gravel road, past the Mills Creek café and Mobile gas station and a campground filled with trailers, following the directions Doug Flint had given him. He stayed on the road till he came to a mailbox with Nelson's address.

Just beyond the mailbox, Santana could see a stack of chain-sawed tree trunks. *Private Property* and *No Trespassing* signs were nailed to the weathered white rail fence that ran parallel to a long dirt driveway. The driveway led to a two-story, ramshackle house set far back from the road. The clapboard house sat on a large expanse of flat land below high green bluffs thick with trees. Behind the house, a tractor and a corn planter were parked between a round corrugated grain bin and a dilapidated red barn.

Santana knocked on the front door and waited in the shade of the wraparound porch, watching the shadows of clouds sliding across a cornfield whose stalks had been pounded by hail. When no one answered, he walked past a flock of chickens to the large barn that smelled of hay and grain. Inside it were empty stalls, a corncrib, a granary, and farm equipment.

"I told you guys I didn't want you coming around here anymore."

Santana's heartbeat jackknifed.

"Get your hands up and turn around."

Santana did as he was ordered. George Nelson, his heavy cheeks pooled with color in the warmth of the barn, was pointing a 12-guage pump-action shotgun at him.

"I think you have me confused with someone else, Mr. Nelson. My name is John Santana. I'm a St. Paul Homicide Detective."

"Homicide?" The distrust in his eyes was unmistakable.

"That's right. If I could reach into my inside coat pocket, I'll show you my badge wallet and ID."

Nelson gave a nod and motioned with the barrel of the shotgun. "Real slow."

Santana pulled out his badge wallet and flipped it open.

Nelson stepped closer, craned his neck, and peered at it. Then he nodded again and lowered the barrel.

Santana released a long breath. "You could get yourself killed pointing a shotgun at someone, Mr. Nelson."

"Snooping around on private property could get *you* killed, Detective."

"I wasn't snooping. I was looking for you."

"Why?"

"You're the man who disrupted the city hall meeting with chickens."

"That a crime?"

"No, sir. I'm investigating a murder that might have some connection to the silica mine. I'd like to talk to you about it."

"Murder, huh?"

"That's right."

"This investigation could affect the mine?"

"I don't know that for certain, Mr. Nelson. But I'd like your help."

Nelson considered it. Then he said, "Let me put my shotgun away."

Outside the barn, clouds were gathering in the afternoon sky that had a yellow cast. In the distance Santana could see a vast expanse of green farmland stippled with red barns. Wind channeled through the tall grass. The driver's side door of a black pickup parked near the barn was open, and dust plumes hung over the driveway. Santana could hear the hot tick of the cooling engine. He waited while Nelson placed the shotgun in the gun rack behind the front seat and then followed him to a shady spot underneath an oak tree.

"You live out here alone, Mr. Nelson?"

"I've got a son away at a technical college. My wife died a few years back."

"Sorry to hear that."

"Best thing," he said.

"I beg your pardon?"

"She suffered from ALS." He shook his head. "Funny how we put a suffering animal to sleep to relieve its pain, yet we won't do the same for our own kind."

Santana let the comment pass. "Who did you mistake me for, Mr. Nelson?"

"Men from the mining company. They've stopped here in the past, wanting to buy my land. I told them to get off my property or the next time I'd put a load of buckshot up their ass."

"I understand you support Virginia Garrison's environmental group."

"What business is it of yours?"

"My business is murder investigation, Mr. Nelson, specifically, Sam Noor's murder. I go where the case takes me."

"I had nothing to do with his death. Hell, he was killed in St. Paul."

"You have a pickup. You can drive."

He thought for a moment. "Okay. I get it. But you're wasting your time with me."

"I never indicated you were a suspect."

"I damn well shouldn't be. Noor and I were on the same side."

"Maybe something I learn from you can help me solve his murder."

"So make it quick. I've got work to do." He removed his camouflage cap, revealing a shaved scalp. The top of his forehead was pale and spotted with perspiration from wearing a hat in the sun. He wiped his forehead with his shirtsleeve.

"What do you have against Select Sands?"

Nelson put on his cap and studied the landscape before giving Santana his full attention. "Too many farmers are leasing their land for silica mining. They stand to make a considerable profit, but neighbors like myself are left to live and farm in the shadow of mining operations without much regulatory oversight. I know sand mining and fracking are supposed to help wean us off foreign oil, but not at my expense."

He paused and looked toward the dead stalks in his cornfield.

"A neighbor of mine sold two hundred acres of property to Select Sands. Never said a word about it. Happened to see a notice in the newspaper. Select Sands paid over two and a half million dollars for the land. That's way above market value and far more than the land is worth. The company intends to mine the property for fracking sand. The mine will depreciate the value of my land."

"So why not sell out to Select Sands?"

He looked at Santana as though the detective were deranged. "My father owned this land and my grandfather before him. I've got a good business here and make a good living despite the occasional crop damage. I don't intend to give up my livelihood for some sand miners." He shook his head and sighed. "Maybe all those tree huggers I once laughed at were right."

"Who are your neighbors who sold their land to Select Sands?"

"Otto and Elsie Vogel. Been friends of mine for years. Not anymore."

Chapter 19

Otto and Elsie Vogel's farm was a half mile east of George Nelson's place. Like Nelson's, the two-story Victorian house with the cross-gabled roof was set far from the road.

Santana loosened his tie as he got out of the Crown Vic. After getting no response when he knocked on their front door, he stepped off the porch and gazed at the barn and fields of stunted corn.

He saw no one.

The wind was dead calm. Thunderheads as thick as oil smoke were building on the horizon. Humidity added weight to the warm air. Santana could feel the hot sand through the soles of his shoes. Flies buzzed around his head. Shriveled rose petals on the bushes planted in front of the house were the color of a bruise.

He checked the garage and saw no car. Perhaps the Vogels were away? Still, his intuition told him something was wrong. His eyes carefully tracked the property, looking for something out of the ordinary, something that didn't fit.

He walked around the side of the house, his eyes alert and scanning his surroundings. Near the back steps he saw a dog chain attached to a spike that was driven into the ground and two large, empty plastic dog bowls for food and water.

Santana went up the steps to the back entrance to try the door, but the lock had been jimmied and the door was slightly ajar. The marks on the lock and doorjamb looked recent. He drew his Glock, eased the door open, and stepped inside.

"Mr. and Mrs. Vogel!"

No one answered.

The kitchen looked clean and organized. Outside, Santana could hear the moan of a distant train whistle and a rumble of thunder. He followed the barrel of the Glock into the dining room and then the living room. Nothing appeared disturbed or out of place.

He went back through the dining room to a carpeted stairway. There was a door at the top of it. He climbed as quietly as he could toward the door, his heart pounding in his chest. Turning the knob, he pushed the door gently with his fingers. It arced back with a squeal on its hinges.

Santana moved along the wall to his left with his Glock at an upward angle, thankful that the carpet runner over the oak floors quieted his steps. When he reached an open door on the opposite side of the hallway, he crossed over and squatted down. He wiped the sweat off his forehead and then stood and swept the large bedroom with his Glock.

A small-boned, silver-haired woman, whose pale skin was lined with blue veins, lay on her back on the bed, her thin legs bent at the knees, her shoeless feet hanging over the side, her face angled toward the door. The bullet hole in her chest stained her simple print dress. Her blue eyes were empty, devoid of light.

A gray-haired man with a heavy, round face lay on his back on the floor, his body perpendicular to the bed.

Santana couldn't let himself feel the full horror of what he saw. He had to focus on the scene. He stepped into the bedroom and knelt beside the man. There was a blackened ring on the man's strap coveralls around the entry wound in his stomach. He had no pulse.

The gun to the man's right was a Smith and Wesson .45 caliber Governor revolver. It had a matte silver barrel and black synthetic handle. Two of the six chambers were empty.

Santana's eyes focused on the gold-framed wedding photo on the dresser of the two dead people in the room as he stood, took out his cell phone, and dialed 911. Though it must have been taken at least forty years ago, Santana thought the Vogels had aged gracefully.

After speaking with the operator, he checked the walk-in closet and the rest of the rooms on the second floor. He saw no indication that anything had been taken and found no suicide note.

He returned to the back entrance and went outside, his Glock hanging from his right hand. Lightning flickered against the black sky, followed closely by a rumble of thunder.

Removing a small Surefire LED flashlight from the left pocket of his sport coat, he twisted the tailcap and played the beam over the dusty ground around the empty dog bowls and chain. Near the end of the chain that attached to a dog collar, he spotted a thin trail of blood leading toward a willow tree behind the barn.

Wind gusts created tiny dust whorls on the dry ground as he followed the trail of blood to a spot behind the trunk of the willow tree, where he found a dead German shepherd, its gold coat matted with dried blood, flies swarming over it.

* * *

An hour later Santana stood beside Doug Flint on the front porch of the Vogels' farmhouse and watched as their bodies were loaded into the back of an ambulance. The rain had stopped, but water still dripped from the gutters.

"The BCA techs will do a thorough job," Flint said, his campaign hat shading his eyes.

The Bureau of Criminal Apprehension in St. Paul handled forensics and crime scenes for Goodhue and other counties around the state. Santana had worked with them before and respected their expertise.

"Bullet wipe," he said.

Flint looked at him.

"Oils were likely wiped off by the clothing as the bullet penetrated, leaving the blackened ring on Otto Vogel's coveralls. It's different than searing on the skin."

Flint nodded.

"Suicides don't typically shoot themselves through their clothing. They usually move the clothing aside or shoot themselves in the head."

"Seen a lot of suicides?"

"More than enough." Santana could see the yellow crime scene tape tied to the porch posts bouncing in the breeze and flashing red lights from squad cars. "I think someone shot the dog, jimmied the back door, took the couple upstairs, shot them, and made it look like a suicide."

Flint watched the ambulance drive away. "My thoughts exactly."

"The Vogels have enemies?"

"They were a nice couple."

"Nice people sometimes have enemies. Their neighbor, George Nelson, is upset with them for selling their land to Select Sands."

Flint tipped his campaign hat back and stared at Santana as though he wanted a closer look. "You think Nelson had something to do with the murder?"

"I don't know. I was at Nelson's farm before I came here. He wasn't there but arrived shortly afterward."

"I know Nelson was upset when the Vogels decided to sell their farm to the mining company," Flint said. "But they were older and had no children. I believe they were planning to move to Florida. If it hadn't been for the lawsuit, they would've been gone by now."

"What lawsuit is that?"

"A year ago a developer alleged that he'd been improperly cut out of a mineral rights deal after Select Sands purchased two hundred acres for two and a half million dollars. The developer argued that he had a binding Mineral Development Agreement in place with the Vogels prior to the sale to Select Sands for well above market value. He felt he was entitled to half of the silica sand proceeds. The Vogels attempted to terminate the contract weeks before filing paperwork with the county. A Goodhue County District Court judge recently ruled in favor of the developer."

"What are the mineral rights worth?"

"Well," Flint said, "conservative estimates are that the site contains over twenty million tons of high-quality silica sand. That's projected to be worth more than two billion dollars."

"So the developer stood to gain a billion dollars."

Flint nodded.

"That's a lot of motive for murder."

"Damages are worth another fifty grand. The Vogels' attorney filed an appeal and then dropped it."

"Why?"

"There was a question as to whether a silica sand mine near Mills Creek would still be economically viable after the developer collected his share."

"Maybe there's another reason?"

"You think the Vogels were threatened?"

"It's possible. Who was their lawyer?"

"A woman named Sally Jenkins. But forget about talking to her. She sold everything she owned and left town. Last I heard, she was living somewhere in Mexico."

"You know who the developer is?"

"Sure. Grayson Cole."

Chapter 20

Early that evening, Santana changed into his gym shorts, a baggy T-shirt, and a pair of Nikes and jogged with his golden retriever, Gitana, for two miles along the road that ran parallel to the St. Croix River—the natural boundary separating Minnesota from Wisconsin. The sun was still above the western horizon, and a crisp breeze blew off the river.

In a perspiration-resistant pouch under his T-shirt, Santana carried his backup Glock 27. The pouch was comfortable and lightweight and had a narrow belt he could strap around his waist. Ever since he had fled Colombia at the age of sixteen, assassins from the Cali cartel had continued to hunt him. He knew they would never quit and that it was better to be armed than dead.

He was looking forward to the weekend and spending time with Jordan Parrish on his 37-foot Mainship, *Alibi,* which was docked at the St. Croix Marina across the river in Hudson, Wisconsin. A former Minneapolis police officer, Jordan was working as a private investigator while pursuing her clinical psychology degree at the University of Minnesota. They had met on a case involving the murder of an Iraq War veteran.

Santana turned off the security system when he returned home and went into the downstairs bedroom he had converted into a workout room. He did three sets of bench presses and curls and hammered the heavy bag and speed bag till he was soaked in sweat and could barely lift his arms. He completed his workout with a hundred sit-ups before showering in the upstairs bathroom.

The doorbell chimed just as he slipped into a pair of jeans. Besides Jordan, Santana rarely had visitors. He looked at his watch. If it was Jordan, she was early, which would be highly unusual. Plus, she had a key.

He went to the computer on his desk and clicked on the application for the security cameras mounted around the house. Four separate rectangular black-and-white boxes appeared, representing the sides of the house. Santana had never met the man standing on the front doorstep, but he recognized the face. He put on clean T-shirt and a pair of deck shoes and went downstairs.

"Detective," the tall man said when Santana opened the door. "I'm Ray Carver." He had thinning gray hair that he combed straight back and eyes that were like those of a hawk. He held out a big-knuckled hand, and Santana shook it.

"I know who you are, Chief." Carver had to be in his early seventies, but he looked in better shape than most men half his age, Santana thought.

Carver handed Santana a standard-sized sheet of white construction paper. On it was a crude drawing of a horned serpent with a long tail. Santana recognized the drawing as an *Unktehi,* the mythical Native American water monster Chaska Youngblood had described.

"You know what that is or why it's taped to your door?"

Santana figured the drawing was meant to be a warning. But he shrugged and said, "Probably neighbor kids fooling around."

Carver nodded in apparent agreement. But Santana could see doubt registered in Carver's narrowed eyes. Then the ex-chief's face returned to a blank mask.

"Sorry to trouble you, Detective, but I'd like a moment of your time."

"I'm expecting company soon."

"This won't take long."

Santana would make certain it wouldn't. Ushering Carver into the house, he said, "Care for something to drink, Chief?"

"Beer's fine, if you have one."

Santana retrieved two bottles of Sam Adams from the refrigerator, popped the caps with an opener, and brought them into the living room. Ray Carver sat on the leather couch in front of the floor-to-ceiling fieldstone fireplace, Santana in a big matching reclining chair.

Carver's eyes tracked the ceiling beams and the painting above the fireplace of the *arriero* with his two mules carrying sacks of coffee down a dirt road in the mountains of Colombia. Santana's childhood friend, Pablo Chavez, was the artist.

Gitana's nails clicked against the hardwood floor as she walked over to Carver and waited patiently until he petted her.

"Nice dog."

"The best."

Carver drank some beer before he spoke again. "You're not surprised to see me."

"I figured we'd be talking at some point."

Carver nodded.

Gitana wandered over to Santana and placed her head in his lap, her eyes half-closed as he scratched her behind her ears.

"I heard Commander Romano asked you to look into the Sam Noor cold case."

Santana looked at him without comment.

Carver drank some beer before he spoke again. "My grandson, Adam, had nothing to do with his father's death."

"You know that for a fact?"

"I do."

"And where's the evidence that he didn't do it?"

"Where's the evidence that he did?"

Santana shrugged. "Romano let you read the murder book."

"Of course."

"Your grandson has some mental health issues."

"Doesn't mean Adam is a killer."

"I understand he assaulted his mother."

"It was nothing, really."

"Yet the two of you had him committed to an institution."

"It was the best thing for him at the time."

"You must be close to your daughter."

"I've been responsible for her ever since she was fourteen, when her mother died."

Santana chose not to disclose the information Adam Noor had revealed to him, that Ray Carver's wife had committed suicide by driving her car into a bridge abutment.

"How did you feel when your daughter married Sam Noor?"

"How does any father feel when his daughter is about to marry?"

"I wouldn't know. I don't have a daughter."

"No father who loves his daughter actually thinks his son-in-law is good enough for her. Mothers probably feel the same way about the women who marry their sons."

Santana recalled feeling the same way about the man dating his sister, Natalia, but he put aside the thought. "Your daughter appears to be doing fine."

"Money solves lots of problems. I never made enough to buy her much."

Department rumors had it that Carver enjoyed betting on the horse races at Canterbury Downs and playing poker at casinos, but Santana moved on.

"If your grandson didn't kill his father, any idea who did?"

Carver shook his head. "Not a clue."

"Well," Santana said, "that makes two of us."

"Your commander insisted that you look into the cold case because of your experience and past success in solving murders."

"I appreciate his confidence."

Carver studied Santana for a time before he spoke again. "I'd like you to keep me informed of your progress."

Santana wasn't comfortable with Carver's request. "Why not get my reports from Romano?"

"I'd rather hear it directly from you. After all, this case involves my family."

Gitana lifted her head off Santana's lap, made two circles, and then with a sigh lay down on the floor at his feet.

"Did you ask that I be assigned to this cold case, Chief?"

Carver shook his head. "My daughter made a request that the case be reopened, Detective. Apparently, my name still carries some influence within the department."

"You were chief for ten years?"

"Eleven, actually. But that was fifteen years ago. Times change. People change."

"Departments change," Santana said.

"So they do." Carver drank some beer, sat back on the couch, and crossed his legs. "The public is more skeptical of police today than when I was coming up through the ranks. They seem to think that most officers get into our line of work to bust heads instead of to protect and serve. The perception that our ranks are filled with psychos, alcoholics, and thumpers is dead wrong, just as it was wrong when I ran the department. The problem is not the individual; it's the institution that conditions and trains our officers. The institution gives officers power for which they're often not held accountable. Some officers are badge-heavy. They abuse that power. You're different, Detective."

"How so?"

"I've heard you're a loner, a man who goes his own way. You belong to the institution, yet you're not part of it. That runs contrary to the blue brotherhood."

"I'm not sure that sits well with the rank and file today, Chief."

"I never gave a damn about what they thought when I was chief." Carver pointed a thick index finger at Santana for emphasis. "There's only one way to control an organization that doesn't want to be controlled. Fear. They were afraid of me. They knew that when I threatened them, I meant it. If you take a few of the bad apples and publicly humiliate them, the rest get the message. If they're terrified of you, they'll do what you tell them to do. They won't like you. You won't change their attitudes, but you can change their behavior."

"You think I'll do what you ask because I'm afraid of you?"

He smiled. "Not in the least. I don't have any power over you now."

"But you said that you still had some influence within the department."

"Does that worry you, Detective?"

"No."

"I didn't think so." Carver leaned forward and rested his elbows on his knees. "Look, don't take me wrong. Humans are capable of some very noble and heroic acts, but also some very shameful and brutal ones. Police assaults were committed during my administration. I've never apologized for the use of police violence, even lethal force, but it has to be guided by the law and the standards of reasonableness."

"I've had to use violence in the past, Chief."

"I'm aware of that. But let's hope that in solving this case, it doesn't come to that." He raised his beer bottle in a toast. "Besides, hope is a good thing, Detective."

"Sometimes," Santana said, "it's all we have."

Chapter 21

Later that evening, Santana ate dinner with Jordan Parrish at the picnic table in his backyard in the sun-spangled shade overlooking the St. Croix. The long yard sloped toward the river and was studded with birch and pine trees. When the breeze blew, it shook the birch leaves and carried the fragrance of raspberry and sandalwood in Jordan's perfume. While they had been dating only a few months, Santana felt as if they had known each other for a long time.

He had grilled two filet mignons. Jordan had tossed a mixed green salad and opened a bottle of Argentinian Malbec, the strong black cherry flavor blending perfectly with the smoky flavor of the steak.

As they ate, they discussed the Sam Noor case.

"So you don't think Romano wanted you investigating Sam Noor's murder," Jordan said, looking at him intently.

He could see the red lipstick print on the edge of the wine glass she held near her mouth. "It's not that Romano didn't want me investigating, but I think it was more Ray Carver's decision than his. His daughter, Kelly, was married to Noor. I think she was pressuring her father."

"Well, it makes sense that she would want it solved."

"It's not Carver's involvement that bothers me so much, Jordan. It's the supposed randomness of Sam Noor's murder and the fact that Clay Buck is at least peripherally connected to both."

"Who's Clay Buck?"

Santana told her about Buck and about the investigation up to this point.

Jordan ran a hand through her medium-length, ash blond hair, giving it a ruffled look Santana found so attractive. "So Clay Buck's sister, Carrie, and Buck's uncle, Chaska Youngblood, are working with Virginia Garrison's environmental group. And you don't believe in randomness or coincidence."

"Not so much in my line of work."

"That's not unusual, John. What appears random or coincidental to one person may not appear that way to another."

"I'm not a determinist who believes there's exactly one way for the world to be, Jordan, that the past and the present dictate the future. But sometimes what you do in the past affects what happens in your future."

"Are you speaking about your own past, John? When your mother was murdered?"

He drank some wine and nodded. "Killing the two men who were responsible set in motion a series of events that still affects my life today."

"Because the Cali cartel continues to hunt you."

"Yes."

"Maybe Danielle Lonetree's murder set in motion a series of events that caused the deaths of both Clay Buck and Sam Noor?"

"Perhaps, but I don't know what the connection is."

Jordan covered his hand on the table with hers. "But if there is a connection, you'll find it."

"Yes," he said. "I will."

They ate without speaking for a time, content in their comfortable silence and the fabric of their relationship. Then, as Santana refilled Jordan's wine glass, he said, "I interviewed Sam Noor's son, Adam, today."

"What was your impression?"

"He's got some mental health issues, but he's smart."

"Sociopathic smart?"

"He's no sociopath. He suffers from depression and schizophrenia and is taking medication. And he reads Schopenhauer and Nietzsche for pleasure."

"Nietzsche. The 'God is dead' guy?"

Santana nodded. "Adam Noor is definitely an atheist and nihilist."

Jordan cocked her head. "If I remember correctly, a nihilist is someone who thinks the world as it is shouldn't exist."

"Precisely."

"I'm not familiar with Schopenhauer's philosophy."

Santana drank some wine as he considered his response. "People are motivated by their own basic desires and will to live and nothing else. No choice or free will."

"That's depressing."

"Schopenhauer believed that punishment should be used to deter people from committing future crimes."

"Sounds more like revenge."

Santana shook his head. "Punishment is about preventing crimes in the future. Revenge is motivated by what happened in the past."

"How do you know so much about Schopenhauer?"

"One of my favorite authors when I was growing up was the Argentinian writer Jorge Luis Borges. He was a fan of Schopenhauer, who believed that our dreams proved that the past, present, and future exist simultaneously, that life and dreams are leaves of the same book."

"I wondered where your interest in dreams came from."

"Both men influenced my thinking. Borges's short stories are really mind games about dreams, space, and time."

"Maybe Schopenhauer influenced Adam Noor as well."

"Maybe."

"You think Adam Noor might seek revenge for his father's murder?"

"It's possible."

* * *

In a dream that night, Santana sees the Thunderbird blanket on the wall in Chaska Youngblood's house. A dark shadow falls over the triangular design. Bolts of lightning forked at the ends shoot from the bird's eyes, and thunder booms as it flaps its wings.

Though his feet remain firmly planted, Santana feels himself sliding backward, away from one wall to another, where he recognizes his reflection in a mirror. The sport coat he wears is backward, and his body is upside down. As his reflection slowly dissolves, he finds himself looking into the half-silvered surface of a one-way mirror.

He observes the hourglass on the coffee table in Kelly Noor's living room, watching as the stream of sand trickling through the narrow neck measures the passage of time and connects the present with the past. Soon a crack appears in the lower vertical bulb of the hourglass, and it splits open like the ground during an earthquake. A wide-open mouth forms and quickly fills with sand. Then, as if he is looking through the lens of a camera, the picture zooms out, and Santana sees the bloated death mask of Sam Noor.

He jerked awake and lay still, listening to Jordan's steady breathing as she slept peacefully beside him, relieved that he hadn't woken her. Slipping out of bed, Santana removed his dream journal from the nightstand and went downstairs to the kitchen table, where he had left Sam Noor's murder book.

He had been taught as a child to trust his intuition and to interpret his dreams, to believe that hidden meanings inhabited the images created by his subconscious. Opening his dream journal to a clean page, he wrote down what he remembered.

Santana knew that mirrors symbolized the imagination and the link between the conscious and subconscious. He also knew that a broken mirror typically signified a troubled period ahead. The one-way mirror indicated that he was coming face to face with some inner issue. Seeing his reflection in his dream represented his true self and that it was time to look within. Yet his clothes had been backward and he had been upside down, as Chaska Youngblood had warned might happen when dreaming of the Thunderbird.

But it was the images of the hourglass and the sand in Sam Noor's mouth that intrigued Santana the most.

He opened the murder book and located the pages containing Noor's autopsy report. It was there that he sensed he would find the connection between the subconscious images in his dreams and the manner of Sam Noor's death—the link that would help him solve the murder.

Chapter 22

As Santana drove to the LEC the next morning, his cell phone rang. It was Doug Flint from the Goodhue County Sheriff's Office.

"What's up, Captain?"

"The Smith and Wesson revolver we found at the Otto and Elsie Vogel crime scene belonged to George Nelson. We brought him in for questioning today."

"What did he say?"

"What do they all say? He said he didn't do it. Claims his gun was stolen two weeks ago."

"Did Nelson report it stolen?"

"No. Said he never really used it much."

"You believe him?"

"As much as I believe anyone suspected of murder."

"It would make sense that his fingerprints were on the gun if he owned it."

"Sure would. And that leaves us high and dry unless the BCA finds forensic evidence tying Nelson to the Vogel murders."

"Nelson was angry that the Vogels were selling their farm to Select Sands."

"Angry enough to murder them?"

"Maybe," Santana said.

When he arrived at the LEC, Santana went to the computer forensic lab on the third floor to talk with Bobby Jackson.

A light-skinned African-American man, Jackson was the department's computer forensics analyst. Well-muscled, with short hair and wire-framed glasses, he was seated on a cushioned swivel chair in front of a computer when Santana entered the room adjacent to the crime lab.

The carpeted room was the size of a large master bedroom. It had laminate counters and cabinets along three walls and a center island in the middle. Neatly stacked intake report forms, hard drives, and the empty shells of seized computers filled the island. Four computers and two forensic towers Jackson used to copy data stood on the counters. Soft jazz played on the Bose Wave music system beside one of the towers.

Jackson turned in his chair. "What's up, John?"

"The Sam Noor cold case. I need to see the data you downloaded from his computer."

Jackson rubbed his chin. "That was nearly a year ago, if I remember correctly."

"Right. Where could I see it?"

Jackson went to a second computer and sat down again. Two minutes later he stood and said, "Sit here, John. I've pulled up all the data. You just need to scroll through it."

Santana sat down and clicked on a folder containing Sam Noor's photos. He scrolled through them till he came to five photos taken on the last day of Noor's life. Three photos were taken near a stream. A fourth was a photo of the Mills Creek café and Mobile gas station. Santana recalled driving past the café and station on the way to George Nelson's farm. He also remembered that a credit card receipt had shown that Sam Noor had purchased gas at the station on the evening that he had been murdered. The fifth photo was a selfie of Sam Noor.

"Can you Google the Mills Creek café and see if they have wireless Internet, Bobby?"

"Sure." Less than a minute later, Jackson said, "High speed Internet is available."

"Thanks. What about the time and locations of these photos, Bobby?"

Jackson came over to the computer.

Santana pointed to the three photos of the stream.

Jackson leaned over Santana's shoulder. "I use Photoshop image editing software to access the EXIF data."

"What's EXIF?"

"Exchangeable Image file."

Santana watched as Jackson clicked on the file menu and then file info. "This allows me to view two types of information about the image," Jackson said, "general and EXIF. When I choose the EXIF option, I get a list of information about the camera used as well as the date and time."

By clicking on each of the three photos of the stream, Santana could see that they had been taken a little after 7:00 the evening that Sam Noor had been murdered. The selfie had been taken at 6:31:18, five minutes before he paid for his gas in Mills Creek—and approximately two hours before his death. The photo of the café had been taken a minute before the selfie.

"The locations of recently used cellular towers are stored in a file on iPhones," Jackson said. With two clicks of a mouse, he found what he was looking for. "GPS coordinates of where a photo was taken are embedded in digital photos. We've also got some mapping functionality here containing the longitude and latitude of the cellular tower locations used by the device." Jackson clicked again, and a map appeared showing the locations of the towers. "Noor was near Red Wing when these three photos were taken."

"That's what I thought," Santana said. But it wasn't the location that surprised him. It was the selfie taken just after Noor had snapped the photo of the Mills Creek café.

Noor's eyebrows were raised, his forehead wrinkled, and his mouth slightly open in an expression of surprise. Three fingers were visible just to the right of Noor's face, as if someone had been reaching for the camera. Santana wondered if someone hadn't wanted his or her picture taken. Maybe Noor had snapped the selfie by mistake. It was easy to do with an iPhone, just an accidental push of an icon.

If the perp thought that Noor had taken a photo of him or her, it might explain why Noor's cell phone had been taken after he was killed. But Noor had already e-mailed the photos to his computer. The perp had either not known the photos were sent or had no access to Noor's computer before Forensics acquired it.

But whether the photo had been taken by mistake or not, someone had been with Noor the night he was murdered.

* * *

Santana used the red phone on the wall outside the SPPD's Forensic Services Unit—formerly called the Crime Lab. One of the female techs opened the door and escorted him into the third floor lab. Tony Novak was seated on a stool, hunched over a file, under the bright fluorescent lights. The room smelled of chemicals and looked like a high school classroom minus the student desks. On the wall above Novak's desk was a framed photo of him as a handsome young middleweight boxer before he had gotten his nose broken a few times and added a few pounds around his middle. Novak's thick mustache and thinning hair were gray. Because of the round bald spot on the crown of his head, Novak's nickname around the department was "Monk," though Santana always called him Tony.

He was the only person from the department that Santana saw outside of work, though the socializing was mostly limited to the boxing matches they attended or watched on cable, and the occasional dinner he and Jordan had with Tony and his wife.

Novak looked up from the file and smiled when he saw Santana.

Santana thought his friend looked different. It took him a moment to realize that Novak wasn't wearing his black-framed glasses with the thick lenses Santana was accustomed to seeing.

"Where are your glasses?"

"Lasik," Novak said with a wide grin. "Best thing since sliced bread. I hated wearing those heavy frames. They were always slipping down my nose."

"If you hadn't been punched in the face so many times, your nose wouldn't be so flat."

"Hey," he said with a smile as he slid off the stool and bounced into a boxer's stance, "I'm still good enough to take you."

"Careful," Santana said. "All that activity could lead to a heart attack."

Novak dropped his hands to his side. "You just came in here to insult me?"

"Primarily. But I also have a question for you."

"Figures," he said, sitting on the stool again. Underneath his unbuttoned white lab coat, Novak wore a black T-shirt. Printed in white letters across the chest were the words SOMETIMES THERE'S JUSTICE. SOMETIMES THERE'S JUST US.

"How much do you know about sand, Tony?"

Novak narrowed his eyes. "Well, I know the composition is highly variable, depending on the local rock sources and conditions."

"What about the sand found along the Mississippi?"

"I don't know much about it. But I have a cousin who's an arenophile. He collects sand samples from all over the world."

"You're kidding."

Novak shook his head. "He belongs to the International Sand Collector's Society."

"They actually have a society?"

"Apparently there's a considerable number of people interested in the variety of textures, colors, location, and mineralogy of sand."

"Who knew?" Santana said.

"We call my cousin the 'sandman.' He always was a little different. But it's good to have a hobby."

"I guess," Santana said.

"What's this all about, John?"

"You remember the Sam Noor case?"

"Vaguely."

"You recall if you took any samples from the crime scene in Hidden Falls Park?"

"Not offhand. But I could look."

"And if you didn't take samples?"

Novak let out a long sigh. "You want me to go to the park and get some."

Santana smiled.

"And what's in it for me?"

"I'll pay for the next HBO or Showtime pay-per-view championship fight."

"At your house?"

Santana nodded. "I'll even throw in the food and drinks."

"This case must mean a lot to you."

"They all do," Santana said.

Chapter 23

Returning to his workstation, Santana called David Shapiro, the business news editor at the *St. Paul Pioneer Press*, and requested information about Select Sands.

"Now why would an SPPD homicide detective be interested in the business operations of a silica sand mining company?"

Santana waited silently.

After a long pause, Shapiro said, "Okay. I happen to know something about Select Sands since I'm writing an article about them."

Santana heard the clicking of a keyboard. "What can you tell me?"

"Well, they're a Texas-based company that mines sand used in shale drilling or hydraulic fracturing. They operate plants in Minnesota, Wisconsin, Nebraska, and Arizona. Kenneth Webb is the majority owner and its founder and chief executive. They produce more than five million tons of sand a year and employ about five hundred people. Their annual sales are about three hundred fifty million dollars. But they're roughly five hundred million in debt."

"That sounds like a problem."

"It is. The company has a high debt load and weak operating results. Investors are skittish. Webb recently hired restructuring advisers."

"Is he mismanaging the company?"

"I think their financial problems have more to do with low natural gas prices. That's forced them to cut back on drilling at the same time that many new sand mines have come online, pressuring sand prices. The average price of sand used for hydraulic fracturing in the US has fallen considerably."

"Is Select Sands in danger of filing for bankruptcy?"

"They *may* file for bankruptcy protection, though my sources tell me they're still looking at opportunities for an out-of-court restructuring. The company's lenders could provide a debtor-in-possession loan in the event of a Chapter Eleven filing. Their spokeswoman told me they were confident in their liquidity position."

"Sounds like something the owner of a professional team might say to the manager just before he fires him."

"Naturally the company is going to put the best spin on their situation. The bottom line is they don't believe a bankruptcy filing is necessary at this time."

"What do you think?"

"If natural gas prices remain at their current level, I think Select Sands could stay in business. Of course, that could change, as could other market factors."

"Thanks for the information."

"What's this about, Detective?"

Santana thanked him again and disconnected.

* * *

Ken Webb's office was located on the second floor of a red brick building in downtown Red Wing, one half block from the historic St. James Hotel.

"Please have a seat," Webb said, offering a bright white smile.

Santana sat in a comfortable cushioned chair in front of Webb's large mahogany desk. A window behind the desk had a clear view of the Mississippi River. Smoke from a cigar balanced on the edge of the glass ashtray on the desktop left a heavy aroma of leather and cedar in the air.

"I'm afraid I haven't been able to locate any record of a meeting with Sam Noor."

Santana hadn't expected Webb to find anything—or admit if he had. But Santana held his tongue. "What happens to your company if the city council fails to approve new permits to mine silica sand?"

Webb looked surprised. "I have no reason to believe new permits won't be approved."

"Say they weren't. What would you do?"

Threads of blue and white smoke floated around Webb as he held the cigar near his mouth, rolling it between his thumb and fingers before setting it on the edge of the ashtray again. "Well, I'd feel bad for the citizens of the town. They'd lose the opportunity for a significant number of jobs and the dollars those jobs would bring to the community."

"What about the loss of dollars to your company?"

Webb tented his hands in front of him and tapped his fingertips together while he looked at Santana. It was the same pose he had struck the first time they had met. Santana figured it was a habit designed to give the appearance that Webb was deep in thought while allowing him time to formulate a well-crafted response.

"Of course we'd lose some money. But this isn't the only mine we operate."

"But it might be the most important one, given your current financial situation."

Webb took in a deep breath and let it out slowly. "This conversation isn't about the possibility of my company losing money or going bankrupt, is it?"

Santana ignored the question.

Webb leaned forward. "Why don't you just get to it, Detective, instead of dancing around the issue? You're still searching for a motive for Sam Noor's murder."

"Has to be one."

"So you think I had something to do with Sam Noor's murder?"

"Did you?"

Santana could see the anger flare behind Webb's eyes.

"I'm not going to dignify that question with an answer." Webb stared at him silently and then rose to his feet. "This discussion is over."

Santana stood. "Thanks for your time, Mr. Webb. I can find my way out."

"Thank goodness," he said. "Because you're certainly clueless about everything else."

Chapter 24

As Santana left Kenneth Webb's office, he was reminded of a Colombian phrase spoken often by his father. *Cuando el río suena, agua lleva.* When the river makes noise, it's carrying water. Santana wondered if Webb's appetite for success might have disabled the moral compass that would otherwise have kept his dishonesty and greed in check, and if that same appetite had driven him to commit murder.

Santana walked north, past the St. James Hotel and the covered garage across the street where he had parked his Crown Vic, then crossed the railroad tracks near the Amtrak depot and Levee Park. The warm afternoon sky was a soft blue and filled with white clouds with dark edges. The air smelled like river water and heated concrete.

As Santana approached the park, he saw Virginia Garrison seated at a shaded white picnic table close to the swollen Mississippi River. Sean Latham was sitting in a wheelchair at the end of the table next to her. There was an open picnic basket on the table and a set of red paper plates, corn chips, sandwiches, cans of Pepsi, and plastic silverware. Latham had spread a paper towel across his lap, and whenever he took a bite of his sandwich, he leaned forward to avoid staining his clothes.

"Thank you for coming, Detective," she said with a warm smile. "Would you care for a turkey and cheese sandwich?"

"I'm fine. But I appreciate the offer."

"Please sit down." She gestured to the bench across from her.

"How 'bout a Pepsi?" Latham said.

"Okay."

Latham gave a nod and wheeled his chair slightly back from the table.

He wore a white T-shirt with the sleeves cut off, and Santana could see the *Semper Fidelis* tattoo on Latham's upper arm and his bulging biceps expanding with effort.

Latham leaned over and retrieved a can of Pepsi from the cooler at his feet and handed it to Santana. "Enjoy," he said with a smile. His wraparound mirror shades were swimming with distorted images of boats docked at the nearby marina.

Santana popped the tab on the ice-cold can and drank.

"I'm sure you're aware that Elsie and Otto Vogel are dead," Virginia Garrison said.

A slight breeze lifted her auburn hair from her shoulders and ruffled her coral-colored tank top. She was deeply tanned, and the sprinkle of sand-colored freckles on her face appeared darker than the last time Santana had seen her.

"Yes. I'm aware of it."

"What do you think happened?"

"Is that why you asked me here?"

"Partly," she said. "But we'd also like to know if you're any closer to solving Sam Noor's murder."

"I can't discuss an ongoing investigation."

"Not even a little?" She gave Santana an encouraging smile.

"I'd like to talk to Carrie Buck, though, if you could give me her phone number?"

"Is it about her brother, Clay?" Latham asked, removing his sunglasses.

"I'm afraid I can't say."

"But Carrie could tell us."

"That's up to her."

"Well," Virginia Garrison said, "it's a nice day for a picnic. We haven't had many nice days given all the rain we've had."

Santana drank some Pepsi and said, "I never asked what you do for a living, Ms. Garrison."

"I'm an RN at the Mayo Clinic."

"In Rochester?"

"No. There's a clinic here in town, too."

"Is that where you met Sean?"

"No," he said, wiping his mouth with a napkin. "We met a couple of years ago at one of the first environmental meetings."

"You've been in the Marines."

Latham glanced at the tattoo on his upper arm. "Served two tours in Iraq after nine eleven. Thought it was the right thing to do at the time. Not so sure about my decision now." His eyes settled on some neutral point in space and then came back on Santana's. "Someone once said that a politician is a fellow who will lay down your life for his country. Seems to be a lot of them in Washington with that attitude."

Santana noted that Latham's right hand shook as he lifted his can of Pepsi. "Were you experiencing silicosis symptoms during your service?"

He shook his head as he drank and then set the can back on the picnic table. "After my discharge, I worked for a sandblasting company. Safety wasn't a priority. When I first met Ginny, I had some mild symptoms. I didn't realize what was wrong. She urged me to see a specialist. She also recommended a good lawyer in town." Latham looked at her and smiled.

"Who are you suing, Mr. Latham?"

"I *was* suing my former employer. But the company went belly up."

"Fortunately, Sean doesn't have much lung scarring," Garrison said, her smoky eyes lit with affection.

Santana wondered why Latham was in a wheelchair if he didn't have much lung scarring.

"I plan to live a long time," Latham said. "But before I die, someone is going to pay for my illness."

Maybe money was the reason for the wheelchair, Santana thought.

* * *

Carrie Buck lived in a small two-story A-frame cabin with tongue and groove walls and a vaulted ceiling. It had a bedroom loft, open kitchen, and a floor-to-ceiling stone fireplace. Sliding doors off the living room led to a deck that overlooked the woods. Hanging on the knotty pine walls were dream catchers and Native American paintings.

One painting in particular caught Santana's attention. It showed a well-muscled warrior in a loincloth mounted on the back of a blanketed, brown-and-white tobiano-patterned pinto. The horse was standing on the edge of a ridge. Its neck and head were bent toward the ground and a back leg was held in the air, as though the horse had come to a quick stop. The mounted warrior was looking up at a stormy sky. His arms were extended above his head. In his hands, he held the whitewashed skull of a steer, as though offering it to the Great Spirit.

"What do you want, Detective?"

Carrie Buck sat on a leather cushioned chair on the opposite side of the fireplace from Santana, her face without expression, her dark eyes flat and emotionless, as though she were looking at nothing.

"Information."

"About what?"

"Let's start with Otto and Elsie Vogel."

"I've never met them."

"But you know who they are."

She nodded. "I read the papers. Most everyone around here knows who they are—or were."

"How did you feel about the Vogels selling their farm to Select Sands?"

"The same as I feel about storing more nuclear waste. Sand mining hurts tourism and visitors to the casino."

"Yet the tribal council negotiated a deal with the energy company that increases the amount of nuclear waste on Prairie Island."

"You get that off the Internet?"

"Does it matter?"

He could see the sudden heat in her eyes. "In exchange for paying us two and a quarter million dollars a year. They've helped us improve emergency procedures and research possible links between nuclear waste and health issues on the island. And they agreed to develop new land for tribal members who want to live a safer distance from the plant."

"Meaning many of the young tribal members like yourself."

"Mostly. But some elders feel the same. It's the best deal we could get for the people of Prairie Island for now. Some kind of compensation is better than none. We hadn't received anything since the plant was built. At least now we have money that we can put away for the future."

"Has Select Sands offered the tribe any compensatory dollars?"

"You mean for digging the mine?"

Santana nodded.

"None of the sites are on our land."

"But you wouldn't be pleased if a new mine was dug on the Vogels' property."

She looked at him for a long moment. "Does it make you feel better, Detective?"

"What?"

"Accusing innocent people of crimes they didn't commit."

"I'm looking for answers."

"And you don't care who you hurt in the process. That's the same attitude I suspect you had the day my brother was killed. You cops are all the same," she said, her eyes sliding off him.

"Maybe the same person who killed Sam Noor killed your brother?"

Her eyes shifted sharply back to him. "Are you saying the two murders are connected?"

"Give me a few more minutes of your time, Ms. Buck." Santana removed a half-folded sheet of paper from the inner pocket of his sport coat and handed it to her. As she unfolded it, he said, "Ever see one of those before?"

"It's a drawing of an *Unktehi*."

"So you have seen it before."

She lifted her chin. "It's an old legend inspired by the fossils my forefathers found in the Badlands. It probably made perfect sense for them to imagine that the Thunderbirds and *Unktehi* once battled and left the bones of their dead scattered across the land. But no one believes in the legend anymore. The bones are dinosaur fossils. Where did you get the drawing?"

"Someone taped it to my front door."

"Really? Why?"

"I don't know for sure. But what if the legend were true?"

Her eyes looked down at the drawing again and then came back to Santana. "You're not serious?"

"I don't mean as a serpent from the water. But as a man."

"He would be evil. Some kind of monster."

"I think he is. I think he's an *Unktehi* come to life."

Chapter 25

That evening Santana sat on a deck chair on his dock, enjoying a cold Sam Adams. Heat lightning forked out of the dark clouds anchored low on the horizon, and the warm breeze blowing out of the west smelled of distant rain. He had spent the last two hours with a power washer, stripping the redwood stain off the sundeck atop the boathouse and nailing down any loose boards. His T-shirt was still damp with sweat, his cut-off blue jeans and old top-siders wet from the spray. Tomorrow afternoon, weather permitting, he would re-stain the deck.

He heard the drone of an engine before he spotted the thirty-foot Bayliner cruiser, recognizable by its wide blue hull stripe. Because of all the June rain and high water, the boat was following the no-wake speed restrictions, heading slowly downriver, away from Hudson, its engine missing badly.

Santana heard the Bayliner sputter along till the engine finally died.

Gitana, lying on the dock by his side, sat up on her haunches. Santana switched his bottle of Sam Adams for a pair of Bushnell binoculars and scoped the boat named the *Double Trouble.*

He could see a couple in their late twenties or early thirties. The woman at the helm on the flybridge had long dark hair and wore a black bikini. She was tall and slender, like a model, and had a perfect beach tan. The man standing in the cockpit had a dark mustache. He wore a baseball cap turned backward on his head and long bathing trunks with a tropical floral pattern. A sleeveless white tank top exposed his tanned, muscular arms. By the look of him, Santana figured he was either a body builder or ex-military or both.

The engine hatch located in the center of the cockpit was open.

As the cruiser drifted toward Santana's dock, the woman yelled, "Jake!" and pointed toward the bow. The man called Jake stepped up and onto the narrow starboard side deck, grabbed the stainless steel handrail, and hurried to the bow, where he released the roller and dropped anchor thirty yards offshore. Then he turned and waved at Santana. "We're having a little trouble here."

"I can see that."

"Think you could give us a hand?"

"I leave engine repairs to professional mechanics."

"How about helping us come ashore?"

"Neither of you swim?"

Jake cast a hand toward the woman on the flybridge. "I do, but Melissa doesn't."

She smiled and waved at Santana.

Placing the binoculars back in the case on the dock, Santana went into the boathouse and retrieved his Intex three-person inflatable raft. He dragged the 10-foot raft to the water's edge, fitted the aluminum oars into the two rotational oarlocks, pushed off, and jumped in.

Gitana tried to jump in after him, but he told her to stay. She whined as he paddled toward the cruiser.

"We really appreciate this," Jake called as Santana approached the stern and tossed him a bowline. Jake caught it and secured it to a cleat. Then he closed the engine hatch.

"Climb down and I'll take you both to shore," Santana said. "There's a mechanic at the marina in Hudson."

"Why don't *you* come aboard," Jake said, aiming a Glock 26 at Santana's chest.

Santana's heart tripped against his ribcage as his eyes shifted from the gun barrel to the man. Up close, Jake's pockmarked face looked familiar, but Santana couldn't place him—until he pictured him without the mustache. Santana had once handcuffed him to a water trough on a farm and taken his AR-15.

Jake smiled. "Remember me?" His face suddenly hardened as he removed his cap. "Come aboard. Now!"

Santana stepped out of the raft and onto a wide swim platform. A transom door on the starboard side led to the cockpit.

The woman called Melissa had come down from the flybridge and was standing beside Jake, a Glock 26 held rock steady in her two hands, her long dark hair lifting in the breeze. She seemed completely comfortable pointing the gun straight at Santana's chest.

"You sure you want to be part of this?" he said to Melissa.

"Shut up," Jake said, his scalp glistening through his crew cut.

Melissa glanced at Jake without comment and stepped back, keeping her distance. Her large, hypnotic eyes were bluer than ice and glazed with a kind of insane excitement. Small waves slapped against the sides of the hull. Santana heard Gitana barking. This woman, Santana thought, was turned on in some twisted way by the vulnerability of another human being.

"Turn around and put your hands behind your back," Jake said.

Santana could feel his palms open and close at his sides.

"Turn around!" Jake said again.

Santana did.

Jake slapped a pair of chain-linked handcuffs on Santana's wrists. Then Jake shoved him toward two steps that led to the cabin below.

At the bottom of the steps Santana's eyes tracked the portside settee and storage cabin. On the starboard side were an enclosed head and a long galley countertop, where the boat's electrical panel was located. A lower helm station was situated in front of the galley counter. Across from the helm and galley to port was a dinette. Under the bow was a V-berth.

Jake pushed Santana forward and had him sit on one of the cushioned seats facing the dinette.

"What do you want?" Santana asked.

Jake smiled again. "What do I want? I want you dead." With his free hand, he picked up the heavy-duty flashlight on the counter and swung it at Santana's head.

Santana turned his body away and leaned back, hoping to deflect or minimize the impact, but the blow caught him just above his left ear. A red wave slid behind his eyes, and then he was tumbling into a dark, cool pit, where there were no thoughts nor feelings, where the rumble of the ancient Thunderbird was only an echo of a distant past, and shifting sands had long since erased all memories.

Chapter 26

Santana gave a shallow, hacking cough and spewed water from his mouth as he awoke. The water was cold—more than he would have imagined—and had a sharp, pungent taste and a strong aroma.

Gasoline!

Pain spiked above his left ear as he sat up quickly, coughing again to clear his throat and lungs, gulping down air, fully awake now from what could have been his last long sleep.

He squeezed his eyes shut till the pain passed and then focused his eyes on his surroundings. He was still in the cabin of the *Double Trouble*. But now he could feel a handcuff biting into his right wrist, cutting off the blood and swelling the veins. The cuff was fastened to a horizontal stainless steel handle attached to the woodwork below the counter stove.

Santana stood and yanked on the cuff, hoping to rip the handle off the woodwork, but the attempt only sent a stab of pain through his wrist. Water had risen to a level above his ankles, and flames were eating away the deck above him. The boat was sinking fast.

With his free hand, he dug into the left pocket of his shorts and retrieved a three-inch galvanized nail, the type he had used to fasten down the loose boards on his boat deck.

The Peerless handcuffs on his wrist were one of the most commonly used because they were easy to apply in a tactical situation. Santana knew they could be beaten with nothing more than a stiff piece of wire or paper clip bent to resemble a crank. But the shank of the nail was too strong to bend and the point too big to pick the lock. He threw the nail away in frustration.

The water level was quickly rising. He felt as if the cabin were closing in on him. His eyes stung with sweat. He pulled up his T-shirt and wiped his face on it. He took a deep breath to calm himself. *Think!*

Handcuffs weren't particularly complicated. When snapped onto a suspect's wrist, the cuffs remained shut because of a simple mechanism. Inserting a universal key, which worked on just about any pair of handcuffs anywhere, disengaged the mechanism and allowed the cuff to open.

Simplicity was not a defect. If an arresting officer was the only one who could unlock a suspect's handcuffs, it would create a logistical nightmare. But there was another way to open a pair of handcuffs besides a universal key or a piece of wire.

As his eyes searched the cabin, at first he saw nothing that he could use. Then his gaze locked on a ballpoint pen on the counter near the helm station. He slid the handcuffs along the handle and reached with his free hand till his fingers grasped the pen.

Water was just below his knees now. He didn't have much time.

Santana drew the pen to him and broke off the clip from the cap. He inserted the flat end of the clip between the notches and the ratchet of the cuff on his wrist, just enough to cover two or three of the ratchet teeth. If he inserted the clip too far, the cuff would jam, and he would go down with the boat. Leaving the shim in, he turned his wrist upward, pulled hard, and the cuffs snapped open—just as he felt the boat listing hard to port.

Steadying himself, he grabbed the flashlight off the counter. It was the same one the man called Jake had struck him with, the same type Santana had on his boat. He knew it was waterproof and would float. Then he waded in waist-deep water toward the stern and climbed the stairs.

Dusk had deepened into darkness. Gasoline streamed across the flaming deck. Flames were licking the edges of his raft. It had been sliced open and lay flat at his feet. He saw no sign of Melissa or Jake, or any lifejackets.

Santana stuffed the flashlight into a jean pocket and dove over the rail and down into the cold black water that smelled of oil and gas. The river seemed to be alive. The current pulled at him like a pair of hands as he rose to the surface. He recalled that nearly every year someone drowned trying to swim from shore to shore. He tried not to think about it.

The *Double Trouble* was burning brightly now from bow to stern. He heard a rush of air bubbles, a hiss of steam rising. Then the boat slid slowly under the water, leaving a red glow on the surface.

Moments later it began to rain.

Raindrops danced on the water and drummed on Santana's head. He treaded water and looked around at the shore lights, orienting himself, drifting away from the spot where the boat had sunk. He figured he was somewhere near the Prescott Narrows and the confluence of the Mississippi and St. Croix Rivers.

Santana had spent much of his childhood swimming in the Cauca River near his family's farm in La Victoria, Valle in Colombia, though he hadn't swum much in subsequent years. The St. Croix River was considerably colder and the current much stronger than what he was used to. His biggest mental challenge now was trying to maintain his composure. It was not uncommon for even very experienced swimmers to occasionally feel panicky in open water. But panicking was the worst thing he could do—no matter what the challenge, no matter what the danger.

In his mind's eye he saw the *Unktehi*, the water monster, the horned serpent, below the surface, reaching for his legs, ready to pull him under. But Santana forced the thoughts of the monster and death from his mind and began swimming toward the Minnesota shoreline. Soon he realized he would tire quickly fighting the continuous current. Fortunately, the river's surface was flat and still, and he could save strength by treading water or by floating on his back.

Then in the distance, he heard the rumble of an outboard engine and saw running lights heading in his direction from the Wisconsin side of the river, the boat moving well above the no-wake speed of five miles per hour. Maybe someone had seen the flames and was coming to help?

When the powerboat neared the location where the *Double Trouble* had gone down, the pilot cut the engine, leaving the boat drifting in the water. Santana thought about calling out and using the flashlight in his pocket to signal for help, but the sound of loud voices caused him to hesitate. Two men were arguing, but Santana couldn't hear clearly what was being said.

Then the glare of a spotlight swept the water twenty yards in front of him. Maybe they were searching for survivors—or maybe they were searching for him?

Santana grabbed some air and went down.

Having no weight belt or flippers, he felt as if his ribs had been pulled free of his breastbone as he slid through a layer of cooler temperature, struggling to gain depth. He stayed down as long as he could before he rose to the surface. The boat was fifty yards from him now. He watched the searchlight sweep the water once more before he heard the engine start, the throttle jam open full out, and saw the running lights receding.

As quickly as the rain had started, it stopped. The clouds were suddenly lit behind a half moon. Thirty yards away, toward the Minnesota shoreline, a round shape, like the back of a large turtle, floated on the surface. Santana swam toward it, one long stroke at a time, breathing sideways, blowing water out his nose, till his hand felt the object, which he immediately realized was no turtle.

Chapter 27

Late the following afternoon, Santana was seated in front of Homicide Commander Peter Romano's desk. Romano had loosened the Windsor knot on his blue striped tie and rolled his shirtsleeves up to his elbows. His thick, olive-skinned forearms were resting on the desktop. Photos of his attractive wife, three sons, and two daughters were arranged on his office walls and on a corner of his cluttered desk.

On the wall directly behind him hung a map with red circles designating parts of the city as crime hotspots. The map was the latest research analysis tool developed to understand why high crime rates occurred in specific areas. Romano operated under the belief that most crime was not random and could be predicted under crime pattern theory. Santana agreed.

"So after the boat sank, you swam to shore," Romano said.

"Some of the way. A few people came out in their boats to investigate the fire and to see if anyone needed help. A very nice older couple picked me up, took me ashore, and drove me to Regions Hospital."

"Tell me their names and I'll recommend them for a Chief's Award."

"I already recommended them."

Romano nodded his approval. "So how are you feeling?"

"I don't have a concussion. But I could use some sleep." Santana gently touched the bandage above his left ear. He had taken two tablets of Aleve to relieve the pain that throbbed with each beat of his heart.

"And the DB in the river?"

"I think she was shot dead, Pete, before she was dumped face down into the water. The air in her lungs couldn't escape, so she floated for a time. Dive teams are out searching, but it might be days or weeks before she surfaces again. She was wearing a bathing suit, so she had no ID on her. But the guy named Jake called her Melissa."

"The boat was stolen from the St. Croix Marina in Hudson."

"Any leads on Jake?"

"Not much to go on. And the name could be a phony."

"I don't think so."

Romano leaned back in his chair and clasped his big hands over his ample belly. "So why the attempt on your life?"

"I'm not sure. But it might go all the way back to Clay Buck's death."

Romano's eyes narrowed. "Who's Clay Buck?"

Santana told him.

"I remember the case," Romano said, nodding his head. "I was working Homicide. The civil suit took a toll on Wendell Hudson."

"I recognized the guy called Jake," Santana said. "He was in one of the vehicles that ran us off the road. I took his AR-15 and handcuffed him to a water trough."

"You sure about this?"

"Positive."

"We've notified departments here and in Wisconsin and given them the description you provided."

"I'm guessing he's ex-military."

Romano shook his head and ran a hand through his jet-black hair. "I don't get it. Clay Buck is dead. The city settled the suit against Wendell Hudson. You think this Jake character has a grudge against you?"

"I'm not sure. But I need to find out."

Romano's brow knitted in concentration as he sat forward and tapped his thick fingers on the desktop. "What happened to you last night can't become a vendetta, Detective. Your task is to find out who murdered Sam Noor. Not to dig up buried cases. If you can't focus on that, then I'll assign someone else."

Santana looked at Romano for a time while he considered his options. Then he said, "You didn't want me on the Sam Noor case because you knew Hudson was the original IO. You knew once Hudson found out, there might be problems again between us."

Romano appeared confused. "You forget, Detective. I was the one who assigned you to work the cold case."

Santana shook his head. "That was Kelly Noor's idea. She spoke to Chief Ashford. Ashford called you."

Romano placed his hands flat on the desk as he stared at Santana. "Kelly Noor doesn't tell me what to do."

"What about Ashford?" Santana could see Romano struggling to find an answer. "Let me do my job, Pete, and stop the threats."

"Sam Noor's murder is a must-solve. I want all your energies focused on that case."

"You know they are."

"I know they'd better be," Romano said.

* * *

Susannah Barnes struck Santana as the epitome of fair-haired polish and cool refinement. She was seated across a shiny dark hardwood table from him in Butler's, the café on the second floor mezzanine of the St. Paul Athletic Club. The club was located in a classic brick building in the central business district near Rice Park in downtown.

The interior of the thirteen-story building had been restored to its original English Renaissance elegance and now housed a boutique hotel. As it was a century ago when it had first opened, executive membership still included many of the rich and powerful of St. Paul society.

"Would you mind if we switched places, Ms. Barnes?"

Slightly tanned and smooth-skinned, clothed in a bright yellow sleeveless sundress, Susannah Barnes blew a blond strand of hair from her unblemished, heart-shaped face and stood. "Not at all," she said with her Southern accent.

When they were seated again, she said, "You always sit with your back to the wall?"

"Whenever possible."

"Wasn't there a lawman in the Old West who used to do that?"

"Wild Bill Hickok. One day he sat at a poker table in a Deadwood, South Dakota, saloon with his back to the door and was shot in the head and killed."

"Well," she said, "it's always better to follow your instincts. Though I think this club is a bit safer than a Western saloon."

"I hope so," Santana said with a smile.

"I'm surprised you remember me, Detective Santana. We only met briefly at Kelly Noor's house. I imagine it's helpful in your line of work."

"What's helpful?"

"Having a good memory for faces."

"It doesn't hurt."

She flashed a smile and stirred her fruit smoothie with a long straw. "You didn't say on the phone why you wanted to speak with me. You know, I've never talked to a homicide detective before."

Santana drank from his glass of Coke and then set it on a coaster on the table. "Where in the South are you from, Ms. Barnes?"

"Atlanta."

"What brought you to St. Paul?"

"I met my husband in Atlanta while he was completing his internship at Piedmont Hospital and I was completing my law degree. He's now a neurosurgeon at United Hospital here in the city."

"How long have you known Kelly Noor?"

"I believe we met ten years ago on the clay court at the University Club. We were in the same tennis league. Fortunately, our membership here entitles us to belong to both clubs."

"You and Ms. Noor still play tennis?"

"I do. Kelly suffers from tennis elbow and quit playing a few years ago."

"But you're close friends."

Her eyes never left Santana's face as she sipped her fruit drink once more and then dabbed her mouth with a cloth napkin, being careful not to smear her pink lipstick. "Was there something specific you'd like to ask me about, Detective?" she said with another bright smile, though this time there was less wattage in it.

Santana suspected Susannah Barnes was accustomed to using her enticing smile as an inducement to achieve what she wanted both sexually and socially. He gave her a smile of his own, hoping it might also serve as an inducement, though he had always had more luck with his gun and badge.

"Did you know Ms. Noor's son, Adam?"

"So this is about Adam?"

Santana let the silence hang between them.

"My, aren't you the reticent one," she said, filling in the silence he had left. "Well, I suppose that comes with the job."

She tapped her bottom lip with an index finger. "I've known Adam for nearly as long as I've known his mother. I also know that it's impolite to speak about your friends to strangers."

"I'm not a stranger, Ms. Barnes."

"Then what are you?"

"A homicide detective."

She sat back. "I'm fully aware of that."

"Then you know I have to ask direct questions if I'm going to find out who murdered Sam Noor. You might be of some help."

"How?"

"By answering my questions truthfully."

"I'm not a dishonest person, Detective Santana. In fact, I pride myself on my honesty."

Santana leaned forward and placed his forearms on the table, narrowing the distance between them. "Then tell me honestly if you think Adam Noor murdered his father."

"Absolutely not. Adam loved Sam."

"What about Kelly?"

"She loved Sam, too."

Santana waited till he saw her eyes widen with recognition.

"That's not what you meant, is it?"

He shook his head.

"Well, I don't believe for one second that Kelly had anything to do with Sam's death. I can't imagine why you'd think that unless . . ." She paused, her blue eyes locked on his, her hand gripping the drinking glass. "Adam thinks Kelly killed Sam?"

"I never said that."

"But why?" she said, ignoring his response.

Santana watched as she sorted through her own thoughts.

"Money," she whispered softly.

He looked at her silently.

"Well, Adam is mistaken."

"Susannah!" a voice called to Santana's right. "How are you?"

Santana saw Grayson Cole approaching, a drink in one hand.

Cole, wearing a white shirt open at the collar, a teal pin-striped seersucker sport coat, and dark blue khakis, hesitated when he spotted Santana. His complexion reddened, and he appeared momentarily lost as to what to do. Then, regaining his composure, he strode confidently to the table, where he kissed Susannah Barnes on the cheek.

"How are you, Grayson?" she said.

"Fine. Just fine."

She gestured toward Santana. "This is Detective John Santana from the St. Paul Police Department."

"We've met," Cole said. He shook Santana's hand, though not as firmly, Santana noted, as the first time they were introduced.

"Really?" she said. "Isn't that a coincidence?"

"Yes," Cole said. "It certainly is." He smiled as his gaze shifted to Susannah Barnes and then back to Santana. "Is this business, Detective, or did you know Susannah before?"

"Business."

"I see." When Santana didn't elaborate, Cole looked to Susannah Barnes for clarification.

"The detective is investigating Sam Noor's death."

"Yes," Cole said. "I was aware of that."

"Kelly and I are good friends."

"Of course."

Cole took a drink and shifted his weight from one foot to the other. "Any closer to solving the case, Detective?"

"I believe so."

"Well," Cole said with a forced smile. "That's good news." He drank again and then glanced at his watch. "I've got to get back to the office. Nice seeing you again, Susannah. You, too, Detective." He raised his glass, spun on his heels, and strode out of the room.

"That was odd," Barnes said.

"How so?"

"Grayson seemed so flustered. Perhaps you being a homicide detective intimidated him," she said with a sly smile.

"Maybe it was something else, Ms. Barnes."

"I'm not sure what you mean."

"Is Grayson Cole married?"

"Never has been to my knowledge."

"Any children?"

"Not that I'm aware of."

"What's Cole's reputation?"

"You mean as a businessman?"

"I think you know what I mean."

Her slight smile had a knowing quality to it. "Grayson is regarded as a ladies' man."

Santana went with a hunch. "Is Kelly Noor seeing anyone?"

Her eyes fidgeted and her gaze slid off his face. She picked up the glass and sipped more of her smoothie while her eyes darted from the English oak paneling to the decorated plaster ceiling and period light fixtures.

"She is seeing someone, isn't she?"

Susannah Barnes eyed him once more. "You don't know, do you?"

"Know what?"

She finished her drink and set down the glass, her eyes holding his. "Sam's been dead for almost a year. Kelly's a very attractive woman. It's natural that she'd be seeing someone."

"Was she seeing this same someone before her husband was murdered?"

"I'm feeling very uncomfortable with this conversation, Detective."

"Who is she seeing, Ms. Barnes?"

"What does this have to do with Sam's death?"

Santana offered no reply.

"You think someone Kelly dated might have killed Sam?"

"Anything is possible."

She thought about it and then shook her head slowly, as if she couldn't believe what she was hearing—or thinking. "Why not ask Kelly?"

"I'm asking you."

"You don't think she'd tell you."

"Maybe not."

"You know I could tell Kelly we had this conversation."

"Go ahead."

Susannah Barnes let out a long sigh. "All right, Detective. Kelly *was* seeing someone."

"And she was seeing him before her husband's death?"

She inclined her head once.

"Who was it, Ms. Barnes?"

"Grayson Cole," she said.

Chapter 28

Early that evening Santana rang the bell and heard it chime deep inside the Queen Anne-style home where Grayson Cole lived. The house had a large porch, steeply pitched roof, half-timbered gables, and turrets at the corners. It sat on a shaded slope overlooking Lake Phalen, northeast of downtown St. Paul.

When the front door swung open, Santana could see the confusion and nervousness in Cole's face. He was wearing a bright blue running suit and a pair of matching running shoes. A white towel was draped over his shoulders. His complexion was red, and he was sweating heavily.

"What brings you here, Detective?"

"Otto and Elsie Vogel are dead."

Cole started to speak and then abruptly stopped, his eyes darting with thoughts. Then he said, "Come in. The maid has left for the night, and I was working out. Fortunately, I heard the doorbell."

Santana stepped into the foyer, which opened to a winding staircase and a large living room and dining room.

"Do you mind if I continue my workout as we talk?"

"No problem."

The corridor leading to the back of the house was paneled in rich amber butternut, the flooring in dark walnut. First-class strength training equipment was lined against three of the mirrored walls in the gym. In the center of the room facing the door were an elliptical machine, a stationary bike, and a treadmill. Mounted on the wall was a large flat-screen television tuned to CNN.

Cole climbed onto the elliptical machine, used a remote to mute the television audio, and looked at Santana. "On days I don't work out at the athletic club, I work out at home."

"But you were at the club this afternoon."

"A business lunch."

"Tell me about the lawsuit with the Vogels."

"Not much to tell," he said, working up a rhythm on the elliptical. "I had a binding Mineral Development Agreement in place with the Vogels prior to the sale of their land to Select Sands. They disagreed and terminated the contract before the sale. A judge ruled otherwise."

"I understand their attorney appealed the ruling and then dropped it. Why would she do that? Why not see it through?"

"It was costing the Vogels money. Had I lost, I would've appealed."

"They had a chance for a two billion dollar payout had they won on appeal."

"Chance is the key word," Cole said.

"Did you know the Vogels' lawyer?"

Cole shook his head.

"Strange that she suddenly decided to quit her practice and move to Mexico. And now the Vogels are dead."

Cole stopped his workout and stared at Santana. "Are you insinuating that I had something to do with their deaths?"

"You stood to lose a billion dollars had the Goodhue County judge's ruling been overturned on appeal."

Cole climbed off the machine and wiped the sweat off his face with the towel. "I'm not a murderer, Detective."

"Someone shot the Vogels' dog and broke into their house."

"Could've been a burglar."

"It appears that nothing was stolen."

Cole shrugged. "Maybe there was nothing in the house worth stealing." He wiped his face again and gestured for Santana to follow.

Across the hall from the gym was a rustic study with the same walnut flooring as in the hallway. The large room was a color palette of brown, gold, and burgundy. Floor-to-ceiling bookshelves filled with hardcovers lined two of the walls. Silver-framed photos showed Grayson Cole on horseback, yachting, and golfing. Two leather-tufted Chesterfield sofas sat opposite a heavy walnut table. Three oversized books on Native Americans were stacked on the table. In the far corner of the room was a horseshoe-shaped bar on which was a plate of fruit and a blender. To the right of the bar was a desk not quite the size of an aircraft carrier. A laptop PC sat on the desktop.

Cole went directly to the bar and invited Santana to have a seat. "Would you care for a fruit drink, Detective?"

"No, thank you."

Cole blended bananas and strawberries and shaved ice and poured the mixture into a tall glass. Then he crossed the room and sat down on the sofa opposite Santana.

A large oil painting depicting Indians on horseback engaged in a pitched battle with blue-uniformed soldiers hung on the wall facing Santana.

"Interesting painting, Mr. Cole."

He nodded but didn't look behind him, as if he had been told that before. "Yes. It's a Charles Russell painting of the Battle of Little Bighorn on June 25th, 1876, one of the most ignominious defeats in American military history."

"I'm familiar with the battle," Santana said, taking out his notebook. "Collect a lot of Native American art, Mr. Cole?"

"Some."

"Any particular reason?"

"Never grew out of the cowboy and Indian phase of my childhood, I guess." His face split in a wide grin. "Plus, I'm a big history buff."

Santana opened his notebook and said, "Tell me about your business."

Grayson Cole drank some of his fruit drink and dabbed his mouth with the towel. "I run a real estate management company for a unique group of historic properties in and around the cities."

"And how did you get involved with Select Sands and silica mining?"

"I'm always looking for opportunities. One can hardly see the future if one is always looking at the past." He smiled again, as if he were pleased with his pithy saying.

"Yet you seem very preoccupied with the past."

"History can teach us much, if we understand it. We can learn from our mistakes."

"Made many of those, have you?"

"No more than the average man, I suspect." He drank the rest of the juice and set the empty glass on a coaster on the coffee table. Looking at Santana, he said, "It's important for a man in my position to know who he's dealing with."

"One might say the same about me, Mr. Cole."

* * *

After leaving Grayson Cole's house, Santana drove to Kelly Noor's home on Summit Avenue. He was thinking about his last conversation with Jordan in which he had said that randomness or coincidence did not exist in the world. Everything that occurred was related to a prior cause or association—like Kelly Noor's relationship with Grayson Cole.

Maria, the maid, whom Santana had met on his first visit to the Victorian mansion, told him that Ms. Noor had gone out for the evening. Santana showed Maria his badge and asked for Kelly Noor's cell phone number. Then he called her and identified himself.

"I'd like to talk to you, Ms. Noor."

"Have you discovered something about my husband's murder?"

"Not exactly."

"What does that mean?"

"If we could meet, Ms. Noor, I could explain."

"Well, I'm at the Wabasha Street Caves."

"I'll be there in twenty minutes," Santana said.

* * *

Located along the Mississippi River underneath a large bluff in downtown St. Paul, the Wabasha Street Caves were actually manmade silica mines first used in the production of glass. Dating back to the 1840s, the seven sandstone caves had been used at various times for growing mushrooms and aging cheese, and as a speakeasy during Prohibition. Later they were home to the Castle Royale, a nightclub and restaurant that opened at the end of Prohibition, and the Castle Royale 2, a nightclub that operated during the disco years of the 1970s. The castle-like exterior and wooden arch entry door were still present, as were the original sixty-foot bar and large hardwood dance floor and stage.

The interior had finished brick walls, stucco ceilings, a carpeted dining space, and tile floors in the lounge area, where Santana found Kelly Noor. The dank, cool odor of the sandstone caves hung in the air.

"Please, Detective, sit down." She gestured with her half-empty wine glass at one of the three chairs at the round table where she was seated.

Santana sat down in the chair directly across from her.

Kelly Noor was wearing a tight-fitting turquoise shift dress with a flowery print, a V-shaped neckline, and three-quarter-length sleeves. Even in the dim light, her shoulder-length dark hair shone like black onyx.

"Would you care for something to drink, Detective?"

"I'm fine. Thanks."

"Are you a fan of swing dancing?"

"I'm afraid not. Salsa is more to my taste, though I don't dance much anymore."

"That's a shame." She finished her last swallow of wine and set the empty glass on the table. "Well, I wasn't much of a fan of swing dancing either till Adam joined a jazz band. They often play here on Thursday evenings. But that's not what you came here to discuss, is it?"

Santana shook his head and leaned forward. Just as he was about to speak, Adam Noor sat down in a chair to the right of his mother. "So what brings you here, Detective? Let me guess. You're really into swing dancing." He laughed at his own joke.

"There's no need to be rude, Adam," his mother said.

"The detective can take a joke, right?" He gazed at Santana with wide, excited eyes, his mouth in a lopsided grin.

Santana wondered if the young man had gone off his medication.

Adam Noor stared at Santana for a moment longer. Then he said, "So what really brings you here? More questions for me?"

"For your mother."

"Fine," he said. "Let's hear them."

"I'd rather speak to her alone, if you don't mind."

"Oh, but I do mind, Detective. There are no secrets in the Noor clan, right, Mother?" He put a hand on her shoulder and gave it a little shake. In most instances it would have been perceived as an affectionate gesture. But given Adam Noor's strained relationship with his mother and the tone of his voice, it came across to Santana as a veiled insult.

"Please, Adam," she said. "Let the detective and me talk privately."

He cocked his head and peered at his mother without speaking, as though he were gazing at something he had seen before but never understood. "No more privacy, Mom." He spat out the last word as if it were an epithet.

Her eyes held her son's for a few beats before she said, "All right, then, Adam. Have it your way." She looked at Santana. "Go ahead and ask your questions, Detective."

Discussing Kelly Noor's relationships with men in front of her son could easily cause problems, something Santana wanted to avoid. He stood up. "We'll talk at another time, Ms. Noor."

She grabbed his wrist as he started to walk away. "The band's first set is starting soon."

Santana followed Adam Noor's gaze to the bandstand, where the musicians were beginning to assemble.

Adam Noor slid his chair back from the table and got to his feet. "I'll be back," he said and strutted off.

"Please, Detective. Sit down and ask your questions."

Instead of sitting across from her as he had before, Santana sat in the chair directly to her right, where her son had sat. "How well do you know Grayson Cole, Ms. Noor?"

"I've heard his name before, but I don't know him."

"I know that's not the truth, Ms. Noor. In fact, I know that you were seeing him before your husband's death. What I don't know is if you're *still* seeing him."

Her cheeks darkened. "Who told you I was seeing Grayson Cole?"

"I can't tell you that."

"Well, whoever said I was seeing him is lying, Detective."

"I don't think so."

"What does Grayson Cole have to do with my husband's death? Surely you don't think he had anything to do with it?"

"I never suggested he did."

"Then what is it you're after?"

"Justice for your husband. You do want that, don't you, Ms. Noor? Justice?"

"Of course."

"Then tell me the truth."

Her eyes searched the room before returning to his, as if the answer to his question were posted on the wall. "Yes, I *was* seeing Grayson."

"Meaning you're not seeing him now?"

"That's right."

"How did you meet?"

"At the club."

"The St. Paul Athletic Club?"

"Yes. We met one evening at the bar. Sam and I had been having problems with Adam's behavior. Sam's coping mechanism whenever there was a problem was to shut off communication and to seek shelter in his work. I wanted to talk it out."

"So how long was this relationship going on?"

"Only a few months. When Sam was murdered, I broke it off."

"So you first met Cole a few months before your husband was murdered."

"My God. This is crazy."

"Did Adam know that you were seeing Grayson Cole?"

"Of course not."

"You're sure?"

Santana followed her gaze as she looked at the bandstand where her son was seated, his saxophone in his lap, his eyes fixed on his mother.

Chapter 29

Jordan Parrish hugged Santana tightly the moment he walked into her condo. "Are you okay?" she whispered into his ear.

He could feel her heartbeat against his chest. "I'm fine."

She broke off her embrace and cupped his face in her hands. "I'd rather hear about it from you than read it in the newspaper."

"I know," he said.

Her hazel eyes were filled with concern. She took his hands in hers and examined his right wrist, which still bore the red marks caused by the tight handcuff. Then she took him by the hand and led him to the couch. "I bought some aguardiente." Imported from the Caldas region of Colombia, the smooth mixture of sugar cane and anisette in aguardiente always produced a comfortable burn in his chest.

"Bring the bottle," he said, stripping off his sport coat and tie.

Jordan returned a few minutes later with a serving tray on which were two plates, two sets of chopsticks, eggrolls, a carton each of fried rice and beef lo mein, two large shot glasses, and an ice-cold bottle of aguardiente. "I thought you might be hungry."

"Thirsty, too," he said with a smile.

While they ate, Santana explained what had happened on the river the previous evening, how he had recognized the man called Jake.

"Do you have any leads?"

"Not yet. But Jake was involved in Clay Buck's murder and the attempt on my life. But why target me now?"

Jordan looked at him a long moment without comment.

"What is it?"

"When I was young, John, I believed in the concept of good and evil. I thought all of us were responsible for our actions because of the choices we made. But I still have a hard time accepting that pure evil exists in the world, or that a benevolent God would allow it to exist."

"That's the paradox, isn't it?"

She nodded. "So what accounts for the evil we see in the world?"

Santana drank some aguardiente as he considered Jordan's question. "The longer I work homicides, the more I believe that no religious, economic, or political system has ever existed that can suppress our basic nature."

Jordan peered at him skeptically. "You're suggesting that all of us are evil at heart?"

Santana was reminded of the demon that had led him down the dark road of revenge following his mother's murder. "No," he said. "But our basic nature is to gather into groups, which are often committed to exterminating other groups for their opposing beliefs, or because of their skin color. Some humans can overcome their dark impulses. Others can't. Nothing will ever make them good. Nothing will ever stop them from killing their own kind."

Jordan was silent for a time before she spoke again. "I think it was St. Augustine who argued that evil wasn't a product of God but an absence of good, that what at first appeared to be evil might eventually turn out to be good." She drank some aguardiente and sat back on the couch, her eyes fixed on his.

"Like casinos and gambling?"

"Possibly."

"How does gambling away their life savings at casinos compensate for the genocide that whites inflicted on Native Americans?"

"It doesn't. But," she said with a little smile, "it is a form of retribution."

"I wonder if Native Americans see it that way."

"So you think racial animosity or evil was the motive for killing Clay Buck and Danielle Lonetree?"

"Maybe their deaths are a cover for something else."

"Like what?"

"I think it's about real estate. The land Select Sands wants to mine is worth two billion dollars."

"Definitely a motive for murder."

Santana nodded. "And a man named Grayson Cole stands to collect half of it."

"How?" Jordan asked.

"Cole negotiated with Otto and Elsie Vogel to collect fifty percent of the mineral rights prior to the sale of their Mills Creek land to Select Sands. The Vogels attempted to terminate the contract weeks before the sale. Cole brought a lawsuit claiming that the contract was still binding and should be transferred with the land during the purchase. A district court judge ruled in favor of Cole. The Vogels filed an appeal and then dropped the lawsuit. Now they're dead."

"Why drop the lawsuit?"

"Maybe out of fear for their lives."

"You think this man called Jake is connected to all these killings?"

"It's possible."

"Sam Noor's murder, too?"

"Jake reappeared when I began investigating Noor's death."

They ate in silence for a time. Then Jordan said, "I know you'd rather talk about the case than about yourself."

"It's that transparent?"

"It is to me." She leaned over and kissed him gently on the mouth. "I don't want to lose you."

"I don't want you to lose me either."

"Then we should talk about what happened on the river yesterday."

"I'm fine."

"No, you're not."

Santana could feel a bubble of anger rising in his chest. He took a breath and drank some aguardiente. When he spoke, he kept his voice neutral. "And you know this because you'll soon have a degree in psychology?"

"I know this because I know you."

"It isn't my first near-death experience, Jordan. Or the first time I've seen a body."

"Then you know that a non-response to a death scene, an autopsy, physical remains, all the ugly things that you're constantly exposed to, is actually a response."

"I understand that. I also understand the roles of good and evil in life and in death. My experience with it began when I was sixteen."

"When your mother was murdered."

He nodded.

"And your repeated exposure to aggression and death has helped you develop coping mechanisms."

"Yes."

"You and I both have taken lives, John. We both have nightmares."

"We're both dealing with PTSD, Jordan."

"But I'm one step removed from the carnage, even as a private investigator. I don't see what you see on a daily basis. That's why I'm worried about you."

He squeezed her hand. "I'll be all right."

She brushed a curl off his forehead and gazed into his eyes. "You need to be all right physically *and* emotionally, John. I'm worried that the more you see of death, the more you're exposed to the darkness, the more difficult it will be for you to find the light."

* * *

Santana slept badly that night, troubled by the dreams of dark water and a woman seated on a flowered swing above a set of gravestones and skulls.

In his dream he remembers the painting above the fireplace in Kelly Noor's mansion, but he cannot see the woman's face now, for she is underwater, yet above him, as though his world is upside down. Soon she rises to the surface and drifts away from him. He swims after her, desperately trying to narrow the distance between them. The water feels warmer the closer he gets to her, almost to the point of scalding him. But he keeps swimming toward her as she floats face down in the water. When he finally reaches the woman and turns the body over, he lets out a silent scream. Then he watches helplessly as Jordan Parrish gradually sinks slowly away from him, disappearing in the darkness deep below the surface.

Chapter 30

The following morning Santana met Tony Novak at Sam Noor's crime scene in Hidden Falls Park. Noor's body had been partially buried near one of the paved trails that ran along the shady, wooded bottomlands next to the Mississippi River, twenty-five yards to the west of the shoreline and ten yards from a large cottonwood tree whose root system was wrapped around its trunk like a serpent spiraling out of a grave. The tree stood as still and as solemn as an onlooker at a funeral, its tall branches appearing to touch the shroud of low gray sky hanging over the misty June landscape.

Fifty yards to the north, through threads of rain as fine as angels' hair, Santana could see canopies that looked like large conical hats sheltering a series of picnic tables. Twenty yards beyond the tables, his SPPD sedan and Tony Novak's crime scene van were the only vehicles in the parking lot.

Raindrops plinking off Santana's poncho and dappling the river's surface darkened the soil at his feet. Thin blades of grass sprouted from the ground that was once a temporary gravesite, but Santana could still see the rectangular patch of earth where the perpetrator had dug.

He was tired, having been unable to make it down into the dark well of sleep after waking from the disturbing dream about Jordan. He wasn't sure of its meaning and hadn't mentioned it to her. But he knew intuitively that the dream was important, and that he needed to keep her close.

Santana squatted in the soft ground beside Novak. "The ME concluded that Sam Noor died of suffocation. All three wounds were post-mortem, Tony."

"Hell of a way to go."

"What about the soil samples?"

Novak thought about it for a time. "The problem with looking at silica, John, is that you'll find it in most sand, though children's sand boxes are silica free now due to parents' concerns about kids ingesting it. So I checked with my cousin, the sandman, and then called a source at the Geological Survey at the University of Minnesota. Essentially, the type of sand simply depends on the mineral content. Magnetite and volcanic obsidian produce very course black sand. In places like the Caribbean, you have white beach sand made from eroded limestone, coral, and shellfish. It primarily contains calcium carbonate."

"And the sand here along the river?"

"It's an arkosic sand containing at least twenty-five percent feldspar. It also contains rock fragments and organic materials."

"Is it much different than silica sand?"

Novak nodded. "Silica sand is made up mostly of silicon dioxide, usually in the form of quartz, typically greater than ninety-five percent. It's more rare, and the grains are well-rounded, like very small marbles. There are four formations that are exposed in scattered outcrops along the St Croix, Mississippi, and Minnesota Rivers and their tributaries, from the Twin City metro area south to the Iowa border and into Wisconsin."

Novak paused and picked up a handful of wet sand. "Most folks looking at it wouldn't realize there's a subtle but distinct difference between the sand in St. Peter sandstone, which is exposed in the central Twin City Metro area, including here in Hidden Falls, and the sand in the silica-rich Jordan sandstone layers in and around Red Wing."

"How distinct is the difference, Tony?"

"Both the Jordan and St. Peter silica-rich bedrock layers are composed of greater than ninety-five percent quartz grains. But the St. Peter layer is measurably finer grained than the silica-rich sandstone in and around Red Wing. St. Peter sandstone has only a very small fraction of coarse-grained sand, meaning grains exceeding five millimeters in diameter. The Jordan sandstone, the most desirable frack sand common to the Red Wing area, is loaded with coarse sand grains, which is one reason it's so desirable for fracking."

"Did you check the sand samples Tanabe took from Sam Noor's body?"

"I did. Bear in mind that comparing sand samples is not as accurate as DNA, John."

"I understand."

Novak's poncho hood had slipped down over his forehead and was nearly covering his eyes. He pushed it back and let his eyes linger on Santana's face. "If the material that suffocated Noor was common river sand, the individual grains would run the gamut from quartz to feldspar to rock fragments. Many of the grains would be quite angular, having sharp edges on them. This kind of sand is common everywhere in the region, including Hidden Falls. If the sand instead was composed almost entirely of quartz grains, and the grains were well rounded, nearly spherical, then it came from one of four silica-rich bedrock formations in the region."

"What did you find when you compared the two samples, Tony?"

"The sand taken from Sam Noor's body was predominantly coarse-grained."

"Meaning it likely came from Jordan sandstone."

Novak nodded.

"So Noor was suffocated somewhere else and his body buried in a shallow grave here in Hidden Falls Park."

"That would be a likely scenario."

"That 'somewhere else' could've been Red Wing."

"Yes," Novak said. "It sure could've been."

* * *

Santana was driving back to the LEC when his cell phone rang.

"I'm so glad I reached you," Kelly Noor said, sounding out of breath.

"What's wrong?"

"Adam stopped by and wanted to know what you and I discussed last night at the club. I didn't want to tell him, but he insisted."

"You told him about your relationship with Grayson Cole?"

"Yes. He was very angry and I think . . ." Her words had been coming as fast as a hail of bullets before she paused.

"You think what, Ms. Noor?"

"I think Adam has gone off his meds. I'm not sure he knows what he's doing. I'm afraid he might harm Grayson."

"Why would he do that?"

"Because he believes Grayson had something to do with my husband's death."

"How long ago did your son come by?"

"About three hours ago," she said.

"Why did you wait so long to call me if you were worried that your son might harm Grayson Cole?"

"I'm sorry. I hope I didn't wait too long."

"I hope so, too, Ms. Noor."

Santana disconnected and dialed Grayson Cole's office. A voice mail message indicated he would return tomorrow.

Santana drove to Cole's house near Lake Phalen and rang the doorbell. He waited and rang the bell again and waited some more. Then he cupped his hands around his eyes, peered through the oval glass on the door, and saw the blood on the entry floor.

Santana drew his Glock and tried the doorknob. The door was unlocked. He went in. The trail of blood on the walnut floor and butternut walls led to the guest bathroom, where he found Grayson Cole face-up in a pool of blood.

Cole was wearing bloodstained boxer briefs and a white terrycloth robe that had fallen open, revealing multiple stab wounds in his chest and abdomen. Santana held the Glock steady in his right hand while checking Cole's carotid artery for a pulse with his left.

The body felt cool to the touch. He detected no pulse.

In his mind's eye, Santana painted a nightmarish picture of Cole's death. Bleeding from the initial attack, he had tried to take refuge in the bathroom, bracing himself against the toilet while he propped his bloody feet against the door to keep it closed. He had pushed so hard he had dislodged the toilet from its base. The perp had forced his way in and killed Cole.

Santana phoned dispatch. Then he cleared the house, room by room.

* * *

The scent of spilled blood in a confined area was like nothing else.

Its sweet, heavy tang hung in the air and lingered in Santana's mouth, filling his throat with the coppery aftertaste of a licked coin. It would stay with him for hours. Something about the way the brain worked, he thought, how the senses were wired together, the molecular memory of the olfactory system.

Standing over the body, Santana refocused his mind and concentrated on the victim, on Grayson Cole. He could see a number of narrow slit-like stab wounds running parallel to the Langer's lines in the epidermis of Cole's skin, and larger gaping wounds running perpendicular to the lines.

"Many of the wounds are superficial," Reiko Tanabe said, looking up at him as she knelt beside the body. "But others show that a knife was thrust with great force into the body. See the wounds that are squared at both ends?"

Santana noted that Tanabe had depersonalized the scene by not using Cole's name.

"The blade was pushed in all the way to the ricasso," she said. "The L and Y-shaped wounds suggest that he moved as the knife was withdrawn. There are defensive wounds on the backs and palms of his hands as well, an indication that he attempted to ward off the thrusts and grab the knife."

Given the brutality, Santana thought, it appeared to be a crime of passion. "How long ago, Reiko?"

"Well, the ambient temperature is steady. The body is still warm and flexible. Given the blood loss, I'd say he died quickly. His rectal temperature measured a three-degree loss. Assuming his body temperature was normal at the time of death, I'd estimate he's been dead about two hours."

"A search of the house and grounds hasn't turned up a knife, Reiko."

"You have any suspects?" Tanabe asked.

"One," he said.

Chapter 31

Santana drove to Adam Noor's loft.

Ray Carver met him at the door. "My daughter called me." Carver gestured toward the couch, where his grandson, clothed in a wrinkled white T-shirt and jeans, lay sleeping.

"I need to talk to him."

Carver shook his head. "I gave him a sedative. You won't get anything from him for a while. Let's talk in the kitchen."

Santana followed Carver into the kitchen and sat down at a butcher-block table.

"Would you like a cup of coffee, Detective?"

"No, thanks."

Carver poured himself a cup, leaned his backside against the counter, and took a sip.

There was a knife block on the counter behind Carver. One of the knives was missing.

"Is your grandson taking his meds?"

"I believe so."

"You talked to him?"

"Briefly."

"Did he mention Grayson Cole?"

"No. Why?"

"Someone stabbed Cole to death."

Carver took in a deep breath and slowly let it out.

"Did you know Grayson Cole, Chief?"

"I knew who he was. How long ago was Cole killed?"

Santana glanced at his wristwatch. "The ME figured two hours. Add another twenty minutes since I left Cole's house."

Carver's eyes jittered as he thought about it. "Tanabe's TOD is just an estimate till she completes an autopsy."

"I know."

"Well," Carver said, waving away any further disagreement. "Adam couldn't have done it. I've been here with him for at least that long. And why would he kill Grayson Cole? As far as I know, he had no relationship with the man."

Santana wondered if the former SPPD police chief was telling the truth, if Carver was aware that his daughter had been seeing Cole. Santana figured Carver would try to protect his grandson, at least till the evidence proved otherwise. Given the bloody scene at Grayson Cole's house, Adam Noor should be covered with blood spatter.

"Was your grandson wearing those clothes when you arrived?"

"Yes."

"You said your daughter called you."

Carver nodded. "She was concerned that Adam might have stopped taking his drugs."

"How long ago did she call?"

Carver started to speak and then stopped, a grin in the corner of his mouth. "Good try, Detective. You wouldn't accuse me of lying to my face. But Kelly called me shortly before she spoke to you. I'm sure her phone records will verify that."

"We've already agreed that the ME's estimate of TOD isn't exact, Chief. Your grandson could've had time to kill Cole and return to his loft before you arrived."

"What's his motive?"

Santana decided he would keep silent about Kelly Noor's affair—for the time being.

Carver peered intently at Santana. "You don't really believe Adam is responsible for Grayson Cole's murder, do you, Detective?"

"Does your grandson own a car?"

"Of course."

"Where is it?"

"I assume it's in the parking garage underneath the building."

"There's a knife missing from the knife block behind you. Know where it is?"

"Maybe it's in the dishwasher or a drawer."

"And maybe it's a coincidence that your grandson's father was also stabbed to death."

"Hold it right there," Carver said, holding up a hand in a stopping gesture. "When we first spoke, my daughter had requested that the department re-open the investigation into my son-in-law's death. The department insisted that you look into the cold case because of your experience and past success in solving murders. I wasn't convinced that you were the right man for the job. Now you're accusing my grandson of a double murder. I guess I was right."

"I'm not accusing him of anything—yet. But maybe the murders of Sam Noor and Grayson Cole are connected."

Carver held the coffee mug close to his mouth for a moment. Then he set the mug on the counter and sat down across from Santana and leaned forward, his eyes focused and intense. "Tell me what you know."

"I'm afraid I can't."

Carver's mouth fell open in shock. He sat up straight. "What'd you say?"

"You heard me."

"I expect answers to my questions."

"You seem to forget that you're not in charge anymore. I don't answer to you."

"I'm sure if I made a phone call to your current chief, he wouldn't agree with your assessment."

Santana stood and headed for the door. "Then call him. I'm getting a warrant to search this place and your grandson's car. Make sure not to tamper with anything."

* * *

Kacie Hawkins got out of her Crown Vic and strode toward Santana. He was leaning against the driver's side door of his sedan that was parked at the curb outside Adam Noor's loft. Hawkins wore tight-fitting jeans and a white cotton pullover under her dark blue blazer. She had played fast-pitch softball in college and had maintained the lean body and long, confident stride of an athlete.

"What's up, partner?" she said, a wide smile brightening her mocha-colored complexion.

Santana quickly summarized the murder scene at Grayson Cole's house and why Adam Noor was a possible suspect. "Ray Carver is with Noor."

"The former chief?"

"Adam Noor is his grandson."

"Perfect," she said with a half-smile and shake of her head.

"You know I'm working Sam Noor's cold case."

She nodded. "You think the kid did his father, too?"

"It's possible."

Hawkins gave a small laugh. "Carver's got to love you."

"Any progress with your cold case, Kacie?"

"Lots of dead ends, John. Not much else."

Santana held up the warrant. "Let's check the kid's car first."

Ray Carver was waiting in the underground garage beside Adam Noor's silver Honda Civic sedan. He looked at Santana and then Hawkins.

Santana saw Carver's jaw tighten and his nostrils flare.

"This is my partner, Kacie Hawkins."

Carver acknowledged her with a slight nod. "Is she working the cold case with you?"

"I'm not mute," Hawkins said. "I can speak for myself."

Carver canted his head, a look of amusement on his face. "I'm sure you can, Detective Hawkins. My apologies."

"She's helping me search," Santana said.

"Always better to have two detectives present," Carver said. "Don't worry. I didn't touch anything. The car's unlocked."

"How do you know that?" Hawkins asked.

Carver held up the keys. "Because I unlocked it."

Santana and Hawkins gloved up and began their search of the Honda's interior. The garage was well lit, but Santana used his mini-Maglite to look under the seats and in the glove compartment and center console. He found nothing but the car manual and service invoices in the glove compartment. The center console was empty. He could see no trace amounts of latent blood, but he wanted Forensics to run luminol or fluorescein testing.

"Nothing on or in the back seat," Hawkins said.

Ray Carver stood near the hood with his arms crossed and a smug smile on his face.

Santana pulled the trunk latch and he and Hawkins, followed by Carver, walked behind the car to take a look.

When Hawkins flipped open the trunk lid, Carver said, "It's clean," with a measure of satisfaction.

"Let's search upstairs," Santana said.

"You're wasting your time, Detective," Carter said. "You should be working on finding the actual perp."

Santana ignored him and headed for the elevator.

He and Hawkins started in Adam Noor's bedroom. In the closet, Santana flipped open a hamper lid and peered inside.

"What do you know," Hawkins said.

Chapter 32

Commander Pete Romano sat behind his desk in the Homicide and Robbery Unit, rubbing his temples with the tips of his fingers as though suffering from a severe migraine. His eyes were closed.

Ray Carver and Kelly Noor sat to Santana's right. The tension in the room was as thick as clotted blood.

"It's a setup," Carver said, his face looking as if it had aged by years in the last few hours. "Someone wants my grandson to take the fall for Grayson Cole's murder."

Romano opened his eyes, rested his forearms on the desktop, and squinted at Carver as though he were looking into a bright light. "You have any proof of that?"

"Well, it's obvious."

Romano peered at Santana, waiting for support.

Santana needed to work the scenario through in his mind and eliminate any doubts before agreeing with the former chief. "Forensics is examining the knife and hand towel found in the hamper," he said, his gaze falling first on Carver and then on Kelly Noor. "But it could be the weapon used to kill Grayson Cole."

Kelly Noor let out a small gasp and wiped her eyes with a Kleenex, though Santana could see no evidence of tears.

Carver turned to his right and patted her gently on the thigh. "It's going to be fine, honey. Trust me."

"It would help if I could interview your son, Ms. Noor," Santana said. "But since he's lawyered up, it's difficult to determine exactly what happened and what he knows."

"You mean interrogate him," Carver said, glaring at Santana.

Santana responded in kind. "You told me he was still on his meds. That clearly wasn't the case when we brought him in here."

"Are you calling me a liar, Detective?"

"Please," Romano said, lifting his hands in a calming gesture. "Let's keep this discussion civil. We're all here to help Adam."

"I don't believe that," Carver said. "I think you've already made up your minds."

Romano took in a deep breath and let it out slowly. His eyes drifted in Santana's direction and then settled on Carver, as if he had made a decision. "Let's get something straight. I respect your right to an opinion, Chief, but that's all it is. I trust my detective to make the right call. You and your daughter are here as a courtesy, not as a right."

"I can go upstairs," Carver said.

"Yes, I'm sure you can and probably will, if you're not satisfied with our discussion here today. But that won't change the fact that your grandson may have been involved in the murder of Grayson Cole. Unless you have something disproving it, I suggest you listen to what Detective Santana has to say. Right now, he's your best hope of saving your grandson."

In his mind, Santana had always characterized Romano with the Colombian phrase *Siempre está cerca del árbol que da más sombra.* He always looks for the tree that gives the most shade. Santana was pleased to see, at least in this instance, that Romano was willing to step out of the shadows and stand up to the former chief.

"What if Adam *is* guilty?"

Everyone's gaze shifted to Kelly Noor.

"Why would you think that?" Carver said to his daughter, his voice filled with shock and disbelief.

"He was angry with Grayson. And if he had stopped taking his medication . . ." Her voice trailed off.

"Why was Adam angry with Grayson Cole?" Carver asked, staring at his daughter.

"He had this crazy idea that Grayson had something to do with Sam's death."

"Why would he think that, Kelly?"

She started to answer and then hesitated.

"You were having an affair with Grayson Cole?" Carver said.

"I *had* a brief affair with him, Dad."

"Why didn't you tell me?"

Kelly Noor looked at her father as though she couldn't believe he would ask such a ridiculous question.

"Why tell your son about your affair with Cole if you knew what he might do, Ms. Noor?" Santana said.

Her eyes shifted to Santana. "I didn't know what Adam would do."

"But you suspected he would confront Cole."

"I don't understand," she said, her eyes uncertain.

"I think you do."

Kelly Noor stood and stared defiantly at Santana. "You can't talk to me like that." Then her eyes rolled back in her head and she sank gently toward the floor, like a dress falling from a hook.

Carver rose quickly from his chair and caught her in his arms. "You're way out of line, Detective," Carver said, his hawk eyes hot with anger.

"Maybe," Santana said. "But maybe not."

* * *

Early that evening, Jordan came aboard the *Alibi*. The breeze was warm and smelled of schools of fish. High above the river gulls glided on the updrafts of air currents, their pointed wings lit by the sun, their keening calls echoing in the air.

Because boats were still operating under the no-wake rule, Santana wondered aloud if it was worth leaving the marina. But Jordan gave him an encouraging kiss and promised special activities were in store in the privacy of open water. When Santana asked Gitana if they should fire up the engines, she barked her support.

Once they left the marina, Jordan grilled two pieces of Copper River salmon and made a spinach salad with blueberries, sliced strawberries, feta cheese, and honey glazed pecans, topped with raspberry vinaigrette dressing. Santana anchored two miles down river near a sandbar and opened a cold Rioja rosé from Spain.

They sat at the dinette in the salon, the boat level in water that was as smooth and flat as a mirror. Despite the companionship and the excellent food, Santana's mind was still busy with the cold case.

If the blood on the knife he had found in Adam Noor's hamper belonged to Grayson Cole, then Noor would almost certainly be charged with Cole's murder. But Cole had been brutally murdered. What had the kid done with his bloody clothes? Forensics might find traces of blood and fibers in Adam Noor's car, though it had looked clean. And why leave the knife in the hamper? Santana puzzled with this for a time and then brought Jordan up to speed as they ate dinner.

He was still troubled by the disturbing dream he'd had in which she was drowning. He wanted to talk with her about it. He refilled their glasses with the last of the wine and suggested they go up to the flybridge to enjoy the beautiful evening.

"It helps to talk it through, John," she said, stroking Gitana, who was lying next to her on the wraparound cushioned seating, her head in Jordan's lap.

"With you."

She smiled and sipped her wine.

"Last night when I stayed at your place, I had a dream. Well, it was more of a nightmare."

"I heard you get out of bed and go to the bathroom."

"I was sweating and wanted to rinse off."

"You want to tell me about the nightmare?"

He nodded, but he didn't know how much he wanted to share. "You were drowning, Jordan."

"That could mean more than one thing."

"Such as?"

"Maybe you're becoming too deeply involved in something that's beyond your control. It could also represent a sense of loss of your own identity, an inability to differentiate who you are anymore."

"Maybe it's a warning."

"About you or me?"

"I think it was more about you."

She briefly looked away.

"What is it?"

"Nothing," she said, sipping more wine.

"Tell me."

She let out a breath. "I believe I'm being followed, but I can't be sure."

"You think it has something to do with a case you're working?"

"I'm not working any cases right now."

"Then it must have something to do with the case I'm working. Unless . . ."

"What?"

"It could be the Cali cartel."

"Why would they want to harm me?"

"Because you're with me. If they can't get to me, they'll try and get to you. That's how revenge works. I want you to move in with me for a while."

She shook her head. "No, John. I can take care of myself."

"It's not about me taking care of you."

"Isn't it?"

"No."

"Then what is it about, John?"

"Well, it's . . ." He couldn't come up with a good answer.

Jordan nodded her head. "I thought so. Besides, if it is the cartel, staying with you puts me more at risk."

"Promise me you'll be careful, Jordan."

"I will. But maybe it has nothing to do with the cartel. Maybe it has nothing to do with the case you're working either. Maybe I'm just imagining things."

"If you're sensing that someone is following you, you're probably right." Santana drank some wine. The twilight sky was streaked with orange and pink. The gentle breeze was cool out of the north.

"What about Adam Noor?" she asked. "He certainly had reason enough to kill Grayson Cole. And he certainly could've killed his father."

"All indications are that he loved his father. It's a different story with his mother."

"You think she had something to do with her husband's death?"

"I get the sense that she supports her son, but she still believes he had something to do with Cole's death. I got a warrant and searched Cole's office downtown after the meeting with Romano, Carver, and Kelly Noor, but nothing turned up."

"Probably because you're not sure what to look for."

"You've got that right."

"Is the Ramsey County Attorney filing murder charges against Adam Noor?"

"I have a meeting Monday morning with Romano and James Nguyen, the director of the Criminal Division."

"You think Nguyen is willing to go against Ray Carver?"

"We'll see," he said, falling silent.

"You don't sound convinced that Adam Noor is guilty."

"I'm not. But Nguyen might be."

"Then focus your energy on convincing him otherwise," she said. "Monday morning."

He looked into her eyes. They had a smile in them and were more green than brown and full of light, like his mother's had been. "What about my energy tonight?"

"Perhaps you could aim it in another direction this week-end?"

"I think I could do that, given some incentive."

Jordan leaned forward and kissed him. "How's that?"

"It's a start," he said with a smile.

Chapter 33

On Monday morning Santana and Pete Romano met with James Nguyen, the criminal division director from the Ramsey County Attorney's Office. The criminal division screened cases presented by detectives and determined whether criminal charges were warranted. They also handled appeals and post-conviction hearings. But their main responsibility was to prosecute all adult felonies in Ramsey County.

Nguyen was second generation Vietnamese, the largest Asian immigrant population in the city after the Hmong from Laos. He was a short man with dark hair and skin, high cheekbones, and double eyelids, typical of many of the Vietnamese, who had immigrated to St. Paul after the Vietnam War.

He was seated in a high-backed black leather swivel chair behind his rosewood desk, his degrees on the wall reflecting in the shiny glass covering the desktop. He wore a tailored dark suit and tie over a white shirt, and small dark-framed glasses.

Santana sat in one of two chairs in front of the desk, beside Pete Romano.

Nguyen fixed his gaze on Romano. "So convince me why I shouldn't file a first degree murder charge against Adam Noor," he said with a slight accent.

Romano fiddled with the knot on his tie. "The kid is Ray Carver's grandson."

Nguyen looked to Santana for clarification.

"Carver is a former chief of police. You were probably just out of law school."

Nguyen nodded. "I see. So you're asking that a suspect who had the possible murder weapon in his possession at the time of arrest, had knowledge that his mother had had an affair with the victim, and who apparently believed that the victim had something to do with his father's murder, should not be charged. Do I have that correct?"

"Well, my detective has some doubts regarding the kid's actual involvement," Romano said.

Nguyen nodded again. "Some doubts?"

Romano cleared his throat. "Yes."

Nguyen paused a beat before speaking. "You both realize, of course, that Mr. Cole was a prominent citizen. This office has received numerous calls for justice. Naturally, given the brutality of the murder, the media has done its part to inflame the public." Nguyen spoke in a clear, calm voice, as though he were talking about the weather rather than a cold-blooded murder.

Romano shifted his weight in the chair and his gaze from Nguyen to Santana.

Santana understood the cue. Romano wanted him to make the case to Nguyen that Adam Noor was innocent. Then if things went south and Noor was later found guilty of Cole's murder, Romano could blame the fiasco on Santana. He was certain that Ray Carver had spoken to Carl Ashford, the current SPPD chief of police, who had spoken to Romano. Ashford and Carver were good friends. Ashford was willing to let the department take the media heat as long as his name was kept out of the spotlight. Romano would never admit that Ashford had spoken to him. But Romano had angered

Ray Carver and upset Kelly Noor by standing up for Santana. Romano would not make that mistake again.

"Someone could be framing the Noor kid," Santana said to Nguyen.

"And what gives you that idea?"

"I believe Grayson Cole's murder is about real estate rather than revenge."

"Would you care to explain?"

Santana told Nguyen about the mineral rights deal between Otto and Elsie Vogel and Grayson Cole, how the Vogels had suddenly dropped their lawsuit, and how he had found them dead. "It was a murder made to look like a suicide," he said.

"But why would Cole kill the Vogels, Detective, if they'd dropped the lawsuit?"

"Maybe he didn't. Maybe whoever killed the Vogels killed Cole."

"That would rule out Adam Noor," Romano said.

"Who stands to gain if Cole and the Vogels are out of the way?" Nguyen asked.

"Select Sands," Santana said. "Neither the Vogels nor Grayson Cole had children. But maybe other relatives."

"Where does Sam Noor fit into this scenario?"

"An environmental group opposed to silica sand mining hired him."

"What you're telling me is all supposition, Detective."

"Maybe so. But shouldn't we at least wait till the lab confirms that the knife was the murder weapon?"

Nguyen studied him without replying.

Having researched the attorney's background, Santana knew Nguyen had higher aspirations. That was his soft spot. "You've got a perfect track record for convictions," he said. "All wins, no losses."

"Something I'm proud of."

"As you should be. But if you charge Adam Noor with first degree murder, what happens to your perfect record and reputation if evidence later surfaces that he's innocent?"

"And you're going to provide that evidence."

"I'm going to keep looking." Santana gestured toward Romano. He needed to offer an additional incentive if he expected Romano to support him. "I know my commander would like more than one unsolved crime off the board."

Santana felt his cell phone vibrate and recognized the ME's number. "Excuse me, I have to take this." He stood and walked into the hallway before answering.

"A floater was found in the St. Croix River," Reiko Tanabe said. "I don't have a positive ID, but it's definitely a woman. The body is in the freezer. You want to come by for the autopsy?"

"Thanks, Reiko. I'll be there in twenty minutes."

* * *

When Santana arrived, Reiko Tanabe went into a small room where tissues were sliced for sampling and then submerged in formalin, a liquid preservative. Most of the samples were stored there, but others were taken to the cooler or the freezer.

Santana recalled how noisy the fans were inside the cooler, where long metal autopsy trays were lined up along the walls. The bodies stored there in blue plastic body bags had already been examined and were in the process of being readied for release.

But Santana knew that Tanabe was headed for the freezer, where decomposing bodies were stored, and where the air was thick with chemicals and an odor unlike any other. Like the refrigerator, there was no outside air coming in. The room was outfitted with sensors to make sure it stayed between 25 and 30 degrees.

Tanabe had once told him that she had gotten used to the smell. Her job was to figure out how the person died. And if she couldn't get past the smell, how could she do that?

Two autopsy technicians wheeled the body into one small, silent autopsy suite that was kept separate from all the others. Tanabe and Santana followed behind the gurney. The walls in the suite were thick. There was a drain in the floor.

Someone who had recently died would be autopsied in a separate brighter suite. Someone who had been missing for weeks or found badly decomposed in the river would be done in here.

The two techs unzipped the body bag and lifted the body onto a clean stainless steel table.

From experience, Santana knew that when a human corpse was discovered on land, the head was typically the first part to degrade. But in water, the head was usually the last part to be consumed. He was thankful that he could still recognize the face.

"I saw her alive four days ago, Reiko."

Tanabe pointed to the entry wound near the woman's heart. "She was probably dead the moment she hit the water."

"Any idea of the caliber?"

"I'll know for sure once I remove the bullet. Only identifying feature might be the tattoo on her upper right arm."

The tattoo was a squared cross with a circle around it. Inked underneath the circle was the name *Melissa.* Santana knew that tattoos often were unique in that those who had one wanted to make a statement or display their love for someone or for an organization in their lives. He might be able to use it to ID her.

"Ever see a tattoo like that before, John?"

He nodded. "Fortunately, I have."

Chapter 34

The SPPD's Missing Person Unit was housed within the Juvenile Unit on the first floor of the department's Griffin Building Headquarters at the LEC. Santana had one of the three officers assigned to the department check recently filed missing person's reports on the hunch that someone might have filed a missing person report and photo on a woman named Melissa.

When that proved to be a dead end, he drove to a series of tattoo parlors in St. Paul. An ex-con named Derrick Booker owned the third one he checked. Framed and unframed designs papered the walls and ceiling. Black and white checkerboard tiles covered the floor. Tiffany lampshades veiled the hanging overhead lights. Two bright red leather barber's chairs sat on a large red patterned Persian rug in the middle of the room. Red velvet ropes hooked to stanchions cordoned off the chairs from the rest of the room and the counter, behind which stood the short, stocky Booker.

"Afternoon, Detective," he said. "Long time, no see."

Booker had shoulder-length brown hair and a thick handlebar mustache. He wore a black T-shirt and ball cap with a skull and crossbones logo, and glasses with black frames. His bare arms were covered with tattoos.

"Derrick," Santana said with a nod. "How's business?"

"Booming. Used to be just military types, gangbangers, and cons wanted tattoos. Now all the athletes and suburban kids want to look like me. Go figure."

Booker had wasted much of his youth doing time for B&E and burglary. But for the last ten years, he had worked as a legitimate tattoo artist while saving enough money to open his own shop five years ago. A large gold-framed picture of Booker with his wife and daughter sat on a corner of the counter.

Santana placed a photo Reiko Tanabe had taken of the tattoo on Melissa's arm on the counter. "Ever design one of these?"

Booker picked up the photo and examined it. "I have."

"Know anything about the symbol?"

Booker peered over the photo at Santana. "It's a short version of the Celtic cross, sometimes called Odin's cross or a sun or wheel cross. It's commonly worn by white supremacists. But you have to be careful here, Detective, and judge it in context."

"Enlighten me."

"Most of the traditional Celtic crosses have an elongated vertical axis that look like a Christian cross. I've designed a few for Irish pride, as well. But Norwegian Nazis used a squared version of the cross with the circle around it. After the Second World War, white supremacist groups and movements adopted the symbol." Booker handed the photo back to Santana.

"The body of a woman was pulled from the St. Croix River this morning, Derrick. We have no ID other than this tattoo. Someone designed it for her."

"Well, it's probably a one-off since the artist added her name. But I'm not the only tattoo artist in town."

"You're the best."

He smiled. "I'd love to design a special one for you, Detective. No charge."

"Thanks, but I'll pass. You remember designing this one?"

He shook his head. "Doesn't mean we didn't do it. I've got two artists working with me now. Let me check. See if I have a picture and address in my records."

Ten minutes later, Booker returned with an index card on which was written the address for a woman named Melissa Cantrell.

* * *

Santana crosschecked the address Derrick Booker had given him for Melissa Cantrell with information from the DMV. Then he used her name and date of birth as descriptors to enter the online National Crime Information Center database. Cantrell had gross misdemeanor convictions for prostitution and fifth degree assault, and a felony conviction for simple robbery, for which she had served a year in prison at the Minnesota Correctional Facility for women in Shakopee. Santana typed a computer affidavit and e-mailed it to the Ramsey County attorney, who forwarded it with an application for a search warrant to a judge.

Forty minutes later, the judge e-mailed Santana a warrant authorizing a search of Melissa Cantrell's house.

Cantrell had lived in a two-story corner duplex in the Dale neighborhood. An alley ran along the right side of the house. Clumps of grass were scattered among the weeds in the mostly dirt yard that was enclosed by a six-foot chain-link fence. A narrow sidewalk led up four steps to a door that fronted the enclosed three-season porch. A thin wine-colored carpet covered the porch floor. There were two inner doors, one for the downstairs and one for the upper level.

Santana pushed the doorbell for the lower level and waited. He heard no ring, but moments later an old woman dressed in a tattered rose-colored housecoat opened the door. She had thinning gray hair and smelled strongly of cigarette smoke. Tiny wrinkles stitched the corners of her mouth, and her dentures looked hard and stiff.

Santana showed her his badge. "I'm Detective Santana from the St. Paul Police Department. I have a warrant to search Melissa Cantrell's apartment."

The woman's rheumy, sunken brown eyes stared warily at his badge wallet, her frail body exuding illness like an infected wound. "Upstairs," she said, pointing with a long, thin index finger.

"Do you have a key?"

"Sure, for my place."

"Did you know Ms. Cantrell?"

"She dead?"

"I'm afraid so."

"Didn't know her. Guess I never will." She stepped back and closed the door in Santana's face.

Santana gloved up and picked the lock with his tools in less than a minute. He closed the door behind him and went up a flight of stairs and into a small kitchen and then into the living room. A narrow hallway led to a bath and two bedrooms across from one another.

He had just returned to the living room to begin his search when he heard a door slam shut and footsteps on the stairs. He drew his Glock and waited in the living room, his back pressed against a wall to the left of the entrance to the kitchen.

Someone tossed a set of keys on the kitchen table.

Santana heard what he thought was the refrigerator door open. He came around the doorjamb behind his gun and saw a blond-headed woman reaching for something inside the refrigerator. Her back was to him. She was bent slightly at the waist.

"Turn around," he said.

The woman gave a frightened start and turned sharply, a peach falling from her hand and landing with a thump on the tile floor.

Santana felt a burst of adrenaline rush through his body. She had changed her hair color and lost some weight, but he still recognized her.

Chapter 35

"Hello, Ms. Ford," Santana said.

April Ford's eyes were wide with shock and disbelief. "What're you doing here?"

"I might ask you the same question."

"I live here."

"With Melissa Cantrell?"

She nodded her head slowly. "Why?"

Santana holstered his Glock. "Sit down, Ms. Ford."

Her eyes drifted toward the door and stairwell.

Santana stepped in front of her, blocking her escape route. "Forget it."

She let out a breath of resignation and sat down in one of the two chairs at the kitchen table. Santana stood near the door with his back against the refrigerator.

"What do you want with Melissa?"

"She was with a man who tried to kill me."

"That's crazy."

"It may be. But it's the truth."

"Well," she said with a wave of her hand, "I don't know where Melissa is. Haven't seen her in four days."

"Melissa Cantrell's in the morgue at Regions Hospital. Her body was pulled from the St. Croix River this morning."

April Ford's eyes narrowed. Her lips parted. She sat perfectly still for a moment. Then she removed the cellophane from a package of Marlboros on the table, slipped a cigarette loose, and lit it with a Bic lighter. Clutching the cigarette between two shaking fingers, she inhaled deeply, holding the smoke before turning her head to one side and blowing a cloud in Santana's direction.

"What happened?"

"Cantrell was shot to death. Her body was dumped in the river. I believe a man named Jake killed her."

April Ford's eyes were elusive as she drew on her cigarette and exhaled. "I don't know anyone named Jake."

To find the truth, Santana figured he needed to come at it from a different angle. "How long have you known Cantrell?"

"A year or so."

"What about her family?"

"Melissa was an orphan."

"How did you meet?"

"What difference does it make?"

"Are you on probation, Ms. Ford?"

"So what?"

"Jake was one of the men who ran us off the road the day Clay Buck was killed. I believe Melissa Cantrell was one of the three people with him. I think Buck's death and the attempt on my life are connected. Jake may also be responsible for the deaths of others. You were in the car that day with Clay Buck, Ms. Ford. Now you're Melissa Cantrell's roommate." Santana placed his hands flat on the tabletop and leaned close to her. "You can answer my questions here or downtown, where I'll have you booked as a possible accessory to murder."

She swallowed with apprehension. "I had nothing to do with Buck's death or the attempt on your life."

"Then you have nothing to fear by answering my questions."

She took another drag on her cigarette, the smoke leaking from her nose, her eyes full of thoughts as they searched his face for deception. Then she stirred the ashes in the ashtray with the tip of her cigarette. "You don't know him," she said. "You don't know what he's capable of."

"You're speaking of Jake."

She nodded while holding her eyes wide and steady on his face. There was a faint gloss of sweat on her upper lip. "Yeah. Jake Fuller."

Santana pulled out the chair across from her and sat down. He took out his iPhone, set it on the table, and pressed the record app.

"I want to record this."

April Ford looked at the phone recorder as though it were an explosive device but didn't object.

"State your name and today's date."

She did.

"What happened in the cornfield with Buck and Wendell Hudson?"

"I don't know. Honest."

"Wendell Hudson didn't shoot Clay Buck, did he?"

She hesitated.

"Who shot Buck?"

Her eyes left Santana's and looked out the window before returning to his face. "After your partner was wounded, Buck picked up his gun, and we ran for the highway. Then a man in a ski mask came out of the corn, like out of thin air. He had a shotgun and told Buck to drop the gun. Buck did. The man picked up the gun and had us turn around. We did. A moment later I heard a shot and Buck went down. I thought the guy would kill me, too. But he didn't. He told me the detective shot Buck and if I wanted to stay alive, I'd remember it that way. I was afraid."

"You're telling me that Buck was shot in the cornfield and not in the stand of trees where I left you two with Detective Hudson."

"That's right."

"What did you do after Buck was shot?"

"I ran to the highway and flagged down a car. Later, the police picked me up."

"You testified that Wendell Hudson killed Buck when he tried to escape."

"You want to keep looking over your shoulder the rest of your life? I don't."

I've spent the last two decades doing exactly that, Santana thought. But he knew April Ford wasn't interested in his problems. "How did you meet Jake Fuller?"

"Melissa introduced us. She dated Fuller. When they broke up, Jake asked me out. Melissa didn't care. She even asked me to be her roommate."

"How did you meet her?"

"We waitressed at the Nickel Joint."

Santana wondered if Jake and Melissa had purposely gotten close to April Ford to ensure that she hadn't—or wouldn't—talk.

"You're not working at the Nickel Joint now?"

"I'm taking courses at a technical college to be a nursing assistant. I'm getting my life together. And now you accuse me of murder."

"You lied on the witness stand, Ms. Ford."

"I was scared."

"Why should I believe you're telling me the truth now? You're still afraid for your life."

"Because I'm not testifying in open court. I'm telling you in private. If anyone ever asks, I'll deny I ever said anything to you."

"You mean if Jake asks."

"Whatever."

Santana held up his phone. "Hard to deny what you said."

Ford let out a breath. "You won't tell Jake."

"No. Did you know he was one of the men in the cornfield that day?"

She shook her head.

Santana showed her the photo of the tattoo on Melissa's arm. "Ever see something like this before?"

"Melissa had a tattoo like that." April Ford's eyes teared, as if she suddenly realized her roommate and friend was dead. She wiped the corners of her eyes with the back of her hand. "Jake belongs to some group that uses that symbol. I don't remember the name of the group."

"Where is Jake, Ms. Ford?"

"I don't know. We quit dating months ago. He moved out."

"Jake Fuller used to live here?"

"He left a few things in a bedroom down the hall."

"I'd like to take a look."

"For what?"

"I'll know it when I see it."

"Suit yourself," she said. "Jake's bedroom was the second door on the right in the hallway. Door's open."

"You take anything out of there?"

"Jake wouldn't like that—if he ever came back."

"You expecting him?"

Fear glazed her eyes as she shook her head. "He's weird."

"How do you mean weird?"

She pointed at the photo. "I went to a couple group meetings with Melissa and Jake."

"Where did these meetings take place?"

"In a small church south of here. All the people there hated Indians."

"You know why?"

"They say the government is giving Indians special treatment. I don't care one way or another. But I didn't like the vibe. I could hardly talk to Jake after the meetings, he was so pissed off. It scared me."

"The police department can protect you."

"That's a laugh." She crushed out her cigarette in the ashtray on the table. "Jake would kill me if he found out I talked to you."

"He'll have to kill me first."

"He will—if you give him another chance."

* * *

There was nothing personal in Jake Fuller's bedroom. No pictures on the walls or framed photos on the dresser. There was a sheet and thin blanket on the double bed. Santana didn't know what he was looking for, so he started in the walk-in closet. A pair of worn jeans was draped across a hanger and another was in the plastic laundry basket on the floor. Hanging farther back in the closet was a black leather jacket, two Harley-Davidson sweatshirts, and Fuller's dress blues from his service with the Marine Corps.

On the shelf directly above the uniform was a white peaked cap. Fuller must have packed some clothes before he left, figuring he would return later for the rest. Santana checked all the pants pockets before moving on to the three-drawer dresser.

The top drawer contained a few pairs of underwear, socks, and folded T-shirts. The next drawer was empty. In the bottom drawer, underneath two heavy wool sweaters, Santana found a shoebox. He pulled out the box, sat on the bed, and removed the shoebox cover. Inside it was a stack of photos held together by a rubber band.

The first photo was a color shot of a squad of Marines running laps under the early morning sun. A caption written on the back indicated it was taken at Camp Leatherneck located in Helmand Province, Afghanistan. A second photo showed Jake Fuller and two unidentified Marines standing beside a mine resistant vehicle at Forward Operating Base

Shir Ghazi in Helmand Province. There was a photo taken through a bullet-riddled windshield of a Marine Humvee, a photo of Marines pinned down by enemy fire, and a photo of battle-weary Marines huddling on the back of a truck, their young faces hardened by battle, dazed looks in their eyes.

Santana thumbed through the photos till he came to one near the end of the stack in which a group of Marines were playing cards in front of tents in the mountains. A shot of adrenaline jacked up his heart rate when he recognized the man sitting to the right of Jake Fuller.

Chapter 36

Santana returned to the Homicide and Robbery Unit in the LEC and checked the National Crime Center Database. Jake Fuller had done time in Minnesota. Santana wrote up a complaint establishing probable cause. He had it signed by James Nguyen, the Ramsey County prosecutor, and then took it to a judge, where he swore under oath that Jake Fuller had attempted to murder him. The judge issued a warrant for Jake Fuller's arrest.

Santana then located Fuller's former parole officer.

"Oh, yeah. I remember Fuller. One very disturbed young man."

"Can you be more specific?" Santana said.

"Hold on while I pull the psych report from his file." Two minutes later the parole officer came back on the phone. "Fuller's mother and father divorced shortly after he was born. The father was later granted custody rights, which is unusual unless the mother has some problems. While Fuller was living with his father, there were allegations of physical abuse, but nothing was ever proven. His father passed away from stomach cancer when Fuller was fifteen. Fuller was placed in foster care."

"Why wasn't he returned to his mother?"

"Fuller was nearly sixteen at the time. According to Minnesota statutes, the judge can grant a reasonable preference of the child."

"So Fuller chose not to live with his mother."

"That's my understanding."

"I wonder why?"

"You'll have to ask him. Anyway, at seventeen Fuller dropped out of high school and enlisted in the Marine Corps. Did two tours in Afghanistan. Was awarded two Purple Hearts, but was later accused of assaulting an officer in a bar and eventually dishonorably discharged. He started using cocaine and held up a liquor store, beating the owner in the process. Fuller was convicted of assault with a deadly weapon and for criminal possession of a firearm, a charge that was reduced from attempted murder. He was fined twenty grand and sentenced to eight years in prison but was paroled in six."

"That's when you first met him?"

"Correct. I was his case manager for two years. Haven't seen him since he cleared parole."

"What was your impression?"

"Similar to his psych report. I'll e-mail you a copy."

Santana printed the three-page evaluation and read it as he sat in his chair, his feet resting on the corner of his desk.

A psychologist had concluded that Jake Fuller had probably suffered brain damage from repeated blows to the head when he was a child. The blows may have altered certain sensory and emotional control centers in his brain. As a result, he had trouble controlling his aggression. Fuller was described as irritable, impulsive, and restless. He often became hostile when dealing with people and was considered to be antisocial. His behaviors were thought to be coping mechanisms for dealing with everyday life and the turmoil he felt from it.

Santana called Jordan. "You all right?"

"Fine."

"You still think someone is following you?"

"I'm keeping my eyes open. Quit worrying. Is that why you called? You were worried about me?"

Santana heard the anticipation in her voice. He felt a pang of guilt, knowing that it wasn't the primary reason he had called her. "Of course I'm worried about you."

"But there's something else on your mind."

"Yes."

"I thought so," she said with a small laugh that was shaded with disappointment. "What is it?"

Santana recounted what he had read in Fuller's psych evaluation.

"Aggressive behavior can be reactive or in retaliation, John, or proactive, as an attempt to provoke a victim. It can also be either overt or secretive. Violence can also occur when someone stops caring about others or the consequences of their behavior. In many cases, the child is exposed to aggression or violence and imitates that behavior, which sounds like what happened to Fuller."

"He's a member of an extremist group apparently known for its racism against Native Americans."

"Well, racism is a form of violence even when there's no physical aggression. In Fuller's mind, the fact that we have different races is reason enough for preferring one person to another."

"Violence is inherent in all humans, Jordan. Not just in racists."

"But not inevitable."

Except in Jake Fuller's case, Santana thought.

* * *

Late that afternoon, Santana met FBI agent Russ Welker. He was seated on a bench along the Mississippi River off Shepard Road near downtown St. Paul, eating a bag lunch, when Santana sat down beside him. The horizon was piled with dark clouds. The bright sun that had lit the sky earlier in the day had dimmed, as if it were a low-wattage bulb.

"We get any more rain this month, I'll need to sell my SUV and build an ark," Welker said, his light blue tie and the lapels of his blue suit flapping in the breeze.

"Keeping busy?"

"Plenty of crime, not enough time." He rolled his heavy shoulders as if preparing for a prizefight.

Santana thought Welker looked as if he kept in shape by lifting small cars. "A little late for lunch, isn't it?"

"It's been a busy day. And because I have this unscheduled meeting with you, I probably won't have time for dinner. And why am I explaining any of this to you?"

Santana showed Welker the photo of Melissa Cantrell's tattoo. "Ever seen a tattoo like this before?"

The agent took a bite of his ham sandwich and inclined his head. "It's the logo for an anti-Native American group calling themselves CERO, or Citizens' Equal Rights Organization. It's made up mostly of third and fourth generation descendants of white people who profited from acquiring Indian lands. They've hooked up with the anti-immigration crowd. Claim they want equal rights for whites. I'd call them the Ku Klux Klan of Indian country."

Santana could hear the hum of traffic along Shepard Road and the squawks of gulls soaring over the river. "Guess I didn't realize whites were oppressed in this country."

"Yeah," Welker said. "You Latinos get all the breaks." His eyes remained focused on the swiftly moving river as he took another bite of his sandwich and chewed his food, the curl of a grin in the corner of his mouth.

"CERO's argument goes something like this, Santana. The government, our employer, has given increased legal powers and jurisdiction to the tribes, which, in CERO's small minds, infringes on the liberties and private property rights of non-

Indian residents on and off the reservations. Their agenda is to roll back Indian rights and terminate all Indian treaties. Put an end to the Indian problem, as they like to call it. Whites, you see, are victims of Red Apartheid, a nicely turned phrase that invokes the legacy of Martin Luther King Jr., don't you think?"

Welker was the only FBI agent Santana had ever met who had a sense of humor, twisted as it was.

"There are now more non-Indians living on Indian lands than there are Indians," he said. "They either own the land outright, or they have ninety-nine-year leases on it. Then you have absentee landowners who use the property as vacation homes, and sport and commercial fishermen."

Welker drank from the can of A&W root beer before continuing. "It scares the hell out of CERO that tribes are re-acquiring some of these lands in order to build an economic base for their people again. They can't stand the idea that Indians would get some land back, no matter how it happens. The group opposes treaty rights that guarantee some tribes' access to resources on lands outside their reservations. And they oppose sovereignty that enables tribes to block projects that might harm treaty resources."

"Like silica sand mines?"

"Why not? Tribes own about twenty-five percent of all the energy-producing lands in the country. Most of which are found on poor lands."

Welker finished his sandwich and crushed the paper bag in his large hands. He drank more root beer and let out a burp, his eyes following a shapely blond woman in a tight T-shirt and shorts as she jogged along the tar path in front of the bench they were sitting on. "Always nice to get out of the office." He tossed the bag into a trash barrel like an NBA player shooting a three-pointer. "You notice the Minnesota Gopher logo on that woman's T-shirt?"

"Sorry. I wasn't staring at her chest."

"Always good to be observant, Santana. Thought you'd have learned that by now."

"Your point being?"

"CERO believes Indian protests against sports team logos and mascots reeks of political correctness. Same with protests against the excavation of mounds and burial sites, and the disrespect of sacred objects. The very idea of a non-Western belief system existing in this country is seen as a major problem."

"So it's a racist group."

"Well, if you believe that Indians today are primarily drunks unfit to govern themselves and benefit from government handouts based on their percentage of Indian blood, I'd say you might have some racist tendencies. But CERO would deny that accusation. They have a more subtle approach."

"Such as?"

"They romanticize past Indian cultures and compare them to modern Native Americans who've adopted white culture. CERO's rhetoric is filled with objections to food stamps and free housing and medical care. They condemn tribes if they're poor, and then condemn them again if they try to get out of poverty through gaming."

"Ever hear of a man named Jake Fuller?"

"Not that I recall. Why?"

Santana handed him a photo of Fuller he had downloaded. "Jake Fuller and a woman named Melissa Cantrell tried to kill me. Cantrell's body was fished out of the St. Croix this morning. I believe Fuller shot her to death and dumped her body in the river."

"You think the attempt on your life is related to CERO?"

"I'm not sure. I'm just following up on Cantrell's death to see where it leads."

Welker nodded, his gaze shifting to Santana before returning to the photo. He angled his body toward Santana and rested his big arm on the back of the bench. "We don't mind working with local law enforcement to keep track of potentially violent actors."

"Gee, thanks."

Welker shook his head in resignation and went on. "You know it's a balancing act, Santana, between civil liberties and the rights of peaceful assembly and dissent, regardless of political positions. The Bureau tries to separate individuals from a particular group who we consider to be capable of direct action."

"You mean terrorists."

He nodded. "My investigating squad is dedicated to uncovering, disrupting, and arresting domestic terrorists."

"That's all well and good, but how does that relate to my murder investigation?"

"You're a hard man, Santana. Ruthless. You push people. You use whatever leverage you can to get them to talk. I was a homicide detective once myself, so I know those are necessary attributes if you're going to be any good at the job. But you agitate the wrong people, you're liable to get yourself killed."

"I'll keep you informed, Welker. Does CERO have a leader or someone who runs the group?"

"A wealthy landowner, part-time preacher, and all-around douche bag named Thomas Starks. He runs his mouth off on a late-night talk show on an AM station he owns."

"Thanks for the tip."

"Here's another one. Lone wolves are more difficult to stop than groups, Detective. And there's only one way to cure a sociopath."

"What's that?"

"Embalming fluid. Remember that when you're looking for Jake Fuller."

* * *

Late that night Santana sat on the couch beside Gitana. He drank a bottle of Sam Adams while he listened to Thomas Starks and a series of like-minded callers rail against Native Americans. The AM broadcast signal was weak and sometimes interrupted by static, but Santana was able to hear much of the diatribe.

"It's their own fault they lost their land and were forced onto reservations," Starks said to one caller. "Their superstition, savagery, and sexual immorality naturally disqualified them from sovereign control of American soil. Of course, the superior battle skills of Europeans gave the white race rights of conquest and the right to control the land. None of the violence would've happened had Indians rejected their old ways and embraced Christianity. Instead, they murdered missionaries in cold blood and rejected our Lord and Savior Jesus Christ."

Starks spoke in a calm, rational voice, as if his words made perfect sense to all who were open-minded and willing to listen.

Santana quickly determined that he would need more than a Sam Adams to get him through the program. He went into the kitchen for a shot glass and the ice-cold bottle of aguardiente he kept in the refrigerator. Then he sat down on the couch again, poured himself a shot, and drank it as he listened to Starks' response to another caller.

"As long as Indians cling to the darkness of indigenous superstitions and refuse to come into the light of Christianity and Christian culture, they'll stay poor and alcoholic and live on reservations. They've got no one to blame for their problems but themselves. You can trace their sexual immorality all the way back to the Lewis and Clark expedition in the early nineteenth century when the savages offered their wives to expedition members for sex."

Starks never explained why the tribe should forfeit claim to the land for their sexual practices—but not the white men who took advantage of them. Santana poured himself a second shot of aguardiente and drank it.

"Americans today are as guilty of abominations as were Indians before they were conquered. Just look at the abortions, homosexuality, adultery, and the sexual immorality in the country today. We're witnessing a huge surge in incest, pedophilia, and even bestiality. I'm warning all of my listeners that if Christians refuse to take a stand against the rising tide of immorality and the unholy practices of savages and sinners, we are morally disqualifying ourselves from sovereign control of our own land."

Chapter 37

The following morning Santana called Doug Flint of the Goodhue County Sheriff's Department. "What do you know about a preacher named Thomas Starks?"

"How did his name come up?"

Santana told him.

"So you think this woman with the tattoo, Melissa Cantrell, was a member of Starks' church?"

"I think her boyfriend, Jake Fuller, belonged to CERO, the organization that Starks runs. You ever have any dealings with Fuller or know where he might be?"

"Never heard of him. But I'll check our records, see if I get a hit."

"What about Starks?"

"He has a large buffalo ranch south of Cannon Falls."

"Buffalo?"

"Quite a few buffalo ranches in Minnesota now. Starks' ministry, if that's the proper name for the bigotry he preaches, began online a few years ago after he joined the anti-Native American crowd. He owns a small AM station and broadcasts a late-night radio show that airs from his ranch. You might pick up the signal on a clear night."

"I listened to his radio program last night."

"Enlightening?"

"I wouldn't characterize it as that."

"Well, I don't believe Starks had any brushes with law enforcement."

"I'll keep you informed."

"Make sure you do that," Flint said.

* * *

Santana drove south on Highway 52 out of downtown St. Paul toward Thomas Starks' ranch. The landscape rose into a succession of low hills before meeting the dead-flat ground of the prairie as he entered Dakota County on the southern rim of the Twin Cities. The pipes, storage tanks, and tall exhaust stacks of the Koch Industries refinery, a major producer of petroleum-based fuels, asphalt, and fertilizer, dominated the view to the southwest, across a patchwork of fields and woodlots. A few miles beyond the refinery, Santana could see a tall white wind turbine and a meteorological tower at the University of Minnesota's wind-energy research station, and five tall chimneystacks that were once part of a World War II munitions plant.

He recalled reading an article in the newspaper about the plant and the ongoing battle between the University of Minnesota and the federal government over who bore responsibility for cleaning up contaminants in the soil and groundwater. Operations of the plant, which were never fully functioning, had ceased in April of 1945 when World War II ended.

Thomas Starks' ranch was nestled among the rolling hills, farmland, forests, and small fast-moving streams of the Sogn Valley. He had built a large chalet into the side of a hill. The chalet had a high, steep roof and a fieldstone chimney. A balcony ran the length of the second floor. Behind the balcony railing was a wall of sliding glass doors facing southeast.

Santana parked on the concrete driveway and got out. The air was cool and heavy with the smell of hay, grass, and manure, and the sound of rushing water in the swollen river near the church.

Tacked high up a tall radio tower beside the chalet was a large rectangular sign with the call letters of Starks' radio station. In the far distance, beyond the tower and four-stranded barbed wire fence, a scattered herd of buffalo grazed in a pasture that stretched to the base of tall green slopes that were studded with trees. A small church thirty yards to the left of the chalet was a rural Carpenter Gothic structure with a tall steeple, arched windows, and white board and batten siding. There was a large red barn and a seven-foot-tall crowding corral made of thick wooden rails. On the far side of the barn was a metal Quonset hut.

An attractive blond woman, who Santana guessed was in her mid-twenties, opened the front door after he rang the doorbell. She was wearing sandals and a yellow short-sleeved dress, and she held an infant in her arms.

Santana introduced himself and showed her his badge.

"You're the detective who called Tom this morning," she said, gazing at him with suspicious blue eyes. "He was preparing his Sunday sermon. Don't know where he's at now. You might try the church first."

Santana thanked her and headed for the church. He spotted two teenage boys sweeping out the barn. They did not look at him or acknowledge in any way that they had seen him. Starks' wife looked too young to have children their age. Santana wondered if Starks had been married previously.

Inside the church, in the shadowy light streaming through the paneled stained glass windows, the air smelled of old wood and candle wax. The pews and wood floor were worn and shiny with polish, the walls painted a faded parchment white. There was a lectern at one end of the altar, but no sign of Thomas Starks.

Santana walked outside and headed for the barn. He didn't find Starks there either, or the two boys he'd seen earlier, and decided to try the metal Quonset hut. The windowless building, which he estimated was 24' x 24', had straight walls and a gable-style pitched roof instead of the traditional semi-cylindrical shape. A standard door in the center was unlocked and opened inward. It was pitch black inside the hut, but Santana found a switch and turned on a set of bright overhead lights.

Mounted high on the wall to his left were antelope horns and the weathered skulls of whitetail deer and buffalo. A big propane stove sat on the floor underneath the skulls. On one of the four burners was a large cast iron pot.

On the wall to his right were the stuffed heads of a lion, leopard, and white rhino. Pegboard hooks to the right of a long workbench held knives, scalpels, aprons, rubber boots, and surgical gloves. Below the hooks were bottles of hydrogen peroxide.

Santana went to the workbench. Boxes of clay, masking tape, super glue, paintbrushes, wire brushes, and one box containing glass eyes of various sizes and colors were scattered across its surface. The eyes ranged in color from caramel brown to very dark brown with a slight hint of red. Santana picked up one and examined it. The white scleral band contained realistic red veins at the corners. The shape and perfect coloration gave it the appearance of a natural eye. He could see his face reflected in it.

"Can I help you?"

Startled, Santana dropped the glass eye onto the workbench and turned toward the voice.

The glass eye rolled off the bench onto the floor and toward a very tall, lean man standing in the doorway. His legs were slightly bowed as though he rode bulls for a living. He wore a blue plaid button-down western shirt, jeans, black leather boots, and a black Stetson. The hat was flat on top, with rounded edges and a flat wide brim, like the hat Kurt Russell had worn when he starred as Wyatt Earp. In fact, Santana thought, with the handlebar mustache and Stetson hat, the man looked like Russell.

Santana held up his open badge wallet. "I'm Detective John Santana. Are you Mr. Starks?"

"I prefer Pastor Starks." He bent over and picked up the glass eye at his feet.

"Thanks for taking the time to see me," Santana said, ignoring the request.

Starks walked to the workbench and dropped the glass eye into a cardboard box.

Santana could see strands of gray threading Starks' handlebar mustache and long sideburns. His close-set eyes were dark and wary. He didn't offer to shake hands.

"What's this all about that you couldn't—or wouldn't—tell me on the phone, Detective?"

"Never been to a buffalo ranch before," Santana said, trying to redirect the conversation and establish some rapport before easing into the topic of CERO. "I had a buffalo burger just the other day. Enjoyed it very much."

Starks squinted and canted his head, as if seeing Santana for the first time.

"Looks like you've hunted some big game, Mr. Starks."

"Still legal in parts of Africa. You do much hunting, Detective?"

"All the time."

Starks paused a moment. Then, as Santana's meaning became clear, a slight smile creased his face. He glanced at the stuffed heads on the wall. "I've got three of the big five from Africa, lion, leopard, and white rhino. I'll get the elephant and Cape buffalo soon."

"Must be quite a rush hunting a lion."

Starks nodded his head once. "Tracking a big cat is a unique experience, Detective. You better kill him the first chance you get. A wounded lion is an ambush predator. If he's hurt and he knows what has hurt him, he'll be intent on doing something about it. The same can be said with a wounded leopard. They're usually hell bent on revenge, and their ability to hide means they hold all the advantages when following their blood trail. They'll choose the time and the place, and more often than not they'll wait till you're literally stepping on them before they charge."

"I imagine it's more dangerous than hunting deer in Minnesota."

"But not as dangerous as hunting people, right, Detective?"

Santana offered no reply.

Starks gestured toward the door. "I'm waiting for the Lord to give me inspiration for my Sunday sermon. Walking helps."

Santana followed him out the door. As they approached the wire fence behind the church, he said, "You've got quite a herd."

"More buffalo today than there have been in a hundred years. I used to raise beef cows. But I can raise a buffalo for about two-thirds the cost. Have to sell about twenty-four head of cattle to equal the price of a single buffalo."

Santana leaned over the top wire.

"Careful, Detective. That top wire is hot."

Santana stepped back quickly. He could hear the grunts and snorts of the nearest animals.

"Breeding season starts in about a month. Bulls are getting restless." Starks gazed at the pasture, a slight grin at the edge of his mouth and a glitter in his eyes, like proud ranchers had looked for hundreds of years, Santana imagined.

"I listened to your radio program last night."

Starks looked at Santana with much more interest now. "That a fact?"

"Have a large congregation?"

"Lots of sinners, Detective. Not many today are willing to heed the call of the Lord."

"You're also head of an organization called CERO."

Starks' eyes narrowed. "On the phone you said you were a homicide detective."

"I'm looking for a man named Jake Fuller."

"That supposed to mean something to me?"

"Fuller was dating a woman named Melissa Cantrell."

Starks shrugged. "So?"

"Her body was pulled out of the St. Croix River yesterday. She had a tattoo on her arm."

He chuckled softly.

"You think that's funny?"

"Lots of young women today have tattoos. I don't approve of it. But what can you do?"

Santana hadn't noticed any tattoos on Starks' wife, a woman he thought half her husband's age. "Most women don't have tattoos of your organization, Mr. Starks." Santana showed him the photo the ME had taken of Melissa Cantrell's tattoo.

Starks' body stiffened slightly, but his expression remained blank. "I'm very sorry that a young woman died."

"She didn't just *die*. She was murdered by Jake Fuller."

"That's unfortunate. But the tattoo in the photo is a Celtic cross. It's a very common symbol."

"Interesting that you're aware of the symbol. I'd guess most people wouldn't know anything about it."

"What's your point?"

"A Celtic cross has a longer vertical axis, Mr. Starks. A sun cross like the one in the photo is often used by white supremacist groups."

"CERO is not a racist organization. We're concerned with the self-preservation of our own people and the promotion and advancement of them. We do not promote or instigate violence. We want Native Americans to have the same rights as everyone else. What's wrong with that?"

"I'm not here to debate you, Mr. Starks. I'm looking for Fuller."

"And you assume that because this woman has a tattoo on her arm, I'd know something about her death?"

"She attended your meetings with her boyfriend, Jake Fuller. I believe you know who he is." Santana tried to read Starks' eyes as he showed him a photo of Fuller, but he couldn't make eye contact.

"I may have seen the man. But I don't know where he is or where he lives."

"You know anyone who would?"

Starks raised his chin and met Santana's eyes. "I'm afraid I don't. But I'll pray for the soul of Ms. Cantrell. The mouths of the dead are filled with dust, Detective. I, and others like me, will continue to speak for them."

Chapter 38

It was a thirty-minute drive from Thomas Starks' ranch to Virginia Garrison's house outside Red Wing. As he was nearing Garrison's house, Santana phoned Dennis Duffy, a confidential informant, and told him he needed information on Jake Fuller and Melissa Cantrell.

"I'll see what I can find out," Duffy said, breaking off the connection.

Santana parked along the curb in front of Virginia Garrison's home, went up the sidewalk, and rang the bell.

"Ginny's working," Sean Latham said, holding open the front door. His long dark hair was pulled back in a ponytail. He was wearing a black tank top, faded blue jeans, and leather sandals. A television was on in the living room.

Santana was surprised to see Latham out of his wheelchair and without his oxygen tank. "I'm not here to see her."

Latham nodded. "Come on in."

Santana followed him inside and waited while Latham cleared newspapers off a high-back panel chair.

"Have a seat," Latham said. "You want something to drink?"

"No, thanks."

"I'll get some coffee and be right back."

Santana took out his notepad and pen and looked at the television. Roman Polanski was cutting Jack Nicholson's nose with a sharp knife in a scene from the movie *Chinatown.*

"You ever see this movie?" Latham asked as he carried a coffee cup into the living room and sat down on a red fabric sofa.

"I have."

"Always liked Nicholson," Latham said. "Something about his rebel-like nature." He picked up the remote, turned off the television, and looked at Santana. "Well, if you didn't want to see Ginny, you must've come here to see me."

"Thought you were pretty much confined to a wheelchair and oxygen tank, Mr. Latham."

"Mostly," he said. "But some days are better than others."

Santana took out the photo of Jake Fuller and Sean Latham he had found in Fuller's bedroom and handed it to Latham.

Latham smiled as he gazed at it. "Seems like a lifetime ago in Afghanistan." He raised his eyes. "How's Jake doing?"

"Not too well, I imagine."

"Did he give you this photo?"

"Not exactly."

"Then where'd you get it?"

"I found it in his bedroom."

Latham appeared confused. "I don't understand."

"Jake Fuller is wanted for murder and attempted murder."

The color drained from Latham's face. "What?"

"You heard me."

Latham peered at the photo in his hand again, as if he might find an answer there.

"When was the last time you saw Jake Fuller, Mr. Latham?"

He looked up from the photo. "I don't know. Must be nine or ten years. Ever since he left the Corps."

"You mean ever since he was dishonorably discharged."

"I heard he was."

"You met while you were in the Marines?"

Latham nodded. "We were in the same rifle platoon."

"How many men?"

"Three rifle squads of thirteen men each and a sergeant."

"So you were close."

"Pretty much have to be when your life depends on one another. Who did Jake supposedly kill?"

"A woman named Melissa Cantrell. You know her or ever hear about her?"

"I told you, I haven't seen Jake in years."

"Maybe he talked about Cantrell while he was in Afghanistan?"

Latham stroked his beard as he thought about the question. Then he shook his head. "I don't recall Jake ever mentioning her name. You said he was also wanted for attempted murder. Who did he try to kill?"

"Me," Santana said, reading Latham's expression. "Does that surprise you?"

"That Jake tried to kill you?"

"That he killed or tried to kill anyone?"

"Well, Jake was always gung-ho, but I never figured him for this. Maybe he has PTSD? Lots of guys do."

"How about you, Mr. Latham? Do you suffer from PTSD?"

Latham drank some coffee and looked out a window before replying. "I never went to the VA. But I have my nightmares and sleepless nights. Hard to forget some of the things I saw over there."

"How long did you serve?"

"Three years," Latham said. "Long enough."

"What was Jake Fuller like when you served with him?"

"He had a lot of guts. He wasn't afraid to die."

"How do you know that?"

"I remember him saying so."

"Lots of men might say it. But do they really mean it?"

"I don't recall anyone besides Jake ever saying they weren't afraid to die. Most never said anything about death, unless they were wounded badly. Never heard a wounded man say he didn't want to live."

"You know a man named Thomas Starks?"

"No, Detective. I don't."

"Ever heard of an organization called CERO?"

Latham shook his head. "What's this all about?"

"Jake Fuller."

"There's more to it. Something you're not telling me."

"Maybe there's something you're not telling me, Mr. Latham."

The front door opened and Virginia Garrison came in wearing hospital scrubs and carrying a bag of groceries. "Detective. What are you doing here?"

"Questioning me," Latham said, his voice flat and without emotion.

She looked at Latham and then at Santana. "About what?"

"One of the guys I knew in the Corps is wanted for murder."

Virginia Garrison set her purse and the grocery bag on the coffee table and sat down next to Latham. Her long auburn hair was pinned in a chignon at the nape of her neck. Without makeup to hide them, Santana could see more of the dusting of freckles across her nose and cheekbones.

"Tell me about it," she said.

Santana did.

When he finished, she said, "The implication is obvious. You believe Sean is involved."

"I never said that."

"But you *implied* it, Detective Santana."

"Jake Fuller is a dangerous man, Ms. Garrison. He's killed at least one person that I know of. Maybe more. Your boyfriend here served with Fuller. Maybe it's a coincidence. Maybe not."

"I've told you I haven't seen Jake Fuller in years," Latham said. "You can choose to believe that or you can choose not to. It makes no difference to me."

"But it makes a difference to me, Mr. Latham."

Chapter 39

Lightning flickered in the dark clouds, and raindrops splattered like bugs off the Crown Vic's windshield as Santana drove from Red Wing back to St. Paul. His thoughts were focused on Sean Latham and whether the ex-vet had lied about his relationship with Jake Fuller. Had Latham told the truth when he claimed that he hadn't seen Fuller since they served together in Afghanistan? Santana had seen no tells indicating that Latham was lying. But a practiced liar could mask those.

Latham's mobility without his wheelchair, and his ability to breathe without an oxygen tank, also raised questions in Santana's mind. How debilitating was Latham's silicosis? He had certainly looked much better than the first time Santana had seen him.

Santana had hoped that showing Latham the photo of Jake Fuller would shake something loose, give him a direction he could follow, a clue that would establish some momentum. Instead, he was left with more questions than answers—and no obvious suspect. His instincts told him that the murders of Clay Buck and Danielle Lonetree were somehow connected to the murders of Otto and Elsie Vogel and the attempt on his own life. Sam Noor's murder, as well as Grayson Cole's, could also be connected to the other murders. But he still needed evidence to support this belief.

When Santana returned to the LEC, he saw a note from Pete Romano on his desktop. He hung his sport coat on the back of his chair and went to Romano's office and stood by the open door till Romano looked up from his paperwork and waved him in.

Santana took a chair in front of the desk.

"I spoke with James Nguyen this morning, Detective."

"About what?"

"Nguyen tells me you filed a complaint against a man named Jake Fuller."

"That's right. He's an ex-con who killed Melissa Cantrell and tried to kill me."

"Any idea of his whereabouts?"

Santana shook his head. "But I'm working on it."

Romano blew out a breath of air and held up the front page of the *Pioneer Press*.

Santana read the headline: GRANDSON OF FORMER CHIEF OF POLICE SUSPECTED OF MURDER.

"The media is having a field day with this, John. I need something for Nguyen. Otherwise, Adam Noor is going down for Grayson Cole's murder."

"Give me more time."

"Either bring me some evidence proving the kid is innocent, or back off," Romano said.

* * *

As Santana was heading back to his workstation, his cell phone rang. He recognized the number for the Forensic Services Unit.

"Stop by the lab, John. I've got some interesting information on the bullet that killed Melissa Cantrell."

"I'll be right up."

Five minutes later, Santana was standing beside Tony Novak in front of a large computer that looked like a giant tower. The computer was connected to the National Integrated Ballistic Information Network, a database of bullets and shell casings from around the country. Paired with the latest software, the system could link a single gun to separate shootings, based on the unique etching on each bullet. They were peering at two side-by-side three-dimensional images.

"The bullets the ME took out of Melissa Cantrell and Wendell Hudson came from the same gun, John. A forty-five revolver."

"You're sure?"

"Take a look at the two images on the screen. They're identical."

Santana wasn't an expert, but he could clearly see that the images looked the same. "Hudson was wounded twice, Tony. The second wound came from a high-powered rifle."

"Only one problem, John."

"What's that?"

"The system can't tell us who pulled the triggers."

"That's my job. Thanks, Tony."

"One other thing before you leave." Novak held up a manila folder. "I've got the report on the vial of water you brought me. I think you should take a look."

* * *

Adrenaline was racing through Santana's system as he took the elevator down to the first floor and headed for his Crown Vic. Things were coming together.

The same gun that was used to murder Melissa Cantrell had been used to wound Wendell Hudson. But Jake Fuller couldn't have pulled the trigger on Hudson. He was cuffed to a water trough at the time Hudson was shot. Fuller could have killed Cantrell with the gun used to wound Hudson, but Fuller and Cantrell had once been lovers. Santana had heard two men arguing on the boat the night Cantrell was shot and her body dumped in the river. Maybe Fuller was arguing with the man who had actually killed her, the same man who had tried to kill Wendell Hudson.

Halfway to the car, he ran into Jane Linden from the cold case unit.

"I was hoping I'd see you," she said. She held a large black umbrella above her head and moved closer to Santana to protect him from the falling rain.

Over her shoulder he could see steam rising from the warm pavement and hear drops as they hit the umbrella. "What's up, Jane?"

"I want to thank you for saving my department."

"What do you mean?"

"You arrested Adam Noor for Grayson Cole's murder."

"He hasn't been charged yet."

"But if Adam Noor killed Cole, he might've killed his father, too. If we can close Sam Noor's cold case and get a conviction, Romano might look more favorably on keeping the unit open."

"You're getting way ahead of yourself, Jane."

"What are you saying? That Adam Noor is innocent?"

"I have to go. Thanks for keeping me dry."

Santana heard her calling after him as he ran toward his Crown Vic parked at the curb, but heavy raindrops hitting the pavement drowned out her words.

Chapter 40

The Mayo Clinic Health System in Red Wing was located just off US Highway 61. Santana parked in the visitors' lot late Wednesday morning and headed for the Garden View café on the lower level, where he met Virginia Garrison. She was wearing her nursing scrubs and eating a sandwich.

"I don't have much time, Detective." She took a bite of her sandwich and a sip of Coke.

"Then I'll be quick, Ms. Garrison. Sam Noor gave Chaska Youngblood a vial of water he'd taken from Mills Creek. Youngblood gave the vial to me. I took it to the crime lab and had it analyzed. I got the results this morning."

"Chaska Youngblood never said anything to me about a vial. Neither did Sam Noor."

"Noor was killed soon after he gave it to Youngblood. Maybe he meant to tell you, but never got the chance."

"Why didn't Chaska Youngblood tell me?"

Santana wondered if Youngblood distrusted Virginia Garrison. But he shrugged and said, "Maybe Youngblood wanted to know if there was anything in the water before he talked to you."

"So is there something in it?"

"The sample contained polyacrylamide."

She put down her sandwich and stared at Santana, her mouth agape.

"You're familiar with it?"

She nodded. "It's commonly used to remove mud, silt, and other impurities while the frack sand is being washed." She shook her head. "Damn. We've been focusing on the wrong problem."

"What do you mean?"

"We've been concentrating on crystalline silica, which can lead to silicosis or lung cancer with overexposure, instead of on polyacrylamide."

"What's the concern?"

"Polyacrylamide contains small amounts of acrylamide, a neurotoxin linked to cancer and infertility. Exposure to it for short periods of time can damage the nervous system and cause numbness and weakness in the hands and legs. Chronic exposure can result in paralysis and cancer."

"And Select Sands is using polyacrylamide."

"Of course. It all begins to make sense now."

"What does?"

"Acrylamide is biodegradable."

"So it doesn't bind to soil."

"Right. That would increase risk of surface or groundwater contamination. But acrylamide has a lower rate of biodegradation in sandy soils than in clay soils, and can more easily contaminate groundwater."

"Like where frack sand mining operations are located," Santana said.

"Yes. And cooler temperatures, like we have in the Midwest for much of the year, can also lower the rate of biodegradation. The EPA has set a national drinking water regulation for acrylamide. But there are no acceptable means of detecting acrylamide in drinking water, and conventional water treatment processes can't remove acrylamide. So any water treatment plant that uses polyacrylamide is required to maintain detailed records."

"So how does all this relate to Select Sands?"

She lowered her voice, as if someone might overhear the conversation. "Even the washed sand poses a risk because once washing is complete, the sand is sent to what's called a surge pile, where much of the water clinging to the sand particles seeps back into the ground."

"I'm still not getting it."

"There's a county ordinance that requires water containing certain mining chemicals to be dumped into a lined pond. If Select Sands were dumping cancer-causing chemicals into an unlined pond, those chemicals could seep into the creek leading to the Mississippi River. Select Sands petitioned the Mills Creek city council to annex the property around the mine. If that happens, the town can issue its own permits for operation, provide its own oversight, and escape the county's regulatory authority."

"Why would the town do that?"

"Jobs, Detective." She paused for a moment, a faraway look in her eyes. "Even then," she said, focusing on Santana again, "Select Sands wouldn't want it known that they're dumping hazardous chemicals into unlined ponds."

"Because of lawsuits?"

"Yes. As far as I know, there's been no litigation regarding the use of polyacrylamide in frack sand operations. But that was before all the frack sand mines were dug around here, and the public became concerned about the possible dangers. If local residents start attributing nervous system ailments to acrylamide exposure, litigation could skyrocket."

"That would certainly impact Select Sands' bottom line."

"It could drive them out of business," she said. "There was a class action suit over the use of acrylamide in West Virginia. Coal preparation plant workers, as well as their children, were exposed to acrylamide when the workers added polyacrylamide to the water needed to process coal.

The suit was settled out of court for nearly fourteen million dollars. Courts have also ruled in favor of workers suffering from neurological injuries from exposure to acrylamide through handling and inhalation."

"You've been a big help, Ms. Garrison. Thank you." Santana stood.

She looked up at him. "You've found your motive for why Sam Noor was killed. But what about the murderer?"

"I'm working on it."

* * *

It was a short drive from the Mayo Clinic building to the Red Wing office of Ken Webb, CEO of Select Sands.

Webb came around his desk and offered Santana his hand. "Good to see you again, Detective," he said, though his tepid handshake and knitted eyebrows indicated just the opposite.

As Webb went behind his desk, Santana took a chair in front of it.

"What brings you here?" He forced a smile and sat back in his chair. Feigning casual. Relaxed.

"You heard Grayson Cole was murdered."

"Yes, I did. It was a terrible tragedy. I can't imagine who would want to harm Grayson, or why."

"What about Sam Noor, Mr. Webb?"

Webb's complexion reddened. "I'm afraid I don't understand."

"I think the murders of Sam Noor and Grayson Cole are connected."

"I told you before, Detective, I have no idea why someone apparently killed Sam Noor or Grayson Cole."

"I have an idea."

Webb leaned farther back in his swivel chair, creating more distance between the two of them. "Would you care to share it?"

"Chemicals linked to cancer and infertility are leaking out of unlined ponds at your mine site and into Mills Creek, which drains into the Mississippi."

"Who told you that?"

"Sam Noor."

Webb cocked his head. "But Noor is dead."

"A sample of water he took from the creek before he was killed contained acrylamide, a neurotoxin linked to cancer and infertility. The creek drains into the Mississippi. I think you knew that and petitioned the town to annex the property so the county couldn't shut you down."

"That's absurd."

"You did petition the town, did you not, Mr. Webb?"

"Well . . . yes. But that wasn't the reason."

"Then what was it?"

"Well . . ."

"Let me help. You knew the town would be open to the idea of annexing the mine because of the jobs it would create. All that could go out the window if the town knew about the cancerous chemicals in the runoff. Your company is in debt up to its eyeballs. If the town rejects your proposal, that could bankrupt the company and put you out of business."

"What are you suggesting?"

"Someone wanted to silence Sam Noor. He was suffocated in silica sand. You had motive and opportunity."

"No," Webb said, shaking his head. "You have no proof that I killed Sam Noor."

"That's an interesting statement, Mr. Webb. You didn't deny killing him. You just said I had no proof."

"You have no proof because I didn't kill him. I'm a businessman, not a murderer."

"You wouldn't be the first to be both, Mr. Webb."

Chapter 41

The Nickel Joint was a windowless brick building and popular biker bar located in the Thomas-Dale neighborhood northwest of downtown St. Paul known as Frogtown.

The town was first settled in the mid-1800s, and Santana had heard two theories as to how Frogtown had acquired its name. One was because of its swamps and the croaking of frogs. A second and more likely explanation, he thought, was that Frogtown was an ethnic slur aimed at the French who had first settled the area. Later, the Irish, Poles, Scandinavians, and Germans arrived. Though Frogtown now had a large number of Hmong, Lao, Cambodian, and Vietnamese, the population was steadily declining. The area had high rates of rentals and poverty. Frogtown was also among the most racially diverse areas in the city. But the patrons inside the Nickel Joint represented a more typical white working-class neighborhood than the changing demographics of Frogtown.

A pinball machine was dinging as Santana sat down at a table across from Dennis Duffy.

"I like the irony of meeting here, Detective," Duffy said.

"You mean in the Nickel Joint."

"No. Frogtown. Don't you Colombians call a snitch a *sapo*, or a toad?"

"We do."

"Then I guess I'm your frogman."

The corners of Duffy's thin mouth wrinkled slightly with the beginnings of a smile. The black marbles that were his eyes were hazy. He had small, yellow teeth, and his unnaturally pale face was flushed from drinking bourbon. The remaining strands of his dark hair looked like tiny black snakes crawling across the top of his head. He wore his hair straight back and kept a comb clipped inside the breast pocket of his bright blue and pink Hawaiian shirt.

"Since you're on duty, you want something nonalcoholic to drink?" Duffy asked, signaling a waitress.

"I'll have a Coke."

Duffy looked up at the waitress, a young, rail thin woman with short brunette hair and a pretty face. "Bring my friend here a Coke and me another bourbon, sweetie."

"I'll bring you the drinks," she said. "But I'm not your sweetie."

Duffy smiled to himself, seemingly unconcerned with her comment. "Whatever you say." When she left the table, Duffy said, "Women are so touchy nowadays. Never used to be that way."

"How are you getting along, Dennis?"

He raised his cocktail glass in a salute. "One drink at a time."

"You making any money?"

"Besides the money I make ratting out perps for the SPPD?"

"No one's forcing you to do it."

Duffy drained the last drop of bourbon and set the glass gently on the table, as if it were a highly prized jewel. "You're right. But I have to survive. It's tough when you've spent half of your fifty-five years in and out of the slammer. At least you've always been straight with me, Santana. I appreciate it."

Duffy was what Santana and the department considered a confidential *reliable* informant. The department used a number of CIs for information. But CRIs like Duffy had proven their reliability over time and were better compensated for the information they provided.

"How long have you been out now, Dennis?"

"Going on eight years. I've given up burglary as a profession. Don't plan on going back."

Santana took out the photos of Melissa Cantrell and Jake Fuller and set them on the table. "Ever see either of these people in here?"

"I recognize Fuller. I've seen him in here. The woman looks familiar, too. Saw her picture in the paper. Her body was pulled from the river the other day."

Santana nodded.

Duffy tapped Fuller's photo with an index finger, his brow creased in thought. "Guy is like a lit firecracker waiting to explode. Most people stay away from him."

The waitress appeared with the drinks and set them on the table. "There you go, sweetie," she said sarcastically to Duffy.

He watched her walk away from the table and then faced Santana again. "She must've gotten up on the wrong side of the bed." His eyes were half-closed as he sipped some bourbon. He held the glass in his hand as he rested his elbow on the table and stared at Santana. "Why you asking about Fuller?"

"He's wanted for attempted murder."

"Who'd he try to kill?"

"Me," Santana said.

"Whoa." The haze clouding Duffy's eyes cleared for a second. "You okay?"

"I'm fine. But I need to find Fuller. Soon."

Duffy pointed discreetly over his shoulder while keeping his eyes locked on Santana's. "See the lanky guy with the vest at the bar?"

There were three people drinking at the bar, but only one wore a black vest over a white T-shirt. He looked to be in his late twenties or early thirties. He had a dark blond beard and matching shoulder-length hair that was swept back from his forehead and held in place by two short ponytails, one on the crown of his head and one at the occipital bone. His sculpted biceps looked like they were carved out of granite. A sun cross was tattooed on his right forearm.

"What about the guy at the bar, Dennis?"

"He hangs with Fuller."

"You know his name?"

"Only heard him called Shooter."

* * *

Santana waited outside the Nickel Joint in his Crown Vic, listening to the drumbeat of rain on the roof. He figured Jake Fuller was a light for other extremists who hovered around him like moths. The man Duffy had called "Shooter" was likely one of them.

Thirty minutes later, after the rain had stopped and the sun had broken through the clouds, Shooter came out of the bar. He removed a rag from the saddlebags on the back of a shiny black Harley parked at the curb and wiped the seat. Then he straddled the cycle and fired up the engine.

Santana keyed the license number into the Mobile Data Terminal and followed him when he drove away. Shooter's actual name was Randy Yates. He had two tickets for speeding, but no wants or warrants.

Yates led Santana to a small two-story Victorian house on a narrow lot along Charles Avenue, where evidence of the sub-prime mortgage crisis and the economic recession was still on display. On one side of Yates's house was a vacant lot. CONDEMNED had been painted on the house on the opposite side. Weathered paper on the front doors of two houses across the street warned passers-by to KEEP OUT: FORFEITED TO THE STATE OF MINNESOTA.

"Mr. Yates," Santana called as he exited his Crown Vic and walked across the lawn overrun with quackgrass.

As Yates turned, Santana saw surprise in his eyes, but he also thought he saw something else. Recognition.

"Detective John Santana. St. Paul PD." Santana held up his badge wallet.

Yates moved into the shade under an oak tree, put a cigarette in his mouth, and cupped the flame of a lighter around it. He snapped the lighter shut with his thumb and said, "Yeah?"

Santana stopped in front of Yates and slid his badge wallet into an inner pocket of his sport coat. "I'd like to ask you some questions."

"What about?" Yates asked, his gray eyes scanning the neighborhood as if he were worried someone was watching.

"You rather we talk inside?"

"Out here's fine."

"All right. You live here alone?"

"This was my parents' home. I grew up here before the gangbangers and slopes moved in and the neighborhood all went to hell." He pointed to the two empty properties across his street. "Two years ago your colleagues used tear gas to empty the crack houses across the street. Now the city owns them. They say they're going to sell the houses to families. That's better than rentals. With rentals, you don't know what you're getting."

"You didn't answer my question, Mr. Yates. Do you live here alone?"

"Yeah. I like living alone."

"I understand you're called 'Shooter.'"

"Sometimes."

"You a veteran?"

He nodded. "Marines."

"Were you a sniper?"

"Why are you so interested?"

"Own any firearms?"

"What's this all about anyway?"

"You belong to a group known as CERO. It's run by a man named Thomas Starks."

"You're mistaken."

"That tattoo on your forearm."

His expression hardened. "What about it?"

"That's the logo for CERO, an anti-Native American group."

"You from the politically correct patrol?"

"Homicide."

Yates's cigarette nearly fell out of his mouth. "Who got murdered?"

"Let's start with Clay Buck."

The color went out of Yates's face. "Never heard of him," he said without much conviction.

Santana stepped forward into Yates's personal space. "Here's what I think. You were involved in the shooting death of Clay Buck while he was being transported from Red Wing to St. Paul. Jake Fuller and Melissa Cantrell were also involved. Cantrell is dead. Fuller might have killed her. I want to know where he is and the name of the other person you were with the day Buck was murdered."

Yates tossed his cigarette and headed for the front door. "You want to talk to me again, Detective, get a warrant."

Chapter 42

Sunlight still lit the upper levels of the downtown buildings, but the streets were already resting in shadows. Santana was sitting in his Crown Vic on Minnesota Street in front of the First National Bank building, which consisted of three towers and spanned an entire city block. The bank had moved to another location, but the large neon red "1st" sign atop the towers remained. The three-sided sign was fifty feet tall and could be seen at night from almost seventy-five miles away and from twenty miles away on a clear day. But what Santana remembered most about the building were the remnants of a ninety-six-foot-long pistol range in the basement. Years ago, bank guards were required to practice twice a week to maintain their shooting proficiency.

In his rearview mirror Santana saw Kacie Hawkins pull up behind him. Hawkins got out of her dark blue Jeep Cherokee and into the passenger side of his Crown Vic. She was dressed in her after work jeans and running shoes. But underneath a lightweight lavender blue blazer, the holster holding her Glock was still clipped to her belt.

"What's this all about, John?"

Santana spent the next ten minutes explaining. Then he said, "Randy Yates is still inside the building. I've been following him since he left his house. In the last hour, he's eaten fast food, filled up the gas tank on his Harley, and stopped here."

"Any idea where he's headed?"

"Maybe to see Jake Fuller."

"What do you think he's doing inside?"

"Visiting Grayson Cole's office."

Hawkins canted her head. "But Cole's dead."

"You think it's just a coincidence Yates is here?"

Hawkins smiled. "There are no coincidences in homicide. You going inside to take a look?"

"Once Yates leaves. After I check out Cole's office, I'll drop off the Crown Vic at the LEC and get my Explorer. Follow Yates, Kacie, but stay far enough back and keep in touch. I'll catch up."

* * *

Fifteen minutes later, Randy Yates' Harley exited the parking ramp. Kacie Hawkins' Jeep Cherokee pulled away from the curb and settled in behind him.

Santana got out of his sedan and entered the street level lobby of the west building with its marble walls and columns, mahogany woodwork, and terrazzo floors. Santana was almost certain that Randy Yates had gone to Cole's office, but he used the touch screen directory in the stand-alone, stainless steel kiosk to search for listings and view tenant information. The tenant mix included law firms, financial management offices, nonprofit organizations, and the State of Minnesota's Department of Employment and Economic Development.

Nothing jumped off the page—besides Grayson Cole's real estate office.

Santana rode an elevator with ornate iron and bronze doors to the 16th floor. Cole's glass-walled office was located directly opposite the elevator.

One end of the crime scene tape that had been stretched across the doorframe had come loose—or had been pulled off—and was lying on the carpeted floor. Cole's office door was unlocked. Santana wondered if Yates had picked it. He drew his Glock and pushed open the door.

The reception area was just as he remembered. There was a mahogany counter and receptionist desk directly ahead. On the wall to his right was a large corkboard with photos and sell sheets describing commercial real estate properties available for rent or for sale. A door to his left led to Grayson Cole's inner office.

As Santana nudged it open, he stood to the side, his left shoulder against the wall, making sure his profile wouldn't be an easy target if someone was hiding in the room.

Cole's inner office was twice the size of the reception area and lit by the early evening sunlight filtering through a wall of windows facing the Mississippi River to his right.

The top drawer of a four-drawer metal file cabinet behind Cole's desk was partially open. Next to the cabinet was a paper shredder. Santana gloved up and went to the cabinet and peered at the manila folders that were arranged in alphabetical order. He recalled looking at the folders when he had first searched the office after Grayson Cole's death, but nothing he saw then had piqued his interest. Now, as he scanned the folders, he noticed that one entitled "Trust" was at a slight angle.

Santana pulled out the folder and opened it.

Nothing.

Would Grayson Cole keep an empty folder in his filing cabinet? Not likely. Santana figured that Fuller had instructed Yates to remove or destroy the copy of the trust document.

He looked through the scraps of paper in the wastebasket of the shredder beside the filing cabinet, but the pieces were so small they were unreadable.

* * *

Kacie Hawkins phoned just as Santana was climbing into his Explorer at the Law Enforcement Center. "Yates is heading south on Highway Fifty-Two."

Santana thought Yates might be headed for Thomas Starks' ranch. "Stay with him."

"You check Cole's office?"

He told Hawkins what he had found.

"So whatever Yates took," she said, "is probably in the saddlebags on his cycle."

"Unless he shredded it. I'm on my way, Kacie."

Santana caught Highway 52 a mile and a half from the 1st Bank building and headed south.

Fifteen minutes later Hawkins phoned him. "I'm on Barbara Avenue in U-Moor Park, just off County Road Forty-Six. It's a strange-looking place."

"It's the site of a World War Two ordnance plant," Santana said.

"Is it safe to walk around?"

"You wouldn't be harmed by the contaminants."

"How do you know?"

"I read an article about it."

"Don't believe everything you read," she said.

"Where's Yates?"

"He parked his cycle and went into a farmhouse near a cornfield. I can't see much from my current position."

Santana glanced at his watch. "It's eight p.m. I'll be there in ten minutes, Kacie. Don't move unless Yates does."

Hawkins had a mind of her own, but she wasn't stupid or reckless. Santana knew she would wait for him.

What he didn't know was what was waiting for the two of them.

Chapter 43

At 8:10 P.M. Santana turned off County 46 and headed north on Barbara Avenue. Thick stands of tall trees and prairie grass bordered both sides of the tar road. He passed a sign on his right that warned:

NO TRESPASSING
Property patrolled by Rosemount Police Department,
DNR, and Dakota County Sheriff's Department

Santana spotted Hawkins' Jeep on the right shoulder, a half block ahead. He parked his Explorer behind it, got out, and approached the driver's side of the Jeep. The doors were locked. No one was inside. He flipped open his cell phone and called Hawkins. Her phone rang four times before turning over to voicemail. He cursed silently, partly out of anger because she had disobeyed his order, but more out of concern that something had happened to her.

Above the trees to the east, five smokestacks, once used to boil water to manufacture the gunpowder for Navy artillery shells, stood like sentinels. On the opposite side of the road fifty yards ahead sat a large white two-story farmhouse. It faced south and was set back about thirty yards from the tar road. Black curtains darkened the windows. Behind the farmhouse was a cornfield. Just north of the cornfield, the tar road came to a T. There was no traffic, only stillness, and the empty feeling of a place where few ventured.

Santana considered calling for backup but quickly rejected the idea. If Hawkins was being held in the farmhouse, calling in an Emergency Response Team would alert whoever was inside—and could be signing her death warrant.

Returning to his Explorer, he opened the hatch and removed his sport coat and tie. He put on a soft ballistic-resistant vest under his SPPD raid jacket. Then he pulled back the rubber mat covering the jack and spare tire and located the two 15-round magazines that were nestled in the tire rim. He put one in each of the pockets of his raid jacket. The standard magazine capacity for his Glock 23 was 13 rounds, but the factory 15-round magazine for the larger Glock 22 functioned in the Glock 23.

As he closed the hatch and locked the Explorer, he saw Hawkins trudging out of the woods and high grass to his left, a set of binoculars in her hand. He breathed a sigh of relief.

"I asked you to wait for me, Kacie."

"I wanted a closer look."

"Why didn't you answer when I called?"

"I had the ringer on vibrate. I was worried someone might hear me talking."

"You sure you weren't spotted?"

"I don't think so."

He could see that she had exchanged her blazer for a soft ballistic vest and raid jacket as well. "You carrying extra ammo?"

Hawkins reached into a jacket pocket and took out a magazine. "Great minds think alike," she said with a grin.

"Let's hope we don't have to use it. You spot anything?"

She shook her head. "Yates went into the farmhouse. But I haven't seen anyone else. You think Jake Fuller is in there?"

"Only one way to find out."

Figuring there was less chance of being seen if they approached the farmhouse along the border of the trees to the west, they crossed the road and headed north for fifty yards to a clearing. There, they each squatted behind the trunk of an ash tree and surveyed the location once more.

Randy Yates' Harley was parked in the dirt driveway behind a battered pickup. A narrow sidewalk split the small, weedy lawn in half. Three steps led to an open railed porch that ran the width of the house.

"Read me the truck plate number, Kacie."

Hawkins raised the binoculars to her eyes and recited the number to him. Santana called dispatch. A minute later he said to her, "Truck is registered to a man named Jorgen Lundgren."

"Probably the farmer who owns the place."

"Keep your phone on vibrate and work your way around back," he said, pointing to the west. "That way you'll stay away from the road. When you're at the back of the house, use the cornfield for cover and call me. Watch the back door. I'll flush whoever is in there out your way."

Hawkins nodded. "Roger that. See you soon."

"Count on it."

Santana watched as she made her way around the house, hoping he wouldn't have to provide cover fire. A minute later, his cell phone buzzed.

"I'm here," she said.

"See anything?"

"Curtains are closed over the back windows."

"I'm going in," he said.

He closed his phone and shoved it in a jacket pocket. *Too much open ground between the edge of the trees and the porch,* Santana thought. But he had no choice. He dashed into the clearing, holding his Glock tightly in his right hand, staying low as he ran toward the house, the soles of his shoes thumping on the ground, his heart thudding in his chest, the day bleeding into night. He ran up the sidewalk leading to the steps and leapt onto the porch, the paint-peeled wooden boards sagging slightly beneath his weight, his eyes darting to the windows on each side of the front door.

Nothing moved behind the curtains.

He inhaled deeply and released a breath, trying to slow his racing heart. The screen door opened with a squeak of rusty hinges. Santana knocked on the door, stepped back, and waited. Then, as he leaned forward to knock again, he heard the threatening slide of a shotgun shell racked into the chamber.

Santana dove to his left a moment before the door exploded into splinters. He rolled once, rose to one knee, and aimed the Glock. The screen door had been blown off its hinges and was tumbling down the porch steps. Through the smoke he could see a fist-sized hole in the front door. The small spread pattern indicated that the shooter had been standing close to the door. Santana fired four quick rounds into the door, each shot flashing out the barrel like a bolt of lightning. He remained on his knee, his Glock still pointed at the door, the echoes of the shotgun blast and the rain of bullets from his gun storming through his head.

Someone moaned.

He stood and kicked the main door open and went in behind the gun barrel.

Randy Yates lay on his back on the hardwood floor, both his hands pressed against a wound in his left side, trying to stop the leaking blood. On the floor beside him was a pump action shotgun. Santana slid it away from Yates with a foot. Then he bent down and felt Yate's pulse. It was fast but strong.

"Anyone else here, Yates?"

"Fuck you, man."

A dim light came from a floor lamp in the corner. It took a moment before Santana's vision adjusted to the shadows, and he saw someone seated on a battered couch on the far side of the room. He dropped to a knee and raised his gun to fire but hesitated when he realized it was a man slumped against the right arm.

The floorboards creaked as Santana stood and moved closer.

It was an older, gray-haired man dressed in coveralls and work boots. *Jorgen Lundgren*. Part of his head had been blown away.

Santana's phone vibrated.

"You okay, John?"

"So far, Kacie. But Yates isn't. Neither is Jorgen Lundgren."

"Is Fuller in there?"

"I'm checking. Stay where you are."

"You can't leave me here to die," Yates said, looking at Santana with eyes the size of quarters.

"Sure I can."

"All right. Jake is in a room at the back of the house."

"He armed?"

"Damn right."

Santana's hand tightened around the butt of his Glock. He wiped the sweat from his face with the sleeve of his jacket and looked at the flight of wooden stairs to his left and down the narrow corridor straight ahead. In the dying light of day he could see four doorways, two in the middle on opposite sides of the hallway, and two at the end of it, one on each side. He listened but heard nothing besides his own shallow breathing. The dryness in his throat made it difficult to swallow.

He walked by Yates as he headed for the corridor.

"Hey, Santana. I need an ambulance. Call 911."

"You keep your mouth shut, I will."

Santana pinned his left shoulder against the wall, both hands on the butt of his Glock, and inched along, ignoring the voice in his head that urged him to turn and run before it was too late.

Halfway down the corridor, as he passed the kitchen on his left and the bathroom on his right, a door on the opposite wall at the end of the hallway creaked open. Light spilled out of the room and onto the floor.

Santana took aim and waited.

The light went out.

He waited some more.

Then a gun barrel appeared around the doorjamb. Santana fired three quick rounds and dropped to his chest on the floor just as an eruption of gunfire ripped through the hallway. Bullets punched holes in the walls and scattered plaster and wood chips that pricked his face.

He returned fire, forcing the shooter to tuck back around the frame.

Knowing he needed cover before tactically reloading, Santana stood and continued firing as he backed down the hallway into the kitchen under a mist of dust falling from the ceiling, the reverberation of gunfire ringing in his ears, the pungent smell of gunpowder swirling in the air.

He flattened his back against a kitchen wall, ejected the magazine, and slammed a fresh one into the butt of his gun. He put the partially depleted magazine into the pocket of his raid jacket and peered around the doorjamb and down the hallway.

He called for backup and paramedics, hoping he could keep Fuller pinned down till support arrived. Then he phoned Hawkins.

"You all right?" she asked, tension and concern ringing in her voice.

"I'm good. I called for backup."

"They better come soon," she said.

Santana heard glass breaking. "You hear that, Kacie?"

"He's climbing out the window!" she yelled into the phone.

"I'm coming," Santana said, jamming the phone in his pocket.

Gunfire erupted from the back of the house as Santana raced to the door at the end of the corridor, stepped back, and drove the sole of his shoe into it. The latch bolt broke away from the striker plate, and the door swung open on its hinges and banged against the wall.

Whoever had been in the room had escaped through the broken bedroom window. Santana climbed out and then knelt in the grass beside a Sig Sauer P229. The slide had locked back when it ran out of ammo.

"Kacie?" he called.

"Here, John." Her voice came from the edge of the cornfield.

"You hit?"

"No, but I think I twisted my ankle when I scrambled for cover. I might have wounded him. He was limping when he headed towards the munitions plant."

Forty yards to the east, Santana could see a man running toward the abandoned munitions plant. He knew that he would need to go into the darkness of that place to get Jake Fuller.

"Wait for backup," he said. "Yates is in the living room with a gunshot wound in his side. Help him till the paramedics get here."

"Why don't we both wait, John? We'll send ERT after Fuller."

"I don't want to wait. We might lose him."

Kacie stared silently at him for a moment. "You want to take him, don't you, John?"

Santana nodded and took off running, keeping Fuller in his sights.

Chapter 44

The hood of darkness had fallen over the landscape. A full moon was on the rise, dusting the landscape white. Wisps of ground fog hung like spider webs over the high native grass. Trees appeared silver in the ambient light, and their shadows layered the landscape. The night was windless and soundless, the air cool against Santana's skin as he pursued Jake Fuller through grounds honeycombed with the weathered architectural remains of the old ordnance plant, the ghosts of a nation at war. Most of the buildings were at least partially gone, leaving foundations, basements, and jagged chunks of walls standing among the grass and woods, like the eerie vine-choked ruins of a Mayan civilization.

Santana figured he would soon overtake the limping Fuller, though he needed to approach with caution. Fuller could still be armed.

He was reminded of Thomas Starks' description of a wounded lion or leopard, hiding in ambush, hell bent on revenge, choosing the time and the place, waiting till a hunter was literally stepping on him before he charged.

A large crumbling concrete structure with ten-foot-high walls loomed up ahead. When Santana suddenly lost sight of Fuller, he slowed. Five yards from a wall, he saw a hole wide enough and tall enough for a man to squeeze through.

Santana stopped, wondering if Fuller was waiting for him on the other side. He fired three quick rounds through the hole and then stepped quickly through it, tracking the barrel of the Glock as he swept an area that was littered with wood and rubble. Fuller was running for a small thicket of trees twenty yards ahead. It would be a difficult shot at best. Santana sprinted after him.

Despite the cool night air, his body was sheathed in sweat. The vest didn't help. He slowed as he came to the stand of trees, worked his way cautiously through it, and then stopped when he reached a dirt road. It ran perpendicular to the trees and was soft from recent rains. Santana saw no movement other than the slow, sinuous rise of ground fog—but he did see a set of fresh footprints. He followed them for about twenty yards before the tracks veered to the left into the woods. He had lost sight of Fuller again, but he could hear him running through the trampled grass. Santana knew he was close now.

He passed a series of large concrete formations that resembled bridge supports and came to a clearing he estimated was thirty yards by thirty yards. Thick, ten-foot-high concrete columns were aligned in rows, like Greek ruins, each column separated by five yards. Santana sensed that Fuller was here among the columns.

He squatted in the grass behind the first column in the front row and wiped his face with the back of his gun hand. He breathed deeply to maintain his steady heart rate.

He considered using his mini-Maglite but rejected the idea. The moment he turned on the flashlight, his night vision would be gone, and everything would turn black around him. And the light would make him an easy target, especially if Jake Fuller had another gun.

Instead, Santana closed his eyes tightly and applied slight pressure with his palms to reset his night vision. After about five seconds his vision turned white behind his eyelids. He waited till the white dissolved and the black returned before opening his eyes again. He noticed an immediate improvement in the clarity and depth of his vision.

He stood and carved his way carefully around each of the five columns in the first row, his eyes darting from side to side as he moved slowly forward behind his Glock. If Fuller was here, he would have to reveal himself.

Santana's nerve endings tingled. The sound of blood pumping in his ears was like listening to his heartbeat through a stethoscope. It interfered with his hearing. He knelt and sucked in a long breath of air and slowly released it, regaining control of his breathing again. Now he could hear the rustle of knee-high grass as he crept through it and the *hoo-hoo-hoo* of an owl.

He had cleared half of the ten rows of columns when, out of the corner of his eye, a shadow came alive.

Fuller moved fast.

So fast that Santana nearly missed seeing him. He spun, his gun raised, his body reacting on its own, without conscious thought.

A blade glinted in the moonlight before it slashed the back of his wrist. Santana slid to his right, opposite the direction he had been moving, his fingers involuntarily releasing the Glock as Fuller rushed by.

There was no pain. Not yet. Not with all the adrenaline in his system. Just the knowledge that he had been cut, that he was bleeding—and that he had lost his gun. Santana glanced at the ground but didn't see it. He hoped Fuller couldn't see it either.

Fuller charged him again. Santana dodged the hissing arc of the blade and backed away. He needed distance, though there was no such thing as a safe distance from an edged weapon. An attacker with a knife in his hand could cover twenty-one feet in one and a half seconds. And Fuller was no more than ten feet away. He had proven he could attack swiftly, even with his bad leg. Santana knew he was in the zone of death. Time was all he had on his side. Time to move. Time to think.

Fuller circled him like a wolf hunting a wounded prey. He held the knife low, like a street fighter, like someone who knew how to use it.

Santana shielded his body behind a column, keeping his eyes locked on Fuller. If the knife had cut the ulnar or radial artery on the palm side, Santana knew he would be bleeding more. Much more. And he knew that if he moved in and tried to catch the knife, he would likely be cut again.

The vest slowed him down. It wasn't stab proof but provided some protection—the only protection he had right now.

The best solution was to dodge and weave, stay balanced and in motion, retreat out of striking range, and wait for an opportunity to counter attack. And always have his next move in mind.

When Fuller chased him away from one column, Santana retreated behind the next one. They moved from column to column till Fuller feinted left, then moved quickly right, catching Santana off-guard, slashing him across the abdomen just below the vest, ripping open his skin.

"Got you!" Fuller said.

Santana pressed his hand against the wound. Blood leaked out. With all the adrenaline in his system, he wasn't sure how bad it was, or if he would lose consciousness. He slipped out of his raid jacket and vest. He tossed the jacket but held onto the vest.

"You can't keep this up all night," Fuller said.

In the distance, Santana heard the welcome wail of sirens. "I don't have to keep it up all night. ERT is coming."

Fuller hesitated, then straightened up.

"You can't outrun me," Santana said, hoping Fuller didn't know how badly he was cut, how much blood he was losing. "We've already determined that. As long as I keep a column between us, you can't cut me again either."

"Don't count on it."

Fuller charged, but instead of retreating, Santana stepped out from behind the column and held the vest in front of him like a shield. Seeing the vest but having already thrust the blade at Santana, Fuller tried to stop in mid-motion—but it was too late. The blade plunged deep in the vest. Santana yanked the vest toward him, pulling the knife out of Fuller's hand. As Fuller grabbed for the vest, Santana tossed it into the shadows.

Fuller fell back a few steps and let out a small laugh. "I guess it's just you and me now, Santana. *Mano a mano,* as you Spanish like to say."

"I'm Colombian."

Fuller shrugged. "Just another spic." He waved Santana forward. "Come and get some. I owe you."

Santana knew it was his last play. He felt lightheaded and would lose consciousness before ERT arrived. Once he did, Fuller would kill him. He had to take Fuller now.

Fuller went into a fighting stance, knees slightly bent, his left leg forward, his body slightly turned, his hands up just below eye level, demonstrating that he had had some martial arts training—and that the wound in his leg wasn't debilitating.

That's not going to make this any easier, Santana thought.

Fuller moved in and launched a sidekick with his front leg toward Santana's solar plexus. Santana swatted the leg away, danced to his right, and backpedaled on the flat ground. His legs and arms felt heavy, as if he were carrying weights on each limb. But he knew that if he stopped moving, he would never move again.

Fuller lifted his left leg once more, as though he were about to launch another sidekick. Santana guessed it was a decoy. When Fuller planted his left foot and let fly a round-house kick designed to take off Santana's head, he was ready.

He stepped back just enough that the outstretched leg missed his chin, but close enough that he felt a rush of air as the powerful kick flew by. Then he stepped forward and drove his right fist into Fuller's kidney. Fuller bent over in pain and tried to clinch, but Santana stepped back and hooked a left to the jaw. Fuller spurted blood and swung a slow, heavy right hand. Santana ducked under it and dug his right fist into Fuller's gut. Fuller went down to one knee. The blood flowing from his mouth looked black in the moonlight.

Santana was dizzy now. The landscape swayed in front of his eyes. But in his mind's eye he saw the body of the old farmer, half his head blown off, heard the demon inside him screaming for vengeance. He set himself and, putting every-thing he had behind it, he threw a hard right that caught Fuller squarely on the jaw.

Bones cracked. Fuller's eyes rolled up in his head. He fell forward and landed on his face. He did not move.

Santana collapsed to his knees and pressed his bloody hands against the wound in his stomach. From out of the fog came the sound of approaching sirens, the revolving red lights reflecting off the grass and shrubs and trees.

He took the pair of handcuffs off the back of his belt and locked one cuff around Fuller's wrist and the other around his own.

Then he closed his eyes and let the darkness take him.

Chapter 45

Santana is in the cloud forests of Colombia, high in the Andes. The air is ripe with the rich scent of coffee beans and ozone from an approaching storm. Black clouds move like shadows across the moon. He hears a rumble of thunder, the incessant buzzing of chicharras, and the sound of his breathing. He feels the first cool drops of rain against his face and then a forearm pressed hard against his throat. Struggling to breathe, his consciousness slipping away, he hears the distinctive click of a switchblade, sees lightning fork across the sky, the glint of a shiny blade above him. He reaches up and grabs the man's wrist, pushing with both hands with all his strength, trying to keep the knife away from his body. But the man who has pinned him to the ground is too strong. The blade comes ever closer. He feels a sharp pain in his stomach as it rips open his skin.

Santana woke with a start.

"It's all right, John."

It takes Santana a moment to realize that the hazel eyes he is looking into are not those of his mother or his sister, though the eyes have the same radiant quality. He is not sixteen and in Colombia. He is in a recliner in his living room. The beautiful eyes belong to Jordan. She is leaning over the recliner, adjusting the blanket that is draped over his stomach and legs.

"You had a nightmare," she said.

He took a deep breath and let it out, trying to slow his racing heart. He adjusted his position and immediately felt a second stab of pain in his belly.

"Be careful. You don't want to pull out the stitches or tear off the dressing."

He remembered now that she had insisted on picking him up at the emergency room two days ago and watching over him till he was back on his feet.

He looked down at the bandage on his stomach and the one on his right wrist. *Maybe the scar on his wrist would match the one on his right hand. Matching scars. How perfect.*

Gitana was sitting on her haunches beside Jordan, staring at him, her big brown eyes, like Jordan's, registering concern.

"I'm fine," he said.

Gitana stood and wagged her tail and came to him. He reassured her by gently stroking her head.

"Hurt much?" Jordan asked.

"Only if I move," he said with a crooked smile. "Less than yesterday. But my head feels like it's filled with helium."

"Probably due to the morphine you're taking." She handed him a mug of hot chocolate and a time-release pill. "Drink this with your meds."

"Give me two Advil instead."

"It might not be strong enough."

"There's a bottle in the medicine cabinet. I'd rather experience some pain than be so doped up I can't think straight."

Jordan started to protest and then appeared to change her mind. "I'll be right back. Don't move."

"Very funny. I'd laugh, but it would hurt too much."

He drank from his mug of hot chocolate and looked out a window toward the river. Dark clouds. Stiff wind. Heavy rain. Cool temps. It was more like late September than June. But he couldn't leave the house or drive anyway, at least not for a couple more days.

Jordan returned with the Advil.

Santana swallowed two pills and a sip of hot chocolate.

"Kacie Hawkins called."

"What did she say?"

"She asked how you were."

"How is she doing?"

"Better. Her ankle is a little sore. But she's more upset that she wasn't with you than she is about the ankle sprain."

"Any news on Jake Fuller?"

"Kacie didn't mention Fuller. Why?"

"My guess is he's lawyered up and isn't talking. But whether he talks or not, he's going down for murdering Jorgen Lundgren."

"The farmer?"

"Uh-huh. I'd like to get him for more than that one."

"Who else?"

"Maybe Danielle Lonetree. Maybe Otto and Elsie Vogel in Red Wing. Maybe Melissa Cantrell."

"Why would he kill them?"

"That's the question, Jordan. I don't know what Fuller's motive was. What did he have to gain by killing all these people? Did he act alone?"

"Randy Yates was with him."

"At the farmhouse. And I think Yates was one of the four people who ran Wendell Hudson and me off the road when we were bringing Clay Buck from Red Wing back to St. Paul."

"But Fuller was with you when Clay Buck was killed. It had to be one of the other three."

Santana nodded. "Randy Yates, Melissa Cantrell . . ." Santana let his voice trail off.

"You don't know who the fourth person was."

"No."

"You might never know."

Santana shook his head. "I'm going to keep looking till I do."

Jordan sat down on the big leather chair across from him. She lifted a mug of hot chocolate off the end table, her eyes never leaving his face.

"What is it?"

"You shouldn't return to work for a while, John. You need to rest. You need some time."

"I can't waste time."

"Getting healthy again isn't wasting time. And Fuller is in custody. He's going down for murdering the farmer. You said it yourself."

"I need to see this case through."

"You keep chasing this darkness, John, this darkness made flesh, eventually it will catch up with you. It's already nearly killed you."

"It's my job, Jordan. It's what I do." He noticed the open murder book on the table near the kitchen. "Have you been reading about the Sam Noor case?"

"A little."

"Why?"

"Because I'm worried about you. I want to know what's going on."

"Stay out of it, Jordan."

She drank more hot chocolate, her eyes shifting to the windows and the storm outside and then to his face again. "What was your nightmare about?"

"It was nothing."

"Don't say that."

"Colombia," he said at last.

"Just Colombia?"

"The men who killed my mother."

"The men who almost killed you."

"Yes."

She let out a heavy sigh. "You have PTSD, John."

"I know."

"This latest fight with Jake Fuller isn't helping."

"I've dealt with PTSD since I was sixteen. I can handle it. The question is, can you?" The words sounded harsher than he had intended. He could see the hurt in her eyes. She had once saved both their lives by killing a woman who was about to kill them. But the taking of a life—even if it was justified—had cost her.

"Unlike you, John, I've been going to counseling. I have my PTSD under control. I rarely experience nightmares now."

"That's not what I meant."

He could see the recognition in her eyes. "You mean can I deal with a reoccurrence of your PTSD?"

"Yes."

"After what we've been through, I don't see how you can even ask that question. It hurts that you would even think it."

"I'm sorry. With all the meds, I'm not myself."

"This has nothing to do with your meds." She paused and gazed out the window again. Then her eyes returned to his. "I think you're conflicted."

"About what?"

"Our relationship."

"How?"

"You're being hunted by the Cali cartel. My being with you puts my life in danger."

"It does."

"But you've told me you love me, and that creates a conflict. You want to be with me, yet you're worried that you might not be able to protect me. It's the same worry you have about your sister."

"All that's true."

"And now you're wounded and can't protect me. I'm protecting you, and you don't like it. So you want to get back on your feet and back to work. But it's too soon. You know it is. So do I."

"A murderer is still out there, Jordan. Maybe I'm the only one who believes that. Maybe I'm wrong. But I have to be sure. And I can't be sure if I'm sitting around here filling my head with pain medication."

"And Kacie can't help because she's injured."

"Exactly."

"What about me? I'm an ex-cop and a licensed private investigator. I could do some legwork while you're recovering."

"No," he said, shaking his head.

"Why not?"

"Fuller tried to kill me twice."

"But he's in jail."

"Are you still being followed?"

"I don't think so."

"If I'm right, Jordan, and a killer is still out there, I won't put your life in danger."

"It already is just by being with you."

"And you're comfortable with that?"

She set her mug down on the end table, stood, and walked over to him. "I'm here, aren't I?" She leaned over and kissed him gently on the lips. "You can't get rid of me that easily."

Santana wondered if Jordan realized the irony in what she had just said. Breaking up to keep her safe was one thing. Staying with her and getting her killed was something entirely different.

Chapter 46

Five days after his mandatory three-day Officer Involved Shooting suspension was up, Santana was seated in a comfortable chair in Karen Wong's office, located in her 19th century brownstone in St. Paul's Crocus Hill neighborhood. Her clients used a separate, discreet side entrance.

The stitched wound in his stomach still screamed whenever he moved quickly or bent over. Just tying his shoes caused him to break out in a cold sweat. Switching from morphine to Advil had released the helium from his head and allowed him to drive, though he had to endure the occasional stab of pain that shot through his body like an electrical current. His wrist was healing quickly.

"How are you feeling, Detective?"

"Much better."

The SPPD required officers involved in shootings to attend one therapy session in order to obtain information on resources available to them. Firing a gun in the line of duty was the only criteria, whether an officer hit anything or not. Santana had seen Karen Wong before and trusted her, at least as much as he could trust anyone whose psychological diagnosis could determine his future as a homicide detective.

"I haven't seen you in quite a while," she said.

"That's a good thing, isn't it?"

Wong nodded and smiled. She was an attractive Asian woman with a heart-shaped face, delicate features, and full black hair that was cut even with the nape of her neck. She wore it brushed across her forehead so that it drew attention to her large brown eyes.

She glanced at the open file on her black lacquer desk. "I understand you were injured."

"I'm healing."

"Physically, I'm sure. What about emotionally? Still having nightmares?"

"Not so much anymore," Santana lied.

"Any since your recent incident?"

Santana thought "knife attack" would have been a better description than "incident." He almost spoke up but held his tongue. Despite his amicable past history with Wong, being confrontational in a therapy session could buy him a quick ticket to desk duty with the rubber gun squad, as it was derisively called.

"I had one nightmare a couple days after the . . . incident." He kept the sarcasm out of his voice. "But nothing since then."

"You're feeling well enough to return to work?"

"Absolutely."

"Are you taking any medication?"

"Advil."

"Did this case affect you more than past cases?"

Santana thought it was an odd question. "They all affect me."

"How?"

"Someone has taken a life or lives, as in this case. It's my mission to find them and to bring them to justice."

"I noticed you said 'mission' instead of job."

He nodded. "I don't think you can work effectively in Homicide and consider it just a job."

"So you believe not every police officer can do it."

"No."

"And why is that?"

"Homicide detectives work long hours. We also have large caseloads. Sometimes it seems like draining the ocean with a thimble."

"There's more to it, Detective. Tell me about it."

Santana wondered if Wong was trying to bait him into saying something she could use against him. He was reminded of the Colombian saying, *por la boca el pez muere,* by the mouth the fish die. But not answering her question could cause problems for him as well.

"The responsibility is great," he said. "You feel pressure because you want to do something to help make up for the loss the family and friends of the victim feel."

"Go on."

He could tell she had no intention of letting him off the hook. "I see the worst that human beings are capable of on a daily basis. This is a job that can take a severe psychological toll. Not everyone can handle it."

"And you feel you can?"

"Yes."

"What do you consider 'justice,' as you call it?"

"Prison."

"Anything else?"

Santana knew where she was heading. "If you mean death is justice, I would say yes. Sometimes death is justice."

"Who makes that decision?"

"Sometimes I do."

"Some might say that what you're describing is a god complex, Detective."

He shook his head. "Someone with a god complex believes he's infallible, Dr. Wong. I've seen that attitude in some of the perpetrators I've hunted. But I'm not infallible. I've made mistakes. Becoming a homicide detective wasn't one of them."

* * *

No one was sitting at the workstations in the Homicide and Robbery Unit the following Monday morning when Santana knocked on Pete Romano's open door.

"Good to have you back," he said, welcoming Santana in with a wave.

Santana tried to get comfortable in the hardback chair in front of Romano's desk. "Good to be back," he said.

"That was a hell of a situation out there. You and Hawkins were fortunate you didn't get killed."

Santana knew by the tone of Romano's voice where the conversation was headed. "I called for ERT."

Romano held up a file folder. Santana assumed it contained the report he had written while on suspension. "You called for backup *after* you'd engaged the subjects."

"I knocked on the door, Pete. We just wanted to talk to Randy Yates."

"And to find out who else was in that farmhouse. Like Jake Fuller."

"We had no way of knowing if Fuller or anyone else besides Yates was in there. Once Yates shot at me, I had no choice but to return fire."

Romano dropped the folder on his desk.

"I want to speak to Jake Fuller."

"We'd all like to speak to Fuller, Detective. Seems his jaw is wired shut. But he and Randy Yates are going down for the murder of the farmer."

"What about Adam Noor?"

"The blood in the knife handle you found in the kid's kitchen didn't match Grayson Cole's."

"Really?"

"It matched Sam Noor's. The kid murdered his father. He used bleach to degrade the DNA, but you know it's difficult to swab a knife thoroughly. The lab doesn't need much to build a DNA profile."

"What about Grayson Cole?"

"Have you heard anything I just said, Detective? Or has the pain medication fried your brain?"

"I'm thinking clearly."

"You could've fooled me. The kid probably did Cole, too. If he confesses to both murders, Nguyen will work out a plea deal with the kid's attorney." Romano began rearranging the files on his desk, a clear sign that the conversation was over.

Santana knew further debate would lead to a dead end. Romano was weighing the probability of another prime suspect—other than Adam Noor—emerging against the need for Santana to work current cases and to shoulder his share of the department's caseload.

"If you have another suspect in mind, Detective, you're free to work the Noor and Grayson Cole case as much as possible. Frankly, if you could prove that the kid was innocent, it would get the media off the department's back and make them look like the opportunistic jackals they are. But as of today I'm moving the two cases from full-time status to part-time."

Romano picked up a second file folder off his desk and offered it to Santana.

"What is it?"

"Your next case. Someone posing as a police officer is pulling over cars for alleged offenses and extorting money by claiming the fine can be paid on the spot to avoid further legal consequences. Shouldn't be too hard to crack."

Santana reluctantly took the folder. But when he left Romano's office, he dropped it on his desk and went to the SPPD property room. He requested the evidence log listing the description of each item collected by the Forensic Services Unit at the Grayson Cole crime scene. Santana looked over the list, but nothing struck him as unusual. The search warrant was still valid for another eight days. He left the LEC and drove to Cole's house.

Chapter 47

An SPPD black and white was parked along the curb in front of Grayson Cole's house. The patrol car belonged to the uniformed officer guarding the front door. Officers would monitor the entrance twenty-four hours a day till the crime scene was cleaned and no longer active. A van with a CTS DECON legend on the side was parked in the driveway. The van belonged to a former paramedic turned businessman named Ricky Shelton. The acronym stood for Crime and Trauma Scene Decontamination.

Cleaners like Shelton, hired by insurance companies, removed fingerprint dust, ripped out and discarded blood-soaked carpeting, upholstery and rugs, scraped brain matter off of walls, and collected any bone fragments embedded in the drywall. In cases of liquefied decomposition, maggots were often left behind after the ME removed the body. Shelton had to find and burn them because the maggots carried pathogens.

Santana showed the uniform at the front door his badge and signed the crime scene log before entering the house. Santana recognized the lanky, affable man cleaning the entryway, despite Shelton's filtered respirator and HAZMAT suit.

Shelton removed the respirator. "Hey, Detective," he said.

Scattered around the area were large heavy-duty plastic bags, mops, buckets, spray bottles, sponges, brushes, disinfectants, deodorizers, a wet vacuum, and an ozone machine that removed particulates, odor, and bio-hazardous materials from the air.

"You working alone, Ricky?"

"Another guy quit on me last week," he said with a shake of his head.

"It's a tough job."

"Like yours, Detective."

"How's that?"

"We both walk that fine line between detachment and sensitivity. Not everyone can do it."

Santana had once believed that he could wipe the disturbing images of bloody crime scenes from his mind. But he never could. Nor could he ever forget the familiar stench of death, the stink of a decomposing body. Even after he had showered and was at home eating dinner, a whiff would drift up to him, faint but distinct.

"Always get a few voyeurs and creeps who apply for the job," Shelton continued. "They love the gore. Depressives are lousy candidates for the job. So are the empaths. Can't get too emotionally involved in the situation, right, Detective?"

"Hard not to sometimes, Ricky."

He nodded. "Psychological tests we have to take before training eliminate most of the candidates. The few that are left have to pass the gross factor test. Make sure they can handle the work without heaving. Then there's the Hepatitis B vaccine and spending hours in a plastic suit. You know death has no schedule, Detective. I'm on call twenty-four seven. Meth labs are taking up more time. So are the trash houses. Still, bodies keep me in business. But the burnout rate is high."

"So why do it?"

"Good money."

"That it?"

Shelton considered his answer for a moment. "Well, when people think about dying, they don't think about becoming a puddle on the floor. Not really a pleasant thought to even consider. I perform a valuable service. But how do you manage it, Detective?"

"The hours?"

He shook his head. "I can handle the hours. It's the human race I'm talking about. I try not to be cynical. But when a grandmother is left rotting for weeks, and then you see family members fighting over her belongings, it's hard to have a positive view of humanity."

Santana understood. If he focused on the death itself, the carnage that humans continuously inflicted on one another, rather than on the death work, eventually he would suffer street fatigue, reach a point where he couldn't do the job anymore.

"I've seen hundreds of kinds of death," Shelton said. "I'm sure you have too, Detective. There's one thing that's the same about almost all of 'em—the murders, the drinkers, the suicides, and the decomps."

"What's that?"

"At the end of their life, there was nobody there to help them. They died alone. I want to be with someone when I die, not be just a spot on the floor waiting for a cleaning crew to suck what's left of me into a wet vac."

* * *

Santana waited till Kacie Hawkins arrived before beginning his search. Defense attorneys were notorious for accusing law enforcement of planting evidence. For that reason it was better—and faster—to have two detectives conduct a search.

"You're looking better than the last time I saw you, John," Hawkins said with a grin.

"You, too. How's the ankle?"

"It's much better. The soreness is gone. What're we looking for?"

"I'm not sure."

Hawkins smiled. "That's helpful."

"I'll know it if I see it. Let's start in Cole's study."

They walked down the hallway that Ricky Shelton had immaculately cleaned and into the study.

"Wow," Hawkins said when they entered the room. "I could move everything I own into this room and still have some space."

"The desk," Santana said.

Hawkins took the three drawers on one side, Santana the center drawer and the three drawers on the other side of the desk.

A few minutes later, Hawkins said, "Nothing in here besides office supplies, John. Did Cole have a home computer?"

"Forensics took it."

"Might be something on the hard drive."

Santana nodded. "Let's check the master bedroom upstairs."

Shelton was scrubbing bloodstains off the wall in the foyer when Santana and Hawkins passed him and took the stairs to the second level. The large master bedroom had a double-sided fireplace that separated the bedroom from a seating area. The king-size, four-poster bed had wood columns that matched the wood-beamed ceiling. There was a leather ottoman at the foot of the bed.

"I have to get a second job," Hawkins said.

"You'd need a third and fourth to afford a place like this."

"I think you're right."

"Search the walk-in closet and bathroom, Kacie. I'll take the nightstands and dresser drawers."

There was something unpleasant about rummaging through a murder victim's personal effects. Santana had never grown comfortable with it. He had often wondered what items victims might discard if they knew death was waiting for them around the next corner. He was reminded of Wendell Hudson's impending death and wondered whether Hudson had gone through his personal effects and rid himself of any embarrassing or shameful items that might further tarnish his reputation.

Santana recalled that Kelly Noor had once told him that we all have secrets. He wondered now if she had been talking about herself or about the population in general. Perhaps it had been both. Perhaps Grayson Cole had secrets, secrets that would cast a shadow over his otherwise positive life. And perhaps, like so many victims Santana had encountered, it was Cole's life in the shadows, his life in the darkness, that had led to his death.

"Hey, John," Hawkins called. "Take a look at this."

Santana went into the walk-in closet that was filled with expensive-looking suits, sport coats, pants, and shoes.

Hawkins handed him a 4" x 6" photo. "There's a wall safe in the corner behind the clothes. I found this photo on the floor underneath the safe. Cole must've dropped it."

Santana peered at the photo and then looked at Hawkins. "I'm betting there are more in the safe."

"Is it important?"

"Very," he said.

Chapter 48

Sherilyn Lonetree looked much the same as she had when Santana first knocked on her door. Her hair was still parted in the middle, though now, instead of framing her light-brown face, the long dark strands were entwined in a braid that hung down her back. She wore tight-fitting faded jeans and a sleeveless white pullover that accentuated her shapely figure.

"Hello, Ms. Lonetree." He showed her his badge as she held open the front door of her house, her onyx-colored eyes lighting with recognition.

"Detective Santana, isn't it?"

"Yes. May I talk to you for a moment?"

She hesitated before responding, as if she might refuse his request. But then a small smile graced her pretty face, and she stepped back and gestured him in.

Santana sat on the couch, where he and Hudson had sat when they told Sherilyn Lonetree that her daughter had been murdered. She took the chair opposite him. He remembered the painting on the wall behind her of eight tepees on a desolate prairie under a purple sky at sunset.

She studied him for a time before speaking. "Would you like something to drink?"

"No, thank you."

There was an uncomfortably long pause as Santana thought of a way into the conversation. "How have you been?"

"I take one day at a time. Like a recovering alcoholic."

Santana nodded and decided there was no easy way to say what he knew. He would just plunge ahead and see where it led. "I'm sure it's difficult losing a daughter—and her father."

"Yes, it has been . . ." she paused. "Excuse me. You said father?"

"I did. Grayson Cole. He was Danielle's father."

Her body stiffened. "What are you talking about?"

"Your photos of Danielle." He handed her the photo Hawkins had found on the closet floor in Grayson Cole's bedroom. Forensics had sent out a locksmith to open the safe after a judge had signed a warrant. Santana had looked at each of the photos Sherilyn Lonetree had sent to Grayson Cole. She had written on the back of them, describing the significant events in Danielle's life, the first time she had walked, her first day of school, her birthdays, and Christmases.

Sherilyn Lonetree stared at the photo in her hand and then searched Santana's face. "Where did you get this?"

"It was in Grayson Cole's safe. Along with the other photos you sent him over the years."

She handed it back, as if she couldn't believe this was happening, as if by acting like she hadn't seen it, she could pretend that it didn't exist.

Santana took out his notebook. "Why don't you tell me about it, Ms. Lonetree?"

"I think you should leave." She started to rise.

"I think the same person who murdered your daughter murdered Grayson Cole."

She dropped back in the chair as if a great weight had suddenly landed on her shoulders. "Clay Buck killed Danielle."

Santana shook his head. "I don't believe so."

"But the media, the police—everyone said that he did it."

"Not everyone."

Her eyes hardened. "Why didn't you tell me this before?"

"All the evidence pointed to Clay Buck."

She stared at Santana as though she were deciding something. "I know why," she said at last. "It was your partner, the one called Hudson."

"What about him?"

"He was accused of killing Clay Buck. If it were discovered that Clay was innocent, that he hadn't killed Danielle, it would've been awful for your department. That's why you didn't tell me, isn't it?"

"Believing something is true doesn't make it so, Ms. Lonetree. I needed more evidence."

Sherilyn Lonetree pointed to the photo in his hand. "And you think you have the evidence now?"

Santana had told her the truth. He had never had a concrete lead till recently. Still, he felt a stab of guilt, wishing now that he had trusted his instincts and continued to pursue the case. "I need you to tell me about your relationship with Grayson Cole. Then I might know what I actually have."

Her dark eyes stayed on him for a moment and then looked away. "We met when I bought this house. Grayson was my realtor."

When her eyes returned to his, he could see that her gaze was inward, as though she were reliving a time in her life long ago.

"We were both young," she said with a wistful smile. "He was just starting out in the business. We fell in love." She took in a breath and let it out slowly. "But I was married."

"To whom?"

"A man named Frank Fuller."

Santana looked up from his notebook. "Did Fuller have a son named Jake?"

Her dark eyebrows rose in surprise. "Yes . . . and no," she said.

"I don't understand."

"I never sent any photos of Jake to Grayson. How could you possibly know about him?"

Santana wasn't ready to talk about Fuller and the crimes he might have committed. Yet he worried that Sherilyn Lonetree could once again accuse him of withholding information if he didn't reveal what he suspected.

"Explain to me why you answered yes and no when I asked you if Frank Fuller had a son named Jake," he said. "Then I'll tell you what I suspect."

Her face grew still and composed before she spoke again. "Jake Fuller *is* my son, Detective Santana. I thought Frank was his father."

"You thought?"

She nodded. "Jake came to see me a year ago."

"Before your daughter's death?"

"Yes. Not long before Danielle's death."

"Why did he come to see you?"

"He wanted a DNA profile done. He claimed that he knew Grayson Cole was his biological father."

"You didn't know this?"

Her eyes slid off Santana's for a second. "I was having sex with my husband and Grayson. I was never certain that Jake was Grayson's child. Soon after he was born, Frank found out about my affair and filed for divorce. Later, when Jake was six, Frank filed for custody. He told me that if I fought for custody, he would make sure my affair with Grayson would become public." She shook her head, as if embarrassed by what she was about to say.

"Grayson was a good man. He always looked out for me. Provided for me. I didn't want to put him through the embarrassment of a court hearing. I gave up my legal and physical custody rights. Jake went to live with Frank." Tears welled in her eyes. "My son never forgave me."

Santana peered at his notes and waited.

She pulled a tissue from a pocket and dabbed her eyes. "Frank took a job in Phoenix after he gained custody of my son. I called and went to see Jake every chance I could. But when he grew older, he refused to see me. I know Frank encouraged him to reject me. He blamed me for the breakup of our marriage. What could I say? Frank began drinking. I believe he physically abused Jake. I think he suspected Jake wasn't really his son. He looked nothing like Frank, who was blond, but a lot like his father, Grayson. Frank wanted to punish me by taking away my son."

"Why didn't you seek custody of your son when your ex-husband died?"

"I did seek custody. Don't you think I tried?"

"I was just asking, Ms. Lonetree."

"Haven't you ever made a mistake, Detective? Haven't you ever regretted something you've done?"

"We all have regrets."

"Then maybe you have some idea of how I felt. I pleaded with the judge. But Jake was nearly sixteen at the time. He told the judge that he had no desire to live with me, that if he were returned to me, he would just run away. The judge placed him in foster care."

"Why did Jake believe that Grayson Cole was his father?"

"On Frank's deathbed, he told Jake that he wasn't his father. It was his last act of revenge, of cruelty."

"Cole agreed to a DNA test?"

She nodded.

Santana glanced at his notes before continuing. "Danielle was your second child with Grayson Cole?"

"Yes. Grayson and I continued seeing each other through the years. He made sure I was comfortable financially. And he provided for Danielle when she was born."

"So your relationship never really ended."

She shook her head. "Grayson never wanted to marry. I knew it from the beginning. That doesn't mean he didn't love me, nor I him."

"Did your daughter know that Cole was her father?"

"I never told her."

"But Jake Fuller knew about your daughter."

"Yes."

"Did he ever see her or talk with her?"

"Jake was ten years older than Danielle. We rarely spoke by the time she was born. But I told him Danielle was his sister."

Santana wondered if Jake Fuller's hatred of Native Americans, his hatred of his mother and himself, had driven him to join CERO, had driven him to kill his sister—or if there was something else behind his actions.

"What about when Jake Fuller came to see you? Was your daughter here?"

Sherilyn Lonetree thought about it. "Yes, I believe she was getting ready for a date."

"Did she hear any of the conversation?"

"Danielle never mentioned it. But she might have."

"You said she was getting ready for a date. Was it with Clay Buck?"

"Yes."

"Then she might have told Buck what Fuller said."

"I suppose she could have."

"Was Jake Fuller here when Buck arrived?"

She reflected for a time before responding. "I believe he was. But only for a short time."

"You said your son hated you for sending him to live with Frank Fuller. What did he say when he came to see you about the DNA testing?"

"He was angry. He felt Grayson and I owed him." She peered down at her hands.

"Money."

She lifted her eyes. "Yes. And he was right. So I talked to Grayson. He said he would take care of it."

"Do you know if Grayson Cole had a will?"

"Yes."

"Are you the executor?"

"No, Grayson's lawyer, Susannah Barnes, is."

"But you're a beneficiary."

"Ms. Barnes contacted me after Grayson's death and told me I was."

"Did Ms. Barnes tell you when she planned to file the will in probate court?"

"She didn't give me a date, but she said it would be soon."

"I don't want to wait till the information becomes public, Ms. Lonetree. I'd like to see the will now."

"Then talk to Ms. Barnes."

"She's under no obligation to tell me. And I can't force her to. But as a beneficiary, she'll tell you."

"Why do you want to know what's in the will?"

Santana closed his notebook and stood. "Thank you, Ms. Lonetree."

"Wait a minute, Detective. I told you about my ex-husband and my son. You promised to tell me what you suspect."

Santana had hoped she might forget his promise. He reluctantly sat down again and opened his notebook. There was nothing written on the page, no words that would be helpful in this situation. But it gave him some time to compose his thoughts.

"I need to talk with Susannah Barnes before I know for certain, Ms. Lonetree."

"Know what for certain?"

"The person responsible for your daughter's death."

"You're sure it wasn't Clay Buck."

"I'm sure."

"Then who . . ." she stopped. There was a change in her face. Santana wasn't certain if it was fear or maybe recognition, but something had changed.

Sherilyn Lonetree's hands went to her mouth, as if to stop the words from coming out. "My God. You think Jake killed Danielle."

"I'll be in touch," Santana said.

* * *

That evening Santana surreptitiously trailed Jordan as she walked home from work. If someone were following her, Santana believed he would spot him. He had considered telling Jordan beforehand, but he wanted her to act naturally and to follow her normal routine. No deviations.

Her office was located in the historic brick and stone St. Anthony Main building, set just across the Mississippi River from downtown Minneapolis.

It was early evening, and people were on their way home or to dinner along the cobblestone street near St. Anthony Falls. A northern breeze cooled the air.

Santana wore a Twins cap pulled down on his forehead, a windbreaker with the collar pulled up, jeans, and running shoes. He stayed well back from Jordan as she crossed the Stone Arch Bridge, which connected Father Hennepin's Bluff Park with Mills City Ruins Park on the other side of the river. Built by railroad magnate James J. Hill in the late 1800s as a railway link to the Union Depot, only emergency vehicles, pedestrians, and bicyclists were permitted on the bridge now.

Santana hung back as joggers, bicycles, and men and women in business suits with briefcases and laptop bags slung over their shoulders passed him, making it difficult for him to spot a tail.

The bridge ran a third of a mile in length, curving as it neared Mill Ruins Park on the west side of the river. Santana's eyes carefully tracked the bridge and the park, searching for anyone who looked out of the ordinary or who was focused on Jordan as she neared the building where her condo was located.

He watched till she was safely inside before heading back to the bridge. Halfway there his cell phone rang.

"Want to come up?" Jordan asked.

"Come up?"

"Yes," she said. "As long as you're here."

"You spotted me."

"Hard to miss since I know you so well."

Disappointed that he had been spotted, Santana headed back toward Jordan's condo. "It was that easy?"

"I've been very diligent."

"True. That makes me feel better." When she didn't respond, he said, "I'm just looking out for you."

"I don't know whether I should feel angry or grateful."

"If it were me, I'd go with the latter."

"No," she said. "You wouldn't. You'd be angry with me for thinking you couldn't protect yourself."

"That's just me."

"Maybe it's me, too."

Santana detected a hint of anger in her voice. "You still want me to come up?"

"I'm rethinking my offer."

"I'll make it up to you."

"How?"

"Let me in and I'll show you."

Chapter 49

The following day, Susannah Barnes met Santana at the door of her large, two-story home in Woodbury, an upscale community east of St. Paul.

"We've had such lousy weather," she said in her Southern accent. "Let's sit out on the patio where we can enjoy a rare beautiful day."

Santana followed her through the spacious foyer, past the cascading double staircase, along the gleaming oak floor, through the sunroom with four walls of windows overlooking the golf course, and onto a wraparound flagstone patio with a rectangular pool and diving board. A low hedge separated the patio and pool from the golf course.

They sat in fabric swivel chairs at a round glass-topped table under the shade of a Cinzano umbrella. The afternoon was bright and sunny. The humidity was high. The slight breeze felt warm. Santana slipped out of his sport coat and let it fall over the back of the chair.

"When you called, I made a fresh pitcher of lemonade. I figured margaritas were out of the question." She smiled. "Would you care for lemonade, Detective?"

"Please."

She reached for the shiny metal pitcher on the serving cart beside the table, filled two glasses with ice and lemonade, and handed one to Santana. The refraction of sunlight off the mirrored pitcher looked like shards of glass on her skin.

"Would you like a straw, Detective?"

"No, thanks."

She gave her head a flick to get the blond hair out of her face. Her eyes were more gold than brown in the sunlight.

"Sherilyn Lonetree said on the phone that I should speak to you about Grayson's will," she said as she peeled the paper off a plastic straw and stuck it in her glass. "You understand that I don't have to give you any information, Detective Santana." She spoke matter-of-factly, as though talking again about the weather.

"No, you don't, Ms. Barnes. But you know what a judge would say if Ms. Lonetree requested that you provide her with the information." Santana drank some lemonade, enjoying the refreshingly tart taste.

She slid a cigarette out of the package of Virginia Slims in front of her and lit it with a gold lighter. She inhaled deeply, tilted her head back, and blew a stream of smoke. "Why can't you wait till I file Grayson's will in probate court? It becomes public information at that point."

"Because I'm trying to catch a murderer, Ms. Barnes."

She didn't flinch but paused briefly before she drew on her cigarette and exhaled the smoke. "Exactly how can I help you?"

"I know that Grayson Cole had two children with Sherilyn Lonetree—Danielle and Jake. I'm sure you know that as well."

"Go on."

"Did Grayson Cole leave anything for his children in his will?"

"The answer to that question is no."

"You're sure?"

She nodded her head. "Why do you ask?"

Santana wasn't comfortable sharing his suspicions about Jake Fuller with Susannah Barnes. He wondered if he could get the information he sought without revealing what he suspected.

He looked back through his notes and then at her again. "I asked you when we first met at the St. Paul Athletic Club, Ms. Barnes, if Grayson Cole had any children. You told me you weren't aware of any. Yet you're the executor of his will."

"This is a very private matter, Detective Santana. Discretion is important."

"But Sherilyn Lonetree said that Cole promised to financially provide for his two children."

"Grayson left them something in a secret trust."

Santana recalled the empty file in Grayson Cole's office, the file that Randy Yates had probably looked at. "So despite your claim of honesty, Ms. Barnes, you lied to me when I asked you before if Cole had any children."

Her complexion reddened despite her tan. "You do understand that a secret trust is just that, Detective."

"You're the lawyer, Ms. Barnes."

She took another puff of her cigarette and then crushed it out in the ashtray on the table. "Basically, a secret trust is used when a grantor such as Grayson Cole wishes to leave a legacy to someone without causing pain or embarrassment to himself or his family."

"In Cole's case," Santana said, "the pain or embarrassment of having illegitimate children."

"You could say that."

"I just did."

She sipped her lemonade through the straw as she gazed at him. "It must be nice to be perfect, Detective."

"I never said I was."

"And I told the truth when I said Grayson's children were not named in his will."

Semantics, Santana thought. "What exactly did Cole leave his children?"

"Property."

"Where?"

"Outside of Red Wing, near Mills Creek."

"The mineral rights on that property could be worth two billion dollars if the silica mine is dug."

"I believe so," Susannah Barnes said.

"Does Jake Fuller inherit a billion dollars if both Cole and his daughter are dead?"

Susannah Barnes nodded her head slowly. "Grayson rewrote the trust after Danielle's death. Jake Fuller would get the billion."

"Who gets the other billion now that the Vogels are dead?"

"The Vogels' children, if they had any."

"They didn't."

"Then, according to Minnesota law, the money would go to their parents if they're still living. If not, the money would go to their siblings."

"What about Sherilyn Lonetree?"

"Grayson left her stock and other real estate investments. She'll be well compensated."

"Did Cole ever say whether he told Jake Fuller about the secret trust?"

"I believe when the DNA test confirmed that Jake Fuller was his son, Grayson told him about the trust."

"If a sibling was convicted of murdering another sibling, what would happen to the money in a secret trust, Ms. Barnes?"

As she sipped some lemonade, her eyes never left Santana's face. "Well, that's a bit more nuanced and complicated than you might expect. Minnesota statutes provide that a person who feloniously and intentionally kills another is not entitled to any benefits under the will or intestate estate of the decedent. The statute does not specifically address if a beneficiary of a trust kills another beneficiary. However, the policy behind the statute is that a killer should not benefit from his or her murder of another. A Minnesota court probably would also apply this statute to a trust as well to fulfill the public policy. I can't definitively say that the sibling who killed the other would not receive the murdered sibling's share of the trust, but I would bet heavily that he or she would not be able to do so."

"So if the surviving sibling could not collect the money in the trust, who would collect it?"

"It depends on the terms of the trust document. The murderer will be considered to have predeceased the deceased sibling. The terms of the trust document may dictate who receives that share in the event of death. Otherwise, the share may be subject to the deceased sibling's estate. If the deceased sibling had a valid will, then that would determine to whom the trust share is distributed or divided. If the deceased sibling did not have a will, then that trust share would be subject to the laws of intestacy."

"Which would mean what?"

"The surviving spouse is the primary beneficiary of the estate—although it may be altered if stepchildren are involved—then descendants if no surviving spouse, and then parents if no surviving spouse or descendants, etc."

Santana stood. "Thanks for your time, Ms. Barnes. You've been a big help."

"You believe Jake Fuller murdered his sister, Danielle, don't you, Detective?"

Santana wasn't sure—not until he knew the name of the fourth person involved in the murder of Clay Buck.

* * *

Randy Yates was handcuffed to a metal bed rail in the Ramsey County Sheriff's Security Unit at Regions Hospital, the sun cross tattoo on his right forearm clearly visible. A sheriff's deputy stood guard in the hallway outside the room.

"Looks like you'll be fine, Yates," Santana said.

"No thanks to you."

Yates' dark blond beard had been trimmed. His shoulder-length hair had been cut to an inch. He was watching *Forensic Files* on television.

Santana picked up the remote on the side tray next to the bed and turned off the television.

"Hey!" Yates looked sharply at Santana. "What the hell you doing?"

"We need to talk."

"I don't think so." He grabbed for the remote, but Santana held it out of his reach.

"Deadly force against a police officer means you're going to prison for ten to twenty years, Yates, with no chance of parole till your full sentence is served. Unless . . ." Santana had Yates' full attention now.

"Unless what?"

"Unless you're willing to deal."

"Talk to my lawyer."

"I'm the cop you assaulted. My recommendation to the Ramsey County attorney carries weight." Santana wasn't certain that it did. But if Yates cooperated, he would pitch a plea deal to James Nguyen.

"Like I'm going to trust you, Santana."

"Who else you going to trust? Jake Fuller?"

"Unlike you, Jake's my friend."

"Great. You two can hold hands while you're walking into Stillwater. You'll have plenty of time together. He'll be doing life. You'll serve closer to twenty than ten."

Yates thought about it. "What do you want?"

"Ten months ago my partner and I were bringing Clay Buck back from Red Wing. He was wanted in connection with the murder of Danielle Lonetree, a seventeen-year-old Native American girl. A Cadillac, a pickup, and a van ran us off the road. There were four individuals. One of those individuals was your friend, Jake Fuller. I know this because I took away Fuller's AR-15. Another one of the four was Melissa Cantrell, Fuller's former girlfriend. She and Fuller recently tried to drown me in the St. Croix River. That same night, someone shot Cantrell and dumped her body in the river. You were one of four people in the vehicles. I want to know who the fourth person was, and which one of the three killed Clay Buck."

Yates stared at the blank television monitor. Then his gaze returned to Santana. "You said there were four people, Santana. Now you say one of three people killed Buck. You better get your facts straight."

"There were four. But Jake Fuller was handcuffed to a water trough when Clay Buck was shot and killed. That leaves you, Cantrell, and number four."

"I don't know what you're talking about. You can't prove I was in that cornfield."

"Whoops," Santana said. "I never mentioned a cornfield. How would you know Buck was killed in a cornfield, Yates, unless you were there?"

His eyes were darting back and forth, searching for an answer. "Go to hell, Santana."

"Is that the best you can come up with?"

"I don't need to come up with anything."

"Maybe your good friend, Jake Fuller, can help me."

"Jake won't say anything."

"Maybe he's smarter than you."

"Meaning what?"

"Maybe he's looking for a way out of life in prison. Maybe he'll finger you for the Buck killing."

"I never killed Clay Buck."

"Then who did?"

Santana saw the growing fear in Randy Yates' eyes. "I don't know," he said, turning his head away.

But in that moment, Santana knew Yates *did* know. He was just too afraid to say.

* * *

Santana drove back to the LEC and took the walkway on the second floor from the Homicide and Robbery Unit to the Adult Detention Center. Minnesota State Statute required that the Ramsey County Sheriff's Office operate the 500-bed ADC, commonly referred to as the Ramsey County Jail. The ADC housed individuals being held for probation or supervised release violations, immigration and customs enforcement, and those arrested and waiting court disposition.

When an individual was booked into the ADC following his or her arrest, personal property, clothing, and jewelry were inventoried and stored. Santana asked to see Jake Fuller's personal property, which consisted of the clothing he had worn the night of the shootout and a mostly empty wallet. Inside the wallet, Santana found Fuller's driver's license and a membership card for CERO, the anti-Native American Citizens' Equal Rights Organization.

Santana figured Fuller wouldn't talk now that he had lawyered up. And even if he were willing, it would be difficult given that his jaw was wired shut. But Santana thought he might be able to access the information he sought through another means.

He returned to the Homicide and Robbery Unit and called Jake Fuller's former parole officer again.

"How can I help, Detective?"

"Is there anything in Fuller's file that mentions his foster parents?"

"Give me a minute."

Santana could hear a file drawer slide open and papers shuffling.

"Let's see. Well, after his father's death, Fuller lived with a foster family for a year before enlisting in the Marine Corps at seventeen. The foster family signed the consent form, allowing him to enlist before the age of eighteen."

"What was the name of the family Fuller lived with?"

"Starks," he said. "Thomas Starks."

Chapter 50

Randy Yates was asleep when Santana returned to Yates' room at Regions Hospital. The television was on. Santana shut it off again.

Yates woke up and blinked at Santana, who was standing at the foot of the bed. "What do you want now, Santana?"

"Thomas Starks."

Yates' body jerked, and his eyes opened wide. "Who's Starks?"

"Jake Fuller's foster father." Santana decided to go with a hunch. "And the fourth man in the cornfield the day Clay Buck was murdered."

"I don't know anybody named Starks."

"That's not what Fuller said."

"Jake wouldn't talk to you."

Probably true, Santana thought. But Yates didn't know that for certain. Santana could tell by the panic and desperation in Yates' eyes now. He just had to offer Yates a reason to confess.

"How do you think I found out about Starks?"

Yates thought about it. "What did Jake tell you?"

"That you killed Clay Buck."

"That's bullshit! I didn't kill Buck!"

"Tell that to a jury. Too bad you didn't talk to me when you had the chance, Yates. But the good news is, you and your best buddy will spend the rest of your lives together behind bars." Santana turned to leave.

"Wait a minute!" Yates swallowed hard. "I didn't kill Buck. Starks did."

"Why should I believe you?"

"Because I was there. I saw him do it."

"What if it's Starks' and Fuller's word against yours?"

"Starks shot Buck with a forty-five caliber."

"I already know that."

"But what you don't know is that Starks still has that forty-five Colt revolver. It belonged to his father. He never would get rid of it. You find the gun. You'll have the evidence he did it."

"You helped Starks carry Buck's body out of the cornfield and back to the stand of trees at the edge of the woods."

Yates nodded.

"Who killed Jorgen Lundgren, the man who owned the farm near the munitions plant?"

"Jake did. I told him we should just tie up the old man. But he wouldn't listen."

"What about Otto and Elsie Vogel? The farmers near Mills Creek?"

"I think that was Starks and Jake."

"And Melissa Cantrell?"

"Jake told me Starks killed her. You were supposed to drown. Starks was worried she might talk about your death."

"What about Danielle Lonetree?"

"Starks killed her."

"Fuller wasn't involved in her murder?"

"Maybe. I don't know for sure. He never said he was."

Santana remembered the crime scene. The hot white lights, the shallow gravesite where Danielle Lonetree's half-naked body was dumped. How her face was painted red, the bone color of her bare legs. He remembered thinking that the killer was someone for whom cruelty and sexual pleasure were interchangeable. Someone who not only killed for enjoyment, but who experienced an unnatural feeling of power and control over another human being, as if he believed he was God.

"Did Fuller tell you she was his sister?"

Yates cocked his head. "Danielle Lonetree was Jake's sister?"

Santana nodded.

"That means he's . . ."

"Native American," Santana said. "Your best buddy, who hated Native Americans, was one."

Yates shook his head slowly in disbelief.

"Who killed Grayson Cole?"

"Jake killed Cole."

Santana nodded. It all made sense now. "What about Sam Noor?"

"I've never heard of Sam Noor."

"Come on, Yates."

He held up a hand. "I swear. I don't know."

Santana watched Yates' body language. Then he said, "If what you've told me is true, Yates, I'll talk with the Ramsey County attorney. See if he'll cut you a deal."

"You going to Starks' ranch now?"

"Soon as I get a warrant."

"Starks probably knows you're coming."

"How would he know that?"

"We've been watching you and your lady friend."

Santana felt a cold place in his gut. "Who's 'we'?"

"Members of CERO. Jake knew you and your partner would follow me to the farmhouse."

"So it was a setup."

"I didn't want any part of it, but Jake had too much dirt on me. I really had no choice."

"There's always a choice, Yates."

Santana took out his cell phone and called Jordan's cell. It went to voicemail. He tried her office. Another voicemail. *Could be she's busy with a client.*

He started out the door and then thought of something. "Who tacked the drawing of the *Unktehi* to the front door of my house?"

"Jake did." Yates looked like he wanted to say something else.

Santana waited.

"I don't know why Starks and Jake killed all those people."

"I do," Santana said.

Chapter 51

Santana and Kacie Hawkins met Captain Doug Flint of the Goodhue County Sheriff's Department on a county road a mile from Thomas Starks' buffalo ranch. The sky was slate gray, the temperature in the mid-fifties, cool for June. The wind had died. The still air felt like a warning.

Flint got out of his patrol car and strode up to Santana and Hawkins.

Santana introduced Hawkins. "Starks might know we're coming," he said.

Flint nodded. "Things go south, I can call out our Emergency Response Team."

"Good to have backup."

"You figure on driving in and handing Starks the warrant?"

"Knocking on the door probably isn't a good idea."

"Sure would be easier."

"Might be easier to get shot, too," Hawkins said.

Santana pointed to the hills. "Kacie and I will reconnoiter the ranch first. If things look quiet, we move in. Otherwise, we call you and wait for backup."

"Sounds like a plan."

* * *

Santana could smell the fresh scent of pines that studded the woods and the faint scent of river mud. Birds sang in the trees that were so tall and dense at the top that the forest floor was mostly bare and dark with little undergrowth. In some places the trunks were so close together neither he nor Hawkins could squeeze between them.

They worked their way uphill and headed straight west for a quarter mile till Santana smelled wood smoke and saw the light at the edge of the forest. Squatting in a copse of trees with Hawkins beside him, he removed a pair of Bushnell binoculars from the case hanging from a strap around his neck and scoped the chalet. It sat in a clearing below them near the river.

"See anything?" Hawkins asked.

Santana lowered the binoculars and looked at Hawkins. "There are three SUVs in the driveway."

"If Starks is waiting for us, he might have people in the area."

"I don't see anyone."

"Doesn't mean they aren't here," Hawkins said. "I don't want another shootout."

"Me neither."

"So what's the plan?"

"If we can plug the chimney, smoke will back up into the chalet and drive everyone out."

"Means one of us has to get on the roof."

"I'll circle around behind the chalet and stuff something in the chimney."

"Like what?"

"Give me your raid jacket."

"Come on, John."

"If it makes you feel any better, I'll use my jacket, too."

She stripped off her raid jacket and handed it to Santana. "For what it's worth, I don't feel any better. Plus, it's chilly."

He handed her his binoculars. "Watch the roof. Once I plug the chimney, call Flint and tell him and his deputies to head for the chalet." Santana moved off through the woods, staying low.

It took him fifteen minutes to work his way around the chalet. From the high slope behind it, he got a running start and leapt onto the roof. He felt a sharp pain in his stitched stomach wound when he landed. He took a moment to collect himself, breathing deeply till the pain subsided. The roof was steep but covered with wood shakes that provided good footing under his rubber soles. He made his way up to the roof ridge and scrambled along it to the chimney. The wood smoke was thick and hot.

Slipping out of his raid jacket, he wadded it up with Hawkins' jacket and stuffed them both into the flue. Five minutes later, from his vantage point, Santana saw Flint and his deputies arrive, their light bars flashing red, Hawkins right behind them in the Crown Vic.

Flint took out a bullhorn and ordered everyone out of the chalet.

Three minutes later, Starks' wife emerged from the chalet holding an infant in her arms. The two teenagers Santana has seen on his first visit and three men Santana didn't recognize were right behind her.

He didn't see Thomas Starks.

Santana slid down the back slope of the roof on his rear and jumped to the ground. The impact sent another shiver of pain through his body. Then he saw Starks emerge from a trap door in the ground at the side of the chalet and head for the slope, toward Santana.

"Hold it, Starks!" Santana stepped out from behind a tree, his Glock pointed downhill.

Starks hesitated a second and then took off running toward the buffalo pasture.

Santana cursed to himself, holstered his Glock, and worked his way carefully between the trees and down the slope, the stitches in his stomach needling his skin. By the time he reached level ground, Starks had a fifty-yard advantage. Out of the corner of his eye, Santana saw Kacie Hawkins racing after Starks, her arms pumping by her sides, her long legs cutting the distance between them, showing no signs that her ankle still bothered her.

Without the wound and stitches in his stomach, Santana knew he could run down Starks. But he hadn't run or worked out hard recently. He would follow, but he was slow. It was up to Hawkins now.

Starks scrambled over a gate into the pasture. Hawkins climbed over it seconds later. Santana opened the gate when he reached it. The buffalo herd was scattered, but they raised their huge heads as Starks and then Hawkins ran across the pasture. Santana could hear the herd grunting and snorting. They began moving together.

Hawkins was closing fast, maybe twenty yards from Starks, when he stopped, turned, and fired a shot at her. She dropped to one knee, slid her Glock out of its holster, aimed with a good two-handed grip on the Glock, and returned fire. They both missed, but the gunshots spooked the herd. The ground shook under their heavy hooves as they swarmed together. Then they turned and rumbled toward the north end of the pasture, sending up mini clouds of dust and clumps of prairie grass, straight at Starks and Hawkins.

Santana yelled at her. Hawkins stopped and turned. He pointed to his left. One look at the oncoming buffalo and Hawkins was sprinting toward him and the safety of the electrified fence, the Glock still in her right hand, trying to reach the edge of the herd before they were on her.

Santana could tell she wouldn't make it.

He pulled his Glock and fired two shots over the heads of the buffalo. Like a long brown wave, the herd turned away from Hawkins.

But Starks wasn't so lucky.

Caught in the middle of the pasture, he got off two shots before he was overrun. The last thing Santana saw was Starks' flat Stetson hat bouncing across the backs of the buffalo before it, too, was trampled under their thundering hooves.

Chapter 52

While the Goodhue County Medical Examiner removed Thomas Starks' broken body from the buffalo pasture, and Doug Flint and his deputies questioned Starks' wife and the two teenagers and three men who had been inside the house, Kacie Hawkins searched the metal Quonset hut near the barn. Santana searched the chalet.

Despite the open windows and cool air blowing in, the chalet still held the heavy odor of smoke. Santana recalled the fire that had damaged the kitchen in the family house in the valley when he was eight. The smoke smell had lingered for weeks. Years later, when an addition was added and walls were torn open, workers had commented on the smoke smell still in the wood.

Santana began his search in the second floor master bedroom with the sliding doors that opened onto the balcony.

He found the Colt .45 pearl-handled revolver he was looking for in a holster hanging from a peg in the walk-in closet. He was certain that it was the gun used to kill Melissa Cantrell and wound Wendell Hudson.

He put the revolver in an evidence bag and filled out the chain of custody information.

Farther back in the closet, Santana found a lock of dark hair in a plastic bag. He figured the hair had belonged to Danielle Lonetree and that Starks had kept it as a trophy. He placed it in another evidence bag.

Kacie Hawkins came into the room. She was out of breath, as if she had been running. The look on her face was one Santana had never seen before, a mixture of horror, dread, sadness, and pain.

"What is it?"

She started to speak and then stopped. Tears formed in her eyes.

Santana placed the evidence bags on the bed and hurried to her. "What's wrong?"

She attempted to speak again, but the words wouldn't come. Heavy tears tracked her cheeks.

Santana took her gently by the shoulders and looked into her eyes. "Tell me."

"Jordan," she said.

"What?"

Hawkins pointed a shaky hand toward the door. "The Quonset hut."

Santana felt as if a nail had been driven into his heart. He stepped around Hawkins, but she moved to block his path.

"Get out of the way, Kacie."

"Don't go there, John."

He pushed past her and raced toward the Quonset hut.

Chapter 53

For years Santana had found comfort in his house overlooking the river. The copper sunsets, the still water, the bright colors of fall. Even alone on chilly, rainy days like this one, he could find solace and peace in front of a warm fire, away from his job, away from the death that had darkened much of his life.

But he could find no solace and no peace in his house today.

Gitana knew something was wrong. For the first time, Santana yelled at her in anger because she would not leave him alone. She backed off but soon returned, sitting beside him, her head in his lap, licking him as she would a pup.

He finally gave up and let her be.

Santana felt that he had become the inside-out-upside-down man Chaska Youngblood had warned him about. Nothing made sense. Alternating between bouts of rage and sorrow, he had no energy. Everything he attempted took too much effort. Eating. Sleeping. Conversing.

The caged demon inside him, the demon that had emerged from the darkest corner of his soul after his mother's murder, the demon that he'd thought he had under control, demanded revenge. But Thomas Starks was dead. Jake Fuller was going to prison, probably for the rest of his life. Santana had no outlet for his rage, a rage that burned like hot coals inside him. Instead, he drank shots of aguardiente and wandered from room to room in his bathrobe, as though searching for something he could not find.

At one point, he found himself in front of the bathroom mirror, looking at his unshaven face, dark with a heavy beard, at his eyes that were more bloodshot than blue, at the scar near his heart where a bullet had nearly taken his life, at the scar on his right hand from the sharp thorns of a guadua tree when he had fought for his life in the high mountain forests of Colombia, at the latest scars on his wrist and stomach from the knife wielded by Jake Fuller. But he was less concerned about the external scars than those he could not see, the deep internal ones that had scarred his soul.

When the liquor was gone, he sat for hours, staring at nothing, trying not to think, trying not to remember. But the horrifying images of Jordan's body worked their way into his consciousness anyway, like a worm into an apple.

Jordan and the old Indian had both warned him.

When you seek the darkness, the darkness seeks you.

Santana had trouble remembering the details of Jordan's funeral service, as though it were all a long-forgotten dream. He did remember it had rained that day and for two days since. Santana had sleepwalked his way through the service. He had met Jordan's parents before but barely knew them. Still, he felt they blamed him for their daughter's death, at least her father, an ex-cop, did. And Santana didn't have the strength to debate the unspoken accusation. What was left of Jordan had been cremated and the ashes given to them.

Everyone in the department rallied around him. Pete Romano told him to take as much time as needed. Tony Novak's wife made a casserole, and the two of them brought it over. Kacie Hawkins called and offered to stop by. Santana appreciated the well wishes and condolences, but he chose to retreat into himself, reluctant to share the all-consuming grief with anyone, as he had not shared when he'd lost his mother. So the casserole sat untouched in the refrigerator. The phone calls remained unanswered, the doors locked.

Now, Santana stood in the living room and stared out the window at the gray light falling through the glass, the water that rattled down from the roof, the misty clouds that hung over the river, the drops pooling on the leaves of the birch trees and forming concentric circles on the water's surface. Like a stone thrown into a river, a murder created an ever-widening circle that touched the lives of his colleagues and friends, anyone close to him.

He recalled the painting he had seen in Kelly Noor's house of the beautiful woman sitting on a flowered swing above a graveyard. In his mind's eyes it was Jordan who was seated on the swing now. That was what his dream, his subconscious, had been telling him.

But why kill her?

She was an ex-cop turned private investigator. Starks must have thought she was the last possible link in the chain leading back to him. The signs had been there. But he had been so focused on solving the case that he had ignored them. Jordan had mentioned she thought she was being followed. He had caught her looking through his case file. She had offered her assistance after he was wounded. He had talked with her about the case. Once forgotten moments that played over and over in his mind, moments that he now wished would burn away like an old reel of film dissolving in a fire.

* * *

The following morning it stopped raining, the clouds parted, and Santana forced himself to get out of bed and take Gitana out for a run—though it was more like a fast walk. The landscape glistened under the bright sun. The air felt fresh and clean. But after only one mile, he and Gitana were both breathing hard.

Santana stopped, bent over, and put his hands on his thighs. Tears suddenly began to trail down his face, and his breath came in short gasps. He sank to his hands and knees and let the tears come, let the gasps wrack his body till he could cry no more.

A passing motorist stopped and rolled down her window and asked if he were okay. He nodded and waved her on.

He felt dizzy when he struggled to his feet again, Gitana's leash still in his hand. The dog held his eyes and tilted her head, as if she didn't know what to make of him.

"I'm a mess, huh?" he said to her.

She wagged her tail and brushed up against his leg, asking to be petted.

He knelt down in front of her, held her head, and let her lick his face. Sweat soaked his body, but it wasn't from the running. He could smell the odor of alcohol seeping out of his pores.

He saw his own image in the dog's large eyes, and it triggered memories of the glass taxidermy eyes on Starks' workbench and of a photo he had once seen.

When he returned home, he skipped the weights but promised himself he would lift tomorrow. His stomach wound had healed nicely. He would try some sit-ups tomorrow as well.

He showered and shaved and ate half his breakfast of eggs, toast, and hot chocolate. The fog that had clouded his mind for days began lifting, and as it did, a lingering thought that had been lost in the wreckage of Jordan's death became clearer in his mind.

Why would Jake Fuller or Thomas Starks kill Sam Noor? Neither knew about the contaminated water in Mills Creek. Grayson Cole had already promised the land dedicated for silica mining to Jake Fuller and Danielle Lonetree in the secret trust. Randy Yates had claimed he'd never heard of Sam Noor. Yates had confessed to everything else. If he knew who was involved in Noor's murder, why wouldn't he have admitted it?

Despite the blood evidence on the knife he had found in Adam Noor's loft, Santana had never felt comfortable with the idea that the kid had murdered his father. Adam Noor was angry with his mother and grandfather for having him committed to an institution. He was angry that his mother had had an affair with Grayson Cole. But Jake Fuller had killed Cole. Once Danielle Lonetree and Cole were dead, Fuller stood to inherit all the money from the secret trust, and, by extension, Thomas Starks for CERO.

Santana believed his mission wasn't complete. There was something yet to prove. He knew he could not rest until it was finished.

He dressed, typed his tardy summary reports, and drove to the LEC.

* * *

"Hey, John. You back?" Bobby Jackson said.

Santana nodded.

"How you doing?"

Santana understood that small talk was a bridge designed to ease his colleagues' discomfort with Jordan's death, a way to avoid discussing an uncomfortable and potentially embarrassing situation.

"I've been better," he said.

Jackson nodded and appeared at a loss for words.

"You remember the cell phone photos you downloaded from Sam Noor's phone?"

"Sure do," Jackson said, clearly relieved to be talking about something else.

"I'd like to take a look at them again."

Jackson hurried over to a computer. A few minutes later, the photos Santana had requested appeared on the screen. Jackson stood and offered Santana his chair.

"Looking for something in particular, John?"

Santana opened the folder containing the photos, clicked through them and stopped at the photo of Sam Noor's face. "This one."

"Someone's fingers are in the photo."

"I want to know who that someone is."

Jackson pointed. "Look closely. What do you see when you look into Noor's eyes?"

Santana wasn't sure at first. Then he saw it. "Someone's face." *Just as I saw my own face in Gitana's eyes this morning,* he thought, *and in the glass taxidermy eyes on Starks' workbench.*

"Exactly," Jackson said. "The pupil of the eye is like a black mirror. What you're seeing is a bystander image or a reflection image that forms on the cornea of the eye. Whenever you look into someone else's eyes, John, you see a tiny doll-like version of yourself reflected back. The word *pupil* actually comes from the Latin word *pupilla,* which can mean young girl or doll. I've started using photos for crimes like hostage taking and child sex abuse in which the vics are photographed."

"You can identify the perp, or whoever took the photo."

"That's the idea."

"Is there a way you can enhance this image, Bobby?"

Jackson got another chair and sat down beside Santana. "It'd be easier if the photo was taken with a high-resolution thirty-nine megapixel camera. Your standard iPhone camera is only eight megapixels. But the extracted face image doesn't have to be of high quality in order to be identifiable. And Noor is looking directly at the camera. That's a plus. We should be able to see a face reflection if I zoom in on his eyes. But you'll have to be familiar with the face to recognize it."

"Nothing to lose by taking a chance."

"All right. Give me a few minutes. I want to use Adobe Photoshop to improve definition and enhance the contrast in each frame."

Five minutes later, Jackson said, "I converted it into a movie format for viewing. Watch this."

Jackson clicked an arrow on the screen, and the computer imaged zoomed in quickly on Sam Noor's right eye. "The face is a little fuzzy, but do you recognize it?"

"Yes," Santana said. "Yes, I do."

* * *

Heads bobbed up as Santana walked through the Homicide and Robbery Unit. He acknowledged the waves and smiles with a forced smile of his own.

Kacie Hawkins got up and gave him a hug. "What are you doing here?"

"Getting back to work."

"You need some time to yourself, John."

"I've had plenty of that. And I'll have time for plenty more."

"You're sure?"

He nodded.

"How 'bout dinner tonight? My treat."

"I'll call you."

Hawkins put her hands on her slender hips and let out a sigh. "Like you returned my calls after the funeral?"

"Sorry, Kacie."

She patted him on the arm. "Don't worry about it. If you feel like dinner, just let me know. I haven't got any plans."

"Thanks," he said.

Santana hung his sport coat on the back of his chair and knocked on Pete Romano's open door.

Romano appeared surprised to see him.

"Can I come in?"

Romano stood. "Of course, John."

Santana pulled up a chair and sat down in front of Romano's desk.

Romano eased himself down into his chair. "How you holding up?"

"Haven't slept much."

"That's to be expected. You take whatever time you need. Rest up. We'll cover for you. Hell, I'll even go back on the street if I need to."

He was grateful for Romano's offer and informality. But he was here to talk about something else besides his emotional state. "I appreciate it, Pete. But there's no need. I'm ready to come back."

Romano's jaw dropped. "It's too soon."

Santana shook his head. "I'm doing nothing at home but staring at the walls." Santana dropped a manila folder on the desktop. "I typed my reports. It gave me something to do and got me thinking."

"About what?"

"Sam Noor."

"We're back to that again?"

"Look, Pete. Randy Yates will testify that Thomas Starks and Jake Fuller were responsible for the murders of Elsie and Otto Vogel, Melissa Cantrell, Grayson Cole, and Danielle Lonetree. Fuller and Lonetree stood to inherit over a billion dollars because the land their father, Grayson Cole, owned was rich in silica sand used in fracking. Her boyfriend, Clay Buck, knew that. If he and Lonetree married, Buck would own half of her share. Jake Fuller wanted that money. And so did Thomas Starks, Fuller's father figure, to finance CERO, his anti-Native American hate group. Starks plotted to kill Danielle Lonetree and pin the murder on Clay Buck. Starks, Fuller, Cantrell, and Yates went after Buck when Wendell Hudson and I were transporting him from Red Wing back to the LEC. Starks killed Buck in the cornfield and framed Hudson for the murder."

"Why go after Buck when he was already the prime suspect in Danielle Lonetree's murder?"

"Because Buck saw their faces. He could identify them."

"Then where does Sam Noor fit in?"

"He doesn't, Pete. But Noor knew Select Sands was dumping contaminated water into Mills Creek, which flows into the Mississippi."

"So you're suggesting that neither Starks nor Fuller killed Noor?"

"Neither of them knew what Noor had found."

Romano spread his hands. "So then we're back to Adam, Sam Noor's kid."

Santana shook his head. "No. It was someone else." He tossed the photo of Sam Noor that Bobby Jackson had downloaded on Romano's desktop. "There's the person who killed Sam Noor."

Chapter 54

The maid escorted Santana to a gable-end glass conservatory at the back of Kelly Noor's mansion. He sat down in a white wicker cushioned chair that matched the white beams in the ceiling and the walls. The floor was made of granite tiles with a high gloss finish. Thick green plants were placed throughout the room.

Santana imagined how bright the conservatory would be on a sunny day. Now, dark afternoon clouds deadened the light in the room, and raindrops blurred the glass.

Kelly Noor folded her arms together as if she were cold, crossed her legs, and leaned back on the wicker couch across from Santana. "You've been in the news lately, Detective. I was sorry to hear about the loss of Ms. Parrish."

Each time someone mentioned Jordan's name, Santana felt a dull ache in his heart. "How did you know about my relationship with her?"

"My father. He has friends in the department."

"I'm sure he does."

"It's difficult losing someone you love. Even worse when that someone is murdered and your son is accused of the crime."

"You lost your mother when you were young."

She nodded. "Did my father tell you he raised me?"

"Yes."

"Well, I was fourteen when my mother died."

"I lost my father when I was twelve."

"How did he die?"

"A drunken driver struck his car."

Kelly Noor nodded again as her eyes studied his face.

"What was it like being raised by your father, Ms. Noor?"

She was quiet for a time before speaking. "He was very protective."

"How did he feel about you marrying Sam Noor?"

"He wasn't crazy about it, but he came around."

"What made him come around?"

She offered a thin smile. "To be honest, Sam inherited a substantial amount of money."

"Was your father aware that your husband was planning to divorce you?"

She straightened up, a hard look on her face. "Who told you that?"

"Your son."

"What are you getting at, Detective?"

Santana told her.

* * *

Ray Carver lived in a story-and-a-half craftsman on Magoffin Avenue in St. Paul, close to Hidden Falls Park. The house had shake siding, brick masonry, and a wrap-around porch with thick columns. The rain had stopped, and the clouds that had darkened the afternoon sky were dissipating, like gray smoke from a fire.

Carver was kneeling on a rubber pad, weeding his garden along the side of the house, his blue denim shirt, jeans, and running shoes smudged with dirt. He stood when he saw Santana approach. He removed his soiled gloves but didn't offer his hand.

Santana hadn't expected him to.

"I'm surprised you had the guts to come here, Detective."

"And why is that?"

"Not only haven't you solved my son-in-law's murder, my grandson is now accused of killing his father. Frankly, we were better off with the first detective. At least Adam wasn't in jail on a first degree murder charge."

"Your grandson is innocent."

Carver's laugh sounded like a hard cough. "Well, that's really helpful. I'm sure once the prosecutor hears that, he'll drop the charge."

"Let's step inside, Chief."

"What for?"

"I know who murdered Sam Noor."

Carver's gray eyebrows rose as he gave Santana a skeptical look. Then he turned and headed for the side door.

Santana followed him into a small kitchen and into a living room where he sat on a cushioned armchair. Carver sat across from him on a well-worn couch.

"Who's the perp, Detective?"

"You are."

"That's ridiculous. Why would I kill Sam?"

"Because he was about to divorce your daughter. You'd always looked out for her, protected her after her mother's death. But you were in no position to financially support her. Not with your gambling habit. So you killed her husband to prevent the divorce."

"Kelly would've gotten money in a divorce."

"I'm sure she would have. But she was cheating on her husband. After a long, ugly divorce and substantial legal fees, I think her income would've dropped considerably."

"You're crazy."

"Your daughter wanted her husband's case reopened, not you, Chief. But you had to go along with it. Once I was assigned to Sam Noor's cold case, you came to see me. You wanted me to feed you information so you could stay one step ahead. When I wouldn't cooperate, you got worried. You knew your grandson was angry that you and your daughter had him committed. You were also concerned that he might harm your daughter. He'd attacked her once. You had access to his loft. You decided to set him up for his father's murder."

Carver stared at Santana and offered no response.

"You rode with Sam Noor to the proposed mine site near Mills Creek. There was a struggle. You suffocated him. You drove his car back to Hidden Falls Park and stabbed him to make it look like a robbery gone wrong. Then you walked home."

"This is pure speculation."

From his briefcase, Santana pulled a copy of the Sam Noor photo that Bobby Jackson had enlarged and set it on the coffee table. "Take a look at this."

Carver picked up the photo and looked at it. Then his eyes shifted to Santana. "It's a photo of Sam."

"A photo taken the evening he was murdered. Sam Noor was suffocated in silica sand. What you didn't count on was that the silica sand at the mine site was different than the sand at Hidden Falls Park."

"How does this photo prove I was with Sam in Mills Creek?"

Santana took a second enlarged photo from his briefcase and handed it to Carver. "Look into the eyes, Chief, and tell me who you see."

Carver stared at the photo and then at Santana. "I don't recognize anyone."

"It's you, Chief. And the eyes you're looking into belong to Sam Noor. When Noor stopped for gas in Mills Creek, he took this photo. You didn't want Noor taking your picture. Those are your fingers reaching for the camera. You accidentally hit the selfie icon on the iPhone. Noor took his own picture. After you killed him at the silica mine site, you got rid of his phone. But Noor had already sent the photos to his home computer using the wireless service at the café and gas station in Mills Creek."

"Let's say I was with Sam Noor that evening. This photo doesn't prove that I killed him."

"Sam Noor took three photos of Mills Creek around seven that evening, after he left the gas station. It's an hour and ten-minute drive back to the city. That puts him in town a little after eight p.m. Very near the time of death."

"*Estimated* time of death, Detective. TOD is not an exact science."

"Close enough. When you felt I was on the verge of discovering the truth, you placed the bloody knife in the hamper in your grandson's loft. You'd kept the knife for insurance in case you ever needed it. You knew that forensics couldn't match the blood on the knife with Grayson Cole's DNA. But they matched it with Sam Noor's DNA. You once told me that your grandson was being set up for murder. What you didn't tell me was that you were the one who had set him up."

"You think you've got it all figured out, don't you, Detective?"

Santana nodded. "I'm not crazy, and neither is your grandson, Chief. You are."

Carver stared silently at Santana for a long moment. Then he reached behind a couch pillow and pulled out a Glock.

"You going to kill me, too, Chief?"

Carver held the gun in his lap, the barrel pointed at Santana's chest. "I could."

"Go ahead. It doesn't matter to me. You're going down one way or another."

Carver didn't move or say anything for what seemed like a long time. "You know what it's like losing someone close to you, Detective. I lost my wife many years ago. You lost your lady friend. I suspect you may have lost others who were close to you as well. We have something in common."

"I'm not you, Chief."

"You don't have any children, do you, Detective?"

"No."

"My daughter is all I have. She means the world to me."

"You have a grandson."

Carver shook his head. "He'll never be right. I know about the disease."

"Your wife was schizophrenic, wasn't she, Chief? She took her own life. The gene runs in the family."

Carver's eyes drifted to the Glock in his lap and back to Santana. "A man with nothing to lose is a very dangerous man, Detective. From the sound of it, you don't seem to feel life is worth living anymore. I don't either."

Ray Carver raised the Glock to his head and pulled the trigger. His head exploded, the roar of the gun like a clap of thunder in the confines of the room.

Epilogue

Santana located Wendell Hudson at a nursing home on the east side of St. Paul. Hudson was sitting at a 45-degree angle in an adjustable bed, his thin black hands resting on top of a blanket, his eyes fixed on the screen of a television bolted to the upper wall opposite the bed, listening to *Jeopardy*.

Santana hardly recognized him.

Hudson was completely bald and could not have weighed more than one hundred twenty pounds. His skin had the brownish-yellow pallor of his nicotine-stained teeth. His lips were dry and cracked. A nasal cannula hissed oxygen into his body. He turned his head on the pillow as Santana came toward him, his rheumy eyes widening as though he had seen the face of the Grim Reaper, then narrowing again as he recognized his former partner and offered a weak smile.

Santana saw no point in asking how Hudson was doing.

"Been going downhill fast, John. Tried to hang on a little longer. Didn't think I'd live long enough to hear that I was cleared of the Clay Buck shooting. I can go in peace now. Thanks."

Hudson's voice was gravelly but surprisingly strong, despite his deteriorating condition and the strong medicinal smell about him.

"I wanted to make sure you knew, Wendell. Not for my sake, but—"

"No need to explain, John. I can only watch television now. Reading tires me out. You've been all over the news."

Hudson coughed once and then couldn't stop.

Santana could smell the fetid breath of death. He handed Hudson a water-filled Styrofoam cup from the bed table.

When his coughing fit stopped, Hudson set the cup on the bed table and said, "I was real sorry to hear about your lady friend."

Santana felt a familiar stab of pain in his heart.

"I'd tell you that she's in a far better place, but you don't believe that, do you, John?"

Santana shook his head.

"I've always believed. Still, the closer you get to the end of your life, the more you hope your belief hasn't been a cruel joke. But I have nothing to lose, nothing else to believe in now, except you."

"I'm no god, Wendell."

"Never said you were. But you're very good at what you do. And you're a man of your word. Not many of those left. I speak from experience. A man loses those closest to him maybe because of what he does, and he starts questioning his purpose, his mission in life. But you have to speak for the dead, John."

"Why me?"

"Because you can."

"So can others."

"Not like you. You have a gift."

"More like a curse. People I care about keep dying around me."

"Not your fault. Take some advice from a dying man. Stay true to yourself. Do what you do best. What God put you on this earth to do."

* * *

The evening after Wendell Hudson's funeral, as twilight settled over the landscape, Santana sat on the cushioned seat on the flybridge of the *Alibi* with Gitana by his side, reflecting on the case.

Randy Yates had cut a plea deal with James Nguyen for a reduced sentence. Jake Fuller would likely go to prison for the rest of his life.

Nguyen had dropped all charges against Adam Noor. His mother, Kelly, had mentioned to Santana that she might again pursue her dream of acting, even if it were only in local theater. Perhaps without her father's influence, she and her son might repair the torn fabric of their relationship.

Virginia Garrison's group had convinced the courts to issue a moratorium, temporarily stopping Ken Webb and Select Sands from opening more silica sand sites till the environmental issues were resolved.

The mineral rights money that Thomas Starks had plotted to get from Jake Fuller for his racist organization would all go to Sherilyn Lonetree, if the silica mine ever opened, but no amount of money could replace the loss of her daughter, Danielle, or soothe the pain caused by her troubled son, Jake.

The cold case unit was closing, despite Jane Linden's efforts to keep it open.

Chaska Youngblood, his niece, Carrie, Virginia Garrison, and Sean Latham had knocked on Santana's door the day after Ray Carver's funeral.

"We once spoke of the *heyoka,*" Youngblood said. "A Lakota who moved and reacted in an opposite fashion to the people around him."

"I remember."

"It's important that you remain an upside-down, inside-out man, Detective."

"And why is that?"

"You ask the difficult questions and encourage your colleagues to think about things that they haven't thought about. You look at things in a different way. You are a mirror for others."

"I was wrong about you," Carrie Buck said. "You proved my brother, Clay, was not a murderer and that your partner didn't kill him."

"You are a voice for the voiceless," the old man said. "You speak for those who have lost everything. You must be the one who asks 'why?'"

"But who asks for me?" Santana said.

"You do, Detective. A *heyoka* asks for all of us."

* * *

From the *Alibi's* flybridge, Santana could see a broad arch of rosy light along the horizon, the afterglow caused by fine dust particles suspended in the high regions of the atmosphere. Streetlights reflected on the surface of the river and gilded the leaves of the trees near the marina, softening the dark edges of growing shadows.

He had long ago come to believe that the dead spoke to him through his memories and in his dreams. When alone, he often heard his mother's voice and his father's laugh, as if they were alive and in the room with him. These incidents used to disturb him, but no more. While he doubted the existence of heaven and hell, choosing to believe that life was what each of us made of it, he felt that the restless spirits of the dead, those whose lives had been taken before their time, still walked among us. They would often come to him in his dreams, seeking justice.

And though he had lost his faith at the age of sixteen, he still believed that evil existed in the world, monsters like the *Unktehi* come to life in the form of man—monsters born of the same gene pool that had created all of us. Were those without conscience created in the womb, or were they shaped by dark events in their lives? It was a mystery he had not solved.

Santana did not want to be a *heyoka,* as Chaska Youngblood had described him, or to carry the burden for those who could no longer speak. The weight of it all, the loss of those close to him, was becoming a weight too great to bear. He thought if he walked away from it all now, turned in his badge, he would at last be free from the darkness that shadowed his life.

But he knew he would never be free of the assassins sent by the Cali cartel. And without his badge, he could not go where he needed to go, do what he needed to do, ask the questions he needed to ask.

No matter how much he denied it, how much he wanted to avoid it, he knew what he was and always would be: a darkness hunter. His mission was to speak for Danielle Lonetree and Sam Noor, for all the spirits that had come before them and those that would come after, spirits of loved ones like Jordan Parrish, spirits that would haunt him forever.

ACKNOWLEDGMENTS

Many people contributed to the writing of this novel. Thanks to Lt. Lee Edwards, former Homicide Commander, Minneapolis Police Department; Sgt. Mark Bolster, Goodhue County Sheriff's Department; Deputy Thomas Wolner, Goodhue County Sheriff's Department; and Captain Pat Thompson, Goodhue County Sheriff's Office, Criminal Investigative Division.

Thanks to Rosie and Paul Schluter for setting up the tour of the Goodhue county LEC and for your wonderful support.

Thanks to Tony Runkel, Chief Geologist, Minnesota Geological Survey, University of Minnesota, for sharing his time and knowledge of silica sand; to attorney Chad Roggeman for sharing his time and knowledge of secret trusts and wills; and to his father, Gene, for the introduction.

Special contributions were made by the following, without whom this book would not exist in its present form: Linda Donaldson, Lorrie Holmgren, Peg Wangensteen, Jenifer LeClair, Dave Knudson, and my wonderful editor, Jennifer Adkins. Thank you all for your time and suggestions regarding the manuscript.

Many thanks to my beautiful wife, Martha, for her love and inspiration.

Thanks to my growing family of readers for your wonderful support and e-mails, and to all the book clubs and bookstores who have graciously hosted discussions and signings.

AN INVITATION TO READING GROUPS/BOOK CLUBS

I would like to extend an invitation to reading groups/ book clubs across the country. Invite me to your group and I'll be happy to participate in your discussion either in person or via the telephone. (Reading groups should have a speakerphone or Skype.) You can arrange a date and time by e-mailing me at cjvalen@comcast.net. I look forward to hearing from you.

Not Sure What to Read Next?
Try these authors from Conquill Press

Jenifer LeClair
The Windjammer Mystery Series
Rigged for Murder
Danger Sector
Cold Coast
Apparition Island
www.windjammermysteries.com

Chuck Logan
Fallen Angel
www.chucklogan.org

Brian Lutterman
The Pen Wilkinson Mystery Series
Downfall
www.brianlutterman.com

Steve Thayer
Ithaca Falls
www.stevethayer.com

Christopher Valen
The John Santana Mystery Series
White Tombs
The Black Minute
Bad Weed Never Die
Bone Shadows
Death's Way
The Darkness Hunter
www.christophervalen.com

Coming Soon
Broker by Chuck Logan
Windfall by Brian Lutterman

For more information on all these titles go to:
www.conquillpress.com